DEATH COMES GIFT WRAPPED

by

Pat Herbert

OTHER NOVELS by PAT HERBERT

Reverend Paltoquet Supernatural Mysteries:
The Bockhampton Road Murders
Haunted Christmas
The Possession of November Jones
The Witches of Wandsworth
So Long at the Fair
The Man Who Was Death
The Dark Side of the Mirror
Sleeping With the Dead
The Corpse Wore Red
Seeing Double

Barney Carmichael Crime Mysteries:
Getting Away with Murder
The Murder in Weeping Lane

Acknowledgements

I wish to thank Darin Jewell and Judith Sturman for all their help and support, without whom this book would never have been written.

1

She could hear the man talking, she could even understand the individual words. The only trouble was they weren't joining together in her brain to make a coherent whole. She stared at the ring on the little finger of his left hand. It glinted in the late autumn sunlight. The dust motes streaming in through the window caused her to cough.

She sat beside her husband, her gloved hand in his. The solicitor's words continued in a seemingly endless reel of legalese. Grant Vaughan turned his handsome head to look at her and the expression on his face left her in no doubt about what she was hearing. English wasn't her first language so she had comforted herself that she had misunderstood what was being said. But she hadn't.

Pilar had lived in London now for nearly sixteen years and her command of English had even been good when she first arrived. Now it was probably better than most native Londoners who spoke incomprehensibly about 'apples and pears' and 'whistles and flutes'. Those on the market stalls did, anyway, when they weren't talking Urdu or Arabic, of course. On balance, she preferred the apples and whistles.

Why was the man still talking? she wondered. Surely, he had told them what they wanted – or rather had not wanted – to hear? That the money her mother-in-law had left, together with her sizeable property portfolio, wasn't going coming to them after all.

Grant Vaughan turned his gaze from his wife to the solicitor, who was at last showing signs of winding up. It hadn't been a profitable half-hour: it could all have been said in one sentence: *The old girl hasn't left you a bean.* Or words to that effect. He was sure the old solicitor was chuckling to himself. It was probably making his day.

Martin Preston had been Mrs Vaughan's solicitor for as long as Grant could remember, an old and creaky individual of indeterminate years but with at least four and a half decades under his belt, he suspected. He had to admire him, carrying on in business as if he was still forty and seemingly possessed of all his faculties.

"I'm sorry the news isn't what you wanted to hear, Mr Vaughan," said Preston, rising shakily to his feet.

Grant could see a smile start to hover around his crinkly eyes as he shook his hand. I bet you are, he thought. It was probably the only enjoyment he got these days, telling people bad news.

"Thank you anyway," said Grant. "It's rather a blow, of course. I suppose there's no chance of challenging the will on grounds of diminished responsibility?"

"Did your mother show any signs of – er – not being in full command of her faculties, Mr Vaughan?"

Damn the man, thought Grant. "Mad as a March hare," he said with conviction. "Always was." He laughed to ease the tension as poor Preston looked decidedly ruffled now.

"I believe you jest, Mr Vaughan?"

"I wish I did, Mr Preston," said Grant amicably.

The solicitor didn't seem amused. "Oh, by the way," he said, just as he was showing them out, "I nearly forgot. I have a sealed letter for you." He returned to his desk and unlocked a drawer. He passed a manila envelope to Grant who took it as if was about to explode.

"Thank you," he said, as he examined it carefully. "Do you know what's in it?"

Preston's eyebrows shot up. "Of course not. It is addressed to you, marked 'personal'." He looked offended.

Indeed it was. Grant recognised his mother's spidery scrawl. "From my mother, I see," he said, stuffing it into the top pocket of his jacket.

"Yes. I hope it explains the reasons why Mrs Vaughan left you out of the will," he said. "I'm sure she was completely in her right mind," he added firmly. "I admired your mother greatly and I'm sure she meant well towards you, despite everything. I was sorry you didn't visit her more often, although I know she derived much pleasure from your daughter's visits."

"Yes, they got on well. I only wish I had."

Grant Vaughan took his wife's arm and headed towards the door, turning back suddenly to the solicitor. "I understood the will stipulates my daughter will receive a legacy in due course when the present legatee dies or when Amanda-Thérèse reaches maturity, whichever is the sooner. I think that's what you said? What you didn't tell me was who that legatee actually is."

Preston coughed and fished a lozenge out of a packet on the desk. "I'm not at liberty to divulge that information to you, Mr Vaughan. I'm sorry."

Pilar, who had been silent for most of the interview, spoke up now. "Come on, dear," she said to her husband, "we have taken up too much of Mr Preston's time as it is. Goodbye, and thank you." She held out her hand to the solicitor.

Preston smiled at her. "Goodbye, Mrs Vaughan, it was a pleasure to meet you."

"Come on, dear," said Grant grumpily. "I think it only fair to tell you, Mr Preston, that I'm seriously thinking about contesting the will."

"That's your privilege, of course," said Preston, his thin lips set in a straight line as he sucked on his throat sweet. "However, you will find it won't be easy, and will be very costly."

He drove erratically through the quiet lanes of Lower Slaughter. Pilar, at his side, looked at her husband with concern. "Please be careful, dear," she admonished him, "you nearly ran over that cat."

"Blast the bloody cat!" cried Grant, banging the steering wheel with his bunched fist.

Pilar knew, when her husband was in such a mood, there was nothing to be done until he had had time to calm down. She watched the poor cat reach the safety of the low Cotswold stone wall of the cottage opposite and sighed with relief. She loved animals, cats, dogs, anything, apart from snakes. Her love of animals was one of the main reasons she had left Spain. She had no wish to be associated with a country that derived sport from tormenting bulls to their deaths. The fact that England went in for hunting foxes for sport had given her cause for concern, but she had salved her conscience with the assurance that foxes at least had a sporting chance of escaping a gory death. Unlike the poor bulls.

She looked again at her husband who was still driving recklessly and whose face was a mask of controlled fury. She began to wonder if they would arrive home in one piece. But she knew he was an excellent driver and trusted him completely when he was at the wheel so she began to relax. Her thoughts now turned to old Mrs Vaughan's letter which she could see poking out from the top pocket of her husband's jacket.

Just what was in it? she wondered.

Grant Vaughan had been so buoyant all through the last couple of weeks, looking forward to the reading of his mother's will. Her demise hadn't caused him any real sorrow, only for a life imperfectly lived. Now she was gone, his only thoughts concerned how much she would have left him, even though they had never seen eye to eye. It hadn't been a factor. He was her only son, after all, so who else was she to leave it to? Besides, his daughter, Amanda-Thérèse, had spent at least one afternoon a week of her school holidays at old Mrs Vaughan's, reading to her, listening to the old woman's reminiscences, sympathising with her aches and pains, and making her endless cups of tea. That alone would have ensured his legacy, or that was his rather twisted logic.

He had been happily planning how to spend all his new wealth. And, in his mind, he'd already sold the old woman's home. The great, rambling barn of a place where he'd been brought up held no fond memories for him. He looked back on it as a house of correction for the little boy who, according to both parents, couldn't do anything right. His hated father died of a heart attack in his mid-forties and that should have drawn him and his mother closer together. Instead, however, Mrs Vaughan took on all her husband's fearsome aspects, wielding the strap whenever poor Grant committed some misdemeanour or other.

His escape was sweet when it finally came and he'd managed to get a place of his own as well as a wife to put in it. But his new-found independence, far from pleasing his mother, only served to estrange her even more. When the marriage ended in bitter divorce, old Mrs Vaughan hadn't concealed her delight at one more failure on his part. Her delight had been short-lived, however, because within a couple of months he'd introduced her to his second wife. It was a double blow to her, as this new wife turned out to be some sort of 'foreigner'.

Things changed somewhat when Pilar Vaughan gave birth to their daughter. Grant recalled the grudging congratulations his mother doled out to him. Amanda-Thérèse had been a beautiful baby, perfect in every way. Even the old woman couldn't fault him on that. As his daughter continued to grow, her beauty was matched by her obvious intelligence, and his mother continued to approve. But this approval soon became limited to only her granddaughter, while the rift between mother and son continued to burgeon, seemingly insurmountable by both parties.

As he pulled up in front of their home, his thoughts still whirling around his head, he realised that, if it hadn't been for their daughter, there would have been no legacy at all. Little Amie, as she was affectionately called, had saved the day.

But just who was going to enjoy his mother's wealth in the meantime?

2

She surveyed the small congregation carefully. She hadn't been in this church before, and everyone here was a stranger to her. This was how she liked it, for there were rich pickings to be had, she felt sure.

In the first row of pews, she spotted one couple and two women on their own. No need to bother with the married couple, of course. She turned her attention to the two women who were both of a similar age, she reckoned, in their mid-sixties to early seventies, or thereabouts. Yes, she would definitely find an excuse to talk to at least one of them after the service.

She looked around the rather dimly lit church and shivered. St John's in the small parish of Bibury, picturesque though she supposed it was, was decidedly chilly. Why couldn't these country churches be a little warmer? she wondered, hugging deeper into her winter coat. It was still only late autumn, but she had taken the precaution of wearing it that morning in the eventuality that the church would be as cold as indeed it proved to be.

The weather outside was mild for the time of year, but not an atom of its warmth was permeating the interior. She sat, shivering, listening to the droning of the organ as people continued to arrive. She watched the vicar with amusement, who seemed to be having trouble with the sleeves of his surplice. Too long for him, she could see, for he was only a short man, no more than five foot four or five.

There were several other middle-aged and elderly women on their own filing in now. Yes, she thought, they look promising. One in particular who looked like she'd been crying. That was always a good sign.

"Nice service," she said companionably to the two women from the front pew. She had waited for them to make their way to the entrance and followed casually behind them. They were obviously friends, or acquainted with one another at least. All to the good. Two birds with one stone. She liked that. Zelda would be pleased with her.

Both women smiled at her. It was a similar smile. She thought they could easily be sisters, twins even. But their smiles were sad, and that made her happy.

"Yes," said one. "Our Reverend Chalmondley does a good sermon. Not too preachy and, more to the point, not too long."

"No," agreed her companion. "He knows we have the roast beef in the oven."

Faith Desmond smiled. It seemed a long time ago when she had last had a roast dinner on a Sunday. Not since her poor Eddie had passed over. "Are you in a hurry to get home?" she asked them.

The two women looked at each other. Faith could see even more of a resemblance between them now. They even seemed to be wearing the same clothes.

"Er, well, no, not right away. The beef's on a low setting – just in case."

"Would you care to come and have a coffee with me?" she asked. "I noticed a nice little café just down the road."

"Oh, that place," said one of the women dismissively. "That's purely for the tourist trade. We know a much nicer place, don't we, Olive?"

"Oh, yes, much nicer," echoed the woman called Olive. "Cheaper too. Off the beaten track."

"Oh, but it's not open on a Sunday," said the first woman.

Olive looked sad. "No, of course not. Suppose we'll have to go to the Olde Tea Shoppe after all."

"Never mind," said Faith. "My treat. I really could do with getting off my feet before I go home."

"You don't live around here, then?" asked Olive, when all three women were settled in the café with a large pot of coffee between them. They hadn't ordered any cakes or sandwiches as they didn't want to spoil their lunch. Faith, who didn't have roast beef waiting in the oven for her, resisted the cream cakes on account of her ever-expanding waistline.

"No, I live in Stow – well, just outside it, actually," she replied. "My name's Faith Desmond, by the way. You're Olive, I know. And you are?"

She looked at the woman as yet unnamed.

"Sylvia, dear. Sylvia Harmon. And Olive's my sister. She's Olive Dickinson."

"So, you're both married?" Faith sipped her coffee, which was a little too strong for her taste, but nonetheless welcome after the chill of the church. She was thawing out nicely.

"Well – we were," said Sylvia, blowing on her coffee to cool it down. "We're both widowed."

"Oh, I'm sorry," said Faith. "How long – I mean, how long since….?"

"My hubbie's been dead two years now," said Sylvia. "But poor Olive's husband has only just died. Four weeks ago."

"I'm sorry," repeated Faith. "I'm a widow too. My husband's been dead for five years, so I'm used to it."

The three women were silent for a little while as they all concentrated on their coffee. A sort of widowy companionship seemed to envelop them. The café was filling up now and there were several children among the new patrons. It was getting noisy.

"That's what I don't like about this place," observed Olive. "The kids. There seem to be more and more of them these days. Any woman of child-bearing age seems to have at least half a dozen of them in tow. The tourists, that is."

"Yes. The parents don't seem to have any control over them, do they?" agreed Faith. "Do you have any children?"

Both women shook their heads.

"Nor me," said Faith, finishing her coffee.

"Tell me," said Olive, leaning forward and looking seriously at Faith. "If you live near Stow, why were you in church here today? A bit off the beaten track for you, isn't it?"

"Oh, no particular reason," lied Faith glibly. "I like a change, that's all."

"Are you a committed Christian?" asked Sylvia, searching in her bulky handbag for something which turned out to be a handkerchief.

"Er, well, I wouldn't say *committed* exactly," replied Faith thoughtfully. "I do believe in *something*, I suppose. We have to, don't we? Otherwise what are we all here for?"

"That's true." Sylvia blew her nose and returned her hanky to her handbag. "Olive's not so sure now."

Faith turned her attention to Olive. At close quarters, she could see she was slightly younger than her sister. "Oh, why is that, dear?"

Olive shrugged. Faith could see tears standing in her tiny brown eyes. Like a bird's, she thought.

"My Harry died," she said with finality, as if that explained everything. Which it probably did, thought Faith. It was often the case that when a loved one died, the one left behind became disenchanted with God and all things religious.

"But you were in church?" Faith was puzzled.

"Oh, that's Sylvie. She made me. Thinks I'll get over it. But I'll never get over it. Not Harry dying, as such. I know we all have to go sometime. No, it was the *way* he died."

Faith could feel the tension building along with the noise of the children's excited voices all around them.

Two five-year-olds were running up and down the café now, shrieking with delight or maybe it was pure frustration at being trapped in a small space while their parents, oblivious, tucked into sandwiches and chattered to one another.

Faith felt her anger rising. Why couldn't parents care for their children properly these days? They were falling over themselves to bring them into the world, but apparently lost interest in them soon after, preferring the company of friends and their inevitable mobile phones.

"Shall we go?" Faith said, taking out her purse to pay the exorbitant price of the coffee. "It's getting too noisy in here. Maybe we could continue our chat somewhere else?"

"Well, there's a nice park just round the corner," said Sylvia. "It's quite a nice morning, we could go for a stroll round there."

Faith had hoped to be asked back to their home, for she was sure they lived together. Why wouldn't they, being both widows and sisters? It would have been nice to sit in a warm parlour, she thought, still feeling chilly. Her bones seemed to absorb the cold these days, reluctant to let it go once absorbed. The hot coffee had helped but not enough. Still, best foot forward, she told herself. She didn't like walking much at the best of times, usually relying on her Austin mini to get her from place to place.

They entered the pretty park and began slowly walking along the designated paths. The trees were all shades of golds, reds and browns. Faith had to admit they looked beautiful in the autumn sunshine.

"My Harry had cancer," said Olive suddenly, without any prompting.

"That's rough. I'm sorry." Faith made suitable sympathetic noises, trying not to appear too interested, nosey even.

"Well, lots of people get cancer and lots die of it," said Olive. Her sister got another handkerchief out of her bag and handed it to her. They all waited while Olive blew on it and wiped some stray tears from her eyes.

They continued along a path which took them around a bunch of overgrown rhododendron bushes. There was a vacant bench in their sights.

"Shall we sit for a moment?" asked Faith, who'd already had enough of walking. She knew she should exercise more but, when it came down to it, she couldn't be bothered. Who had time these days, anyway? There was always so much else to do.

They managed to squeeze themselves onto the rather narrow bench. It was made to seat three normal sized individuals comfortably, but all three women were overweight, Olive particularly so.

"As I was saying," said Olive now, seemingly glad to unburden herself to a stranger, "he died a horrible death."

"Yes, well, cancer's a horrible disease," said Faith quietly. Her own husband had died of it too. He was only forty-two.

"Pancreatic cancer's the worst," said Olive vehemently.

"Yes, I've heard it is pretty horrible." Faith felt the woman was blaming her personally for the virulence of her poor husband's disease. "But don't you think he's in a better place now? No more pain? Free?"

"Bollocks!" said Olive. Sylvia touched her sister's hand.

"Hush, dear!" she said sweetly. "Sorry, Faith love. She doesn't usually swear."

"Excuse me. I'm still here, you know. Who's 'she'? The cat's mother?" Olive looked as if she was about to swear again, but then suddenly laughed.

Sylvia joined her sister in the laughter, and they both seemed more relaxed now. Faith saw her opportunity at last. "Wouldn't you like to know if your husband's happy now, Olive? After all the pain?" she asked, as casually as she could.

Olive stared at her. "What do you mean? He's dead. He can't tell me anything, let alone how happy he is."

"Well, dear," said Faith softly. "That's where you're wrong and I intend to prove it to you."

3

Grant Vaughan continued to fume all day after his visit to Preston, Preston and Underwood, and all through the following day too, which was Sunday. Despite a delicious dinner provided by his wife, despite all sorts of other delightful distractions she provided, he couldn't get his mind off what he saw as the injustice of his mother giving away his birthright to a complete stranger. Just who was this person who had got it all? And why?

"Why don't you open the letter?" Pilar asked for the umpteenth time as her husband obstinately refused to do so.

"What's the point?" he grumbled, picking up the envelope old Preston had given him. He stared at the handwriting: *Mr Grant Vaughan – to be opened after the reading of the will.* His mother's spidery scrawl had always struck the fear of God into him. He knew, even before he opened a letter from Mrs Vaughan, what it would contain. And he was always right. She had only ever written to him when she wanted to reproach him with something. First, when he was at boarding school and then when he was married and no longer under his mother's roof. Letters complaining about something he hadn't done and should have, or had done and shouldn't have. Her script was even more spidery now due, he supposed, to the arthritis she'd been moaning about for years.

"There's a lot of point, surely?" Pilar came and sat on the arm of his chair. The imitation gas log fire beside them gave out too much heat and it was warm for November. "Do we need this on?" she asked. The central heating was up full blast too.

"I'm cold," he protested, still fingering the unopened envelope. "I'm always cold these days."

She ruffled his hair. "Whatever you say, dear," she said softly. She leaned over and took the letter from him. "Shall I open it?"

He snatched it back. "No!"

"Why don't you want to see what your mother has to say? It may be another legacy, for all you know."

He snorted with derisory laughter. "You're joking, of course?"

"Maybe you should have visited your mother more often," said Pilar. "She was a lonely old woman. I'm glad Amie went to see her when she could."

"No doubt she'll be glad too when she comes into her grandmother's legacy." Grant looked at the log effect fire now and kicked it irritably. "Why is this thing on? It's much too hot in here."

Pilar bent down and switched it off without speaking.

"Look, I know I'm being annoying," said Grant as he watched his wife's trim figure unbend, showing off all her perfectly proportioned assets. Even at her age she was a stunning woman and he never tired of looking at her. But she couldn't cheer him up today.

"Why don't you open the letter? Go on." Pilar tried once more.

But he was reluctant to know its contents, fearing even more bad news, although he couldn't imagine what that could be. After all, he already knew the worst, didn't he? "All right, all right," he said at last. "You open it, if you like."

Pilar took the envelope from him and smiled. "I'm sure it won't say anything that dreadful," she said coaxingly. She tore it open and Grant watched as her eyes scanned the letter.

"Well?" he said, impatient now to find out what his mother had written to him. Pilar passed the letter to him without a word.

He started to read:

Dear Grant

You will by now have received the news that I'm leaving you out of my will. It gave me no pleasure to do this, contrary to what you no doubt believe. All my life I only tried to do my best for you. I was probably too strict by today's standards, but it was my way and I cared for you more than you probably will ever realise.

Your daughter was the consolation of my old age, and I have you and Pilar to thank for that. Which I never did. I didn't want you to marry her, and I didn't like her. She was too beautiful. I didn't think she'd stick by you. I was wrong. I'm sorry now we never got on.

Now to the information I know you really want to know. I have left my house to someone who gave me much comfort in my last years. Zelda Caldicot is a medium and she got in touch with your father for me. I was able to contact him through her on many occasions and I go to my death happy in the knowledge he is waiting for me on the other side. Thus Zelda – Madame Zelda as she is known professionally – is my beneficiary. She will not be allowed to sell the property but she will be able to rent it out until Amie reaches her majority. This, I understand, is eighteen years and not twenty-one as I erroneously thought. Times change and not usually for the better.

As you know, I invested wisely over the years. Your father taught me well, even after his death. There is a large legacy to come to Amie, but for now it is entrusted to Madame Zelda. Again, when Amie is eighteen, this will come to your daughter, apart from the profits made by Zelda herself out of this money. I think that is only right. It should be a tidy sum on which she should be able to live comfortably for the rest of her life.

In the event that Madame Zelda dies before Amie reaches her eighteenth birthday, then all will revert to yourself for the duration. I do not expect this to happen, as Madame Zelda is only in early middle age and in good health, as far as I am aware. If, however, she dies sooner than expected, I will expect you to hold in trust all the investments and profits thereof until Amie comes of age. I am confident you inherited your father's financial brain and so will look after these investments wisely. You will be at liberty to continue renting out the house until Amie comes into her fortune and can decide whether to sell it or not.

I have nothing further to say now. My hands are painful and this rather long letter has taken me several hours, on and off, to complete.

Think kindly of me, if you can.

Grant read his mother's letter three times before he said anything to Pilar. Meanwhile, she busied herself with stacking the dishwasher and tidying the kitchen. Sunday lunch was a ritual for her, and involved the use of every pot and pan in the well-equipped kitchen, as well as every work top surface visible to the naked eye. She had little else to occupy her, so she enjoyed making a mess and clearing it up again.

However, her mind wasn't on her work this afternoon. Grant's mother's letter was a bit of an eye-opener for her, almost as much as for her husband. He had always spoken bitterly of the old woman and, although Pilar privately thought he should try and mend fences, she also privately thought Mrs Vaughan was rather an old cow. When she had first met her, she could sense her icy antagonism immediately. She had tried to ignore it at first, however, and paid her many visits during the first two years of her marriage to

Grant, bringing her cakes, magazines and other little gifts. But it had been a waste of time.

Then Amanda-Thérèse was born and, when she first brought her to see old Mrs Vaughan, a layer of chill began to lift. It was clear from the start that the old woman doted on the baby, but somehow Pilar still wasn't included in that affection. At best, she was tolerated, as baby Amie wasn't, of course, able to visit the old woman on her own.

Pilar had long since given up trying to persuade Grant to try harder with his mother. She had found knocking her head against a brick wall too much of a negative activity and, besides, she couldn't really blame him. Now the letter revealed something about her mother-in-law she hadn't expected. The woman had actually cared for her son, after all. But it didn't make Pilar soften her attitude towards old Mrs Vaughan; it had made her more angry with her, if anything. Too much stuff had gone on, and her husband, for all his outward bravado, was a damaged soul.

Grant had been plainly moved by his mother's letter, and she could only imagine what a shock it must be to find out he wasn't the son of the wickedest fiend that ever lived, after all. Grant had told her how his mother had beaten him as a child, especially after the death of his father who, up to then, had been the one to administer the frequent corporal punishment, and this had shocked her deeply. But the old lady had explained in the letter how she had only been strict for his own good and had brought him up in the way she thought was right. She was from another generation, Pilar conceded. Things were different then.

She returned from the kitchen to find her husband still holding the letter and staring into the now turned-off gas fire. The room felt chilly now. She switched it on again and retired to the kitchen once more, leaving him alone with his thoughts.

"We must find this Zelda woman," said Grant suddenly later that evening over a supper of cold roast beef and pickles.

"Must we?" asked Pilar, her heart sinking. Far from being sad now at the loss of a mother he had never really understood, he seemed to be concentrating on his lost legacy again. "What good would that do?"

He shrugged. "I'd just like to meet her, that's all. A psychic medium, I ask you! What a load of rubbish. She's obviously a fraud, preying on deluded women like my mother. Now she's got her hands on all her money."

Pilar reached across the dining table and touched his shirt sleeve gently. "You must try to get over it, dear," she said soothingly. "Amie will come into it all when she's eighteen, and that's only three years away. She'll not see us starve." She tried a little laugh, but her husband obviously didn't see the joke.

"I don't want to be beholden to my daughter," he growled. "Don't you think I've got my pride? I was looking forward to chucking the job and doing some travelling. Wouldn't you have liked that?"

"Of course I would, and I know how the job gets to you. But in three years' time we'll be able to do all that. It's not so long to wait."

"Will we? Maybe Amie will have other ideas. She'll be the one doing the travelling, I shouldn't wonder."

"Amie will have more money than she'll know what to do with. Be sensible, dear. And she loves you. She loves us both. You only have quarrels about your mother."

It was true. Young Amie had often tackled her father about his lack of filial affection, but otherwise the bond between father and daughter was deep and strong. Pilar often felt excluded when they were all together and, although she had objected when Grant had decided Amie should go to a private boarding school, she was more often glad rather than sorry about her daughter's long absences from home.

"And what if this stupid woman blows the lot on bad investments? We have to find her, I tell you."

Pilar could see there was no help for it. "Well, if she's a professional medium, she'll no doubt advertise in the local papers. She'll probably have a website too."

"Come on then, let's look online," he said, getting up from the table, his meal hardly touched.

4

Charlie Caldicot was a bit of a novelty in the Cotswolds, being a Londoner born and bred and as 'cor blimey' as they come. A handsome, pulsating pile of testosterone, he had gone through two wives and was now estranged from his third at the relatively young age of forty-one. Having given marriage his best shot, he had since decided a mistress might be a better option, and so had now got himself one of those instead. Generally speaking, therefore, he was a contented, if not an exactly happy, man.

He had been happy not all that long ago. Wife number three was fairly well off and he'd had no need to work, which suited him down to the ground. His motto had always been 'why work if you don't have to?' There was always someone else who would, save him the bother. His fondness for the high life had proved his undoing, however, as wife number three's private income had soon begun to dwindle. Even though she had a profession of sorts which brought in extra cash, she had expected him to contribute to the household expenses. That's when he'd decided to look for a mistress.

He didn't have to look too far for her as it turned out. The woman who took his fancy was a close friend and confidante of his wife's and, far from giving him any qualms about the ethics in the case, he had begun a charm offensive on her without a second thought. She wasn't as attractive as his wife, but he'd decided she'd suit him, mainly because he was too lazy to look further afield. And, before too long, he had moved from the marital home to his mistress's far smaller, but nonetheless, comfortable abode.

So, life was reasonably sweet for him now, as he sat by the fire in her picturesque cottage in an equally picturesque Cotswolds village not far from Stow-on-the-Wold. Except today he was alone. It was Sunday afternoon and the clock was just striking two-thirty. She had been gone for over four hours, when at last he heard the key in the lock.

"And about time too!" he shouted as he heard the familiar footsteps in the hall. "Where 'ave you been till this time? My guts 'ave been rumbling something rotten. You said you were going to church. 'Ow long do services go on for these days?"

"Look, Charlie," said Faith Desmond, as she removed her scarf and stuffed it into her handbag. "You know I go to church every Sunday. We have this row every week."

"Not every week. Not when you come 'ome at a reasonable time and get my lunch on. A man needs 'is grub, woman."

She clipped her handbag shut and stared at her mobile phone without replying.

"Don't keep checking your phone every five minutes neither," he moaned. "It's bloody annoying. I bet it's my bleedin' wife again."

"I just sent her a text and I wanted to see her reply. That's all." Faith didn't raise her voice. "What do you want for your lunch then?"

"I suppose we're 'aving bleedin' pasta again," he grumbled. "You know I 'ate the stuff. I'd 'ave joined the bleedin' Mafia if I wanted to eat that all day."

Faith smiled and came over to him. She kissed him lightly on the forehead. "I've got some chops," she said. "Won't take a jiffy. I suppose it was beyond your powers to peel a few spuds?"

"I ain't 'ad time."

"Yes, I see you've been busy," she said snidely, eyeing the pile of Sunday papers on the table beside him.

"Anyway, you 'aven't told me where you've been to this time."

"I've been talking to a couple of possible clients, if you must know. I'm late as well because I drove out to Bibury. We need some new clients and there were some good prospects there. Lots of widows."

"You're always runnin' round 'er like a blue-arsed fly!"

"You're forgetting she pays me for that. If it weren't for her, we'd be in shtook. *You* don't bring in much."

Charlie Caldicot squirmed. 'Ere we go, he thought. She's beginning to sound like my bleedin' wife. He hadn't missed his 'bleedin' wife' for a single moment, and he'd missed her son by her first marriage even less:

a great hulking teenager with a brain that had obviously stopped working when he'd reached the age of seven.

Zelda Caldicot was a professional medium and Faith was employed as a sort of procurer for her. It was all rather dodgy, but it hadn't bothered him unduly as long as the money kept rolling in. His wife had been a genuine psychic in her earlier days, or so she had told him, but by the time he married her she was having to resort to underhanded methods to maintain her reputation. Those methods mostly involved Faith befriending the recently bereaved to find out all about their dear departed and priming 'Madame Zelda', as she called herself, accordingly.

"I do gardening and odd jobs," he pointed out as Faith continued to give vent to her annoyance at his idleness. It was true that he occasionally got himself out of his armchair to help some of the neighbours when they needed a hedge trimming or a sink unblocked. As the calls on his services usually came from women, he never had much trouble in doing a substandard job and then charming them out of twice what the job was worth.

Faith sighed. "Oh yes, of course you do. Well, I'd better get the dinner on, hadn't I? Make yourself useful and open the wine, will you?"

This was a job that he actually liked. He followed her into the kitchen and searched the wine rack. He prided himself on being a bit of a wine buff, grinning as he selected a four-year-old Macon and blew the dust off it. Just the thing to go with the chops, he thought with satisfaction. The smell of them frying was comforting now, as he watched her peel the potatoes. He uncorked the wine to let it breathe.

5

Luke Caldicot stared at his mother as he watched her coming up the garden path carrying a dog lead completely empty of dog.

"Where's Meg?" he yelled at her. "What have you done with her?" He followed her into the house, nearly treading on her heels.

Zelda Caldicot sighed. She was still crying, even though she had left the vet half an hour ago. She had loved Mystic Meg just as much as her son, but he would never believe it now. With a mental age of only seven, despite being a decade older, he couldn't, or wouldn't, understand why she had taken his pet to be killed.

She looked at her only son with his gentle, intelligent face and masculine beauty and, as always, was shocked by what she saw and by her overwhelming love for him. What would she do if he wasn't there? What would she do if she couldn't protect him from the world or from the fact of death?

He had never known his father, who had died in a car crash shortly before he was born. The tragedy had brought on her early labour, and she blamed this on Luke's stunted mental development. But it was his very innocence that made her love him so much, as well as his vulnerability and need for her love which he had always returned unquestioningly. Until today.

Now she realised she was powerless to protect him from unhappiness. Death had come to him at last. His beloved pet of eleven years had been taken from him and there seemed to be no way she could explain it to his seven-year-old brain.

"Luke, darling, you know she was old and ill, don't you? I kept telling you it was cruel to keep her alive when she was in so much pain. She had cancer, darling."

Luke stared at his mother through teary eyes. "But Granny had cancer and you didn't take *her* to the vet!"

Zelda didn't know what to say to this. She almost wanted to laugh. Instead she put her arm around his heaving shoulders as he sobbed his heart out. She joined him.

After a while both their sobs began to subside. "You – you just put Granny to bed when she had cancer," he accused her.

"But Granny said she would have rather gone to the vet like poor Meg, dear. Don't you see? Meg was luckier than Granny. She didn't have to suffer half so long."

Luke seemed to take this in and Zelda was almost sure he had understood. But the hatred in his lovely brown eyes still remained. "You killed my Meg!" he cried as if she hadn't said anything at all, and stormed up the stairs to his bedroom, slamming the door. The next thing she heard was loud thumping music.

Although she liked Simon Rogers, the boy who lived next door, she wasn't entirely sure he was good for her precious, unworldly son. Of course, she was pleased Luke had a friend of his own age, in years at least, but Simon was a normal sixteen-and-a-half-year-old and into the usual things boys of that age indulged in. Luke didn't understand half of it, of course, but that didn't stop Zelda worrying.

The choice of music was a case in point. Harmless enough in itself, but somehow disturbing to her soul. Up until Simon's influence, Luke had preferred gentle classical music, like Tchaikovsky's *Swan Lake* and *The Nutcracker Suite*. Now it was loud, tuneless thumping house or garage, maybe even handbag music for all she knew. Chopin and Mozart might never have even existed as far as Luke was concerned now.

Sighing, she decided to leave him alone for a while. He'll get over it, she thought. Maybe she should get another dog, except nothing could replace their beloved Mystic Meg, she knew that. If only Luke could understand just how heartbroken she was too by the dog's death.

Going into the living room, wiping her eyes, she remembered Faith Desmond. She had asked her to 'babysit' while she was at the vet. Her friend rose from the sofa to greet her.

"Hello, Faith," said Zelda, hastily shoving her wet hanky up her sleeve. "Thanks for holding the fort."

"Don't worry," said Faith kindly. "I'm happy to oblige. Poor you and poor Luke. He was beside himself. Was there no other way?"

"No, I'm afraid not. Meg was suffering. I had to make the decision. I hated doing it, but it was kinder. I know Luke doesn't understand though, no matter how many times I try to explain. It goes in one ear and out the other. I think he really hates me now."

"He'll come round, I'm sure. He just loved that dog."

"So did I, Faith. So did I!" She burst into tears, allowing Faith to put a comforting arm around her and lead her to the sofa. Zelda wasn't sure who she was most sorry for: the dog, Luke or herself.

"What you need is a nice cup of tea," she heard Faith say. The universal panacea trotted out at every conceivable disaster: wars, famine, floods, death.

"No, no, I'll be all right. I've got three clients coming. The first one is due any minute."

"She's already here, dear," said Faith.

"Oh, well, she's a little early. Did you show her into the back room?"

"Of course. Oh, by the way, there was a phone call for you. I answered it, I hope you don't mind."

"No, of course not." Zelda gave her a faint smile. "After all, you *do* work for me."

"Not as a secretary, I don't," Faith smiled back.

"Who was it?"

"Some solicitor or other. Preston, I think his name was. He asked you to call him. I wrote the number on the pad there."

"Thanks." Zelda picked up the pad beside her on the small table. "I don't know any Preston," she said thoughtfully. "I wonder what he wants?"

"He didn't say."

"How's Charlie?" Zelda asked suddenly. "Still as idle as ever?"

She'd been deeply hurt when her husband had left her, and even more hurt when she'd found out who he had left her for. She hid it well, however, determined not to let either party see her pain. Faith had been a good enough friend to tell Zelda where Charlie was, which had helped to heal a rift that had threatened to separate them. The fact that both women needed the other helped to produce an uneasy truce, although hostilities were always on the brink of breaking out.

"You know Charlie," Faith laughed, a little nervously. "About the only job he likes is opening the wine."

"And then drinking most of it?"

Faith laughed. "Naturally."

The two women exchanged smiles now.

"I'll get you that tea," said Faith, heading for the door. "Oh, by the way, did you get my text yesterday?"

"Yes, thanks."

"Two more likely prospects for you. I've given them all your details and I'm sure they'll be in touch."

She returned for her handbag and drew out a piece of paper. "I've jotted down the details about their husbands there. Names, what they died of, et cetera. Same deal as before?"

Zelda studied the paper. "Olive and Sylvia. Nice widowy names," she said. "Thanks, Faith. Yes, same deal as before. *When* they book, of course."

"I'll be on my way once I've made the tea, if you don't mind," said Faith. "I need to do some shopping."

"All right. Thanks for looking after Luke while I – you know."

"No worries, love. I don't think I was much comfort to him, though."

"No, as you can hear, he's sulking in his room." They listened to the noise from above their heads, which seemed to be getting louder by the minute.

"I don't envy you," said Faith. "I never liked that heavy metal music, even when I was Luke's age. That special school doesn't seem to be doing him much good these days."

"No, it's not the school. I think it's that Simon Rogers from next door. I'm grateful that he seems to have taken a liking to Luke, but I don't like his taste in music, if you can call it that. I'm sure Luke only listens to it because he thinks it's cool."

"Well, you've certainly got your hands full," said Faith a few minutes later as she handed Zelda a mug of steaming tea.

She picked up her handbag and pecked her on the cheek. "See you tomorrow," she said. "No, don't get up, I'll see myself out."

Zelda sipped her tea as she watched Faith walk down the front path. She had a clear view of her through the window from her vantage point on the sofa. Not for the first time, she wondered what her erring husband could see in her. Her gorgeous Charlie whom she still loved, despite everything. What had Faith

Desmond got that she hadn't, apart from a reasonable mode of living and presumably enough income to keep him in the style he was accustomed to? She had a nice face, she supposed, but she could do with dropping a couple of dress sizes, that was for sure.

Finishing her tea, she looked again at the telephone number on the pad. What could an unknown solicitor want with her? she wondered. She decided to wait until after her clients had left before ringing. Anything even vaguely legal made her nervous.

6

Grant Vaughan sat outside the headmistress's door, feeling for all the world like a naughty schoolboy waiting to be caned. In reality he was the proud father of Amanda-Thérèse, star pupil at St Mary's, the exclusive girls' day and boarding school especially chosen by him. The fees were crippling and, despite Pilar's constant protestations that they couldn't afford to keep their daughter there, he managed somehow to find them each month. He was determined his precious Amie would have every privilege money could buy. Of course, if his mother's will had come to him, any worries on that score would be at an end. He stood up and paced the long corridor, impatiently awaiting the bell to signal the end of lessons for the morning.

The bell, which was more of a siren, eventually sounded and girls of all ages and descriptions poured out from the classrooms on either side of him. He eagerly searched their young, happy faces for the one he loved best. And there she was. He caught his breath as she appeared, almost a head taller than most of her classmates and by far the most beautiful, with her flashing dark eyes and deep brunette hair inherited from her Spanish mother. Her lithe slimness added to her beauty, as did her soft, full lips and long dark eye lashes. He marvelled that this beauty seemed unhampered by the dowdy uniform the girls all had to wear, although the black stockings certainly did something for him.

"Hi, Dad," she greeted him, giving him a kiss on his slightly rough, unshaven cheek.

"Hello, my darling," he replied, stroking her hair lovingly. "I swear you get prettier each time I see you."

"But you only saw me last week at the funeral," she protested, laughing, but looking pleased nonetheless. She gave him a hug. "So, where are you taking me for lunch? I hope you, like, got permish from old Iron Drawers."

"Old Iron Drawers" was the nickname of Miss Bingham, the strict headmistress who, despite her manners and the epithet applied to her, was well respected, even liked, by most of the pupils under her care. They liked her better than the matron, anyway, a sour-faced creature given to dosing the girls with syrup of figs at every conceivable opportunity. Why she hadn't been put out to grass long ago was a mystery to the girls, but somehow she remained a fixture.

"Oh, Miss Bingham was no trouble. Said you could stay out as long as you want."

"Like, I bet she fancies you, Dad."

Grant laughed self-deprecatingly, although he was quite used to the admiration of the opposite sex. With a full head of silver hair and standing well over six feet tall, he wore his age well. He could pass for forty-five in a favourable light.

"She's bound to," insisted Amie. "All the girls in my class think you look like George Clooney. I think you look more like Cary Grant myself."

Grant laughed again. "I'm surprised you even know who Cary Grant is," he said, as they made their way to where he had parked his car. It was, in fact, right next to Miss Bingham's smart Audi.

"Come off it, Dad. Like, we've all seen the old films on telly. You made me watch them with you, remember?"

Grant Vaughan remembered those cosy evenings watching all the old black and white films only too well. Films he had collected lovingly over the years, first on video cassette, then on smart new DVDs. Not to be left behind, he had now graduated to Blu Ray and Netflix. Pilar was glad about Netflix as her husband's film collection was threatening to take over the house.

He smiled as he ensured his daughter was safe inside her seat belt and switched on the engine.

"So, Dad, to what do I owe the honour of this visit?" She rummaged in the glove compartment for the Polo mints she knew her father always carried. She sucked contentedly as they moved out onto the high street.

"I'll tell you all about it when we get to the restaurant," he said. "Now, before I tell you *my* news, what about yours? How's school?"

"Okay," she said, lowering the window. The heater was blasting up her black stockinged legs. "I like chemistry best. Mr Kenwright, that's the chemistry teacher, says I've got a talent for it. He's given me the key to the lab so I can go and do experiments whenever I like. I'm going to find a cure for cancer one day."

Grant gave her a sidelong glance. It was full of pride. "That's wonderful, darling. But – " He hesitated.

"I know what you're going to say, Dad. 'Like, what am I reading at the moment'?"

It was a sore point between them. Amie didn't like reading and she avoided it whenever possible. There was a time when her father had been hopeful she would get to like it. It was when she had read all the *Harry Potter* books in quick succession. But then she stopped. It didn't encourage her to pick up any other books, and Grant had reluctantly come to the conclusion that she had only read the *Potter* books because she didn't want to be excluded from a party everybody else was enjoying. J K Rowling had a lot to answer for, in his opinion. There was a wealth of literature his darling daughter hadn't even heard of, let alone read.

"Yes. What *are* you reading? A set book for GCSE?" That only made matters worse, of course. If his daughter was forced to read a book, that would only put her off the more.

"Boring!" she sighed, elongating the word as she closed the car window. "Some ugly old man, Quaglino or something, rings the bells at Notre Dame cathedral and, like, falls in love with this gypsy girl. Goes on for pages and pages and pages."

Grant smothered a laugh. "Quaglino? I think you'll find that's a restaurant in London, darling. It's famous."

"Whatever," she said, looking at her mobile phone. It had pinged several times during the past few minutes.

"I think you mean Quasimodo, and it's a wonderful story. I've got it on DVD somewhere. Charles Laughton and Maureen O'Hara."

These names from the dim and distant vaults of movie history weren't unknown to Amie. She had been schooled well by her father who had managed to instil in her a love of old films, if not books.

"It's a beautiful film. Maureen O'Hara never looked more beautiful." He sighed dreamily. One of the reasons he had first been attracted to his Spanish wife was her resemblance to the lovely film star. The colouring was all wrong, of course, O'Hara being flame-haired and green-eyed.

"I'll watch it with you, Dad, in the Christmas hols," she said, her fingers texting furiously. He wondered how she could do it so fast. He could only manage one finger at a time, but he didn't text that often, not if he could help it. He still preferred pen and paper, or typing at a push. The young today, he thought indulgently.

"I'll look it out especially. I think it will help you appreciate the book more." That was a vain hope, of course.

They pulled into the car park at the back of MacDonald's. "I suppose you want to eat here, darling?"

She smiled. "Natch," she said.

"Okay, Dad, tell me why you've come to see me." She squirted tomato sauce over her burger until it began to look like a traffic accident or the field after the battle of

44

Waterloo. Grant's stomach turned over. He had played safe with some fries and a strawberry milkshake, but he didn't fancy either now.

"It's about your granny's will," he said slowly.

"Oh yes, all that lovely money. She had stacks and that great old house. Are we, like, going on a world cruise? Are you getting a Jag or a Porsche?"

Grant held up his hand. "Hold your horses, love. I don't get a penny."

He watched her face as her jaw visibly dropped and she nearly choked on a chip. "What? Do you mean she was broke after all? I know she, like, had a flutter at the bookies sometimes, but she wasn't silly about it. She was always telling me how much she'd got in stocks and shares."

"Oh, she had plenty of money all right, only she's given it to someone else. At least, some of it. You'll get the bulk when you're eighteen."

"Oh Dad, I'm sorry," she said, reaching for his hand and giving it a squeeze. "Still, if I'm to inherit later on, then you'll have as much as you want then."

"That won't be for three years though. In the meantime, this woman's got the house and is earning money from renting it out. At least, I presume she is, as the will stipulates she can't sell it and it will come to you on her death. She also gets a smallish annuity for life, which I understand is what is euphemistically called a 'tidy sum'."

"What's happening to the stocks and shares then? Does she get them as well?"

"No. They're being invested wisely by your granny's solicitor and held in trust until you reach maturity."

"Only three years, Dad. Not so bad."

"I was just hoping to get hold of it now as I really want to give up work. I hate the bank, you know that. And then I wanted to make sure there was enough to pay all your school fees. Money's getting tight."

"Oh, Dad, I'm sorry. But I'll go to a state school, if that's the problem."

"Over my dead body you will."

"Well, Dad, I don't know what to say. Perhaps if you'd, like, visited her a bit more…" She pushed her plate away which was empty now apart from streaks of tomato sauce. She sucked at her milk shake. "Who's the beneficiary then? Do you know?"

"I was coming to that. Some clairvoyant called 'Madame Zelda'."

"Madame Zelda? Oh, that kind of makes sense. Gran was always going on about her. Took me with her a couple of times towards the end. Like, when she was getting too frail to go on her own. Poor Granny. Why did you hate her so much?"

"I didn't hate her exactly. But she never showed me any affection all my life. Never gave me a hug when I was a boy. Not once."

"She did love you, Dad. I know she did. She just couldn't show it. She wasn't a demonstrative person. She, like, only managed a peck on *my* cheek when I visited her, but I knew she loved me."

Grant Vaughan had kept the letter his mother had left him with her will and could quote by heart the bit where she told him she always did her best for him. As she saw it, anyway. If only she had told him just once that she loved him, all could have been different. He saw, perhaps for the first time, that his mother was starved of affection herself. His father hadn't shown any towards her, he remembered. He hadn't really noticed at the time, as he had been more concerned for himself then. Both his parents hadn't liked him, he had always been convinced of that. Now he began to see what a miserable life Mrs Vaughan must have had.

This Madame Zelda obviously told her what she wanted to hear; probably said her dead husband had always loved her more than anything in all the world. No wonder she felt so grateful to her. And then there was Amie, of course. Amie had gone to see her regularly every holiday. Suddenly he was glad she had cheered his mother's last days. He had always resented his daughter visiting his mother, seeing it as a sort of betrayal. But now he saw things differently.

He was starting to forgive his mother for all the years she hadn't shown him any love. It would take some time but, yes, he could do that eventually, because he now knew she had cared for him after all – in her own way.

But not for leaving him out of the will. No, he could never forgive her for that. Never.

7

Zelda Caldicot sat opposite the old solicitor, her mouth open. The little man poured out a glass of water and handed it to her, trying not to spill it. His arthritis wasn't getting any better; he'd soon have to retire and leave the work to his son and partner. But he wasn't quite ready to do so. He returned to his chair and looked through some papers while the lady in front of him collected herself.

He had been surprised by the woman's appearance when he had opened his office door to her ten minutes ago. He had expected a little old lady in pince nez, hair done up in a bun and probably draped in a lacy shawl. Instead, here was a woman in early middle-age, wearing that age well, tall, lithe, articulate and, above all, stunningly beautiful. His own experience of clairvoyants and their ilk didn't encompass the idea of Zelda Caldicot in the slightest.

When he had told her about her good fortune courtesy of Mrs Ada Vaughan, he thought she was going to faint. Now she sat drinking the water, her hand which held the glass visibly shaking. And not from arthritis, thought old Preston. Not like himself. Ready for the knackers' yard, that's what he was.

"I'm sorry to spring this on you, Mrs Caldicot," he said, when she had emptied her glass and seemed more composed. "It has come as a shock. Didn't you have any idea Mrs Vaughan had made you a beneficiary?"

"No, I had no idea at all," she said, "I never expected anything like this." She gave him a warm smile. Old Preston gave her a wintry smile in return. At his age, sunny ones were difficult to manage.

"It's a lot of money," he continued. "But you must understand that the property cannot be sold and will be transferred to Miss Vaughan on her eighteenth birthday. In the meantime, you can enjoy the profit from it by renting it out. It is a large, detached house, with five decent-sized bedrooms. Or, you might want to live in it yourself. It is a bit remote, though, and needs a bit of work on it. And then you might have to vacate it in a few years if the owner decides to sell."

"Oh, I don't think I'd want to live there myself," she replied. "It's not in Stow itself, is it?"

"Er, no, it's about a mile outside just before Upper Slaughter."

"Nice spot," she said.

"Also, you receive a small annuity for life which amounts to just over two thousand pounds a month," said Preston. "Not to be sneezed at, eh?"

"No, indeed. I need never work again. I had no idea she was so rich." Zelda Caldicot looked even more startled now.

"I think you must have given her more comfort than you realised," said Preston. He pressed the intercom on his desk which was answered immediately by a lot of crackle and a voice which was just recognisable as feminine. "Can we have coffee, please, Dulcie?"

Zelda emerged from the solicitors' office twenty minutes later still in a mild state of shock. She had never expected, in her wildest dreams, that such good fortune would come her way. She made a reasonable living out of clairvoyance, but Charlie Caldicot's expensive tastes had eaten into her private income. Ada Vaughan's legacy was a godsend.

Charlie. She thought of him now. He had left her because she'd had the temerity to ask him to contribute something more tangible to the marriage than just himself. Her friends had warned her when she'd married him that he was a waster. Good looks weren't everything, they had pointed out, and she knew they were right. But it had made no difference: she wanted Charlie under any conditions.

And the novelty hadn't worn off as quickly as everybody had thought either, mainly due to Zelda's unswerving love for him. She had been prepared to let him live off her money for as long as it lasted, although she hadn't expected him to desert her the minute she couldn't support him anymore.

She sat in the car but didn't start the engine. Did she really want him back? Because she had no doubt that the idle, good-for-nothing Londoner would be back as soon as he knew she was loaded once more. No, she told herself, enough was enough.

But then, of course, there was Faith. Her so-called friend and partner in the business. She'd lost no time in taking Charlie away from her. That would show her, when he came scuttling back to her. And she knew, deep down, she wanted him back. He was a rough diamond, but to Zelda he was the Koh-i-Noor.

She smiled as she stroked the steering wheel with her gloved hands. She didn't want to go back home just yet. She had a client at four o'clock, but until then she was free. Free to buy up Harrod's if she wanted. Well, that was an exaggeration, of course. But at least she could treat herself to a cup of coffee and a pastry at Hilda's Pantry. Hilda overcharged outrageously, but her clientele was mostly tourists so that was all right.

Today everything was all right with Zelda. She would enjoy a coffee and cake at Hilda's and even enjoy being fleeced for the privilege.

8

Simon Rogers splayed himself out on Luke's bed, reaching for the iPod station as he did so.

"That's enough of that row," he said firmly. He flicked through the menu until he was satisfied he had hit upon the loudest track he could find. "That's better."

Luke, who had been seated on the bottom of his bed to allow as much room as possible for his friend, jumped up and started to dance. It wasn't long before Zelda put her head round the door.

"Please turn down the volume, boys," she pleaded. "I have clients downstairs."

"Sorry, Mrs Caldicot," said Simon, all politeness and contrition, but as soon as Zelda had returned downstairs he raised the volume again.

"You'll get a smack," warned Luke, staring at the door with eyes like a rabbit caught in a car's headlights.

"She wouldn't smack me," smirked Simon. "I'd soon show her." However, he made a slight concession and fiddled with the volume so that it was somewhere between the loudest setting and the one below it. "Anyway, I think she fancies me."

"Fancies you?" Luke, with his child's mind, didn't quite grasp Simon's meaning, although instinctively he knew. "Do you like my mummy?"

Simon laughed. "Like her? Well, I suppose I do. She's fit, actually. I wouldn't say no."

This last comment was quite beyond Luke's brain so he decided to ignore it. "I hate her. She killed Meg."

Simon reached for the iPod and found another track to his liking. "Poor dog, but she was ill, Luke. I already told you that. Your mum was only doing what was best. It was suffering. You were being cruel trying to keep it alive."

Luke stared at Simon in horror. "You're wrong!" he screamed and flung the iPod, complete with its station onto the floor. The music continued to play as he burst into tears and proceeded to throw one of his tantrums. "How would she like it if I killed *her* like she killed Meg?"

He started to beat the duvet with his balled up fists. Simon, who was a nice lad despite his penchant for terrible music, tried his best to calm him down. "Come on, mate," he said, patting him on the back which was heaving with dry sobs, "you can't mean that. Your mum's all right. I'm sure she'll buy you another dog if you ask her nicely."

Luke still sobbed but with less passion now. He sat up and looked at Simon enquiringly. "'Nother dog?" he asked him, wiping his dripping nose on his sleeve and sniffing loudly. "I don't want another dog! I want Meg!" He began to wail again.

"Oh, give over!" Simon got up from the bed. Patience had never been his best quality. "You get on my tits, you do. I'm going."

Luke was in a panic now. He loved Simon and he loved his company. Now that he had sent his mother to Coventry for her dastardly crime, he only had Simon to talk to. There was Faith Desmond, of course, but she didn't really count. She was a grown-up, after all.

"Don't go," he pleaded. "I don't like being on my own. You only just got here."

Simon's hand was on the door handle, his other one was fixing his iPod's ear piece into his ear. He removed it and returned slowly to the bed. Flopping down on it, he propped himself up on one elbow and smiled at Luke.

"I've told you before about your tantrums. I won't stand for them. If only you knew how stupid you look when you get into one. I'll stay if you behave yourself."

Luke loved Simon because he didn't talk down to him all the time. A casual observer would look at the two boys and see very little difference in their appearance. Simon was a year older than Luke, but he was really a decade older in wisdom. Luke would never progress beyond his seven-year-old brain. Even though he was a strikingly handsome young man, no girl would ever love him as he ought to be loved. Once he opened his mouth, they would realise his problem at once and either pity him or just walk away.

Luke didn't bother about girls, not in the way Simon did. When Simon said a girl was 'fit' he saw someone good at skipping or climbing wall bars. When the epithet was applied to his mother, as Simon just had, the image became confused. Surely Zelda Caldicot was too old for such frivolous activity?

Simon was Luke's only real friend. The boys and girls at his 'special' school were all somehow removed from him. He had tried making friends with one or two of them but they had their own issues and couldn't relate to him in the way he wanted. Only Simon understood him properly and he couldn't bear to see him walk out on him in a huff.

"I'll try to behave, Simon, I will, I promise."

The rest of the evening was spent pleasantly enough after that. Simon helped Luke draw a picture of a tree and then an aeroplane. Luke's talent as an artist was non-existent but, with Simon's sure hand to help him, the pictures turned out rather well.

"I must get back now, Luke," said Simon eventually, looking at his diver's watch. It could do everything apart from make the tea and help with his homework and Luke was very envious. Christmas was coming and he had already dropped several hints to Zelda that he would like one just like it.

"But it's only half-past seven," protested Luke.

"Yes and I've got to get back for supper. Your mum will have yours ready too, won't she?"

Luke sniffed as if he was about to cry again. "S'pose," he said.

"Well, then. I'll see you tomorrow, okay?"

"Okay," said Luke. But it was far from okay. All he had to look forward to tonight was a silent supper with his mother and no dog to make a fuss of. The future, to poor Luke, was decidedly bleak.

"How much longer are you going to keep up this silent treatment?"

Zelda put a plate of fish fingers and chips in front of him and sat down opposite at the kitchen table. He didn't reply. She watched her handsome son as he poured HP sauce all over his chips and then shook more salt than was good for him over them too.

"Luke, dear, would you like another dog?" she asked, pouring out a glass of milk and passing it to him. He drank thirstily. He still said nothing.

She began on her Welsh rarebit with little appetite. "I shall have to finish off that dead tree tomorrow," she said, more to herself than to him. He had watched her as she had removed the dead branches of the old damson tree in the front garden, helping her to clear them away until only the dead stump of the trunk was left to deal with. That had been last week, when he was talking to her. Before she had murdered his precious Meg.

"I've got some special stuff from the garden centre. They told me it would poison the root. I hope so. I'd like to plant another tree there so that we'll have some nice blossom in a few years. That tree was such an eyesore. I told Charlie time and again to get rid of it, but could he be bothered?" She looked at her son as if expecting him to respond which of course he didn't. "No, of course he couldn't. The idle toe rag."

Silence continued to reign, the only sound coming from the scraping of cutlery on plates as they ate their supper.

"Now, Luke, I know you're not talking to me but at least you can listen," said Zelda, as she finished her meal. "There's a bottle under the kitchen sink which has a black and yellow sticker on it with a skull and crossbones. Now, do you know what that means?"

If Luke knew, he didn't let on, but she noticed a spark of interest in his eyes now.

"Now, you mustn't touch it and, in no circumstances, must you drink it. It's poison. It's for killing the root of the damson tree. Do you understand?"

Luke, for answer, stood up and left the kitchen.

9

Faith Desmond counted out the pound notes which had been handed to her by Zelda Caldicot.

"Just right," she said, wishing, not for the first time, that the amount agreed for each new client introduction was more. She had been paid the same for over five years now, and the cost of living wasn't getting any less. She resolved to say something next time as she put the money in her purse.

"Wine?" asked Zelda, proffering a half-full bottle of Merlot. "I'm having one. Although I think it should be champagne."

Faith was taken aback. It wasn't entirely unknown for Zelda to give her a glass of wine when she came for her money. It depended on what sort of mood she was in and what time of day it was. However, it was rare enough for her to wonder to what she owed the pleasure this evening.

"Thank you," said Faith, taking the glass. It was a favourite wine of hers and she drank it with relish. Charlie Caldicot had been particularly trying that day and she was in no hurry to get back to him. She rested her head on the back of the sofa and began to relax. "Why should it be champagne?" she then asked, curiosity getting the better of her.

"I suppose I should tell you, but I don't want the whole world to know. Besides, if I don't tell someone I'm going to burst."

"Tell me what?" Faith held out her empty glass for a refill and Zelda obliged.

"You mustn't tell anyone – not yet. Especially not Charlie, although he'll find out soon enough." There was a meaningful look in her eye as she said this.

"Cross my heart and hope to and all that," said Faith, ignoring the look. "I'm good at keeping your secrets, remember? What is it? You seem very happy tonight."

"I am. And with good reason. Do you remember that phone call you took for me last week?"

"Phone call? Oh, yes. Some solicitor wasn't it?"

"That's right. Well, apparently I've got a legacy from a grateful client."

"A legacy? That's nice."

"It's more than nice. It means I'm practically set up for life. I could stop doing this ridiculous job for a start. I'm also getting a sizeable income from the client's property. 'Loadsa money', to use an expression."

Faith was distinctly envious now. It was probably a client she had introduced her to and found out all about before she saw her. No wonder the client was grateful. Too bloody grateful.

"Congratulations," she managed to say through gritted teeth. "So are you going to give up this 'ridiculous job' as you call it?" Faith could see her sole source of income slipping away from her. Not only that, once Charlie knew about Zelda's good fortune he'd go back to his wife like a shot, leaving her precisely nowhere.

"I don't know. Not yet, anyway. In fact, I've rented a room for my sessions not far from here. It's much better as Luke's always playing loud music and disturbing the clients. There's someone else on the floor above who also deals in psychic matters. I haven't met him yet. It's the right sort of place. Don't you think that's a good idea?"

Faith thought it probably was. Mrs Moneybags was going up in the world, no doubt about that. "I think it will be the making of you," she said, trying very hard to keep the acid out of her tone.

"The making of *us*," said Zelda, picking up the wine bottle and seeing it was now empty. "I want you to share in my good fortune."

"You do?" Faith suddenly felt very warm towards her. She had always said Zelda Caldicot was a generous soul. Salt of the earth.

"We can definitely make the consulting room look fantastic," said Zelda. "Clients won't have to put up with that poky room downstairs anymore, not to mention the din from upstairs." She laughed. "Shall I open another bottle?"

"That would be nice."

The fresh bottle was soon uncorked and poured out. "Here's to you, Zelda," said Faith, clinking her glass.

"To *us*," said Zelda, clinking back.

So, thought Faith, as she happily sipped her wine, which tasted even nicer than the first bottle, the time was right to ask for an increase. She cleared her throat.

"Yes, dear Faith." Zelda was quite drunk, having downed half of the first bottle of wine before Faith arrived. "You shall receive more money for your introductions in the future. As long as you keep them coming and don't give the game away." She giggled.

"What game would that be then?" Faith felt quite tipsy herself now. They both giggled.

"Here's to us," said Zelda, hiccupping as she clinked Faith's glass.

"To us," returned Faith. "Just how much are you going to pay me, by the way?" She wasn't drunk enough yet to forget the essentials.

"Oh, lots!" said Zelda, waving her hand at nothing in particular. The many bracelets on her arm jangled.

"Precisely?"

"Oh, I'll work it out and let you know. I shall consult my solicitor."

Faith could see Zelda liked saying that. 'Consult my solicitor'. It sounded very grand, as if she was already enjoying her newly acquired status, which, of course, she probably was.

"Okay, thanks. But Zelda you were – *are* – a good medium. You have the gift or at least you did have once upon a time."

"Oh yes, I did have a lot of things once upon a time." Another meaningful look came Faith's way.

"You mean Charlie, don't you?"

"Do I? I suppose I do."

"He'll come back to you when he hears about your legacy."

"Do you think I'd want him back on those terms? You're welcome to the lazy sod."

Faith sipped her wine thoughtfully. Who did she think she was kidding? she wondered.

10

Cornelius Gray looked out of the window. What's all that commotion downstairs? he wondered. The source of the disturbance was soon apparent. A small white van was parked in front of the building and various items of furniture and what looked like red velvet drapes were being unloaded. Standing beside the two men doing all the donkeywork was an extremely attractive woman. Just my type, he thought.

He had been a professional medium all his working life, having been aware of his gift from the early age of eleven when he first saw a black cloud over one of his classmates. A few days later that boy was dead, crushed under the wheels of a lorry. Since then he had predicted the deaths of literally hundreds of people. It wasn't a gift he relished, but there was a certain appetite for knowing the worst and he had tapped into it when, as a young man, he set himself up as a clairvoyant in the King's Road, Chelsea. It was a happening place then. He wondered if it still was.

He had moved to the Cotswolds some time later with his young wife and small son. He predicted their deaths too. A widower for many years, Cornelius Gray had decided not to get attached to anyone else in case he saw the black cloud.

Predicting death wasn't his sole talent, but it was what he was best at. He could also see the future in other ways, but most of the predictions were dire and he often watered them down when passing on the information to his clients.

He stared down at Zelda Caldicot as she prepared to enter the building. The last of her possessions had obviously been taken inside now. If only he could let himself fall in love again, he could fall very easily in love with her. Still, she was probably married so what was the point? A woman that attractive was sure to be spoken for. However, he reasoned, at least he could introduce himself and see if she needed anything.

When Zelda took his proffered hand, she gave him a smile that sent his stomach lurching all over the place. Get a grip, he told himself. She's only a woman. They were ten a penny in his profession. Which was true, as most of his clientele consisted of women. Women of all ages, shapes and sizes, and he had never been tempted once, even though some of them were very attractive and obviously lonely and in need of friendship. But somehow this new woman had reached a spot no other woman had. Not for a long time. Not since his wife died. Maybe it was time to fall in love again. Life could be a lonely business without someone to care for.

He realised he was still shaking her hand and released it at once. "Sorry," he grinned, "hope I didn't squeeze too hard. I was miles away."

"Yes, I thought so," said Zelda, still smiling. "I'm Zelda Caldicot and I've taken the room on the ground floor. I see on the plaque by the front door that you're a clairvoyant too. I noticed that when I decided to rent here. I hope you don't think I'll steal your clients or anything."

By now, Cornelius would have let her steal the floor from under him and the roof over his head and he wouldn't have batted an eye. She was adorable. He tried to focus.

"Er, no, not at all. I might poach yours, you never know." He laughed and she joined in.

"Can I make you a cup of tea?" he asked, as he escorted her into the hallway. It was impressively spacious with a small waiting room off to the right. It was also very warm and inviting. "My next client isn't due for twenty minutes."

"That would be very nice," said Zelda, and she followed him up the stairs to his rooms.

That was the beginning of their friendship. Zelda had liked Cornelius Gray from the moment he had shaken her hand and crushed all her fingers together. He was the very antithesis of her husband, which she could only see as a good thing. And she could see he was smitten with her, but she was cautious. Although he was personable if not exactly handsome, he was charming with astonishing blue eyes. And tall. But, even so, she didn't see him as a prospective lover.

Cornelius was obviously a much better bargain than cheerful Charlie. How could she still be in love with the bugger? she wondered. He'd never done a hand's turn all the time he had been living under her roof. Take, take, take, that was what he was good at. A past master at it. Now here was a man who actually worked for a living. That was a novelty in itself. If only she didn't still love her husband.

Whatever her mixed-up feelings were, she was happy to spend time with Cornelius Gray. They enjoyed visits to the cinema and theatre, finding their tastes coincided more often than not. They were almost twin souls: laughing at the same jokes, despairing at the state of the world and at the silly people in charge of it. They had several expensive dinners together too, at the best restaurants in Oxford. He spared no expense in giving her a good time. A good time that he also obviously enjoyed. She always let him pay, determined not to make the mistake of telling him how well off she was. No man was going to take her for a ride again. Charlie Caldicot was the only one who could do that.

Then something changed. Cornelius had arrived one evening towards the middle of December to take her to the Oxford Playhouse to see a production of *The Curious Incident of the Dog in the Nighttime*. She had been looking forward to it and had dressed herself with especial care for he had proposed dinner afterwards as well. She had also half made up her mind to accept his invitation to coffee at his place to round off the evening. He had tentatively asked her last time they had gone out a few nights previously, but she had refused. Why had she? she had wondered. After all, Charlie Caldicot was out of her life for good, wasn't he? What was she holding back for? Cornelius Gray was an attractive man and she was a woman with needs just like anyone else.

Yes, she had finally decided, that night would be the night to take their relationship on to the next level. She had made him wait long enough.

But, as she greeted him at the door his face had taken on what she could only describe as a mask of horror. It had quickly vanished, however, and been replaced by an uncertain smile.

Was her makeup on straight? she had wondered. She'd had trouble with her lipstick and had had to wipe it off twice. She remembered hoping she didn't look like Coco the clown.

The play was a success but the dinner following was a distinct failure. He had been distant, cold almost, and had hurried her out of the restaurant without ordering coffee or liqueurs.

What had happened? She had finally trusted him enough to confide in him about the inheritance. Surely he wasn't the kind of old-fashioned, chauvinistic male who couldn't bear the woman having more money than the man?

She cried herself to sleep that night, hoping Luke couldn't hear her. Even though she wasn't in love with Cornelius, she had loved the idea of being in love with him as well as the idea of him being in love with her. She smothered her sobs in the pillow.

11

Luke opened the cupboard under the sink and looked inside. Yes, there it was, where his mother had left it. He picked it up and showed it to Simon.

"There! See I told you. Poison!" He said the word 'poison' with relish.

Simon took it from him and read the label carefully. "It's poison all right," he concluded.

"I keep telling you it is!" cried Luke impatiently. "She showed it me. Said I was not to touch it."

"Well of course you mustn't," said Simon. He passed it back to Luke. "Now, put it away," he said. "That stuff's dangerous."

Luke did as he was told and closed the cupboard door. Standing up, he looked around the kitchen as if he expected someone to pop out from one of the units or from behind the fridge. "Sshh!" he whispered.

"Sshh? Why?" Simon followed Luke's eyes around the room. "There's no one here. Anyway, why are we whispering?"

"No one must hear what I'm going to say, that's why," said Luke.

"Okay, if you say so."

"Poison kills people, doesn't it?"

"Can do, if you use enough of it or know what amount to give, I suppose. Depends."

"How much would you say is in that bottle? Enough to kill a person?"

Simon scratched his head. "I don't know. It says on the label it's for poisoning roots. Japanese knotweed, that sort of thing. No mention of human beings. But then, it's hardly likely to tell you how much you'd need to kill a human being." He laughed. "Now, come on, Luke, what's all this about?"

"I'm going to kill Mummy!"

Simon stared at him. "What? What did you say?"

"She killed Meg so I'm going to kill her. It says in the Bible that I have to."

They were back upstairs in Luke's room now. Simon flung himself down on the bed and propped himself up on one elbow. He watched his companion's excited face for a while before speaking.

"You're nuts," he said. "Bats in the belfry."

"Bats in the belfry to you too! It says in the Bible 'an eye for an eye'. I learnt that in Sunday School. I loved Sunday School till Mummy made me leave it."

"She only did that so people wouldn't laugh at you," said Simon. "Sunday School is for children and you had grown too big."

"I loved Miss Wiley. She was kind – not like Mummy. She wouldn't have murdered my dog."

"Miss Wiley? Who's she?"

"She was my Sunday School teacher. She told me what 'an eye for an eye' means."

"Did she? Did she also tell you what else it says in the Bible?"

Luke shrugged. "She told me lots of things in the Bible."

"I'm sure she did. For example, what about the Ten Commandments?"

"Oh, them…" Luke looked uninterested.

"Yes – them. One of them is 'thou shalt not kill'."

"So, then, Mummy shouldn't have killed Meg!"

There was no arguing with Luke's childish logic, but Simon persisted.

"Then there's the New Testament. She should have stuck to the New Testament and told you all about Jesus."

"She did tell us about Jesus – 'course she did."

"Right – and that he was a good person? He said that if someone smacked them on the cheek then they were to let them hit them on the other cheek – sort of."

"That doesn't make sense."

"Yes it does – it's kind of allegorical." Simon was struggling with words now, words that Luke could understand. He had another go: "Jesus talks about forgiveness all the time in the Bible. Your Miss Wiley should have told you that."

"She didn't. She'd understand that I have to kill Mummy. My mummy's wicked."

"No, she's not. She's kind, Luke. She was kind to your dog. She put it out of its misery. I don't know how many times I've told you that. Now stop talking such rubbish and listen to this."

He produced his smart new iPhone and plugged it into Luke's ears. "Great eh?"

Luke was diverted by the sound for a while. But when the track finished, he returned to the subject of matricide.

"I'm going to kill Mummy, you can't stop me."

"You can't! Anyhow, how are you going to do it?"

"I'm going to pour some of the poison in her tea."

"She'll taste it. That won't work."

"Then I'll put it in her food – somehow."

Simon got up to go. It was time for his supper. "Look, Luke," he said, as they both clattered down the stairs. "I've been thinking – "

Just then, the front door opened and Zelda came in, looking windswept, eyes shining.

"Hello, boys. How are you, Simon? Off home?"

"Yes, Mrs Caldicot."

"Your supper will be ready. I'll get yours, Luke. Give me ten minutes."

Luke followed Simon out of the front door. "What was you going to say?" he asked as he watched his friend clamber onto the fence which divided their properties.

"I was thinking that, if you're really determined to kill her, then you'd better let me do it." Simon propped himself precariously astride the rickety fence.

"You?" Luke seemed taken aback, then he smiled. "You can do it? You'll know how much poison to give her and how to give it to her so she won't taste it? Enough to kill her?"

"Yes. Enough to kill her. Now, you just forget all about it and leave it to me."

"But you'll need the poison," Luke pointed out.

"Oh, yes, of course. I'll get it tomorrow. Remind me."

He jumped down off the fence with a thud into his own front garden, just avoiding the Michaelmas daisies. "See you, Luke," he called. Then he was gone.

Luke grinned with satisfaction. Simon was a good friend. He had understood why he had to kill Zelda Caldicot. She had to learn she couldn't kill his dog and get away with it. It would teach her a lesson she'd never forget. See how she liked being killed, for a change.

12

Cornelius Gray sipped his morning coffee thoughtfully. He was between clients. He looked out of the window for the fourth time, hoping to see Zelda Caldicot. Where was she? he wondered. He had last seen her two nights ago, since when he had made a point of not meeting her at their joint place of work. He had, however, known she was seeing clients yesterday and that she was there on the floor below. Somehow that thought had comforted him, but this morning there had been no sign of her. No clients either. Why did he read anything sinister into it? he wondered. She hadn't come because there weren't any clients to see. Simple.

But something was wrong and he knew it. His sixth sense was working overtime on her behalf. Ever since he had seen the black cloud over her head when he had called for her to take her to the play. It had been unmistakable and very distinct which meant, in his experience, death would occur within a matter of days, or at the very most, a couple of weeks. He had wanted to go home and think what to do. He had left her in a hurry, and he knew he had upset her. But he couldn't think with that black cloud hovering in front of his eyes.

He had set his heart on marrying her eventually. Yes, he had jumped as far ahead as that. She had told him all about her feckless, no-good husband. He had left her when the money was running out, she had told him.

Then she had told him about her inheritance and the reason she had been able to afford the new premises where they had fortuitously met. She had a generous annuity for life, apparently, and she had laughingly said that old Charlie would be back like a shot if he knew about it. But she wasn't going to tell him, so that wasn't going to happen. She had been reassuring, but Cornelius was a 'sensitive', in more than one meaning of that word. He knew she was still in love with her husband and that he had a mountain to climb if he was to win her in the end. Her fortune meant nothing to him; he was comfortably off. Charlie Caldicot was likely to return to the marital home if or, more likely, when he heard about the money and, despite her feeble protestations, she would take him back. It didn't take a clairvoyant to predict that.

Now, of course, things were all up in the air. There was no future for her sham of a marriage and no future at all, of course, for her. All the secret plans he had been visualising for their future together were pointless now.

He finished his coffee as his intercom sounded, heralding the arrival of his next client, a sad widow who was dying herself, although he hadn't had the heart to tell her. She was the last of the morning and he suddenly made up his mind to pay Zelda a visit after she had gone. He couldn't leave things as they were. And what if she was already dead?

He was relieved to find she was still in the land of the living, but not so relieved to be told that news by her husband. A handsome, dark, curly-haired brute of a man with shining white teeth answered the door. Zelda's description of her erring husband was right on the money: a cleaned-up version of Bill Sikes. Even if he hadn't recognised Caldicot, the animosity between them, born of instant rivalry, would have told him who he was.

"Yeah?" Charlie Caldicot stood in the doorway, glaring at him. "What d'you want?"

The man was insufferably rude and his rough cockney manner didn't endear him in the least to Cornelius Gray. "Hello, I just came to see if Zelda was all right. I didn't see her this morning at the rooms."

"Why shouldn't she be all right?" came the reply. "What's it to you anyway? Who are you?"

"My name's Gray. I'm a friend of Mrs Caldicot. She and I are – well, we're sort of seeing each other. A bit." He tried not to appear nervous, but the steely stare of the man was getting to him and he was almost apologising for calling at all. No, he thought, I won't let this lout intimidate me. "So I just came to see if she was all right. Okay by you?"

"I'm 'er 'usband," said Charlie now. There was menace in his tone.

"Er, yes, I supposed you were. But she gave me to understand you were separated."

"Nah, just a blip. You'd better come in." He stepped aside and Cornelius entered, making sure he didn't brush up against him as he did so. There wasn't a lot of room in the passage.

"She's 'ad one of 'er turns," Caldicot informed him as he led the way.

"One of her turns?"

"Yeah. She's got a bit of a dicky ticker. Didn't she tell yer? The quack's with 'er at the moment, so you'd better come into the kitchen. Suppose you want a cuppa?"

Zelda's doctor tutted under his breath as he returned his stethoscope to his bag. "I suppose you haven't been taking your medication, Mrs Caldicot?"

Zelda, who was sitting by the fire with her feet up on a pouffe, smiled weakly at him. "I – always mean to, but sometimes I forget. Then I ran out yesterday and I haven't got round to ordering another prescription."

She looked pale but interesting to Dr Crabtree, who had always admired her beauty. He could never keep up his pretence of being cross with her for long, even though she was one of his most difficult patients when it came to taking medical advice.

"Well, you know you can't ignore your condition with impunity, Mrs Caldicot," he said, sitting down in the chair opposite. "I'm glad your husband is here, anyway. I'm sure he'll make you take your medicine properly."

"Charlie? Remind me?" She laughed, but it turned into a pathetic cough. "He'd forget his own head if it wasn't screwed on."

The doctor grinned. "Oh well," he said. "I shall just have to keep my beady eye on, shan't I?" He tried not to sound like he was flirting with her, but it wasn't very successful.

Just then Charlie came into the room, followed by Cornelius. "You got a visitor, love," said her husband. He said it as if he were introducing her to some kind of inferior life form.

Cornelius stepped forward and took hold of her limp hand. "Are you all right?" he asked in concern. She didn't look at all well.

She shot him a look which seemed to say 'as if you cared'. "I'm all right. Just a bit of a faint, that's all. Don't fuss."

"Shall I look after your clients for you?" Cornelius felt surplus to requirements all of a sudden.

"No, thanks. That's all right. They've been taken care of." Which was true. Faith had managed to ring and cancel her bookings for the rest of the week.

"Well, you look after yourself," he said. Charlie Caldicot and the doctor were standing staring at him, as if waiting for him to leave. "I – I hope you get better soon," he finished lamely.

"I'll be fine in a couple of days," she said. There was no smile for him, however, and he knew he couldn't blame her. Not after the way he had treated her the other night.

Cornelius left the house with the doctor. "Is she really going to be all right?" he asked him.

"Yes, if she takes her medicine regularly."

"What – what's the matter with her?"

Dr Crabtree climbed into his car. "She'll tell you herself, I'm sure," he replied coldly.

He switched on the ignition. Pausing before pulling away, Dr Crabtree stared out of the window at the retreating figure of Cornelius Gray. Another poor victim of the woman's charms, he thought wryly. He didn't have any time for Charlie Caldicot, but he was her husband, after all. So who was this other man? he wondered.

He drove to his next patient, still concerned about Zelda. Her heart condition wasn't a serious one, but it could become so if she continued to ignore his advice and pretend she didn't have a problem. She was too lovely to die young, even though he knew it was the ones the gods loved that did that. Dr Crabtree couldn't help thinking that the gods would definitely love someone as beautiful as Zelda Caldicot.

13

It was two days later when Zelda was well enough to venture out once more. She had a special trip to make now her husband had come back to her. This had happened the day after Cornelius Gray had so unceremoniously dumped her, which had made Charlie's return opportune. She had tried not to look pleased to see him, but she knew he hadn't been fooled. He was a cocky bastard.

"So you know about the will, then," she had said. There was no question in her tone.

He had tried to appear surprised. "Will? What will? What are you on about?"

"Come off it, Charlie," she had sighed. "You wouldn't be here if you hadn't heard about it."

"Well, I sort of 'eard about the new premises from Faith. You could never afford a separate place for your clients before."

"And I suppose she then told you about the annuity."

Charlie had made another attempt at ignorance but Zelda hadn't been taken in.

He had shrugged by way of a reply, then added: "Faith and I are finished, anyway. She ain't my 'ammer at all. You know I only love you, you silly bitch, don't yer?"

Zelda could have argued the point, especially about being called a 'silly bitch', but she had felt too weak for that. Her heart was thumping inside her rib cage and it wasn't long after that she had blacked out, regaining consciousness to find Dr Crabtree looking down at her with concern.

Now she was feeling much better and taking her medication 'like a good girl' as Charlie had instructed her. She had to see old Preston, the solicitor, today before anything else happened to her. She had often felt vulnerable when her heart didn't behave itself, and on her black days she would convince herself she was never going to make old bones. Today wasn't exactly black, but she had to know just what the full terms of the will really were. If, God forbid, anything *did* happen to her, she wanted to make sure Luke was provided for. At the back of her mind was Charlie, of course. Wouldn't she be a fool to leave him in charge of the money? She knew it was a crazy thing to do, but it would be one sure way of keeping him. Now he was back, she couldn't bear the thought of being alone again. She realised, apart from anything else, that she was actually frightened. Frightened of what, exactly? Loneliness? Death?

She had decided not to drive to the solicitor, just in case. She was still feeling a bit wobbly after her attack. She had had these attacks before, but this one had been much worse than the others. The taxi was waiting outside the house, and the driver politely opened the cab door for her. She gave him one of her dazzling smiles as she climbed into the back seat. Fiddling with her seat belt, trying not to appear stupid, she gave him another smile, less dazzling now. "Never can get the hang of these back seat belts," she said apologetically.

"Do you need any help with it, madam?" he asked, tapping the driving wheel as if anxious to be off.

"No, it's all right," Zelda replied, as she felt the click of the belt at last.

The taxi moved off smoothly, and she leaned back against the upholstery, trying not to notice her heart had started thumping again. After about a mile, however, it settled down to a more normal rhythm and she sat up again. She thought wryly that, if she wasn't worried that her heart would misbehave, she wouldn't get the palpitations. A vicious circle, that's what it was. Calm now, she fumbled in her handbag and withdrew a small mirror. She gazed at herself. She was still pale, but she was glad to see the dark circles under her eyes had begun to fade. She didn't look ill anymore, thanks to her artistry with make-up. She was as fit as the next woman, or so she told herself.

The taxi drew up outside the premises of Preston, Preston and Underwood. The sun peeked out from behind a dark cloud as she stepped out of the cab, only to disappear almost immediately. In its place, a burst of violent rain skittered down the pavement at her, threatening to drown her unrealistically high stilettos.

Paying off the cab, she tottered up the steps of the solicitors' office and pressed the intercom. A noise that could have been a human voice responded and Zelda announced herself. The door buzzed and she pushed it open with an effort. It was solid oak. She wished her heart hadn't started racing again.

"So, Mrs Caldicot, how are you?"

Old Preston's watery eyes had lit up at the sight of Zelda's exotic appearance. He liked her looks, they reminded him of Dorothy Lamour, a film star he had loved ever since he was a small boy in the front row of the Gaumont Picture House. The star was long dead but that didn't diminish his admiration one bit. She was luminous. He still had a film annual with a picture of her on the cover. Today's stars didn't begin to compare; nothing topped a dusky, dark-eyed maiden dressed in a sexy sarong. Zelda, to his faded eyes, was almost the personification of his beloved Dorothy and he had been looking forward to her appointment all morning. But he was sorry to see that she didn't look as well as the first time they'd met. In fact, she looked decided *un*well.

After he had settled her with a cup of tea (she had sensibly refused coffee), he leaned forward confidentially and smiled at her. "Now, Mrs Caldicot, what can I do for you today?"

"It's the will, Mr Preston," she replied. "I need to know exactly what the conditions of my fortune are."

"Conditions?"

"Yes. I mean, if I were to die – er, I need to know what will happen to my money. The – er, the annuity, as well as the property. I mean, I know the property will revert to someone else on her majority, but what will happen to it if I die before that? You see, I have a son who is, well, dependent on me."

"Sons usually are," smiled Preston, enjoying the joke. "At least until they get to be adults – one supposes."

"Well, in my son's case adulthood won't make any difference. You see, he's mentally handicapped. I don't suppose you can say that these days, but I don't know how else to describe his condition. He's sixteen but has a mental age of about seven. Doctors say he won't progress any further."

Preston felt ashamed of his flippant comments now. "My dear Mrs Caldicot, I'm so sorry."

"There's nothing to be sorry about. My son is probably much happier than normal boys of his age. Can you remember what it was like to be seven? I'm sure the world was a much simpler place then."

"Well, I do have trouble in remembering that far back," said Preston, trying not to give his client a flirtatious wink. "I'm sure you only have to cast your mind back a few years."

Zelda smiled, but Preston could see she wasn't in the mood for pleasantries that morning. "Er, would you like some more tea?" he tried.

"No thanks. I just came to find out exactly what I'd be worth dead and to make a will."

"Haven't you already made a will, Mrs Caldicot?"

"No, to my shame. But I should like to do so now. You see, I have a heart condition. Nothing immediately life threatening, but I think it would be wise to make some provision for the future."

Poor Preston felt out of his depth all of a sudden. The woman before him appeared not to invite sympathy, but he wanted to condone her troubles. In the old days, he would have offered her a cigarette, even with her heart condition. No one knew the dangers of nicotine back then. In the end, he decided to opt for a business-like approach. That much he could do. He was an experienced solicitor with especial expertise in drawing up wills, the more complicated the better.

"Very well, Mrs Caldicot. Very wise. Now, first of all, I can inform you that Mrs Vaughan's will stipulates that you were to have control of her property to do with as you like – live in it or rent it out – but that you weren't to sell it. Then the property would revert to her granddaughter on reaching her majority, which today is eighteen."

"I always think eighteen is too young to be an adult," she said. "You can vote and fight for your country, both of which should be in the hands of more sensible people, don't you think? Definitely older, anyway."

"I do so agree. The young today are very immature. Much more so than in my day."

Zelda smiled at the benign old man. "Anyway, what about the annuity? Two thousand pounds a month is a nice sum. I have been investing most of it."

"Very wise," he repeated. "That annuity is yours for your lifetime and then, according to the will – " He paused as he studied the document in front of him. "You can bequeath it on. Any investments that have accrued, together with the continuation of the monthly income."

"So, if I died before Mrs Vaughan's granddaughter reaches eighteen, then the property would – would – ?"

"Would – let me see – oh yes, it would go to her only son. He would have control of it until his daughter's eighteenth birthday. You couldn't, I'm afraid, bequeath Mrs Vaughan's property to your son or whoever you intend to be beneficiaries of your will."

"I see. Well, that makes everything much clearer." She seemed content.

"Now, Mrs Caldicot, let's draft your will. Firstly, do you own your own home?"

"No, it's rented, I'm afraid. I'll need to renegotiate the conditions of the lease soon too. Which shouldn't be a problem now that I know the annuity is safe." She smiled again.

Charlie Caldicot was smiling too later that day when Zelda told him about the will she had made.

"Everything comes to you," she told him, "so that, if I die, you can ensure Luke is taken care of. I've invested the monthly income I've been getting from Mrs Vaughan's will, and that should build up nicely. You and Luke should be comfortably off."

"I don't want you to die," said Charlie, caressing the pale skin around her cheeks and chin and kissing her lightly on the lips. "You must look after yourself."

"I intend to. Don't worry. I'll just go and have a lie down now."

"You do that, love. I'll bring you up a cuppa later on."

"Thanks, Charlie. You – you won't leave me again, will you?"

"No, of course I won't. You're stuck with me now, old girl."

Later, as she lay on top of the duvet waiting for much-needed sleep, she wondered if she had done the right thing by telling Charlie how much he stood to gain by her death. Suddenly she felt afraid.

14

Amie loved her boarding school, but was never happier than when she was away from it, back home for the holidays. Her favourite holiday season was Christmas and the first snow of the season was dusting the Cotswold stone as she drove with her father through the picturesque villages towards Stow-on-the-Wold. Grant Vaughan had announced his intention of visiting Zelda Caldicot the day after his daughter returned from school, and Amie expressed her desire to accompany him.

"She'll probably remember me," she had said as they set off. Pilar had insisted her precious daughter wrap up warmly on that cold December morning, and now Amie was in the process of unwrapping herself as the car sped towards its destination.

"Oh, yes, I'm sure she will."

"She always, like, made me a hot chocolate drink when I came with Gran to visit her. She also gave me the latest copies of *Hello* and *Vogue* to read while she was, like, giving Gran a sitting. I didn't like her though. I'm sure she's a fraud. I didn't like the way she gave poor Gran false hope. Like, I mean, telling her her husband was watching her, waiting for her and happy. LOL."

"LOL?" he repeated.

"Oh, Dad, get with the zeitgeist. Like, it means 'laugh out loud'."

"I see. Yes, well, I suppose it is laughable. Your gran must have got something out of her visits to this woman; otherwise why would she have left her fortune to her? Just to spite me?"

His face was set in a grim expression, seemingly concentrating on his driving and narrowly missing a rabbit as it hopped on what looked like only three legs across his path.

Amie, taking his father's questions as purely rhetorical, took another tack. "Like, she's very pretty – beautiful even," Amie continued, once she was sure the rabbit was safe. "Lovely black hair just like mum's. In fact, she looks a bit like her."

"Does she indeed?"

"Yes, but you won't like her. I know you won't." Amie stared out of the window. The snow was getting heavier now, settling on the road in front of them. The world looked like the song: a winter wonderland. She started humming the familiar tune.

"I've got no reason to like her, have I?" said her father.

"She shouldn't keep the money, should she, Dad?"

"No, of course she shouldn't. Your gran wasn't in her right mind when she made the will, I'm sure."

"Yeah, but how can you prove it?"

"Not easy. I shall just have to try and appeal to Zelda's better nature – if she's got one."

They both laughed. They were driving along Zelda Caldicot's road now, and Amie recognised the house at once. "Pull up just here, Dad," she instructed.

The snow was easing now, but the sky looked threateningly grey, full of more snow to come. "Let's hope we can get back home before the roads become impassable," said Grant.

He rang the doorbell and they waited on the doorstep, stamping their feet to keep warm. It was freezing. Amie was now glad of the scarf her mother had made her wear. She huddled into it as she tucked her arm into her father's.

Faith Desmond opened the door after Grant had rung the bell a second time. She looked at them enquiringly. "Can I help you?" she asked.

Grant looked at Amie. Surely this wasn't Zelda? She looked nothing like Pilar. Amie understood the look.

"No, Dad," she whispered. "This isn't Zelda."

"Hello," said Grant to Faith. "Is Zelda – er Madame Zelda – at home?"

"Do you have an appointment?"

"Er, no. I've come to see her on a purely private matter." Grant's voice was politeness itself.

"She's having a lie down," said Faith.

"Who is it, Faith?" came a voice from within.

"Someone to see Zelda," she called. "Not a client – apparently." Turning back to Grant, she asked: "Can I have your name?"

"The name's Vaughan," he replied.

"It's a Mr Vaughan," Faith called to the voice within.

Charlie Caldicot appeared at the door now. "Vaughan, did you say?" he asked.

"That's right."

"You'd better come in."

"My wife ain't been well," said Charlie as they were shown into the front room. It was warm and inviting, an open fire blazing on the hearth and the attractive bay windows looking out on a wintry scene that wouldn't have disgraced a Christmas card.

"I'm sorry to hear that," said Grant.

Caldicot eyed the coltish young girl by Grant's side lasciviously, obviously appreciating what he saw.

Faith came into the room and smiled at the visitors. "Would you like a hot drink?"

"Yes, please," said Amie at once. "Hot chocolate?"

"Make that two," said Grant. "Er, will Madame Zelda be able to see us, do you think?"

"Yes, I've just told her. She's awake and feeling better. She'll be down directly."

The hot chocolate had been produced and appreciated before Zelda made her appearance. A pale, dark beauty, who seemed almost ethereal, met Grant's gaze. What a looker, he thought. It's a pity she's such a grasping cow. They shook hands.

Zelda turned to Amie. "I've seen you before, haven't I?" she smiled.

"Yep," was Amie's monosyllabic reply.

"Well, Mr Vaughan, what can I do for you?"

As if she didn't know, thought Grant. "Er, can we have a word in private?"

"Of course." Zelda turned to Faith and Charlie. "Can you make yourselves scarce?"

They both looked uncertain. "You sure, love? I don't want you upsetting 'er," Charlie growled at Vaughan. "She's been ill and only just recovered. You're 'ere to make trouble, ain't yer?"

"What makes you say that?" Grant adopted a supercilious tone. This brutish man was very possessive. A refined woman like Zelda couldn't be married to this animal, surely?

"You're 'ere about the will, ain't yer?"

"Please, Charlie," Zelda interrupted. "Let me handle this."

Faith tugged at Charlie's sleeve. "Come on," she said. "Let's leave them to it."

By a combination of pushes and pulls, Faith managed to drag him out of the room.

"You'd better go too, Amie."

"Dad!" she protested.

Zelda escorted her to the door. "My son will look after you," she said. "Luke. Come here a moment, please."

A booming sound that had been issuing from one of the upstairs rooms became louder as a door opened to reveal a handsome teenage lad leaning over the banisters. "What do you want?" He sounded sullen.

"Come and look after this young lady, please."

Luke started to walk slowly down the stairs. He stared into the beautiful brown eyes of Amie Vaughan as she stared into his almost equally beautiful blue ones.

"All right, Mr Vaughan," said Zelda calmly. "What is it you want?"

"I want you to reconsider accepting my mother's bequest," he said bluntly, determined not to be distracted by her good looks. Beautiful though she was, she had stolen what was rightfully his. He watched her features register surprise, then mild anger. There was a flush on her cheeks which gave her a feverish glow. He saw now that she looked unwell.

"And why should I do that? It was plainly her wish that I should have the money. I understood your daughter will come into the legacy when she's eighteen. I'm sure she'll lend you a bob or two then."

Grant ignored the flippancy of her remark with difficulty. "My mother wasn't in her right mind at the end. My daughter can vouch for that. She used to visit her regularly until her death and she told me how absent-minded she had become. Besides, your 'profession' as you no doubt would like to call it is a load of bunkum. It preys on people like my poor mother. You should give the money back. The property belongs in the Vaughan family and you haven't a leg to stand on. If I got a solicitor onto it you'd lose, I can assure you."

Grant could see the strained veins around Zelda's eyes as he uttered these words, words he didn't even entirely believe himself. Legal advice hadn't exactly been promising. He knew he would have a fight on his hands if he carried out his threat. Going through the courts was a last resort, but he could see that this woman wasn't prepared to listen to reason. He supposed it was obvious, really. If *he'd* been given a fortune by someone, no matter how undeserved, he would hang on to it for dear life.

"Do your worst," she said firmly. "Now, would you mind leaving?"

Grant stood his ground. "Look, at least you can understand my position, can't you? It's not for my sake I ask you to refuse the bequest. Think of my daughter. I haven't even got enough money to see her through private school."

"Send her to a state school, then," was all the reply. "I hear some of them are quite good."

He could see there was no point in pursuing the matter further. "I only hope you can live with yourself," was his parting shot.

"Come on, Amie," he called up the stairs on his way out. "We're leaving."

"Okay, Dad." She clattered down the stairs, looking flushed.

"Have you been in that young man's bedroom?" he asked, aghast.

Before Amie could reply, Faith stepped out into the passage from the kitchen. "You needn't worry about that, Mr Vaughan – it *is* Mr Vaughan, isn't it?"

"Yes, that's right. And who might you be?"

"Come into the kitchen. Both of you." Amie had joined her father in the hall.

Entering that room, they beheld Charlie Caldicot scrabbling around under the sink, muttering to himself.

"What are you doing, Charlie?" asked Faith with impatience. "Can you go and see what Zelda wants. I think this visit has rather upset her."

"In a minute. I can't be in two places at once. She's told me to poison the roots of that dead tree in the front garden."

"Well go and do it then. She's been asking you to do it for days."

"I can't find the stuff to do it with. She told me it was under the sink."

"Oh, don't bother. That tree's as dead as a dodo anyway. It won't be doing any growing at this time of year."

Charlie stood up and grunted. "Obsessed with that blinkin' tree, she is."

"Get along, Charlie," said Faith, shoving the big man out of the door. "Go and see that Zelda's all right."

Still muttering to himself, he allowed her to push him out of the kitchen and even turned to give her a playful peck her on the cheek. "Enough of that, Charlie," she hissed, smacking him on the arm. "You and me are finished. Remember?" She stared round at the visitors, but they didn't seem to have noticed anything.

Giving her a wink, Charlie left the kitchen at last. Grant and Amie remained where they were standing while Faith bustled around them, finding suitable chairs. "Please, do sit down. Take no notice of Charlie. He's harmless."

Grant grinned. "He didn't look all that harmless. I wouldn't like to get into a fight with him."

Faith grinned. "Well, who would? Anyway, you've quite a few years on him, haven't you?"

"What is it you want to say to us?" asked Grant ignoring her comment. "We got our answer just now. Your friend is being unreasonable."

"She's no friend of mine," sniffed Faith with venom.

"Er – I presumed she was? A relative, perhaps?"

"No, no relation. I suppose we're what you'd call business partners, if you want to give our relationship a name. I do her dirty work for her."

"Tell me more," said Grant, leaning forward.

"So she's a complete fraud," said Grant with satisfaction. "Madame Zelda isn't entitled to a penny of your grandmother's money."

He was driving a little too fast in the driving snow, but he couldn't slow down, he was too full of adrenaline. "The evil bitch," he spat. The windscreen wipers were having trouble keeping the snow off the glass, but he increased his speed nonetheless.

"Slow down, Dad," admonished Amie, removing her ear plugs and sitting up straight, ensuring her seat belt was fixed properly.

"Sorry, love," he said, easing the car more slowly along the white road. Luckily there was little traffic about. "But you heard what that Faith woman said? She gets her to find out all about prospective clients then recommends Zelda, telling them she can get in touch with their loved ones from beyond the grave. It's a scam. Your gran never got in touch with your granddad at all. Not that I ever believed she did, of course."

"So what are you gonna do, Dad?"

"God knows. I wish I did. Changing the subject, what were you and that boy doing up in his bedroom?"

"That Mrs Desmond told you, didn't she? He's mentally retarded." There was a dreamy look on her face. "Doesn't look it, though. Looks just like Justin Bieber."

"And that's a good thing?"

"Oh, Dad – you!" She punched him playfully on the arm.

"Watch it! I'm driving!" He laughed, despite his anger and frustration over his fruitless visit to Zelda Caldicot. He'd been a fool to even think he'd get her to hand over her inheritance.

"You're right about her being an evil bitch though, Dad." Her tone was serious now. "Luke told me she killed his dog. Like, and I'm not even joking."

15

"What are you doing here, Charlie?"

Faith stared at Charlie Caldicot who was standing on the doorstep looking frozen but friendly.

"You haven't even got a coat on," she challenged him, trying not to soften her approach, but not altogether succeeding. He had braved the winter weather, coatless, to come and see her, or at least she told herself that. But she knew there was always an ulterior motive with Charlie Caldicot.

"You've still got your key, haven't you?" she asked him, as he entered her flat.

"Didn't seem right to use it," he said, "… in the circumstances, like."

"The circumstances being that you've left me and gone back to your wife, just because she's suddenly loaded."

"Come on, Faith, love. You know you're the only girl for me. 'Ow many times d'you need telling?"

It sounded unconvincing, even to her. She wanted to believe him and had done so in the past. Not anymore. The human yo-yo could protest as much as he liked. The worm had turned.

"Hmm," she said, as he swept past her into the sitting room. "So what brings you here? Think you can come back to me, do you? Just a few words and you think I'm putty in your hands. Well, I've got news for you. I haven't just come up with the daisies, to use your quaint cockney expression. I suppose she's seen sense and chucked you out, hasn't she?"

"Nah, 'course she ain't. Got 'er wrapped round me little finger, 'aven't I?"

"Well, what do you want then?" she said, a little deflated.

"A cup of Tetley's wouldn't go amiss."

"I've only got PG Tips, so you're out of luck." Faith was even more determined to resist his charms now. But she couldn't help worrying about his lack of an outdoor coat.

"That'll do," he grinned, sitting down by the fire. "Could do with some more wood," he observed. "Shall I go and chop some?"

"No, Charlie. You can't get round me this time. The minute you heard that Zelda was in the money, you went back to her. The words were hardly out of my mouth. You're a rat, Charlie, and no amount of wood chopping will change that."

He held up his hands in mock supplication. "I'm sorry, Faith. But I told you why a thousand times. I get back in 'er good books and she leaves me money in 'er will. Money for *us*. She ain't got long – you saw the state she was in. One more attack like that'll see 'er off."

"You're an arse hole, Charlie. Haven't you got any feelings? All you care about is money. It's a pity you don't work for it. Maybe you'd be rich in your own right by now. You've got a brain in your head, and you're able bodied. How you've got away with skiving

98

all these years, I'll never know. Oh, wait, yes I do. It's by living off poor gullible women like me and Zelda."

"That's a bit off," sniffed Charlie. "Look, I ain't come 'ere to argue the toss all day. I wanna know what you said to that Vaughan bloke yesterday. When you shoved me out of the kitchen. Made me look a right berk."

"Oh, so that's what this visit's all about." Faith took the kettle off the stove before it had a chance to boil. He can whistle for his tea, she thought grimly.

"Well, like, I thought it was a bit funny. You and me never 'ad no secrets before," he continued.

"Well, now we have. If you must know I told Mr Vaughan that Zelda's a fraud. Thought it might help him if he was going to contest the will. I liked him. He's very good looking too." She hoped this last comment would make Charlie jealous but he seemed not to have heard it.

"You done what?" he screamed, leaping from his chair and grabbing her by the shoulders. "You mad or what?"

"Or what, I think." She wasn't frightened of Charlie Caldicot but he was looking very mean at that moment. "Get your hands off me. I hate her! Why did she take you back? She can't have any pride, that's all I can say. I want her to lose her fortune. It's not hers by right."

This little speech made Charlie more angry still. "You little bitch! You jealous little bitch!"

He released her and slumped back in his chair. "What 'ave you bloody done, girl? We could 'ave been rich. You and me."

"Just you, you mean. If Zelda kicks the bucket and you get her money I wouldn't see you for dust."

"That's not true, Faith. I love yer, you silly cow."

"What a pretty speech. Get out, Charlie."

"I 'ope for your sake Vaughn don't go to court over this. If 'e wins I'll bloody kill yer."

Faith returned the kettle to the boil and made herself a cup of tea after Charlie's departure. She sipped it slowly, her mind racing. She hadn't meant to give the game away, really, but she was angry with Zelda. She'd promised her more money, but she hadn't seen a sign of it so far. Then, of course, there was Charlie. He was living back with her and, no matter how often she reminded herself that he was a waste of space, her pride couldn't stand that.

She finished her tea and took the empty cup through to the kitchen, washing it up absent-mindedly. She had nothing to reproach herself with, she thought. Charlie and Zelda were as bad as each other. They deserved all they got, or didn't, more to the point. She'd been a muggins too long.

She had been friends with Zelda since their school days, but it was always Zelda who had the upper hand. She had been better at maths, better at games and, what was most galling, better at getting the boys. As they grew older, it was the same. And Faith had always been jealous of Zelda's psychic gift too, even when they set up the business together. It was clear from the start that her role in her friend's life was always going to be as second fiddle.

It had been a rare moment of triumph when Charlie had left Zelda for her. She had never been under the illusion that he preferred her to his wife, but he had seemed genuinely fond of her, even so. It had been good while it lasted.

She sighed. Charlie hated her now. She stiffened her shoulders as she put on her hat and coat in preparation for a morning's shopping. Well, whatever happened now, she couldn't change it. The damage was done.

If Faith and Charlie had been flies on the wall of Grant Vaughan's solicitor's office, they would have been relieved. While they were having words, Grant was consulting his solicitor and receiving no reassurance from him.

"So, you're saying I'm unlikely to win if I take her to court over the will?"

His solicitor, an old family friend, shook his head. "I fear not," he said. "You see, whether or not this Madame Zelda is a fraud is irrelevant."

"But surely, if she can be exposed as a fraud, then the will's invalid." Grant stomped up and down the office, a disappointed man.

"I'd be a poor friend – and a poor solicitor – if I offered to take on your case. You don't have a hope of winning. I'm not going to take a fat fee for a case I can't win."

"But I *want* you to. I'm *instructing* you to!"

The man shrugged. "Forget it, Grant. Your daughter will come into the money and property soon enough."

"But I need some money now! I can't continue to pay the school fees for one thing." And for another, he thought, I want to travel the world with my wife and live it up for a change. However, he was wise enough not to say this out loud.

"I wish I could be more positive," his solicitor was saying. "But look at it logically. Even if Madame Zelda is the fraud you think she is, and I agree, she probably is, that doesn't alter the fact that she made your mother happy in her last years. And – forgive me for saying so – that was more than you did."

Grant Vaughan stopped pacing and came up to the desk. He thumped it hard, just like Patrick McGoohan always did at the beginning of each episode of *The Prisoner*.

"How could you say that, Brian? You know the score. My mother and I didn't see eye to eye. We didn't get along. She didn't want anything to do with me."

"Yes, I'm sorry, I know you had your differences. But she was a frail old woman at the end. Didn't it ever occur to you to try and make your peace with her?"

"Bollocks!"

Grant Vaughan stormed out of the office, determined to find himself another solicitor.

16

"Can I go, Dad, please!"

Mealtimes at the Vaughans were usually pleasant, harmonious affairs, due mainly to the influence of Pilar, who insisted they all ate together as a family. Something to do with her Spanish upbringing that still lingered.

But that morning, five days before Christmas, there was a distinct atmosphere around the breakfast table. Amie Vaughan wore the expression her mother and father hated the most: half sulky, half defiant.

"Mr Kenright said I could use his lab while I'm not at school. Why can't I go? Dad, you could give me a lift. It's only in Bourton. Go on. Plee-ee-eease!"

"I've never met this Mr Kenright. How long has he been a teacher at your school?" asked her father, swallowing his tea.

"Oh, ages. Since the beginning of term. He's brilliant – taught me more chemistry in a few weeks than I ever learned in three years. Like, I'm his star pupil. He said I could use his lab any time I wanted during the holidays."

"That's all well and good," said Pilar, pouring out more tea for her husband. "We know nothing about him."

"What d'you mean?" asked Amie, still defiant and angry now. "Do you think he's a paedo? Not everyone's a paedo!"

"No of course we don't think that," interposed Grant Vaughan, although his facial expression conveyed otherwise.

"Look, Dad," said Amie, trying to keep calm now. "He's not even going to be there. He and his family are going away for Christmas. He's left me the key to his shed – where his lab is. I'm dying to see it. He's given me some homework and all the stuff I need is in there. You must let me go."

Grant looked relieved. "Oh, that's a different story," he smiled. "Why didn't you say that in the first place?"

Pilar was smiling too. "Of course you can go, darling," she said. "But be sure you wrap up warm. I don't suppose the shed has any heating."

"Oh, Mum, don't fuss," said Amie, getting up from the breakfast table and checking her backpack. "Come on, Dad. I'm ready. Let's go."

"Give me a minute to finish my tea," protested Grant Vaughan. "Eager beaver."

Driving through the snow-covered roads ten minutes later, Grant looked sideways at his daughter. He adored her, never more so than when she was fired with enthusiasm as she was that morning.

"You really love chemistry, don't you?" he said.

"I told you, Dad. I'm going to find a cure for cancer one day."

"I know you will, darling," he smiled, manoeuvring the car around a tricky bend. "But in the meantime, remember you're still my little girl."

She gave him a knowing look. "Little girls tend to grow up, Dad," was all she said.

17

Zelda Caldicot's health continued to improve as Christmas approached and with that, so too did the relationship with her husband. By ten o'clock on the evening of the 24th of December, they were by the fire, in each other's arms, admiring the newly decorated Christmas tree. And the presents beneath it.

"It looks a treat, love, don't it?"

"Yes, Charlie. It looks a treat." Zelda kissed him on the lips with some enthusiasm. He received her affection warmly. As his octopus hands stole over her receptive body, she began to believe he was back with her to stay. She even began to believe he was actually still in love with her.

He had come back to her, hadn't he? She tried not to think of the probable reason. Instead she thought of his happy willingness to decorate the tree with Luke. She had watched them with delight. She had always feared Charlie didn't much like her son, but tonight they had got on very well, even laughing together as an occasional bauble hit the floor and smashed into pieces. The only blight on her Christmas horizon now was her son's continued determination not to speak to her.

She had wrapped up the pretty dog collar for her son and it was under the tree. The puppy due to inhabit that collar hadn't been wrapped up, of course, and was in fact next door with Simon and his family. They had already fallen in love with it, and Zelda hoped she wouldn't have any difficulty retrieving it the following morning. This present, she fervently prayed, would help her son to get over poor Meg's death and heal the rift between them.

"Stop worrying about the boy," said Charlie sleepily, as he finished off his third scotch and soda. "'E'll love the bleedin' thing. 'E'll soon forget Meg."

"I hope you're right," she said thoughtfully, pushing his hair back from his forehead. "You need a haircut," she observed fondly.

"I like it like this," said Charlie, pushing her off his lap as gently as he could. Unlike his wife, the whisky bottle was out of his reach and he needed a refill.

"Makes you look like Lord Byron," she said.

"Lord who?"

"Ignorant bugger," she laughed. "Don't make out you don't know who he is."

"Well I ain't read none of 'is bleeding poems," laughed Charlie, a full glass once more in his hand. "And I don't intend to, neither."

"No, I don't suppose you do."

She climbed back on his lap. "Now that we're alone," she said, "shall we open one little present each?"

He grinned. "What about Luke? Shall we call 'im down?"

"No. Let him stay in his room," she said. Although she wanted Luke to forgive her, she wanted Charlie even more at that moment. "He's still not talking to me and I don't want this evening spoilt. Let's you and me open one present each."

Charlie grinned as he jumped up again and riffled through the gaily coloured parcels under the tree. As he was doing this, Luke burst into the room.

"Have you seen my charger?" he pointedly asked Charlie, ignoring his mother. He watched as Charlie returned to Zelda on the sofa with two packages in his hands. "Are you opening your presents now?" Luke asked.

"Just one each," said Charlie. "Do you want one?"

"No. Just my charger," said Luke sulkily. He glared at his mother.

"Here it is," said Zelda, handing it to him. "You left it plugged into the socket by the tree."

He snatched it from her without a word, but remained in the room. "Did you buy that for her?" he asked Charlie, as he handed the parcel to Zelda.

"*Your mother*, d'you mean, you ungrateful bugger? And yes, I did. Because I love 'er, like you should love 'er too."

"Don't go on at him, Charlie," said Zelda, as she looked at her present and the gift tag attached. "You only put my name," she said, "and even that's printed." She seemed upset.

"I must 'ave forgot," said Charlie, seemingly unapologetic for the oversight. "Go on, open it."

She did so, and an expensive-looking box of chocolates was revealed, Belgian ones. "Oh, Charlie, darling. They're my favourites!"

Luke watched her as she proceeded to open the box, then turned swiftly on his heels and left the room.

"That kid wants a bloody good 'iding," said Charlie, as he unwrapped Zelda's gift to him. It was an electric razor. "Cheers," he said, "just what I needed."

"Glad you like it. Have a chocolate."

"No ta, can't stand them Belgian ones. What's wrong with good old Cadbury's? I'll 'ave another whisky though. What's on the box?"

"Nothing much," said Zelda, reaching for the *Radio Times*. "I'm going to put on my favourite DVD in a minute. You know – the one I play every Christmas."

"Oh not that bleedin' thing again," sighed Charlie. He downed his fifth whisky in one. "I think I'll turn in."

"But it's only early. Aren't you going to watch the DVD with me? It's Blu Ray actually. I bought it yesterday."

"Don't make me wanna watch it just because of that. Why don't we watch some more *Game of Thrones* instead? I got the latest series as a Christmas present to meself, like."

"That's not very Christmassy, is it?" She smiled at him indulgently. "If you're so keen, why don't you watch it with Luke in his room? He loves that kind of thing. Make sure it's not too violent, though."

"Give the kid a break, Zelda," said Charlie as he poured himself another whisky. "He's old enough to know what goes on. You can't keep 'im wrapped up in swaddling clothes forever."

"I know, love. I just can't help it."

He kissed her on the cheek. "Goodnight, then. And don't worry, love. I'll make sure 'e ain't too upset by anything in it."

"Thanks, Charlie," she said, pulling him on top of her, reluctant to let him go now.

When Charlie had left the room about half an hour later, she arranged herself on the sofa more comfortably. She was still worried about Charlie's lack of understanding where Luke was concerned, however. But then she remembered his philosophical gem of only yesterday: "'E ain't such a bad kid. Don't know what it's for, poor thing, but 'appy in his skin which is more than can be said for most people these days." She smiled at the recollection.

She inserted her precious Blu Ray disc into the player and sat back against the cushions, his present open beside her. She couldn't remember the last time he had bought her a present, if he ever had. She supposed he was doing his best to stay in her good books. There was no doubt about it: having money was a powerful thing.

The film started as she picked out a delicious-looking truffle and popped it in her mouth. She was soon immersed in the woes of a snow-covered James Stewart as he contemplated suicide. She always cried when she got to that bit, where he declared that the world would be a better place if he had never been born. Oh no it wouldn't, Jimmy, dear, she told him. Oh no it wouldn't.

18

Cornelius Gray woke up on Christmas morning feeling as if he had a heavy weight on his chest. He had been dreaming all night, or so it had seemed, of Zelda Caldicot. In most of his disjointed dreams she had met her death. It had come in various ways: illness, road accident and even murder. He climbed out of bed and stared, bleary-eyed, into the dressing table mirror, a piece of furniture he had meant to replace ever since his wife's death, but had never had the heart to. As he stared at himself, he saw his wife sitting there, brushing her hair vigorously like she had done every night of their marriage. "A hundred strokes," she had said, "it keeps the hair shiny and in good condition."

He blinked back a tear. His wife was gone, but Zelda was still alive. He was thinking of her now, knowing with absolute certainty she was going to die very soon. He opened the dressing table drawer and withdrew the wrapped bottle of perfume he had bought her as a Christmas gift.

He must go and give it to her, before it was too late. However, he knew his visit would be an intrusion; that great brute of a husband of hers was back on the scene and likely to punch him on the nose, Christmas or no Christmas. She had asserted she would never take him back, but she had obviously changed her mind. He sighed. What did it matter now, anyway?

He had a quick shower and dressed with care. He found he had no appetite for breakfast, but managed to down two cups of strong coffee to keep out the cold, he told himself. His doctor had told him to cut down on his caffeine intake, so he had dutifully foregone his usual third cup.

He looked out of the window and saw, true to form, the winter wonderland which had enveloped the Cotswolds for the past two weeks had turned to slush just in time for Christmas day. He couldn't remember the last time there had been a white Christmas. A weak sun was glinting through an ominous cloud. Oh well, he thought, that was the best they were going to get, he supposed. He thought that, if he ever managed to get in touch with Bing Crosby in one of his séances, he'd make sure he didn't tell him how the words of his song hardly ever came true. It would probably upset him.

He drove slowly towards Stow, thinking furiously and feeling tired. His broken dreams had taken it out of him. His psychic powers extended to his dreams sometimes, and he had often predicted national disasters because of them. He had known about the seven-seven bombs on the morning before they happened. He often wished his extra-sensory powers extended to preventing death instead of just predicting it.

As he drew up outside Zelda's house, he saw a car parked just opposite that looked vaguely familiar. He had seen it before, and then he remembered that it belonged to the Caldicot family doctor. Oh God, he thought, was he already too late?

The door was opened by a tear-stained Luke and Cornelius Gray knew the worst. His prediction was only too accurate as usual. His lovely Zelda was dead.

"Hello, young man," he said, trying to be upbeat. After all, he didn't know for sure, did he? "I wonder if I could see your mummy? I just came to wish her a merry Christmas – and you too, of course."

"Mummy's dead!" yelled Luke. "Simon killed her!"

While he tried to take in these two facts, Dr Crabtree came out of the sitting room, clipping up his medical bag. The expression on his face gave nothing away.

"What – what's happened, Doctor?" asked Cornelius, pushing past Luke who went to sit on the stairs. "Luke tells me Mrs Caldicot's – dead?"

"I'm afraid it's true," replied Dr Crabtree, heading for the front door. "I have made all the necessary arrangements for the – er – body to be removed. I'm sorry. Were you a close friend?"

"I – I haven't known her very long, but I like to think so. What happened to her?"

"Her heart, I'm afraid. She wouldn't take her medication regularly. I was always telling her."

"Is – is she still here? Can I see her?"

"Her husband's with her," said the doctor, a warning note in his voice. "And her friend – Faith, I think she's called."

"I just want to say my goodbyes," said Cornelius, the perfume he was carrying in his pocket feeling like a lead weight now. He had spent a long time choosing it, and now she would never wear it.

"I don't see any harm in that, Mr – er?"

"Gray. Thank you, Doctor."

He went through to the sitting room and saw Zelda lying peacefully on the settee, her husband and friend seated in the matching chairs, staring at her. The woman was crying, but the man was strangely still and dry-eyed.

Charlie Caldicot rose as Cornelius entered the room. "What the 'ell are you doing 'ere?" was his 'friendly' greeting. "Can't you see this is an 'ouse of mourning? What right 'ave yer to come in 'ere at a time like this? Get out!"

"Stop it, Charlie," Faith was standing too now. "He only wants to see her. They were friends."

"Friends? Hmmph!"

"Charlie! She had a right to have friends." Faith blew her nose loudly, and stepped up to Cornelius. They shook hands. "Th-thank you for coming," she said. "How did you know?"

"Know?" Cornelius was puzzled. Then he realised what she meant. "Oh, no, I didn't know she was dead. I just came to wish her a happy Christmas and to give her – this." He withdrew the present for Zelda from his inside pocket.

"How kind," she said.

"Wish 'er an 'appy Christmas? You joking or what?" Charlie Caldicot looked like he was about to hit him.

"I didn't know she was dead. How could I?"

Faith pulled Charlie back down into the chair and pressed her hand on his chest. The body language between them was unmistakable to Cornelius, but he ignored it. They couldn't hurt Zelda now.

He toyed with the idea of giving the perfume to Faith, but changed his mind. After all, he hardly knew her. He'd find someone he could give it to one day.

He left the sitting room without waiting to be shown out. He wanted to talk to Luke.

The boy was still sitting on the stairs, sobbing quietly now.

"Hello, Luke," he said. "I'm so sorry about your mummy."

Luke sniffed. "Simon killed her!" Those three words again.

Cornelius sat down beside him. What would the poor lad do now? he wondered, now that he had no mother to steer him through life. He knew Luke's real father was dead and that Charlie Caldicot was a poor replacement. Zelda had often complained about that. But it seemed that Charlie Caldicot was all Luke had now.

"What do you mean, Luke? The doctor said she died of heart failure." Cornelius sat down beside him. "You mustn't go making up stories, you know."

"I'm not! She *was* poisoned."

"Poisoned? Why on earth would you say that?"

"You go and ask him. He took the poison from under the sink."

"Ask who?

"Simon Rogers. He lives next door."

Of course it couldn't be true. Dr Crabtree had stated categorically that Zelda had died a natural, if untimely, death. Nevertheless, Cornelius Gray was puzzled. Maybe he should just forget all about it. Forget about Zelda, forget about Luke, Charlie and Faith, the whole damn lot of them. After all, they were nothing to him. He didn't need to get involved. He probably wouldn't even get an invitation to the funeral.

But, as he was thinking these thoughts, he found himself parked outside Oxford Police Station.

19

DCI Hayley Pascal was good at her job. Everyone said so. She had been fast-tracked because she'd had a university education and because she was a woman. She had no illusions about that, and she had to work hard to prove she was up to the job. In fact, it was soon clear she was better than most of her male, less well-educated, counterparts and consequently had earned the grudging respect of her team.

It was an inescapable fact she was divorced, which she couldn't help, and that she was rather attractive, which she also couldn't help. Most of her male colleagues had tried their luck with her, in one way or another. She didn't mind some of the attention but the endless invitations for drinks after work got on her nerves most of the time. If she accepted any of them, it usually meant she had to fight off their advances at the end of the evening.

She had opted for duty on Christmas day this year because her daughter Natasha wasn't spending it with her. She had promised to spend the New Year with her mother and Hayley was very much looking forward to that. Now, however, she was content to sip coffee in her office and trawl through various cases that still hadn't been solved. Christmas was always a quiet time at the station, and it was an ideal opportunity to see if there were any clues that had been overlooked.

Today there were two unsolved murders to study: a beating up outside a nightclub that had resulted in brain trauma and eventual death. No one had apparently seen anything. Suspects had been interviewed again and again but nothing stuck to any of them. There seemed to be a wall of silence, and everyone had an alibi. Then there was the poor widow who had been battered to death for the sake of a few pounds and her wedding ring. Life was cruel, thought Hayley. No, she amended, it was *people* who were cruel.

She was expecting her new DS this morning too, something she wasn't looking forward to. He, like her, had had a university education. But this had been at Oxford and before that he had been at Harrow. Another fast-tracker like herself. But he was damned before she had even met him. He'd obviously had all the advantages of a first-class education because his family was rich and not because he had earned it. He probably had a title as well, even if he had the good sense not to use it. 'Artie Frobisher'. She tried the name on her tongue. It tasted bitter.

Then the door opened and DS Artie Frobisher was there in person. What she saw pleased her even less than her inner vision of him. He was a smallish man, of a height that years ago would have banned him from the police force. His face was all wrong too: his eyes too small, his mouth too large. Added to these unforgivable defects, was a distinctly receding hairline. And she had to work with this thing?

"Hello," he said, smiling at her. The smile helped, she had to admit. It almost transformed him from a frog into a prince. Almost but not quite. Maybe a minor baron at best. "Artie Frobisher at your service. Pleased to meet you."

"Hello," she replied. They shook hands. "Take a seat. Let's get started right away. Look through this file, will you?" She flung the murdered widow case file at him. "See what you make of it."

"Certainly," said Artie. "Can I get you a coffee or anything first?"

"No time for coffee," she grunted. "Just get on with that."

"Certainly," he said again. He opened the file and began reading.

Two hours later, they were still reading in silence, the only sound was the turn of the pages. Hayley sighed and closed her file. The poor girl kicked to death outside the nightclub was probably the only person who would ever know who her attacker had been, she concluded. She watched Artie Frobisher who was still diligently reading the battered widow file.

"Er, any thoughts?" She broke the silence, realising she was bored now. She could have been at home, opening Christmas presents with her daughter and eating a huge turkey, if only it had been Natasha's turn to come to England this year. She wouldn't have been bored then.

"Well, it's a sad case," said Artie. "Very sad. A few paltry shillings and a piece of jewelry. Some petty thief who probably got angry when he couldn't find anything else so he took it out on the poor woman. Probably didn't mean to kill her. Just lost his temper."

"And that makes it all right in your book?"

"Of course not." He closed the file and stared at her. "You don't like me, do you?"

"Not much, no."

"You've got lumbered with me, haven't you? You think I got here just because I went to the right schools, don't you?"

"Pretty much."

"Well, let me tell you I had to work hard to get this job. My parents wanted me to go into the Foreign Office. My father and grandfather were both high up at the FO. I broke with tradition and they didn't like it. I think they'd rather I'd gone on the stage than joined the police. I'm a great disappointment to them."

For the first time, Hayley saw a human being sitting there in front of her, not a bundle of clichés. He was right, she had assumed he got there by means of school ties and old boys' networks but no, she realised, he was there because he wanted to be. He wanted to make a difference.

"Everyone here thinks I'm just a posh bastard," he grinned. Again, the grin. He was really quite attractive, she thought.

"Oh no, I wouldn't say that," she grinned back. "You're not posh at all."

They looked at each for a moment, then burst out laughing in unison. She could feel the tension between them lift. There was one thing she could say for him, at least. He had a sense of humour.

The day wore on slowly, interrupted only by an indifferent lunch in the sparsely populated canteen. The Christmas decorations were already looking sad.

They returned to the office together and were about to reopen the old case files which they almost knew by heart by this time, when Hayley noticed a folded up piece of paper on her desk.

"Hmm," she said when she had read it. "Apparently there's a Mr Gray waiting in the interview room."

"Yes?"

"He wants to see someone in charge."

"Guess that's you," grinned Artie.

"Suppose so. I wonder what he wants? Still, it'll break the monotony."

Cornelius Gray stood up as Hayley entered the room. She saw a tall, elegant man who looked ill at ease, as if he had closed his eyes and found himself there by mistake.

"Mr Gray? I'm DCI Pascal." She shook his hand. "How can I help you?"

Once they were seated, Cornelius Gray coughed nervously. "I think I'm probably wasting your time and, if so, I apologise in advance."

"We're not exactly rushed off our feet, Mr Gray," said Hayley. "Perhaps you'd like to tell me why you're here?"

"Well, it's about a death," he began.

Hayley's antennae pricked up at the word 'death'. "Go on," she said quietly.

"I'm sure it's all above board and there's nothing suspicious about it, especially as the doctor diagnosed heart failure…"

"Are you fond of practical jokes, Mr Gray?" Hayley snapped.

"No, I do assure you," said Cornelius anxiously. "Please – please bear with me. I haven't told you exactly why I decided to come and see you."

"Very well," she said. "Carry on. But get to the point, please." She was in no hurry, but she wasn't going to tell him that. Time-wasters weren't popular with the police at the best of times.

"You see, her son is convinced she was poisoned."

Hayley's antennae were working overtime now. She hadn't had a juicy poisoning across her desk in a long while. In fact, she had consigned deaths by arsenic, cyanide, et cetera to the Victorians. She remained outwardly calm, however. "Poisoned? What makes him think so?"

Cornelius Gray shrugged and looked around him quickly. "I feel a bit of a fool, actually," he admitted after a moment. "You see, Luke – the son of the dead woman – is – "

"Is what, Mr Gray?"

"I don't know what the politically correct thing to say is but, well, he's sixteen, I think, about that anyway, but he's got a mental age of seven."

"I believe you are wasting my time, after all, Mr Gray," said Hayley, looking dangerous.

"I probably am, but the boy was very upset and seemed convinced. He even told me *who* poisoned her."

"And who might that be?"

"The boy next door. Yes, I know it sounds far-fetched and I'm sure I'm barking up the wrong tree, but I do think it's worth investigating. You see, Mrs Caldicot was a friend of mine and – well, she wasn't well but I don't think her condition was terminal."

"All right," said Hayley, after a moment's reflection. "Give me the address."

She wrote it down. Surely she had better things to do than go on what was very probably a wild goose chase? But it was Christmas day and, thought Hayley, murder was traditional on Christmas Day. Just as much as the turkey, stuffing and tree.

20

Artie was gratified to be doing something other than sitting in a not too warm police station going through files so old they hadn't even been entered on the police computer. When Hayley instructed him to get his coat, he obeyed at once.

"Where are we going?" he asked, as she jumped into her car.

"Get in. I'll explain on the way," she said crisply.

They pulled up outside Zelda's house shortly after two o'clock. The blinds were drawn. It was a house of mourning, a house of death and hopefully, thought Hayley, a house of murder. She was longing to get her teeth into something new. Battered women were sad but the crimes against them were insoluble. What wouldn't she give for a crime that was solvable, and one she got all the credit for.

She showed her ID to Charlie and barged past him before he could utter a word. Faith stared open-mouthed as the two coppers entered the sitting room where Zelda's body was still waiting to be removed to the funeral parlour. It had a quite different destination now.

"I hope you haven't touched anything," said Hayley with authority. "We have reason to believe this lady's death wasn't entirely natural."

"What you on about?" said Charlie, almost baring his teeth at her. He looked like a pitbull ready to pounce. "Who the 'ell are you, barging in 'ere like you own the bloody place? Ain't you got no respect? My wife's just died."

Hayley gave him the benefit of one of her best smiles, the kind that had won the heart of her ex-husband, Jean-Pierre, but Charlie Caldicot seemed unimpressed. "I ask again, who the 'ell are you?"

Hayley showed him her ID card once more. "DCI Hayley Pascal, Thames Valley Police, sir."

"You? A bleedin' DCI?"

"Who were you expecting? Inspector Morse?"

"Nah, you're kidding. You ain't a proper copper, not in them 'eels."

DS Frobisher was trying not to laugh as this interchange went on. Faith Desmond, who had been watching and saying nothing, asked what they thought they were doing, calling on them today of all days. She asked more politely than Charlie, but her tone was still confrontational.

Hayley Pascal, when she was on duty, was a force to be reckoned with. She glared at Faith. "We aren't here to share a wishbone with you, I can assure you," she said briskly. "We have a job to do. Any interference from either of you will be treated as obstruction. There are grave penalties for that."

Faith and Charlie both looked stunned as they obediently stood to one side to allow Hayley and Artie to examine the corpse.

"Is this where she was found?" asked Artie.

"Yeh. She died of an 'eart attack sometime last night. I'd gone to bed. The doc said it was 'eart failure.

You don't wanna take no notice of Luke. Tuppence short of a shilling that one." Charlie, unlike Cornelius Gray, had no qualms about political correctness. "You 'ad a wasted journey."

Hayley ignored him. She looked at the open box of chocolates beside the body. There were only about three or four missing, presumably eaten by the dead woman. "Bag that up, Artie, please."

"Now, sir," she said, turning to Charlie. "Leave everything exactly as it is, please. I'm calling SOCO to come and do their stuff. We should be out of your hair soon. It's purely precautionary and, if it proves a false alarm, we will release the body."

"You ain't taking the word of a bloomin' idiot, are yer?"

"We will need to analyse those chocolates," said Hayley, ignoring him. "Also, would you tell us what this lady's last meal was, please?"

"We all 'ad shepherd's pie. We all 'ad the same."

"Good. Anything else? Did you all have the same thing to drink? Any pudding?"

"Cor blimey!" Charlie scratched his head. "Er, we all 'ad some wine. I got it from the off licence on the corner. You can check if you like."

Faith interrupted at this point. "Zelda and I had ice cream after the shepherd's pie," she said. "Straight out of the freezer. This is a nightmare!"

Hayley checked her notes. "Mrs Zelda Caldicot," she read out. "That is the name of this woman?"

"Yeh, 'course it is. She's my bleedin' wife. Least –
she was," said Charlie.

"Okay. I'm sorry for all this disturbance, but we
must check everything out. We'd be failing in our duty
if we didn't go through the motions."

"Can we speak to Luke?" asked Artie. "Is he
here?"

"No, 'e's gone next door, I think."

"Fine. We'll go and see him there. In the
meantime, don't touch anything," instructed Hayley.
She and Artie let themselves out of the front door,
giving a united sigh of relief as they closed it behind
them.

"What an arse hole," said Artie. "Begging your
pardon."

"Don't apologise," grinned Hayley. "I was calling
him worse names than that under my breath. A wife
murderer if ever there was one."

"Except, according to the son, it was the boy next
door who did it."

"We'll see about that. Let's get round there.

21

"He killed her! He killed my mummy!"

The handsome, dark-haired teenager with the babyish voice was wailing on the doorstep of the house next door to the Caldicots. Artie rang the bell, while Hayley attempted to calm the young man with soothing words.

"Is your name Luke?" she asked him when he had quietened down a little. Meanwhile, Artie rang the doorbell again.

"Don't appear to be in, ma'am," he said.

"Don't call me 'ma'am'," grumbled Hayley, still with her arm around the sobbing boy. She saw at once what both Cornelius Gray and Charlie Caldicot had meant, in their different ways, about Luke's disability. What a shame, she thought. Nature could be so cruel, sometimes.

"Do you know where they've gone, Luke?" she asked him.

"Simon said he was going to his auntie's for Christmas dinner," he replied, wiping his sopping face on his sleeve.

"So they will be back later?"

"Ye-es-es. You must put him in prison!"

"Who must we put in prison, young man?" said Artie, sitting down on the other side of Luke. The cold stone step was unwelcoming, but fortunately he was well-padded. Hayley stood up now, realising her rear end was very cold and damp.

"Simon, of course!"

"Well, we can't stand here on the doorstep all day," said Hayley brightly. "And you, young man, need to be inside in the warm. Let me take you home."

Even though it was only next door, it seemed the right thing to say as Luke smiled for the first time and took her hand. She had a sudden maternal surge of feeling, something she usually only felt when she was with her beloved daughter.

"So, what do you make of that?" Artie Frobisher was at the wheel. It was his turn to drive as they journeyed back to Oxford.

Hayley was thinking about Luke, now an orphan. His stepfather was neither use nor ornament (despite his obvious good looks) and she felt sure he wouldn't have a clue how to treat a delicate boy like that.

"Do you think there's any truth in what he says?" Artie was saying. "I mean, he's not exactly Einstein, is he? Probably got hold of the wrong end of the stick."

"We have to take him seriously. For the time being, at least. That young man is a human being, with feelings, and he's not stupid."

Artie seemed about to point out to her that that was exactly what he was, or what it boiled down to, but the look in her eye stopped him in time. "We'll see what the pathologist has to say about these chocolates, then?"

"Of course. If they're all right, then we'll probably go no further. But I want to speak to this Simon Rogers and then I want a word or two with that Charles

Caldicot. I think he knows a lot more than he is prepared to tell us about what happened to his wife."

"But surely the doctor said it was heart failure? Are you saying he's mistaken – or worse, covering up a felony? A murder?"

"No, I don't think the doctor's made a mistake or covering up a murder, Artie."

"So – what are you saying?"

"I'm just saying – I don't know what I'm saying. Look, just drive, Artie, and shut up. We'll know a bit more this evening after we've spoken to Simon Rogers."

Which proved wrong. They returned sometime after eight o'clock that night. Mr and Mrs Rogers both seemed a little worse for drink but, Hayley thought, it was only to be expected. It was Christmas after all, a fact she had almost forgotten. It had been a long day, one of the longest she had known. She had tried to blot out Christmas without her daughter. It was just another day.

Simon Rogers was similar in build and appearance to Luke. Hayley liked him at once, and she could see he was no murderer. Besides, what on earth could the motive be? He seemed very fond of Luke, so murdering his mother would seem a little bizarre, to say the least.

"Poor Luke," said Simon. They were all seated in the warm sitting room, the lights of the Christmas tree flickering on and off. Mrs Rogers had provided some welcome fresh coffee and Hayley, for one, was enjoying herself for the first time that day. Although it wasn't a festive drink, the coffee was good, and she was getting in the Christmas spirit at last.

"He seems convinced you killed his mother," said Hayley. "Now, why would he think that?"

"Oh, that's easy to explain," said Simon. His face was a picture of innocence.

His father broke in. "Simon wouldn't hurt a fly. In fact, I've been urging him to man up for ages. Spends all his time with that halfwit next door."

"Dad!" protested Simon.

Hayley stared at Mr Rogers balefully. He looked intelligent enough, it was a pity his words didn't match. "I think, if you don't mind, it would be better if we saw Simon on his own."

Simon's parents didn't look like they were going to move. Artie went to the door and opened it. "Thank you," he said. "I'm sure you understand. We won't keep him long. Just a few questions."

Hayley smiled to herself. Artie was proving a useful member of her team. She would even go so far as to say her right hand man. She'd always wanted one of those.

Mr and Mrs Rogers walked slowly to the door. "I'm sure Simon would want us to stay," protested Mrs Rogers. She turned and looked hopefully at her son.

"It's okay, Mum," said Simon sweetly. "I don't mind answering their questions. I've done nothing wrong."

"Of course you haven't, darling," Mrs Rogers was saying as Artie closed the door firmly on the two of them.

"Now, Simon, let's get back to Luke's accusation. Can you tell me why he would say such a thing?" Hayley drank some more of the delicious coffee. She didn't like Mrs Rogers any more than she liked her husband, but she had to admit she made great coffee.

"Because I told him I would kill her," he said.

There was a stunned silence. Hayley eventually broke it. "Do you want to elaborate on that?" she said. It was the last thing she expected the nice young man to say, but she had come across so many weird and dreadful things in the course of her career that what people did or said very rarely surprised her. However, this was one occasion when she was.

"Yes, of course," grinned Simon. Hayley could see he was playing with her now and she breathed an inward sigh of relief.

"Go on," she told him, giving him a warning look. He might be able to charm birds off trees, but this was police work. This was serious.

"Er, well, you see it was Luke. He said he wanted to kill his mother – "

"*Luke* said that?" Her world was turned upside down for the second time within the last few minutes. She began to wonder if she was in some kind of parallel universe where everything wasn't normal unless it was standing on its head.

"Yes, you see, Mrs Caldicot took his dog to the vet to be put down. It was because the poor thing had cancer and was suffering. But Luke couldn't understand that. He just believed she killed Meg – the dog – for no reason. It's a shame. I could understand how he felt. But I couldn't let him go on thinking about killing poor Mrs Caldicot. She was a lovely woman. I really liked her. I'm so sorry she died."

"I see," Hayley said, finishing her coffee. "That makes things a bit clearer. But you say you agreed to kill Mrs Caldicot yourself?"

"Yes. To shut him up, basically. I thought that if I said I was going to kill her for him, Luke would be satisfied. And he'd soon forget all about it. Deep down he loves – er, loved – his mother. Now, of course, he's heartbroken. In fact, all would have been well today, because Mrs Caldicot bought him a puppy for Christmas. We're keeping it here at the moment. It was to be a surprise." He looked sad now. "I haven't told Luke about it yet. I think it will make him more upset to know his mother had planned this surprise for him. It's such a mess."

Hayley blinked a tear away. The trouble people got themselves into, she thought sadly. "I'm sorry." She paused, then cleared her throat. There was no room for sentiment in her business. She looked across at Artie who was sitting quietly, sipping his coffee. She could see he was as moved as she was and liked him all the more for it.

"I'm sorry to ask you this," she continued now, "but how were you supposed to have killed Mrs Caldicot?"

"No sweat. Tree poison. Luke showed me the can under the sink. I was to put it in her food somehow."

"Chocolates, even?" broke in Artie.

"Er, well, I hadn't thought that far. I wasn't intending to do it."

"And, of course, you didn't?" Hayley had a moment's doubt now. Was Simon's fondness for Luke enough for him to do the unthinkable?

"Of course not!"

"Presumably we'll find the tree poison can in the place where Luke told you it was? Under the sink? Next door?"

"Well, no," said Simon, a sheepish look on his face. "It's under *our* sink at the moment, actually."

22

The pub was crowded and noisy, but it suited Artie and Hayley, who sat in the quietest corner they could find with their pints of beer. Artie had nearly made a faux pas by remarking that pints of beer didn't suit delicate little, feminine hands like hers, but had stopped himself in time. Their budding friendship would no doubt have taken a sharp decline if he had, and he was sensible, as well as sensitive, enough not to say it. DCI Pascal had spent her entire career being 'one of the lads', he suspected, and was no doubt able to down pints with the best of them.

"I'm surprised to find a pub open on Christmas night," observed Artie.

"Yes, it's only known by the regulars. Kemal keeps an orderly house, too. Nice chap."

"Kemal? Who's he? He's not a Muslim, is he?"

"Yep, he's the landlord," she grinned, pointing at the rather handsome man who had just appeared behind the bar. Artie watched her as she wiped the beer froth from her lips. He noticed that those lips were rather nice. Inviting, almost.

"Unusual," he said with marked understatement.

"Doesn't touch a drop himself, of course. Doesn't know what his right arm's for, but knows when he's on to a good thing. Savvy bugger. While all the other pubs close early on Christmas day, he stays open. He thinks they're missing a trick, because by the time evening comes, most people are sick of cold turkey sandwiches and listening to the mother-in-law wittering on or overtired kids screaming. That's why this pub's so popular. It provides an escape from the ritual."

"I'm guessing you don't like Christmas much, then?"

"Oh, I used to love it. When – when Natasha was small." She looked sad for a moment.

"Natasha?"

"My daughter. She lives with her father in Paris. Comes to me every other Christmas. This year she's with *him*." There was a derisory note in her voice now. The word 'him' was spoken with some venom. "But at least she'll be here for the New Year. I've booked the time off so I'm hoping nothing will prevent me from taking it."

Like a murder, he thought wryly. That would be just her luck. "How old is your daughter now?" he asked.

"Fifteen. She'll be sixteen in February."

"So," Artie chose his words as carefully as he could. "So – your ex-husband got custody then?"

She shrugged. He could see the hurt behind that shrug and lingering in her dark grey eyes. "It was only right, I suppose. Natasha was only five when we split and I did such long hours I couldn't guarantee to be there for her twenty-four-seven."

"And I suppose he could?"

"Yes. He'd taken up with this woman and he was going to marry her when the divorce came through. She's French, like him, and she has a high-powered job at a Paris advertising agency. Something like that, anyway. Jean-Pierre found it easy to transfer his skills back to his home city, being a top-flight criminal lawyer. Lots of crime in France, like everywhere else."

"That's true," Artie interrupted. "Charles bloody Aznavour for a start."

She smiled but didn't respond to his attempt at lightening her mood. She continued. "So, they could give Natasha a stable home – at least they could afford a full-time nanny, which amounted to the same thing, I suppose. I couldn't afford even a part-time one at the time. Or now, for that matter."

"Maybe your daughter will come and live with you now. I mean, she's old enough to decide for herself isn't she?"

"Don't you believe it. Got it made where she is. Besides, I think she resents me giving her up in the first place. She's made me pay for it ever since."

Artie wanted to pat her hand in sympathy, but wisely decided not to. He wondered what would have happened if he had. Besides, a mere pat on the hand wouldn't be enough, he knew. Once he'd made physical contact with her, he would have found it extremely difficult not to take her in his arms and kiss her. Kiss all her sadness away.

Pulling himself together, he drank his beer before saying anything else. The rawness of her sorrow touched him, even frightened him a little.

"Er, well, what do you think? About this Caldicot business, I mean. Do you think Simon Rogers could be a cold-blooded killer?" He felt on firmer ground talking police business. Besides, if he'd probed further into her private feelings, he was worried he'd open the floodgates of her tears. He had never been able to handle a woman's tears.

"You never can tell," said Hayley, finishing her beer. Her eyes, which had looked wet just a moment ago, were dry now. "Some of the most wicked murderers had faces like angels. Anyway, once we've got the path report we'll know more. If they find this tree poison stuff in her system, then – well, it looks very much like we'll need to talk to Simon again. Seems totally improbable to me. Nice boy like that. Didn't go a bundle on the parents, though."

"No, nor me. It doesn't mean they've sired a murdering bastard, though."

"'Course not." They both laughed.

Artie went to the bar for two more beers. He returned with the foaming glasses and a couple of packets of pork scratchings. He'd never tasted a pork scratching in his life. He hadn't even been sure what they were, until tonight.

"Lovely," said Hayley, ripping open a packet. "My favourite." Artie opened the other packet and gingerly put a smallish piece in his mouth. He was surprised by just how much he hated it.

"If she was poisoned – and it's a big 'if' – I bet we won't need to look any further than the husband," said Hayley, continuing to chew happily.

"On the premise that it usually is?" he queried, passing the rest of his pork scratchings to her.

"Probably. He's too good looking, for one thing," she said. That made Artie smile, knowing that was one thing she couldn't accuse him of. "And I bet he's having an affair with that Desmond woman, for another. Didn't like her much, I have to say."

"Seemed all right to me," said Artie, playing devil's advocate. "It's a funny sort of job, isn't it? – being a psychic medium. Perhaps Zelda Caldicot was killed by a dissatisfied client. Someone who thought she was a fraud. That kind of thing."

"It's possible, I suppose."

"I mean, they're all charlatans, aren't they? But there are so many gullible people out there – think they're really talking to their loved ones through a Red Indian called Hiawatha or something. I ask you!"

"Well, if it gives them some sort of comfort, I don't see any real harm in it. Fake or not."

"So, the only possible motive for her murder as I can see then, is that Caldicot and Desmond were having an affair and they wanted the wife out of the way. Funny though. The dead woman was much better looking than Faith Desmond," said Artie. "Even dead she looked better than her."

"Looks aren't everything, you know."

"No, I know. I, of all people, should know that."

"You do all right."

Artie felt a warm glow somewhere below his solar plexus although he wasn't sure how much of a compliment it really was.

"Anyway, you've forgotten the other big motive for murder, Artie. Besides sex."

"Oh?"

"Money, lad. Money."

"Have you got any kids, Artie?"

They were walking along the road together, feeling the chill after the warmth of the pub. They weren't exactly arm in arm, but they were in very close proximity. They looked like a couple to the rare passers-by that night.

"No, which is a blessing."

"Why's that? Don't you like kids?"

"I do, but I'm glad me and Jan didn't have any. It was bad enough, the divorce, without having to fight over the kids as well."

Hayley gave his shoulder a gentle squeeze which he could hardly feel beneath the thick wool of his winter coat. But he was gratified to know her hand was there all the same.

"Right," she said after they'd gone past two turnings. "This is my road. Sorry, I didn't ask. Where do you live?"

"Not here in Oxford," he said. "I'm headed for the station to get my car."

"Excuse me," she said, "how much have you drunk tonight?"

"Only a couple of pints," he said, looking anywhere but into her eyes. "Possibly three. Or was it four?"

"And you're planning to drive home?"

"No, of course not. I'll get someone to drive me when I get back to the station."

"Well, see that you do," she said firmly.

"Of course, ma'am. Anything you say ma'am." He gave her a mock salute and began to walk away.

"And don't call me 'ma'am'!" she shouted at his retreating back.

23

Charlie Caldicot didn't like police stations. He didn't like the police, full stop. But here he was, standing outside the imposing façade of Oxford Police Station, hands in pockets, looking for all the world like he was just passing and not contemplating going in.

The law and Charlie Caldicot were uneasy bedfellows at the best of times. When he was a headstrong teen hanging around the back streets of Shoreditch, he'd got into all sorts of scrapes, avoiding Borstal by the skin of his teeth. As he got older, he realised he was on a hiding to nothing, getting in with the wrong sort. It would have been easy to have thrown his lot in with the kinds of gangs that proliferated in the East End back then: the Krays were gone, but there were always others ready to take their place. But somehow he'd avoided the pitfalls that lay in his path and, by the time he reached his mid-twenties he was more or less on the straight-and-narrow. Even so, any voluntary association with the police was strictly on a needs-must basis in Charlie Caldicot's slightly off-kilter view of the world.

Of course, there were always exceptions to every rule. That Inspector woman, for instance. He wouldn't have minded getting arrested by her. Being handcuffed to her would have been a bit of all right, he thought.

So here he was, going up the steps of Oxford Police Station. No one was forcing him, and he was still unsure what he was doing there. It was the day after

Boxing Day and two days since his wife had been found dead. According to the doctor it was a natural death, but that stupid fool Luke had sown a doubt in the minds of the DCI and her rather odd-looking sidekick. And, worst of all, they had bagged up the chocolates, presumably to have them analysed for any poisonous substances. He had been the one to give his wife those chocolates. He had to stop the police going any further down the route of that enquiry.

He entered the station, looking around him as he did so, ensuring no thick copper was about to jump out and challenge him. No, all was well. He looked respectable enough, anyway. Gone were the days when a policeman only had to look at him to suspect he was up to no good. More confident now, he went up to the reception desk and asked the desk sergeant if he could speak to DCI Pascal.

He was shown into a small, dark interview room and told to wait there. There was one small window just above his head which let in the winter daylight only grudgingly. The one inadequate radiator rattled noisily. Anyone would think he was the criminal here, he thought. He shivered inside his thick Harris tweed.

Hayley Pascal finally arrived about twenty minutes later, followed closely by DS Frobisher. Caldicot smiled ingratiatingly at them. What the hell was he doing here? he was now wondering.

Hayley sat down at the small table on the other side of Caldicot while Frobisher remained standing, the full quota of chairs being been used up.

"Well, Mr Caldicot, have you some information for us?" Hayley was brisk and business-like.

Charlie was already discomfited without this coldness. He had never failed to charm the opposite sex, or hardly ever, but this young woman seemed to have got his number, all right. She wasn't having any of it.

"Er, well, no, nothing new. No."

"Then I fail to see why you are here, Mr Caldicot," said Hayley. Her manner remained severe, more so, if anything.

"Yes, well, you see, I just wanted to know what you were planning to do about – about this business."

"This business? I presume by that you mean the death of your wife?"

"Yeah, you know what I mean. The doctor said she'd died of 'eart failure, so I don't see why you need to waste your time looking into it."

"Yes, we know Mrs Caldicot died of heart failure. That's a given. What we don't exactly know is what caused her heart to fail."

"She'd always been weak in that area," said Charlie, desperate now to leave. He was beginning to think that the usual infallible Caldicot charm wasn't going to help him now. He'd only served to incriminate himself by coming in the first place. "The doctor only last week said she should take it easy and make sure she took 'er medication regularly. She often forgot, you see. That's probably what 'appened this time." Charlie smiled at them nervously. Surely they could see there was no reason to suspect foul play?

"We cannot presume anything at this stage, Mr Caldicot," said Hayley. "Not until all the tests have been done."

"Well, I know you got your job to do, Inspector," said Charlie wheedlingly. "But surely you don't need to examine them chocolates?"

"What makes you say that?"

"Oh, well. They were a Christmas present. 'Ardly likely to be poisoned are they?"

"On the contrary. Chocolates have a strong enough taste to disguise many poisons. If you or I were to decide to murder someone, I think poison in a box of chocolates would be an excellent way to do it."

Outside the station once more, Caldicot shuddered. The cold wind had something to do with it, but it was mainly due to the look the attractive DCI had given him as she showed him out.

"Come on, Artie, we've got a couple of visits to make," said DCI Pascal after Caldicot had left. The brisk manner she had adopted during the interview was still very much in evidence.

"Where to?"

"First off, I'd like to talk to Luke again. Then I want to ask that Dr Crabtree some questions. Let's go."

Luke Caldicot opened the door to them when they arrived shortly after. He looked dry-eyed today, almost as if the tragedy of Christmas day hadn't happened. Or, if it had, only on the television in an Agatha Christie murder mystery. Hayley reckoned that, having the mind of a child of seven, Luke was more resilient than his peers. Or maybe the death of his mother hadn't really sunk in yet.

"Hello, Luke," said Hayley sweetly. "Can we come in?"

She hoped Charlie Caldicot hadn't got back home before they arrived. They were in luck. Faith Desmond told them he had come back but gone straight out again. No doubt to the pub, had been Hayley's correct assumption.

"That's all right, er, Mrs – Miss ?"

"*Mrs* Desmond."

"That's all right, Mrs Desmond. It's Luke we really wanted to have a word with. If you don't mind."

"I think I should stay with him," she said guardedly.

Artie Frobisher grinned at Faith. It had the desired effect. She thawed a little. "Why don't you and I take ourselves off to the kitchen and have a cup of tea?" he said.

When they had left the room, Hayley sat down beside Luke on the sofa. The open log fire was welcoming and cosy.

"Now, Luke," she said, "how are you feeling today?"

"All right," he said blandly. "Why?"

"Well, because of your poor mother, dear."

"Mummy killed my dog."

"I'm sorry about that." Hayley was floundering already. The death of a dog was sad, but the death of a

146

human being was a little bit more important. Except, maybe not to Luke. Did he give his mother poisoned chocolates because she'd killed his pet and did he then put the blame on Simon Rogers? No, it couldn't be right. A seven-year-old would never be able to concoct all that. How would he get the poison into the chocolates, for a start? Wouldn't you need a hypodermic needle or something?

"Do you remember the box of chocolates we found by your mother?" She started again.

"Chocolates?"

"Yes, we took them away to see if there was anything wrong with them. Anything that might have caused your mother's death."

He shrugged, then looked animated for the first time since she had arrived. "Oh them. Daddy gave her them for Christmas. I saw him give them to her."

"I've got some news for you, lad," said Hayley eagerly as they left the Caldicots.

"Snap! So have I," said Frobisher, giving her one of his most terrifying grins. "You were right, what you said."

"Right? What about?"

"You said that one of the main motives for murder was generally money. You dismissed the sex angle. Money, you said. That's at the bottom of it. Remember?"

"Yes. So?"

"Well, Mrs Desmond was very informative. Apparently there's a will and Mrs Caldicot was quite well off, as it happens."

24

Charlie returned from the pub a little the worse for drink. Faith stood looking at him as he slumped on the sofa in front of the fire.

"You still 'ere?" he slurred. "When you goin' 'ome?"

"I just thought you might like me around since your wife has just died." Her tone was beyond sarcastic.

"I don't want no one around. You don't belong 'ere. You never 'ave. You was always insinuating yourself with 'er and me. Thought you could play both ends against the middle, didn't yer?"

"You quite liked me being around once upon a time, remember? Then when you got a sniff of Zelda's money you went crawling back to her. Well, you've made your bed now."

"Oh, get stuffed!" Charlie lolled against the back of the sofa, his eyes unfocussed. "You always was a bleedin' nag."

"I know. Anyway, let me tell you something, Mr Charlie Caldicot, I was relieved when you came back here. I'd had enough of you laying around and doing nothing all day while I cooked your meals and fetched and carried for you as well as Zelda. I don't miss you at all."

"So why are you still 'anging round 'ere then?"

"Oh, don't worry, I'm going in a minute and you won't see me again. I just stayed to tell you that the police know about the will."

"The will?"

"Yes, cloth ears. The will. I think that gives you a motive for killing Zelda, don't you?"

Charlie stood up abruptly and swayed dangerously on feet which seemed too small for him. He made a grab for her, but she ducked away easily, laughing.

"You – you bitch! You sayin' I done 'er in?"

"Well, didn't you? I mean, now you can cream in the rent from that place, can't you? She told me she made sure her will said you'd get the money from that if anything happened to her. And that you'd get the monthly annuity too. Lap of luxury now, eh? And you only had to poison a few chocolates, didn't you? Easy peasy."

"I never poisoned no chocolates! Who said I gave 'er them chocolates?"

"A little bird told me," she laughed. "Otherwise known as Luke. I'm taking him home with me, by the way."

"You bloody well ain't!"

"I think you'll find I am. You never legally adopted him despite Zelda begging you to do so many times. But you didn't want a halfwit for a son, did you?"

She was taunting him now, but he was practically powerless to shut her up. He collapsed back on the sofa and gave a loud burp. The smell of beer and whisky clung on the air.

"Oh, do what you like. I don't want the brat 'anging round my neck. You can 'ave 'im. Don't envy you looking after 'im."

"Right. If that's all, I'll be off. I gave the police the name of Zelda's solicitor, so I don't think it will take them long to put two and two together. Anyway, you fancied that inspector woman, didn't you? Well, she'll be back soon. Bye bye."

While Faith and Charlie were having this heated exchange, Hayley and Artie were making straight for Preston, Preston and Underwood, little expecting that establishment to be open for business in between Christmas and New Year.

"We are an old-fashioned firm," the bespectacled receptionist informed them primly. "This is a normal working day by our calendar. Is it *young* Mr Preston you wanted to see?"

"Er, no, I don't think so," said Artie. "At least, it's *Martin* Preston we need to see."

"That's right – *young* Mr Preston. Take a seat and I will tell him you're here."

When they were shown into the office of 'young' Mr Preston they saw a man of at least eighty-five seated behind a giant mahogany desk. Artie almost giggled, but Hayley nudged him in the ribs just in time. The old solicitor's office didn't look like a place of jollity at the best of times.

"Good afternoon," said Martin Preston. He stood slowly and reached across the desk to shake their hands.

"Thank you for seeing us at such short notice, Mr Preston," said Hayley. "Especially at this time of the year."

Preston's watery eyes gleamed behind his spectacles. "'This time of the year' means nothing to me these days," he said.

Hayley saw she had touched a raw nerve. She wondered if he was missing his family in the same way she was missing hers. Her daughter was never far from her thoughts. "Well, thank you, anyway. We need to find out the contents of one of your client's wills, if you would be so good," she said.

"I believe I know whose will you wish to see," the old man said, before Hayley could elaborate further.

"You do?"

"Indeed. I had a phone call not half an hour ago from Charles Caldicot. Very sad business, very sad."

"Yes, very sad," echoed Hayley. She was used to dealing with unnatural deaths, of course, but she still felt the pain, if one or two steps removed. "Do you think we could know the conditions of Mrs Caldicot's will, please?"

"Do you think Mrs Caldicot's death wasn't a natural one, Inspector?"

DCI Pascal felt sure now it wasn't. She had doubted before, believing that Luke's hysterics were nothing more than that. His childish mind had exaggerated the circumstances surrounding his mother's death. At least that was what she had thought at the time, until the revelation about the will. Artie was proving more of an asset as each day went by, and she had only known him three days. If he went on like that, she thought, she'd have to marry him.

Hayley coughed before replying. "I fear there is a distinct possibility, but we are keeping an open mind. We just need to see the will, please."

Mr Preston also coughed, but it was a louder, more lung-infected one than that produced by DCI Pascal. When he had recovered, he took a large handkerchief from his pocket and wiped his nose so many times, it began to get on her nerves.

"This is highly irregular," he said at last, returning the handkerchief to his pocket and popping a lozenge into his mouth. "If you say you don't have definite prove that the death was – er, shall we say, suspicious, then I don't feel I can reveal the will's details to you," he said between sucks. "Client confidentiality is our byword, you see. As I'm sure you will appreciate."

Appreciate, my arse, thought Hayley. And 'client confidentiality' is *two* words she mentally told him. Time to get tough. She'd show him she wasn't the sort of ineffectual female he was no doubt used to dealing with. "I'm afraid we must insist, Mr Preston," she said. "We can get a warrant, if necessary." She doubted she could get a warrant, but he wasn't to know that. Or, at least, she hoped not. Being a man of the law though, he probably did.

However, this threat seemed to change things. "Very well," said the old solicitor. He got up creakily once more and went over to the filing cabinets in the corner of the room. After a few moments, he returned to his desk with a manila folder.

Hayley held out her hand to take it, but Preston kept a proprietorial hold on it. "I shall read it to you." He cleared his throat.

Hayley and Artie sat in the small café just around the corner from the solicitors' office half an hour later, congratulating themselves over strong hot coffees and chocolate muffins. It had begun to snow again.

"So what d'you think, guv?" said Artie, biting into his muffin with relish.

"Guv? Guv! I'll kill you if you call me that again," said Hayley, grinning all over her face as she said it.

"Sorry, gu- er, ma- er – what the hell do I call you then?"

"How about my name?"

"Hayley," he said softly. "Nice name."

"Yes. My mum named me after Hayley Mills. She was her favourite actress when she was young – my mum, that is. Oh, and Hayley too. They were about the same age. My mum had a scrap book full of photos of her and I must say she was a pretty girl."

"Not as pretty as you, I bet," said Artie, before he realised he had said it.

"Flatterer," she said, but Artie could see she was pleased. Artie wondered if she got many compliments, being in such a high-powered job. He had been nervous himself and had only paid her the compliment instinctively without thinking. He had expected rapped knuckles at the very least, but no, she seemed okay with it. He wondered, for the first time, if she liked him as a man and not just as a colleague. Up to now, he hadn't kidded himself she actually *fancied* him. He knew his limitations, even though he'd had frequent proof he wasn't entirely unattractive to the opposite sex. Unconventional looks sometimes went down well with certain women. There were lots of men who were less prepossessing than himself, and they seemed to do all right.

He finished his muffin and looked over at the middle-aged waitress who was standing by the counter staring at them with disapproval. He wondered what had got up her nose, as if he cared. Perhaps she thought they were having an illicit affair. Chance would be a fine thing, he reflected. Not that an affair would be *that* illicit, seeing as how they were both divorced and free agents. Except she was his boss, of course. That was a stumbling block but one he hoped to get over, given time.

"So, this Charlie Caldicot stands to benefit very nicely from the will," he said. He wanted to pursue a different conversation with his superior, but decided wisely that would be for a different time. Maybe when they had solved this murder, because now, he was sure, that was what it was. Even if the pathology results hadn't confirmed it yet. They would, he was sure.

"Yes," said Hayley, "he certainly does. And if he gave his wife the chocolates and they prove to be contaminated, we have him bang to rights."

"Sewn up like a kipper."

"Trussed up like a turkey."

"No room for manoeuvre."

"None at all."

"And Faith Desmond's no better than she should be," said Artie, "according to what she said. Took him away from his wife, she did. They were shacked up together for a while. I reckon she probably egged him on to get rid of his wife. Wouldn't put it past her, anyhow."

"And what if she was the one who poisoned the chocs? They say poisoning is more of a woman's crime," said Hayley thoughtfully.

"Sure. Good call. Mustn't get ahead of ourselves, though," he said, a warning note in his voice. "Let's just wait for the lab report."

Hayley grinned and sipped her coffee. "Bet you a million trillion pounds those chocolates contain poison. They were got at somehow, you can be sure of it."

Artie looked doubtful. "I don't know. She wasn't a well woman, remember. She could have just died of heart failure. Maybe she over-indulged on the chocolates. That alone could have brought it on. And, anyway, why are we beating ourselves up over this? All we've got is the word of a boy who – well, you know. I mean, how can we rely on that?"

"And what about Caldicot? Why was he so anxious that we drop the case?"

Artie nodded. "There's that, of course."

"And now we know about the will, we've got another reason to suspect it was murder," said Hayley, getting into her stride. "This Grant Vaughan. He could be responsible. The son cut out of his mother's will. Bound to be a bit pissed off about that. And now that Zelda Caldicot is dead, Mrs Vaughan's stocks and shares will revert to him to look after for his daughter. He'll be able to dip his hand in whenever he wants to now. He just won't be able to get his hands on the annuity which goes to Caldicot. That was a clear proviso."

"Hmm. I still think Caldicot had the most to gain. But, yes, Grant Vaughan must be in the frame. And what about the property? Who gets that now? I don't think old Preston made it clear." Artie attracted the stern waitress's attention now. "Bill, please," he mouthed.

"No, you don't," said Hayley. "My shout."

There followed a brief argument, ending in Artie giving in none too graciously. "Women's lib has gone too far, if you ask me," he grumbled.

"Look, Artie, don't be a prick. I'll claim it back on expenses if it bothers you."

"You can?"

"Sure," she grinned. "No problem."

The snow was falling heavily as they left the café and made for the car. "Where to next?" asked Artie, as they sat in its comparative warmth, waiting for the heater to kick in.

"Back to the station, methinks. I wish it wasn't still bloody Christmas. No point in going any further until the lab opens on Tuesday."

"Are you going to take any time off between now and then? I think you said you'd booked the time off for New Year?"

Hayley put the car into gear and turned on the windscreen wipers. "I sure did. Can't wait. Natasha should be here tomorrow."

"Natasha? Your daughter?"

"That's right. I need to get everything ready for her. I'm leaving you holding the fort meantime." The car chugged slowly away from the curb.

"I hope you have a good time," he said.

"Oh, I shall. I haven't seen Natasha since last Easter. She'll have grown so much, I bet."

Artie watched the loving smile spread across Hayley's face as she concentrated on her driving. He could see she prided herself on her road skills but, more than that, he could see how much she loved her daughter. And just how much she was relying on seeing her for the New Year. He inwardly prayed she wouldn't be disappointed.

25

"What are *you* doing here?"

Hayley Pascal glared at DS Artie Frobisher from behind her desk and through her (rarely worn) spectacles. Today, she hadn't been able to face her contact lens; crying all night had made her eyes too puffy.

"I work here, remember?" she snapped.

Artie came over to her desk and perched on the end of it, only to remove himself immediately on catching the look in her eye. "Well, yes, but you booked the time off. It's New Year's Eve, for goodness' sake!"

She stood up and strode around the desk in her precarious high heels. She folded her arms at him. "I'm aware of the date, thank you."

"Then – then – er, why are you here?"

By way of an answer, she picked up her iPhone and proceeded to scroll through her texts, stopping at one and throwing the phone at him.

He read: *Hi mum, love you, ma chère maman.* You don't often see grave accents in a text, he thought. He read on: *Hope u don't mind, darling, but hv been asked to New Year party by this boy I fancy. Will try make it over for Easter. xx*

Why did he know that was what he had expected, but hoped wouldn't happen? He gave her a sympathetic look, but felt inadequate to express what he felt.

However, he made a stab at it. "That's a bugger," he said. "Shall I pop over to Costa for some nice coffee? With caramel and cream and all that?"

"Yes and make it the biggest one they've got and triple cream – triple everything!"

A few minutes later, coffees in front of them, Hayley gave Artie a wan smile. "I believe you're a treasure, Artie," she said. She hugged her coffee cup as she spooned the cream off the top.

"I try to please," he grinned. He sipped his Americano. The sight of all that cream was making him feel queasy, but he was glad his boss was enjoying it.

"Young people, eh?" he said. "Never a thought for the people who love them best. Not when they reach their teens, anyway."

"What do *you* know?" she snapped. He was instantly on his guard. He realised at once she wouldn't tolerate any hint of criticism of the girl who had upset her so badly.

He shrugged. "No, I don't know. Not being a parent."

"Oh, sorry," she said, her voice softening and almost tearful now. "It was just that I was so looking forward to seeing her. She'd promised. I bought her a new iPad and everything."

"Lucky girl," he said with a rueful smile, fighting down the urge to comment that she didn't deserve it. "The young people have to enjoy themselves, I suppose. While they're young. It's what happens. It doesn't mean your daughter doesn't love you any the less or doesn't want to be with you – " He broke off.

"It's that she wants to be with this boy more," she grinned, removing her spectacles. Her eyes were shining with tears but to Artie they were the loveliest eyes he'd ever seen.

"We could have our own New Year's Eve Party, if you'd like," he said, finishing his coffee and aiming the empty cup at the waste bin in the corner.

"I'd like," she said.

They sat in silence now, Artie staring out of the window, Hayley finishing her coffee. The silence was broken by the urgent ring of the telephone on her desk.

"Hello," she said. "Work calls, it would seem."

"Hello," said the voice on the other end of the phone. "Is that DCI Pascal?"

"U-uh," she replied. "Who's this?"

Artie watched her concentrating on what the caller was saying. A grim smile appeared on her face. She replaced the receiver carefully.

"That was the path lab," she told him. "Apparently, there's someone like me who'd prefer working to being on their own."

"Oh?"

"Yep. We're going over to see good old Ronnie Mason. Get your coat."

He got his coat.

"What's the buzz?" he asked as they ran down the stairs two at a time.

161

"We were right, apparently. The Caldicot death was caused by poisoning," she said.

Dr Ronnie Mason surveyed the two (relatively) young coppers. He knew Hayley, of course. A sight for sore eyes, she was. Lovely smile, lovely figure, lovely legs. The man, whom he had never seen before, was a bit on the plain side, but he had a pleasant personality. Neither of them was run-of-the-mill police issue, and he liked them all the better for that.

"Okay, Ronnie, what gives?" said Hayley, business-like and informal at the same time. Ronnie had always admired her ability to effortlessly combine the two. He also knew of old that, although she was a woman in a predominantly male world, she was no pushover. He continued to admire her, but from afar. Many a better man than he had tried and failed.

"It's very interesting," he began. "Do you want to follow me to the mortuary?"

"Is that strictly necessary?"

Ronnie paused in the act of opening the door. Although she appeared indomitable, he knew she shied away from the cadavers whenever possible.

"No, not strictly. Anyway, the thing is we've found an alien substance in the chocolates that's definitely not praline or strawberry crème."

"I don't want to know what it's *not*, Ronnie," she sighed. "Give me a break. What *is* the substance?"

"It's the same substance as that found in the body," he said, dragging it out like some compere on a TV talent show. A hypothetical clock ticked down the seconds as he paused for effect. Whether either copper wanted to punch him in the nose for keeping them waiting, he didn't know or much care. This was his domain where he got to call the shots.

"And it is?" Hayley's stiletto heel tapped impatiently on Ronnie's immaculately clean laboratory floor.

"A form of pesticide known as chlorpyrifos, actually."

"Chlorpy- what?" said Artie, already blinded by science.

"Chlorpyrifos," Ronnie repeated. "Toxic, but not usually fatal."

"I see," said Hayley. "So you're saying that this stuff was somehow injected into the chocolates and from there made its way into her system?"

"Correct. It is a liquid concentrate so it could easily be injected into something like a chocolate."

"According to the box, she only ate about three chocolates," mused Hayley. "That's what you found, didn't you?"

"Yes. There were three empty wrappers."

"So would that have been enough to kill her?"

"In the ordinary way no, probably not. But she was on a beta blocker, so I presume the deceased had a heart condition?"

"Yes. The doctor diagnosed her death as caused by heart failure."

"Which is exactly what it was. The chlorpyrifos or pesticide (shall we say? Bit of a mouthful, I agree) would have caused vomiting in a normal healthy individual, especially considering the limited quantity that was ingested by the deceased. But in this woman's case, it's proved fatal."

Hayley thought for a moment. "So are you saying that whoever put this pesticide into the chocolates meant for her to die?"

"Murder in other words?" Ronnie's eyebrows were raised quizzically. He aimed for one, Roger Moore-style, but they both always rose together, much to his chagrin.

"Yes. Murder."

"I would say yes, if the perpetrator knew about the woman's heart condition. Otherwise – well, then perhaps the poison was there to cause her an upset stomach. Somebody who didn't like her much but didn't intend to kill her."

"I see," said Hayley.

Artie looked from one to the other of them. "So, Dr Mason, can we start treating this death as a murder case?"

"On balance, I should say – yes."

They left the building five minutes later, wrapping themselves in their coats against the blizzard that was now raging. Icy globules insinuated their way down the backs of those coats as they ran the few hundred yards back to the station and made straight for the canteen.

Hot tomato soup was on offer and they both ordered a bowlful.

"So, it looks from where I'm sitting," said Artie between mouthfuls, "that Charlie Caldicot is the boy. He, being her husband, must have known about her heart condition."

"Yes, that's true," Hayley agreed. "But then, I would imagine Faith Desmond would have known too."

"Hmm. But at least it lets this Grant Vaughan character off the hook."

"Not necessarily. Even if he didn't know about Zelda Caldicot's heart condition, he might have been pissed off enough with her to send her poisoned chocolates. Maybe he even thought they *would* kill her, heart condition or no."

"Yes, but you're forgetting what Luke said. He said he saw Caldicot hand the chocolates to his wife."

Hayley soaked up what remained of her soup with a thick crust of bread and chewed contentedly. "Yep. That's right."

"Well then?" said Artie, following suit with the crusty bread and the remains of his soup.

"He could still be innocent. Someone else could have got at the chocolates before he gave them to her. He might not have known anything about it. It's possible. It's up to us to prove it either way."

"Piece of cake, then?"

Hayley smiled but said nothing.

26

A slim, thirtyish woman entered Oxford Police Station the following morning accompanied by a throbbing head and a feeling of nausea. Thankfully, Reactolite spectacles hid the redness of her eyes, but if ever there was a walking example of the morning-after-the-night-before, Hayley Pascal was it. The desk sergeant greeted her cheerfully enough, although he looked almost as tired as she did, if for a very different reason.

"Hello, guv," he said, leaning on the counter as if his whole body would collapse in a heap if he didn't.

Inwardly quailing at the loudness of his voice as well as the word 'guv', she managed a weak smile. It was a definite failure, however.

"Heavy night?" asked the friendly sergeant, despite his obvious lack of sleep.

"Sort of, but probably not as heavy as yours by the look of it."

He grinned and forced himself to stand up straight. "You could say that. I swear I'll take my wife and kids to the Bahamas next New Year. Straight, I will."

"Drunken riots?"

"And then some. Why people can't enjoy themselves without having to get hammered out of their skulls beats me."

Hayley, who had got hammered out of her skull that very night, didn't respond. She made for the lift instead. Her office was only one flight up but her legs were weak enough without the added trauma of introducing them to stairs.

"Have a good day, guv," he called after her, a knowing smile playing around his lips.

"… good show."

She heard these words as she entered her office and felt like screaming. There was her drinking partner of the night before looking bright as a button, chatting up a couple of uniformed policewomen. They were all standing around her office, coffee in hands, laughing.

"'Good show'?" she repeated. "Has Terry-Thomas just walked in? You'll be calling us an 'absolute shower' next. Come on, Artie, we all know you're posh. You don't have to rub it in."

Artie and the two policewomen looked at her oddly. There was an awkward silence for a moment, before Artie Frobisher spoke. "Er, actually I was telling them about 'Jersey Boys' – what a *good show* it was."

"Ah, right." If Hayley could have crawled under the floor boards she would have done so at that moment. Not only had she accused him of being Terry-Thomas, she was aware that, despite her aching head and sore eyes, she was a little jealous of his obvious camaraderie with the female staff. Both women were lookers too, which didn't help.

The two policewomen discreetly removed themselves from the office, allowing Hayley to circumnavigate her desk and sink into her chair behind it. She supported her aching head in both hands.

"Coffee?"

She looked at him through her fingers. "You don't seem to be affected by all that booze last night," she observed.

He smiled and shrugged. "That's probably because I'm an alcoholic and used to it."

"You're an *alcoholic*?"

"Joke. I'll get you that coffee. Very black, I take it?"

He left the office without waiting for her answer. Hayley still sat with her head in her hands, trying not to cry. The night before was a blur now, but she vaguely remembered kissing her subordinate. And it hadn't just been an innocent peck on the cheek either. Tongues had definitely been involved. Oh God, she thought. I'm a complete twit. What was I thinking?

Where was her daughter when she needed her the most? If Natasha had turned up for the New Year like she had promised, she wouldn't be sitting here now with the mother of all hangovers and the ghastly recollection of trying to seduce her second-in-command. What, she wondered, must Artie think of her?

Artie, in fact, thought a lot of her. He was remembering that kiss too as he paid for the coffee. She had come on to him, there was no denying that, but she had been very drunk. He mustn't at all costs, read too much into it. Keep his distance, that was the ticket, until asked to do otherwise. If she was really fond of him, time would tell.

He returned with the coffee and put it on her desk without a word.

"Thanks," she muttered, reaching out for it. After a couple of gulps, she put it down and looked up at him. She had removed her glasses and he could see her eyes were hurting.

"I'd put them back on, if I were you," he said, hoping she wouldn't take what was meant as light-hearted banter as some kind of criticism of the way she looked. Even with those red eyes she was a dish. A 'right bobby dazzler' as his old grandfather used to say.

She did as he suggested and looked at him again. Then she smiled and relief flooded through him. She seemed to be thawing towards him now and he even risked parking his bottom on the edge of her desk.

"I've been thinking," she said. "Now we know for sure it was murder, we need to go and see this Grant Vaughan. He certainly had a motive and we know nothing about him. We have to either rule him in or out. My gut feeling is still that it's Caldicot, but we have to go through the motions. The Super will have our guts for violin strings if we don't cover all avenues."

"Waste of time, if you ask me," said Artie, swinging his rather short, stubby legs as he remained seated on her desk. "Caldicot is our man. Why look any further?"

"I tend to agree, but that's just because we're both a bit prejudiced. We see him as some wide boy from the smoke who'd do his own granny in for a few quid."

Artie was about to protest, but she raised her hand to silence him. "You know it's true, Artie. You've had a sheltered upbringing, but the likes of Caldicot had to get where they are by their wits alone."

"I'm not prejudiced, Hayley," said Artie now. "I admire anyone who can pull themselves up by their boot strings and make something of their lives. It's just the way he was acting when he came to see us. That's all."

"Okay, have it your way. But there are plenty of others who had motives. Well, not so many, I suppose." She began counting on her fingers. "Caldicot, one. Desmond, two. Vaughan, three. Luke, four – with the help of Rogers. Er – anyone else?"

"Dr Crabtree? I mean, he categorically said it was heart failure," said Artie. "He didn't seem to like his diagnosis being questioned."

"Well, I suppose he wouldn't. Anyway, what possible motive could he have?"

"None, I suppose. But you never know, do you? Maybe he'd made a pass at her and she'd threatened to tell the GMC."

"A bit fanciful, isn't it? But I suppose we'd better talk to him. But first," she said, getting up, the coffee having revived her a little – "we'll go and talk to Grant Vaughan."

"Aye aye, Captain," said Artie, grinning at her.

She, in turn, gave him a warning look, as she eased herself back into her coat and pulled her woolly hat down firmly over her ears. "My name is Hayley," she said, "not 'guv', not 'ma'am' and definitely not 'captain'."

She wasn't prepared for the George Clooney lookalike who opened the door to them. Such a man, she thought, wouldn't murder anyone. It was his job to save lives. She had fond memories of 'ER', the TV programme that had made his name, and which even now she sometimes watched on her almost worn-out box set. She had to remind herself now that this man wasn't George Clooney about to sweep her off her feet and pour her a Nespresso. She was a grown-up with a grown-up job to do; schoolgirl crushes must not be allowed to cloud her judgment.

She took out her ID card and presented it beside that of Artie's. "Mr Vaughan?" she queried, trying to remember why she was here. It was difficult, though, with those steely blue eyes staring at her. "Mr Grant Vaughan?" she asserted.

"That's right."

"DCI Pascal and DS Frobisher," she explained. "May we have a word?"

The man looked puzzled for a moment. Hayley watched his features, but they seemed to register only mild surprise. No guilt.

"Er, yes, of course. You'd better come in," he said, stepping aside. "Mind your boots on the parquet," he added, as Hayley and Artie trooped inside, shedding ice and snow as they did so.

As they were shown into the main living area, a beautiful, dark-haired woman of about fifty appeared in the doorway.

"Hello?" she said. Her voice was soft with the faintest Spanish accent.

"Pilar, these are the police," explained Grant Vaughan.

"Policía?"

Hayley smiled at the woman who she assumed, rightly, was the man's lucky wife. "Nothing to worry about. Just a few questions."

"What about exactly?" asked Grant, indicating chairs by the fire for them to sit.

"We understand you know a Mrs Zelda Caldicot?" Hayley began. Artie Frobisher, meanwhile, was staring admiringly at Pilar Vaughan who had seated herself beside her husband on the sofa.

Hayley noticed an immediate change in Grant Vaughan's demeanour at the mention of Zelda's name. His back seemed to arch and his face darkened.

"What about her?" he asked abruptly. Pilar's hand caressed his shoulder.

"Would you please just answer the question, Mr Vaughan?" said Hayley, equally abruptly now.

"Yes, I know her," he said. "Slightly," he qualified.

"I see, sir," said Hayley coldly. "Would you please tell us the exact nature of your acquaintance with Mrs Caldicot?"

Grant smiled, or rather smirked, at his visitors. "I think you know that or else why would you be here?"

"May I request you do not answer my questions with questions? Just tell me what your relationship is with Mrs Caldicot, please." Hayley was feeling a little unnerved now and, although he was a hunk, he wasn't a nice hunk at that moment. She wouldn't trust him as far as she could throw him.

"Of course." Grant Vaughan looked suitably chastened and looked down at his shoes. "She's a beneficiary of my mother's will."

"Thank you, sir. It wasn't that hard, was it?"

Grant Vaughan smiled again. Hayley studiously avoided it. "So, you know Mrs Caldicot for that reason and that reason alone?"

"Yes."

"Even though your mother must have known her pretty well to leave her something in her will?"

"Something? *Something?*" Hayley watched in fascination as his face changed again. It wasn't dark now, it was turning a deep crimson. "*Something in her will!* Just the whole bloody lot, that's all!"

Hayley and Artie exchanged glances. "I see," said Hayley, waiting for Grant to calm down a little. "That must have been most galling for you."

"I'm sorry," said Grant suddenly. He slumped forward as if all the air had been pricked out of him like a balloon. "I'm not angry for my sake. It's my daughter's education that's in jeopardy. I'm going to struggle to pay the fees for the next term, which wouldn't have been a problem if my mother had thought fit to make some provision in her will for it. My daughter gets everything when she's eighteen, but she needs the money now. Or, at least, *I* do. For her."

Hayley chastely crossed her legs and stiffened her posture. The chair she was sitting on looked comfortable, but actually wasn't. Her expression hardened as she stared at Vaughan and his wife. Here, if ever there was one, was a strong motive for murder, just as strong as Charlie Caldicot's. It would have been a shock to have been left out of his mother's will. Why his mother would have given her fortune to a clairvoyant she hardly knew, was a puzzle. No doubt she had her reasons. Probably fell out with her son. He probably didn't visit her often enough. Families! She knew someone too who didn't visit often enough either.

"Anyway, what's all this got to do with the police?" Grant Vaughan's arm was linked through his wife's and seemed to be holding on to her as if she was a lifeline.

"I'm sorry to have to tell you that Mrs Caldicot was found dead on Christmas morning, sir," Hayley told him.

Just then the door opened and a long-legged teenage replica of Pilar Vaughan strode into the room. Amie stared at the two strangers with her large Bambi eyes.

"Er, hi," she said to Hayley. "Dad? Mum? What's up?"

Pilar got up from the sofa and took her daughter by the hand. "I'll tell you all about it, darling. Come into the kitchen."

Hayley watched open-mouthed as mother and daughter left the room. The young teenage girl who had just come and gone could have been her daughter's twin sister.

She came back from her trance to hear Artie explaining the reason for their visit to Grant Vaughan. She gulped in some air, realising she hadn't breathed properly for several long seconds. She now understood why Grant Vaughan wanted the very best for his daughter, and why he was so unhappy he was unable to afford her school fees. She would do anything for Natasha and she knew that Vaughan would do anything for his.

Including murder.

27

Amanda-Thérèse Vaughan had everything going for her: looks, brains and a personality few could resist. Her fifteen (nearly sixteen) years of life had been spent in a cocoon of love and happiness. Until now. What did the police want with her father? she wondered. Why were they questioning him about that Madame Zelda's death? How had they come to the conclusion that he might be somehow involved?

She supposed it was obvious, really. Her father had told her he needed money, money that should come to him through his mother's will, money that would have seen her through her last two years at St Mary's. The school she loved so much. She couldn't bear the thought of not going to St Mary's anymore. She had learnt so much there, and was learning still. What other school would allow her free reign of the laboratory out of school hours because she was gifted in that direction? Even her chemistry master had given her the key to his private lab while he was away on holiday. She'd never be able to pursue her aim to cure cancer if she had to transfer anywhere else.

But her father was no cold-blooded killer, whatever was at stake. It just wasn't in him.

She sat with her mother in the warm kitchen, sipping hot chocolate as the snow started to fall again outside the steamy windows. "Why are the police here?" she asked for the umpteenth time. "What do they want with Dad?"

Pilar Vaughan looked just as concerned as her daughter felt. "I don't know, darling. A mistake, probably. They seem to think he knows something about the death of Madame Zelda. I think that is why they are here."

Amie nodded. She stared into her mug, twirling the dregs of the hot chocolate absent-mindedly. "He couldn't have anything to do with it, Mummy," she said. "He just couldn't. Like, why would they think it?"

Pilar smiled sadly. "Because of the will, Amie love."

"The will. Yes. But I get the money soon, don't I? Daddy can have every penny of it then."

"You won't come into it until you're eighteen. It's a long time to wait if we need the money now."

"For my education, you mean?"

"Yes. Also, your father has other commitments and he wants to retire. Besides, the legacy is rightfully his – it does not belong to a complete stranger."

"I know. But you don't think he killed her for it, do you?"

Pilar stared at her lovely daughter, pushing a stray dark curl from out of the girl's eyes. "Not for a single moment, my darling," she said firmly.

"What did the police say to you, Daddy?" Amie asked him later that day. She had been to the sales in Oxford with her mother as a special treat to cheer her up, and had bought some Jimmy Choo shoes to die for. She could only have the one pair, Pilar had told her, even though she was hankering for the same style in green. Money was beginning to be tight. This time last year she would have been able to buy both.

Grant Vaughan didn't reply to her question at first. "Did you enjoy your shopping trip, love?"

She came over to him and gave him a hug. Still clinging on to him, they both stared into the open fire that made the room so cosy. She remained seated on the arm of his chair. "Yes, Daddy. I got some marvellous shoes. They're bright red. I wanted the green pair too but Mummy said we couldn't afford both."

He looked sad now. "You know we'd let you have both, if we could," he said. "But I'm determined to save as much as possible so you can carry on at St Mary's."

"I won't go there if you can't really afford it, Dad," she said now. She crossed her fingers behind her back. What would she do if he took her at her word?

"Don't worry, chicken," he smiled. He always called her that when he was being extra sweet to her. "We'll be able to afford it now. Once the will has been sorted out. I think probate might be involved, but we can probably get something on account until it's sorted. Enough to keep you at St Mary's. When do you go back, by the way?"

"Next week," she said. She playfully pinched his arm. "Come on, Dad. You didn't answer my question."

"What question's that?" He gently pinched her back.

"Why did the police come here?"

"Oh, it was just routine, nothing to worry your head about."

"You're being evasive, Dad," she said, a serious expression clouding her face. She got up and sat in the armchair opposite. "Tell me."

He shrugged, reaching out for the poker. He stirred the coals and the flames crackled. "There's nothing to tell. The police naturally wanted to talk to me as I benefit from the will now. Indirectly. Mind you, her husband will get something, I'm sure. It wouldn't surprise me if he didn't murder her to get his hands on the legacy."

"Like, why should the police bother with you?"

"They have to do their job. You've seen enough cop shows on the television to know that."

"She's pretty isn't she?"

"Who?"

"That police inspector. Can't be all that old to be in such a senior position. I liked the look of her." She leaned across to him and touched his trousered knee. "I bet you did, too!"

"I hope you're not winking at me, Amie," he laughed. "Yes, I thought she was rather attractive. For a copper."

"So you don't think they suspect you of killing Madame Zelda then?" Amie was serious once more.

Her father's silence was ominous.

"Dad?"

"Between you and me, I think DCI Pascal believes I did."

28

"My money's on Grant Vaughan."

"And mine's still on Charlie Caldicot. He's got two grand a month for doing bugger-all. *I* might even kill someone for that."

Hayley Pascal eyed her colleague with scepticism, not entirely sure whether he was joking or not. The wink he gave her over his indifferent police canteen coffee reassured her, however.

"Grant Vaughan is in love with his daughter," she said thoughtfully. Her bacon roll was congealing as she spoke. It had been sizzling hot when she had brought it to the table, but now it looked ready for the dustbin, cutting out the middle man as a safety precaution.

"*In love* with her?"

"Oh, not in the way you mean," she said quickly. "His love is quite kosher, I'm sure. But I'm convinced he'd do anything to ensure she has the very best of everything, including a first class education. That boarding school is costing him an arm and a leg, so the money coming to him to keep in trust for his daughter couldn't have come at a better time."

Artie had finished his coffee and toasted sandwich and was now eyeing Hayley's abandoned bacon roll. "Hmm, I see what you mean. Are you intending to eat that?"

By way of an answer, she pushed the plate towards him. "I mean, people have murdered for a lot less."

Artie, she began to think, had a cast iron stomach. He was demolishing the roll with relish. "Do you get fed at home?" she grinned.

"Only if I do it myself," he pointed out. "I'm usually much too knackered to bother when I get home. And the cat hasn't learnt to make a cup of tea, let alone a spag bol."

She laughed. "You should get yourself a good woman," she advised.

A silence suddenly fell between them. He eyed her quizzically. "Do you have anyone in mind?"

"Oh, no one special. I don't suppose you're that fussy."

"As long as they've got a pulse." He laughed as he picked at the crumbs from the finished bacon roll.

"Anyway, back to the job in hand," said Hayley now. She was aware the conversation was edging onto dangerous ground. It wasn't that she didn't find Artie attractive; she had to admit she did – rather. But it would never do. Romance between colleagues rarely worked out in the end. And life was complicated enough already.

"Do we cross off the combined efforts of Simon Rogers and Luke?"

Hayley pulled a face as she concentrated on that question. "I think so. After all, Ronnie said the tree poison analysis showed no sign of the stuff that was found in the chocolates and the body."

"Red herring number one dealt with."

"I think we really only have two main suspects."

"Meaning Caldicot and Vaughan?"

"Yep."

Artie leaned back in his chair. The canteen was filling up now and soon their places would be required by hungry bobbies. "But what about Faith Desmond and Dr Crabtree?"

"Yes, I think we should talk to this Desmond woman," agreed Hayley.

"And the doctor?"

"Okay, okay. Your pet theory. We'll talk to him too."

It was, however, Faith Desmond they visited first, having gone back to the Caldicot home only to find she had moved back to her own flat on the other side of Stow. They found her in, but unwelcoming.

"What do you two want now?" was her frigid greeting. She stared at Hayley and Artie, one hand on hip, a duster in the other. "I'm a busy woman. Is it still snowing?"

She asked this as Artie brushed some wet drips from his shoulders. Hayley had a drip on the end of her nose, which she quickly removed with the back of her hand.

"Er, it's sort of thawing, I think," said Artie.

"Do you want to sit down?" asked Faith now. Her attitude continued to be unfriendly, but she was obviously resigned to their presence.

Hayley, who didn't think a cup of hot tea would go amiss, said, "Just for a moment." She sat in the chair nearest the fire, leaving Artie to make do with an armchair further away and in a decided draft.

Faith Desmond reluctantly sat down too, in the one chair left, which was even further away from the fire than that now occupied by Artie. Gallantly he stood and offered her his seat which she declined with very little grace.

"Well, now that you're here, what do you want?" she said, flicking her duster suggestively. "I can't sit and chat all day to the likes of you. I've responsibilities."

"Responsibilities?" Hayley's elegantly plucked eyebrows rose. "And what would they be?"

Faith sniffed. "None of your business," was her helpful reply. However, a fuller answer was unneeded because one of those 'responsibilities' appeared in the doorway at that moment.

"Is my egg on toast ready yet, Auntie?"

It was Luke. Both Artie and Hayley looked at him in surprise. "Is he your nephew, Mrs Desmond?" asked Artie, going over to the boy.

"No, no. He calls me that. I'm looking after him – for the time being. I couldn't leave the poor sod to the tender mercies of Charlie Caldicot."

Hayley was inclined to agree with this rather unpleasant woman who was, at least, doing something useful. Perhaps she had a softer side to her nature than was immediately apparent.

"Artie," said Hayley now. "Why don't you go and have a chat with Luke?"

"Perhaps you'd make his egg on toast while you're at it," said Faith, a sardonic smile on her face. She flicked her duster again.

"My pleasure," grinned Artie Frobisher. He put his hand on Luke's shoulder. "You come with me, lad. I'll make you the best egg on toast you've ever tasted."

"Really? Okay – er, is it okay, auntie?"

"Yes, of course. You can trust him – he's a policeman." This last sentence was said with only the merest hint of sarcasm.

When Artie and Luke had left the room, Hayley turned her full attention on Faith. "All right, Mrs Desmond. Now, just a few questions. I hope that's all right?" The sarcasm was returned with knobs on.

"Go ahead. I've got nothing to hide."

"Did I say you had?"

Faith flicked her duster again but said nothing. Hayley sensed this woman wasn't going to be easy, but she enjoyed a challenge.

"You and Mr Caldicot. May I ask what relationship he is to you – if any?"

"Nosey parker, aren't you? Seems to me the police are all just a bunch of nosey parkers, prying into what doesn't concern them."

"You're not being very helpful," said Hayley sharply. "We have our job to do. A death has occurred and we need to establish all the facts."

"Since when has it been the job of the police to investigate a perfectly natural death? Poor Mrs Caldicot had a heart condition. Her medical records will verify that if you'd bother to find out. Why can't you let her rest in peace?"

"I would like nothing better than to do that, believe me. But before I can do that, I will need to talk to Dr Crabtree about the exact cause of death. In the meantime, I just want *your* version of events and what your position is in all this. You're obviously a close friend of the family?"

"Yes, well, I work – worked for Mrs Caldicot."

"And you got to know her well?"

"Yes. As well as you get to know anybody, I suppose."

"And Mr Caldicot?"

"What about him?"

Hayley watched her reaction to this. If she wasn't having an affair with him, she'd eat her hat. "Just that, Mrs Desmond. You got to know him well, too?"

Faith reached across to the small table by Hayley's chair and picked up the cigarette packet lying there.

"I'd rather you didn't, if you don't mind."

"It's my house. You can clear off if you don't like it." As Faith lit her cigarette, Hayley could see her hand was shaking.

"I repeat, you got to know Mr Caldicot well during the time you worked for his wife. You're even looking after his son."

"Luke's not his son," she snapped, blowing an almost perfect smoke ring. "He never even adopted him, even though Zelda kept asking him to."

"Oh, I see. How long had they been married?"

"Oh, ten years about."

"And in all that time, you and Mr Caldicot had never got to know each other well?"

"We got to know each other. Naturally."

"It's my belief you got to know each other well – very well. As well as one person can know another person."

"If you know, then why ask?"

"Did you and he have an affair? Please just answer the question."

"So that you can take it down and spread it round the town in the next ten minutes? You police make me sick."

"Look, Mrs Desmond, I don't know what you think the police do with information of this nature. But we are not gossip-mongers. We just need to get as informed a picture of this situation as possible."

"So that's it. It's out now. You think I was having an affair with her husband and I killed her so that I could have him all to myself."

"Did I say that? I don't think so, Mrs Desmond. But it's a theory, certainly."

Artie placed a plateful of egg and toast in front of Luke who was sitting with knife and fork poised at the kitchen table, kicking out his legs as if he was five years old. Artie felt sorry for him. The young man, for he was almost that, still had the mind of a child where egg on toast was seen as a special treat and nothing much else mattered until he had eaten it. He watched as Luke chomped happily away.

Then he thought again. Maybe he *was* happy, happier than most normal boys of his age. Going through puberty hadn't affected him in the same way. The 'sulky teen' stage had passed him by, and he was probably all the better for it.

"Are you enjoying my cooking, Luke?"

"Yummy."

"Glad you like it. I make good eggs. Mind you, I'm not much good at cooking anything else."

Luke wiped the egg yolk with some more bread and showed Artie his clean plate. "No need to wash it up," he said proudly.

Artie laughed and took the plate from him. He put it in the sink making sure that Luke didn't see him do it. He then sat down at the kitchen table and poured out the freshly brewed tea he had also made. Not for the first time he thought he would make some lucky woman a wonderful husband, even if his ex-wife would hardly have agreed.

"Now, Luke, do you remember what you said about your friend Simon?" He stirred sugar into Luke's cup and handed it to him. "Careful, it's hot."

"I'll wait till it's cool. Mummy used to let me drink it from the saucer."

Artie tipped some of the hot liquid into the saucer for him. He watched in amusement as Luke slurped happily.

"Now, about Simon," he said, after a few moments.

Luke looked up from his saucer, licking his lips. "Simon?"

"Simon, yes. Your friend who lives next door? The one you said poisoned your mother?"

Luke looked sad now. "Poor Mummy," he said.

"You said you thought Simon had poisoned her?"

"I told him to do it. He *promised*."

"But why did you tell him to poison your mother? Didn't you love her?"

"She killed my dog. I hate her."

"You can't really hate her – not now she's dead."

"No, I suppose …"

Luke got up, leaving most of his tea. "I want to go home," he said.

"I'm sure you can go in a minute," said Artie. "But first, do you still say that Simon killed your mother?"

"He *promised*."

"Do you believe he could have broken that promise?"

"No! You never break a promise."

"No, you shouldn't. But sometimes it's necessary or unavoidable. People make promises for all sorts of reasons and sometimes they have to break them because of things that happen that they didn't expect. Do you understand?"

"No."

Artie sighed. He had to remember he was talking to a seven-year-old, even though all he could see was a young man, taller than himself, with an intelligent face and sensitive eyes. "All right. Now, you said that you

188

saw your daddy give a box of chocolates to your mummy on Christmas Eve. Do you remember?"

"Yes. He did."

"Good. Did he say they were a present for her?"

Luke screwed up his face in concentration.

"Yes. He did. He said they were a special present for Christmas. Because he loved her."

"Because he loved her? He said that?"

"Yes. He did."

29

Dr Howard Crabtree had been a little in love with Zelda Caldicot almost from the moment she had walked into his surgery for the first time a little over six years ago. It was a kind of protective love, not one that would ever see the light of day, of course. He had kept his feelings hidden under the blanket of his respectability and community pillar as an experienced and well-liked general practitioner. Besides, he was a married man and she was a married woman.

However, he had allowed his professional persona to slip just the once, but once had been enough. He had constantly relived that foolish moment, and each time it had seemed to grow in horror until it had taken on the august proportions of the Dresden bombings. He would never live it down, not if he lived to be a hundred.

Zelda Caldicot had looked particularly charming that fateful day, the day he had quarrelled with his wife and daughter. The two facts seemed somehow inextricably linked in his mind, as he looked back on it. He had long since fallen out of love with his wife; rubbing along together was the best they could manage. But that morning he had had enough of her nagging disapproval. It had been made worse by his daughter's harsh words and that had proved the last straw.

If Zelda hadn't been his first patient after that quarrel, all might have been well. But when he arrived at his surgery, still smarting from what he perceived to be the unreasonableness of his trying family, his hatchet-faced receptionist had showed her in with one of her frightening sniffs. It was a sniff that told him Zelda Caldicot didn't meet with her approval. Too much make-up and too heavy on the scent for her liking. It had often occurred to him to get rid of Miss Aucutt as she tended to scare a lot of his patients. But she had been with him for so long and, besides, where else could she go? Who else would employ her?

His heart had started to thump straightaway and his hands were unsteady as he'd listened to Zelda's chest through his stethoscope. As a doctor, the flesh he had to navigate to reach that vital organ had never bothered him. Female mammary glands were just that. Except Zelda's weren't. He had tried his best to focus on what he was hearing through his stethoscope, not what he was inadvertently seeing.

"I'll need to do an ECG," he had said. He had been worried then. Her heart wasn't working properly. He could quote all sorts of medical terms at her, but he had told her bluntly that her heart wasn't working properly.

She had looked as if she was going to faint at the news and, before he could stop himself, he'd rushed around his desk and taken her in his arms. It was then that the mad moment had happened. He had kissed her. Not a little peck. He might have been able to get away with that. No, it had been on the lips, a little too long, although stopping short of tongue insertion.

From that moment she had kept her distance. He had never behaved inappropriately again, but the damage was done. She could have reported him to the

General Medical Council at any time. This knowledge had hung over him like Damocles' sword for longer than he cared to think. Now Zelda Caldicot was dead, that threat had died with her but it gave him no comfort.

As he was thinking this, hatchet-face appeared at his surgery door. "There's a DCI Pascal and DS Frobisher to see you, Dr Crabtree," she said, articulating all three names in her clipped tones.

He stood up. "Show them in," he told her. "If there are no more patients waiting?"

"No, your last patient cancelled," she told him.

Hayley and Artie were soon seated in front of Crabtree's desk. Hayley wondered if she had seen a nervous tic below his left eye, or was it just a trick of the light? Her training as a copper had drummed into her the need to look for signs like these. Signs that could tell you whether someone was innocent or guilty. She had always thought this theory wasn't fair on people with facial palsy, but it was a useful yardstick nevertheless.

"We won't keep you, Dr Crabtree," she said reassuringly. "I know you're a busy man."

"No, it's fine. I've got my rounds to do, but I'm a little early as my last patient didn't turn up."

"Good," smiled Hayley. "Now, you know why we're here, of course. We just wanted to make sure you were exact in your diagnosis of Mrs Caldicot's cause of death."

Baldly put, but for a purpose. The nervous tic again. Maybe Artie was right. Maybe Dr Crabtree bore closer looking into.

"As I told you at the time, I saw no reason to suspect anything. Her death was caused by heart failure. She had been very poorly for some time, and I had been expecting the worst as she often forgot to take her medication."

He seemed to relax a little now, but Hayley wasn't ready to let him off the hook just yet. "So, you stand by your diagnosis? Death was natural. Heart failure. Yes?"

"Yes."

"Except our path lab found a foreign substance in Mrs Caldicot's system which was traced to the box of chocolates she had been eating. Do you have any thoughts about that?"

Dr Crabtree didn't seem unduly flustered by this. Hayley gave him a mental plus point.

"Not having an x-ray machine or ultrasound equipment with me at the time, I had no way of knowing she had ingested any poison. If I had I might have reached a different conclusion."

Hayley had to admit it was a point well-made and she had no comeback. "Quite so," she said, stealing a look at Artie who gave her an encouraging smile, as if to say, 'carry on – you're doing all right'. But she didn't think she was. Dr Crabtree had the upper hand at that moment. She tried a different tack.

"Do you know of anyone who could have had a grudge against her?" she asked.

"I wouldn't know. She was my patient. I didn't know anything about her personal life. Outside of her health issues, of course."

That was that then. It wouldn't be easy to break down this man's defences, she thought, as she and Artie made their farewells. He probably had nothing to hide anyway. Probably.

"Brick walls everywhere we turn," she sighed, later that day in the office. Artie had done his usual ministering angel turn and provided Earl Grey tea and cake. Her favourite today: coffee and walnut. They were comforting, but hardly an aid to her reasoning capacity. Hercule Poirot had his tisane to help his little grey cells, but she guessed he would have turned up his little French nose at the coffee and walnut cake. Stuck up little twat.

"Caldicot's our man," said Artie, his voice firm and authoritative. "Let's haul him in for more questioning."

"Hmmm. Grant Vaughan has just as much to gain as Caldicot, don't forget. He gets the rent from the property now, as well as the investments. Caldicot only gets the annuity which is worth a couple of grand a month."

"Exactly." Artie looked thoughtful. "I'd say it's six of one and half a dozen of the other. Both men have strong financial motives."

"Yes, I agree. But what about Faith Desmond? She's a bit of an enigma. Seems she doesn't care about Caldicot, but I bet she's seething if he'd dumped her to go back to his wife when he found out she'd come into a fortune."

"Yes, that's probably true. But she doesn't look as if she's got the oomph to commit murder. Much too boring."

"Oh, I don't know. Appearances can be deceptive. Look at Crippen. A more meek and mild little man you couldn't wish to meet and yet he chopped up his wife into pieces, hiding parts of her body still not found to this day. A little poisoning in a box of Cadbury's is nothing in comparison."

"Yes. You never can tell about people. But I still think Caldicot's our man. He reminds me of Bill Sikes. Better looking, probably, but he has that brutish magnetism that defines a murderer in my eyes."

"You mad romantic fool you," she laughed, finishing the last of her cake. "You can't arrest someone just because he looks like a Dickens villain."

Artie scrunched up his coffee carton and hurled it at the bin on the far side of the room. It missed.

"Anyway," said Hayley, "we'll talk to him again. Give him a hard time. I'd like to make that cocky bastard squirm."

"If anyone can make a man like Caldicot squirm, my money's on you," said Artie, retrieving the carton and placing it carefully in the bin.

"So I should think," said Hayley, grinning.

30

Charlie Caldicot wasn't altogether surprised to find DCI Pascal and her sidekick on his doorstep once again. He wasn't altogether pleased, either, even if he did fancy the woman. She must be something else, he'd thought when he first met her, to be so high up in the force at so young an age. She couldn't be more than thirty-five, he guessed. The bloke with her was a bit of a geek, though, with that posh accent and crooked mouth. Probably didn't have a lot of success with the birds.

All this went through his mind as he looked at his unwelcome visitors. The fresh flurries of snow were already covering the shoulders of their coats and a few flakes had landed on that cute little nose of hers.

"Well, what is it this time?" he said. "Ain't you got no 'omes to go to?"

"We do and we wished we were there instead of having to talk to you," said Artie, before Hayley could respond.

"Charming! I suppose you'd better come in then." He stood to one side, managing to brush himself against Hayley's body, ever so slightly. She gave him a glare, but said nothing.

When they were seated in the living room, Hayley coughed and began. "Mr Caldicot, we need to ask you a few more questions," she said.

He could do without all this again, he thought. However, it was pleasant enough staring at her black stockinged legs, what he could see of them above her fur-lined ankle boots. The boots were cute too.

"We just need to clarify a few things," said Artie, glaring at Caldicot. The lascivious look in the man's eyes had obviously not gone unnoticed by the young copper.

"Clarify? Oh, right. Well, fire away." Charlie leaned back in his chair, a smile on his face. He wasn't about to be fazed by these representatives of the Long Arm. Not him.

Hayley cleared her throat. "We understand that you gave your wife the contaminated chocolates. That's right, isn't it?"

"Who told you that?" Caldicot snapped. It was clear he had been taken by surprise at this question. "Luke told yer, I suppose."

"Never mind who told us, Mr Caldicot," said Hayley, watching him closely for nervous tics or twitches. "Did you or did you not give Mrs Caldicot the chocolates?"

"Yeah, I did. But I didn't know they were contaminated, for Gawd's sake. I loved the woman."

"Did you?"

"What d'you mean? 'Course I bloody did. You got no right to suggest I didn't."

"Very well, we'll let that pass, for the moment. So, you can confirm that you gave the chocolates to your wife?"

"'Ow many times? I said so, didn't I? I ain't denying it. But they weren't from me. I 'adn't got 'er a

197

present, you see, and it was under the tree with 'er name on but it never said who it was from. So I made out it was from me. Didn't want 'er to be disappointed, like."

Silence followed this revelation. Hayley looked at Artie and nodded.

Artie took his cue. "Let me tell you how I think it really was, shall I?" he said. "You and Mrs Desmond were having a relationship – affair – whatever you want to call it. You had even left your wife to go and live with her. But when you heard about the will, you came back to your wife to make sure you got her money. You also knew she had a heart condition, but you weren't going to wait for nature to take its course. Oh no. You wanted the money soonest. Perhaps you and Mrs Desmond cocked it up together – I make no comment on that. Anyway, I put it to you that you deliberately injected a certain substance into the chocolates and gave them to her as a Christmas present. That's the real truth, isn't it?"

"'Ave you finished?" Caldicot was standing now, looking dangerous. "You can't pin this on me. I swear I never done 'er in."

"In that case, Mr Caldicot, you will have no objection to coming down to the station with us and making a formal statement?" Hayley stood as she said this.

"What? I just told you 'ow it 'appened. What d'you want me to come to the station for?"

"We just need to take a formal statement, that's all." The look on her face was inscrutable.

"Are you arresting me?"

"Not at this stage. Unless you refuse to come voluntarily, of course."

"I'll get me coat."

Walking to the car, Caldicot looked as if he was about to make a run for it. However, Hayley got into the driving seat and watched as Artie took hold of the man's arm and opened the door to the back seat. He gently pushed him into the car, his hand approaching Caldicot's head.

"You do that trick of pushing me 'ead into the car like they do on all the cop shows on the telly and I'll – I'll – "

"You'll what? Assault a police officer?" Artie grinned.

"Oh, fuck off."

Artie sat beside Caldicot in the back seat and Hayley got the car going after the third attempt. There was a blizzard raging around them, and the windscreen wipers weren't coping well.

"Easy does it," advised Artie.

"She a good driver?" asked Charlie, now seemingly resigned to his fate. "I don't 'old with women drivers."

"You're a bit of a Neanderthal, aren't you?" observed Artie with barely disguised distaste. Hayley said nothing as she concentrated on her driving.

"You married?" Caldicot asked.

"None of your business," said Artie, looking out of the window at the driving snow. It was obviously preferable to looking at his companion.

"I bet you are. Or maybe you're divorced? You got the look. Anyway, I bet you sometimes thought about killing your wife, eh? They can 'alf get on your tits, can't they? Can't live with 'em, can't live without 'em as the saying goes."

"Just shut up." Artie continued to stare at the snow.

"What I'm getting at is I've often wanted to strangle the bitch, but I never would 'ave. Not got it in me. Neither 'ave you or most everyone else. I wouldn't know where to get 'old of any poison for a start – apart from what you get in 'ouse'old goods, I suppose. And even if I did, I wouldn't 'ave the first clue 'ow to get the stuff into the chocolates."

"Just keep quiet. You can make your statement at the nick and then you can go home. If you didn't murder your wife, you have nothing to fear." Artie was looking directly at him now.

"If you think I'm falling for that one, you got another think coming, mate."

"Well, do you believe him?"

Artie asked this question as he and Hayley stood together in the corridor outside the interview room watching Caldicot's departing back.

"Hmm, you know, I think I do."

They moved to the lift. Back in their office, Hayley sat behind her desk, while Artie paced up and down.

The radiator made a few clicking noises as if to let them know it was actually on, even if it wasn't giving out any heat. The snow outside made them feel even colder inside.

"Why?"

Hayley looked up from her paperwork. "Why what? Can you stop pacing up and down like a pregnant father?"

"Why do you believe he's innocent?" Artie slumped behind his desk and drummed his fingers on it. "He's got to be our man."

"You're fixated on him, Artie. You've got to get it in proportion, see the bigger picture."

"It's as plain as a pikestaff. It's so feeble a lie about pretending the present was his."

"I don't know. It's so improbable, it's probably true. I know you don't like him, Artie. He's a world away from you. Chalk and cheese. He never had the advantages you had, for a start."

Artie looked about to say something, but remained silent.

"Yes, I know, Artie. Caldicot is every kind of a shit, but I don't see him as a wife murderer."

"Well I do!"

"So you're convinced?"

"Completely."

Hayley looked at him angrily now. Then she sighed. "I bet class is at the bottom of your dislike and suspicion. You must try to be more broadminded, Artie."

"It's not that! Okay, okay. He's not quite the tennis club sort, as my dear mother would say, but that's not the reason I think he's guilty. Look, he gave Zelda Caldicot the chocolates, didn't he? He admits it. This business of no name on the gift tag is rubbish."

"I see we're not going to agree over this. Grant Vaughan is our man, I'm sure of it."

"But why are you so sure? He's a much more respectable character than Caldicot. Upright family man and all that. Lovely wife and daughter. He's got a lot to lose."

"And a lot to gain. He's probably really angry that his mother gave her fortune to a stranger. I think I'd be angry too if it were me. Then there's his daughter's schooling. He dotes on her, you can tell. I believe he'd do anything – and I do mean *anything* – to make sure she has the best."

"Like you'd do anything for *your* daughter?"

Artie had touched a nerve. "Let's leave my daughter out of it, shall we?"

"No, let's not. You said he'd do anything for his daughter. Including murder, I presume. Well? Would you go that far for yours?"

"No, of course not."

"Then why suspect Vaughan?"

"Because it's his mother's will, which he sees as rightfully his, that's why."

"Maybe we should look at other suspects," sighed Artie after a moment.

"On which we can both agree?"

"Yes. At least if we both agree we can eliminate them, that's a start."

"Good thinking."

"Coming up on the outside is that Cornelius Gray bloke. He obviously had a soft spot for her. I bet he was fed up when her husband came back on the scene."

"Now that's stupid," said Hayley. "If he wanted Zelda for himself, he'd murder Caldicot, surely?"

"I suppose so. Not a likely contender, then?"

"No. Not very likely."

"Worth a punt, though?"

"Okay. You go and talk to him. He might know something."

"You're not coming?"

"No, I've got masses of stuff to do here."

"Don't fancy going out in the snow again, guv?"

"Watch it!"

31

DS Artie Frobisher was rather glad Hayley had allowed him to visit Cornelius Gray alone. He had always been wary of psychic mediums, clairvoyants and others of that ilk, classifying the whole of lot of them as charlatans. As a non-believer in any form of after life, he viewed the likes of Cornelius Gray with deep suspicion. They were simply parasites, living off the vulnerability and susceptibility of their clients. They lied to them and got away with it. What other profession did that?

He was determined to give Mr Gray short shrift. He pulled up outside the imposing façade of his consulting rooms and sat still for a moment in the warmth of his car. The snow had stopped now, but the gunmetal sky was heavy with more. Right, he thought. I'll see what you have to say, Mr Gray. And I won't believe a word of it.

As he rang the bell he noticed Madame Zelda's name plate hadn't been removed. She could only have occupied these rooms for less than a couple of months, he thought. The intercom buzzed and a woman's voice asked his business.

Once inside, he looked around the entrance hall and marvelled at its opulence. Clairvoyance obviously paid well, he thought bitterly. A young woman came down the stairs towards him, smiling.

"Mr Gray won't keep you long, Sergeant," she said. "Will you wait in here?" She opened a door to the left and he was shown into a warm, inviting waiting room. It was empty, apart from a black cat which immediately sprang up from its vantage point at one of the large windows and streaked past them into the hall.

"That's Clovis," she said. "We feel he adds to the atmosphere – being black."

"And sinuous," observed Artie. His own cat was also black and sleek. He liked cats. They stood no nonsense from anyone, not like dogs. Always sucking up to you, they were. It was true what that card said, the one he was sent by a friend. 'Dogs have owners, cats have staff.' He liked that, it amused him, and it was also very true if his own feline was anything to go by.

"Can I get you a coffee or anything?" the young receptionist was asking.

"Er, no thanks," he smiled. He noticed she was pretty behind the spectacles. A bit plump, but it suited her.

He sat down and picked up a magazine from the well-stocked table and began to flick through it. It didn't hold his interest for long, being a DIY journal: all four-by-two's and rawl plugs. It was like a foreign language to him. He had never even managed to put up a shelf. Not one that stayed up, anyway. It was one of the reasons, one of the many, why his wife had divorced him.

After about ten minutes the door to the waiting room opened and a tall, distinguished-looking man in his middle years appeared. "Sorry to have kept you waiting," said Cornelius Gray, shaking Artie's hand. "Please, won't you come with me?"

Artie followed him up the stairs, working out in his mind what questions he was going to ask. He hadn't been prepared for the look of the man or the self-confidence of his manner. Here was someone who seemed comfortable in his own skin. His mode of making a living was altogether dodgy, but he acted as if he was a top-flight Harley Street surgeon with a list of life-saving operations under his belt. Artie felt out of his depth all of a sudden. He had expected to find a seedy little man in a seedy little room, someone he could trample into the dust with just a few apposite words. Then he remembered. Cornelius Gray was a suspect in a murder case, even if a fairly remote one.

"Didn't Jennie offer you any refreshment?" Gray asked when they were seated in his plush consulting room. It was exactly what Artie would have expected a clairvoyant's consulting room to be like: all red velvet curtains, soft lighting and ethereal music playing somewhere in the background.

"No – I mean, yes, she did," said Artie. "I didn't want any, thanks."

"I suppose you've come about poor Zelda?"

"Just a few routine questions, sir. You were the one who informed us about the death of Mrs Caldicot, didn't you?"

"Yes. I – I don't think I would have suspected anything, because Zelda had a weak heart. It was just what Luke said – her son."

"About his mother having been poisoned by his friend Simon?"

"That's right. I thought it was all nonsense. The boy isn't exactly normal – I don't mean to be derogatory. But, well, his mental age is only about seven. As I suppose you know."

"I do. So you didn't attach much importance to what he said then?"

"Not at first, no. But it niggled away at me afterwards. I didn't think his friend had poisoned her. I didn't think anyone had really poisoned her, but I just thought I ought to bring the matter to the attention of the police."

"Of course, sir. It was your duty. As it turned out there is cause for some concern about the death of Mrs Caldicot, as I presume you now know?"

"There was a report in the paper – something about foul play not being ruled out," said Gray. "Is it true, then? Was she – was she murdered?"

"We have reason to believe that Mrs Caldicot's death wasn't entirely due to natural cause, yes," said Artie, choosing his words carefully.

"Poor Zelda! Who would want to kill her? I can't believe she had an enemy in the world."

"You were very friendly with her yourself, Mr Gray?" Artie paused, trying to gauge the man's reaction, but Gray's expression was inscrutable. He'd hoped to instill a sense into the man that the police had got his number, disconcert him into saying something he otherwise might have kept to himself. It was a tactic he had learned at Police Training College.

"Yes, we were friendly. Quite friendly, I would say. But we hadn't known each other very long. I met her when she moved into the rooms on the ground floor. She only did her consulting here, you understand. She still lived in her own house. I live on the premises myself."

"I see, sir," said Artie. "So, you wouldn't describe yourself as anything more than just a friend of the victim, then?"

Cornelius Gray smiled and leaned back in his swivel chair, his long legs stretched out before him. Artie studied those legs. They were the sort of legs he would have liked himself. Instead he was saddled with what amounted to little more than stumps, or so they had always seemed to him. His five feet eight inches didn't compare very favourably with Gray's six feet two. He dismissed these irrelevant thoughts quickly as he waited for the man's reply.

"As I said, we were friendly, and I think our friendship would have grown, given the right circumstances."

"So you wanted to become more than friends, then? Even though she was a married woman?" Artie tried to keep the tone of censure out of his voice as he said this. It was the twenty-first century, after all, and pretty much anything went these days. His mother and father were dyed-in-the-wool Tories, and their outlook on life had rubbed off on their only son, despite Artie's attempts to be more liberal in his outlook.

Gray eyed him with obvious disdain. "Yes, a married woman," he agreed. "But her husband was living with someone else when I first met her."

"Quite so. But then her husband returned, didn't he?"

"He did. And she didn't encourage our relationship after that. Which was only right, of course. She was a good woman." There was a faraway look in his eyes now.

"But I presume you weren't happy about that?"

"No, of course I wasn't. I was very fond of her."

"Have you ever been married, Mr Gray?"

"Yes. My wife died."

"I'm sorry." Artie paused once more to study Cornelius Gray's face. There was no sign of strain, no chink in his armour as far as he could see. The interview wasn't going according to plan at all. "So you still wanted to see Mrs Caldicot when her husband returned, but she didn't?"

"In a nutshell, I suppose. Yes."

"What did you feel about her husband?"

"What do you mean? What did I feel about him?"

"Well, you must have been jealous, surely?"

Gray shrugged. Just then the cat slid around the door and stalked across the room. He leapt up on Gray's lap, purring loudly. It jabbed its head under the man's chin in order to claim his full attention. An absent-minded stroke was all it got, however. "Of course I was. I'm human, after all."

There was a silence now. Artie wasn't sure how to proceed.

Gray finally spoke. "You'll be pleased to hear you have a good aura," he said.

Here we go, thought Artie. Bloody auras now. Showing his true colours at last. Perhaps he's about to tell me I'm going to meet a tall, dark stranger or cross the water.

"I'm sorry, I can tell you're not a believer in the occult. But you have a strong aura, despite the heartache you've suffered in the past. Your marriage break-up has taken its toll on you, I know."

How the hell does he know about my divorce? Artie wondered grimly.

"But you'll have a good life from now on," Gray continued, seemingly unperturbed by the look on Artie's face. "You've got someone else in your life now. It won't happen overnight, but it will – one day."

"Thank you, Mr Gray, but I didn't ask for a psychic consultation."

"I apologise. I've been in touch with Zelda, by the way."

Artie stared at him. Was he taking the piss?

"What are you talking about?"

The cat jumped onto the floor and started to rub around Artie's legs. Perhaps this stranger would give it a stroke or two, seeing as how its owner wasn't giving it any. However, Artie, generally happy to stroke felines

210

whenever they came his way, pushed the cat aside. Gently.

"I spoke to her two nights ago," said Gray. It was a matter-of-fact statement, along the lines of 'I went to the pictures the other day' or 'I had to go to the dentist yesterday'.

The cat continued to sit at Artie's feet, but seemed resigned to being ignored now. "You spoke to a dead woman?"

"Yes. I do that for a living, remember?"

Some living, thought Artie. "And what did she say? Is the weather fine where she is?"

"I know you think I'm a fraud," said Gray quietly, "but I *did* speak to her. She is unhappy. In limbo. She can't rest."

"So you knew all the time she had been poisoned?"

"Yes, I knew." Gray looked suitably shamefaced at having misled the good detective sergeant. "But I didn't think my saying I knew because I'd been in touch with the dead woman would go down very well. And I was right, obviously."

Artie, against his better judgment, decided to pursue the turn the conversation had taken. "Did Mrs Caldicot throw any light on who her assassin might be?"

"You're laughing at me," said Gray. "You think I make it all up. You think I hoodwink poor widows out of their money, don't you? Profit from their unhappiness? That's what you think, isn't it?"

"It doesn't matter what I think, Mr Gray," said Artie blandly. He bent down to stroke the cat at last. The purring was deafening. "If you think you can help with this line of questioning, then don't hold back. Did Mrs Caldicot have anything of any significance to say? Anything that could throw any light on her murderer?"

Gray shook his head. "All she kept saying was 'he didn't buy me the chocolates – they weren't from him'."

"And who did she mean?"

"I took it she meant her husband, of course."

"She said she didn't think he'd bought her the chocolates?"

"Yes. That's right. The chocolates weren't from him."

"But her son said he saw him give them to her."

"Oh, yes. I'm sure he gave them to her, all right. But my belief is he just pretended they were from him."

"But why would he do that?"

"Zelda told me – er, I'm sorry, but she did."

Artie grimaced. "You're trying to tell me that you got in touch with her after she died and she told you that her husband hadn't bought her the chocolates – only *gave* them to her?"

Cornelius shrugged. "That is what I'm saying. She knew he hadn't bought them for her. The gift tag only had her name on it. They could have been from anybody."

"But why would she assume they weren't from her husband?"

"Because Zelda told me that Caldicot had never bought her a present in his life."

Artie sniffed. If he took the word of a clairvoyant as evidence, he'd be drummed out of the force as quick as you like.

But he couldn't quite dismiss it, even so.

32

Hayley Pascal grinned as Artie Frobisher recounted the details of his visit to Cornelius Gray.

"So, what was your overall impression of him?" she asked. "Still think he's a fraud?"

Artie was about to nod vigorously, but something stopped him. How did the man know about his messy divorce? Mind you, it wasn't that bad a guess; many men of his age had at least one marriage break-up under his belt. "Well, I suppose I gave him the benefit of the doubt," he said slowly. "He seems a genuine person. As far as that goes."

"Did you get anything useful out of him?"

"Useful? Useful – hmm." Artie thought carefully. Should he tell his boss about the contact he said he'd had with Zelda Caldicot from beyond the grave? It would be like admitting he was taking that kind of thing seriously. Hayley didn't look the type to swallow rubbish like that.

"Yes, useful. As in – well – useful," she prompted.

"I don't know what you'll think about this," he said now. "You're going to think I've lost the plot, but Gray told me he'd been in touch with Zelda. I mean, after she was dead." He waited for the laughter. It didn't come.

"I see," she said showing no emotion. "Right. What did he say she said? Word for word, or as near as dammit."

"Oh, just that she said Caldicot hadn't bought her the chocolates. He hadn't bought her a Christmas present at all."

"What?"

"Which kind of knocks my theory that Caldicot is our man on the head. Doesn't it?"

"Of course it doesn't! Why would you believe a load of rubbish like that? As if she could communicate from beyond the grave. You simple or what?"

Artie laughed. "I thought that's what you'd say. I didn't believe it either."

"Oh, yes you did. You do realise we can't take that as any kind of evidence, don't you?"

"Yes, I realise that."

"Although, if there was any truth in it – which of course there isn't – it would mean that Caldicot is guilty of nothing more than not getting his wife a Christmas present. Bad enough in my book."

"So, what do you think then?" Artie was becoming confused with Hayley's yo-yo comments.

"The bottom line is – and I've said it to you before – Caldicot is not our man. Grant Vaughan *is*."

There was a ping from her phone which jumped slightly on the desk. She glanced at the text message and smiled.

"Something nice?" asked Artie, watching her.

"Kind of. Another one of Natasha's many texts. She thinks if she keeps sending me texts all the time it'll make up for her not being here."

"Still, it's nice to hear from her, though, isn't it?"

"Of course it is. This one's slightly different from her usual. She says there's a surprise waiting for me when I get home."

"I hope it's a nice one."

"Probably another model of the Eiffel Tower. She's always sending me them. I've got twelve different ones so far. Even got one in gold."

"Like in *The Lavender Hill Mob*." Artie was grinning now.

"Oh yes," Hayley laughed. "Great film."

"One of my favourites."

"Mine too."

The 'surprise' turned out not to be another model of the Eiffel Tower. Hayley couldn't believe her eyes when she saw her daughter splayed out on the sofa, surrounded by an open backpack, iPad and a pile of books. She ran across the room and took her in her arms, sobbing. It wasn't long before Natasha joined in the sobbing.

"Oh, Maman, I've missed you so much!" she wept.

"Why have you taken so long to come and see me then?" Hayley wiped her eyes, but immediately started crying again.

Natasha studied her mother's tear-stained face. "Anyone would think you weren't pleased to see me," she observed. She hugged her mother again.

"Of course I am! But why are you here now? You were supposed to come for New Year."

"Well, it still *is* the New Year," smiled Natasha. "Happy New Year, darling Maman."

"I love you," sobbed Hayley.

"Me too."

"But why *are* you here?" Hayley repeated, drying her tears thoroughly this time. "Your school starts soon, doesn't it?"

"I – I want to come and live with you." Natasha was nearly as tall as her mother and she hadn't finished growing. At the moment, though, she looked like a small, unhappy child.

Hayley's heart leapt a beat. It was the one thing she'd always wanted and now at last it seemed her prayers had been answered. But why did her beautiful, beloved daughter look so sad?

"Of course you can! I know a wonderful school you can go to." Hayley was jumping way ahead of herself, seeing a rosy future with the daughter she thought she'd almost lost. "Your room is ready and waiting for you as always."

"Thank you," said her daughter, her voice sounding small and far away. "Thank you."

"What's wrong, love?" Hayley didn't want to spoil the moment, but she knew she had to ask. What had Jean-Pierre been up to now? Or was it that wife of his? She could take a bet Natasha had always come second to her natural sons. Which was only natural, she supposed.

"I don't want to talk about it – not yet," said Natasha, picking up her iPad and books, preparing to go up to her room.

"Darling, you must tell me! Is it your father?"

"No, of course not."

"Your stepmother then?"

"Stop fishing. I'll tell you when I'm ready."

Hayley realised she would have to be content with that. "Can I bring you anything to eat or drink?"

"No thanks. I'll just chill in my room. There's a programme I want to watch."

"Don't stay up too late," instructed Hayley, slipping easily into the concerned mother role she hardly ever had the opportunity to assume.

Natasha smiled at her. "I'm fifteen, Maman. Nearly sixteen. I'm old enough to choose my own hours."

"I know, I know. But you mustn't neglect your studies now you're here under my care."

"How's detective work?"

"It's okay. We've got a murder case at the moment, but we're stumped. As usual."

"Maybe I can be of help?"

"Have you been reading *Maigret* again?" They both laughed.

Then Hayley became serious once more. "One of our suspects has a daughter who's about your age. Looks a lot like you too."

"Poor her."

"No. She's very pretty. Like you."

"Am I pretty? Really?"

"Of course you are. You know you are."

"I know somebody who doesn't think so."

With that, Natasha Pascal left her mother to wonder who that someone was, and what she would like to do to him or her if their paths ever crossed.

33

Faith Desmond didn't much care for Luke. It wasn't his disability that bothered her, though. She could deal with that. There was something about the boy that went deeper. She felt he was watching her every move, as if he knew all about her life and her innermost secrets. Of course, she had reasoned to herself time and again, he only had the brain of a seven-year-old so how could he know? It just wasn't logical, but somehow she just couldn't shake the belief that Luke knew things that other mere mortals didn't. Superstition, perhaps. That's what she put it down to, anyway.

She had taken him on without a moment's hesitation after Zelda died. To leave the poor thing with the likes of Charlie Caldicot didn't bear thinking about. She supposed the police would have the Social Services involved at some point, but in the meantime her maternal instinct hadn't quite been extinguished. She had always avowed to all and sundry, but mostly to herself, that she had never wanted children. That infernal body clock was ticking away, but she continued to ignore it. Luke would do for the time being, even though he seemed distinctly ungrateful to her for rescuing him from Caldicot.

In fact, he continually asked her when he was going home. She had explained to him as clearly as possible that his home was with her now, but it hadn't sunk in.

"But Mummy's expecting me," he had said once, flooring her completely.

She had sat down beside him and removed the iPod plug from his ear. "Luke, dear, your mummy isn't at home anymore. Don't you remember?"

"Why? Where's she gone?"

"She – she died, dear." Faith hadn't been able to find better, softer words for the truth. He had to be told.

"Like Meg? She died like Meg?"

"Your dog was very ill, dear. Your mummy only had her put out of her misery." She hadn't thought Luke had understood that phrase but she hadn't been able to find another way of putting it.

"So Mummy's out of her misery too?"

So he had understood, she had thought. She sometimes wondered if he understood more than he seemed to, or admitted to, possibly. Sly, that was the word for Luke, she had finally decided. Sly. The brain of Britain was throbbing away inside his skull and he was keeping quiet about it.

"That's right," she had said. "She is in heaven now."

"Heaven? But only good people go there."

"And your mummy was good. She was very good."

"Was she? Was she really?" That was something, she had thought. At least he was now speaking of Zelda in the past tense. They were making progress.

"Yes. She was. But now she has gone, you're going to live here with me. For the time being."

"But this isn't my home."

221

Faith had got tired of going round in circles. She had almost decided to take him back to Caldicot, when that individual turned up on her doorstep the day after the police visit. She was still feeling upset by it, although she wasn't sure why. Her conscience was clear.

"You again!" she greeted him. "Never mind. It's good that you're here. Luke wants to come home."

"Come 'ome? He ain't bloody coming 'ome with me. He ain't my son. I'd never spawn a daft turd like that."

"You're unspeakable sometimes. I don't know what I ever saw in you."

They were in her small living room now. He gave a suggestive pelvic movement and grinned lasciviously at her. "Oh, yes, you do, miss 'igh and bloody mighty."

"Never mind all that. Just what is it you want?"

"Thought you might like to come back, like. Now I've got some proper dosh at last. We can 'ave a good time. Just you and me. Like we used to."

"Unspeakable! Can't you get it through that block of wood you call a head that I don't want you anymore? What do I have to do to prove it?"

"Come off it," grinned Charlie. "You did the old girl in so we could be together. Didn't you? I ain't blaming yer. I ain't sorry she's dead. But you *did* poison them chocolates, didn't yer?"

"How dare you!" She stared at him, stumped for a suitable reply. "I wouldn't kill a cockroach if it was crawling all over you, let alone another human being for your sake. I'm sorry to say you're barking up the wrong tree."

He seemed a bit deflated now but continued to grin. "You don't fool me. I know *I* didn't put the poison in them chocs so you must 'ave done. I mean, who else 'ad a motive?"

"I really don't know, Charlie. Maybe the son. Have you thought about that?"

"Luke? Don't be daft! 'Ow could an 'alfwit like 'im do it?"

"Not Luke! I meant the son of Mrs Vaughan. It's to do with the will, I bet. If *you* didn't do it, that is."

"'Course I bleedin' didn't. Wouldn't 'urt a fly, me."

"No, I don't think you would," she said quietly. "You're a complete bastard, but you wouldn't kill anyone."

"That's right. I wouldn't." He looked pleased with himself.

"You haven't got the guts!"

He looked as if he was about to strike her. "You sayin' I'm a coward?"

She backed away from him. "Oh, just get out. You said you couldn't hurt a fly, so please don't try and hurt *me*."

Charlie Caldicot was visibly shaking with anger. "Don't try and be clever, Faith. It don't suit yer."

"Cleverness isn't one of your strong points either," she countered.

The atmosphere was dangerous, very dangerous. Luckily, at that moment, Luke walked into the room.

"Hello, Charlie," he said. He had been carefully and painstakingly taught by Caldicot to call him by his name and not 'dad', 'daddy', 'father' or any other form of that word.

He glared at the handsome youth. "You all right?" he muttered.

"Can I come home now?"

Faith was smiling. "Hear that, Charlie? Luke wants to come home."

"Not on, old son," said Charlie. "Got too much to do. Can't look after you. You stay 'ere with Faith. She'll look after you."

Before Luke could reply, Charlie Caldicot had walked out of the room and out of the house. Faith went over to the young lad and put her arms around him as he started to cry.

"There, there," she said soothingly. "You're much better off with me. As Charlie said, I'll look after you."

"He doesn't want me, does he?"

"He's busy, love. Besides, he can't cook you beans on toast the way you like it, can he?"

Luke brightened at this. "No. He can't. He burnt it last time."

34

Hayley Pascal was trying to concentrate on her work, but she was finding it hard now to even care who'd put the poison in the chocolates or even for the fate of the poor woman who had eaten them. It was tough on Zelda Caldicot, of course, and her assassin had to be brought to justice somehow. But Natasha was home and intending to stay. That, for DCI Pascal, was the top of her agenda at that moment.

Now that her daughter had come home to stay, a suitable school had to be found for her. Not a state school, oh no. Even though some of the best state schools were to be found in Oxford and its environs. There wasn't a sniff of an inner-city education there. But Hayley wanted something even better for her only daughter. She had given her up when she was small, but she wasn't going to fail her now.

Her thoughts turned to Grant Vaughan and, more particularly, to his daughter. She still felt he was the chocolate assassin, but today she thought of him for another reason: Amie's education. He needed money badly to ensure she continued on at the school he'd chosen for her. It must be a good one, the best. Hopefully, though, she thought sadly, not Cheltenham Ladies College. There was no way on earth she could ever afford to send Natasha there. But she had a bit put by, especially saved for the purpose of giving her daughter the best in life she could give her. And she couldn't think of a better use for the money.

With all this in mind, she decided to pay another visit to Mr Vaughan. He didn't look pleased to see her. In fact, he looked rather nervous. Again, the conviction went through her mind that he was her man. If he had nothing to hide, why was he acting as if he did?

"I won't take up too much of your time," she began, smiling sweetly. This did nothing to remove the look of mistrust in his eyes. "I just wanted to pick your brains, actually."

She looked around the room and listened out for the sound of other inhabitants. The only sound she heard came from the radio. That lovely thing from the New World Symphony was playing. It almost broke her heart every time she heard it. She'd already stipulated in her will she wanted this to be played at her funeral. "Going Home" were the perfect words. She refocused on Grant Vaughan. Despite his grim look, he seemed to get more handsome every time she saw him.

"Pick my brains?" He turned off the radio for which she was grateful. It was easier for her to concentrate.

"Yes. You see, I want to send my daughter to a good school. Her 'A' Levels are coming up. It's the most crucial time."

"You're telling me." He seemed to visibly relax. "But why are you asking me?"

"Because you send your daughter to a good school, don't you?"

"Yes, I do. I suppose I must have mentioned it?"

"Yes, you did. Mrs Caldicot's will would have been useful there, wouldn't it?" She was back in official mode now. Even though her visit was more or less informal, she was still on the ball. After all, he might let something slip, something incriminating, while he was in a more relaxed mood. It was, in fact, the ideal opportunity.

His manner became stiff once again. "It would have been very handy, yes. But I didn't put the pesticide in the chocolates, Detective Inspector."

"No, well, I'm not here to question you about that now," she said. "All I really want is the name of the school your daughter goes to."

"Is that all?"

"Yes. That's all."

He gave her the details readily. "Oh, I think I've got an old prospectus somewhere," he added, after he had given her a piece of paper with the name and address of the school. Rummaging in a sideboard drawer, he found what he was looking for without much trouble. "As you can see, it's set in very picturesque grounds."

She looked at the brochure with pleasure. Natasha would love this school, she thought.

"It's Roman Catholic, by the way," he was saying, as she put the prospectus into her bag. "Are you of the faith?"

"Er, me? No. But my husband is and he brought Natasha up as one."

He looked puzzled for a moment. "Oh, I see. You're divorced and your daughter has been living with your husband?"

"Yes. In Paris."

"Paris?"

"Yes, my husband's French."

"Oh, I see."

"Not that it's any of your business, of course."

"No, sorry, it's not."

Hayley began to wish this man wasn't married, happily it seemed, with a lovely daughter. Above all, she wished he wasn't a cold-blooded murderer. Maybe if he wasn't and he was divorced ….

He guided her to the front door as she was thinking these strange thoughts. "Well, I hope you can get your daughter into the school," he said, opening it for her. An icy blast greeted them. Now the snow had stopped, the gales were coming into their own.

"It's going to be a long winter," he observed wryly.

Later that afternoon, Hayley sat down with her daughter and showed her the St Mary's prospectus. Natasha seemed unimpressed, even uninterested. Hayley had noticed her eyes were red too, as if she'd been crying. Something had brought her back to England and to her mother, but she still didn't know what it was.

"Don't you think it's a lovely place, darling?" she tried. They were snuggled up on the sofa together, in front of a roaring open fire. But there was little warmth in the room, even so. The atmosphere was dead as if all the life had been sucked out of it. The friendly flames made no difference at all. Hayley was so happy to have Natasha back with her, but it was obvious that Natasha didn't share her joy.

"Hmm, it's okay."

"Okay? It's more than okay. It has to be, if the fees are anything to go by."

"I don't want you to pay any fees," said Natasha firmly. "I don't want anything from you. A state school is good enough for me."

"But I want to do this for you. I've been saving up especially."

"You needn't have bothered."

"Darling – what's wrong? Please tell me."

"What d'you care? You've never cared before."

Hayley was stung by these remarks, although she understood where her daughter was coming from. To Natasha, it must have seemed she had abandoned her when she was five, so that she could pursue her career in the police. Her career had come before her own little girl, and Hayley, in her heart of hearts, knew this to be true.

She gulped down the lump that had risen in her throat. "I've always cared – more than you know."

"No you haven't. It's just your guilty conscience pricking you now. Save your money, Mum." She stood up and stretched. "What's the time?"

Hayley looked at her watch. "Five o'clock. Why?"

"I've got a hair appointment. It needs cutting badly, as you can see."

"You need it cutting badly? I can do that! No one cuts hair as badly as me."

Natasha's eyes brimmed with tears at her mother's attempt at humour. "Oh, Maman, I *do* love you. Despite everything."

They hugged. Hayley was happy again. Her daughter loved her, and that was all that mattered. The 'despite everything' she would have to think about later.

35

Artie was pleased for Hayley. He liked seeing her smile and she had been unhappy, more or less, since the first day he had met her. That had been Christmas Day, which wasn't that long ago, but it seemed a world away to him now. Now that her daughter had miraculously reappeared in her life, it seemed for good, he couldn't have been more pleased for her. She was making all sorts of plans, including paying out for a posh boarding school. He had never liked his own posh boarding school, still retaining memories of his head down the toilet and the sound of the chain being pulled. But, he hoped, girls' schools were more decorous.

"It's so good to have her home," Hayley had told him. They were getting nowhere with the poisoned chocolates, so they were eating some unpoisoned chocolate cake in the café close to the police station. It was four o'clock, and time for a tea break. They reckoned so, anyway. The Chief Superintendent had come down on DCI Pascal like the proverbial ton of bricks only that morning, instructing her to 'get her finger out' and 'arrest someone – anyone'. That hadn't been very helpful to Hayley, but nothing, not even this commandment from on high, could dampen her happy mood.

"Did – did she say why she'd decided to stay here?" asked Artie, licking the cream from the end of his éclair.

He carefully squeezed the remaining cream into his mouth. He could see his boss watching him with amusement. It seemed that nothing mattered to her now only that her daughter should be looked after and cosseted, as well as sent to the best school money could buy. Catching the perpetrator of Zelda Caldicot's murder was just a side issue at the moment.

"No, not really," she said, catching the eye of the waitress. "Can we have some more tea, please?"

"No more for me," grinned Artie. "I'm awash with the stuff."

"Oh, go on. I don't feel like going back to the station yet. The Chief's still on the prowl, ready to pounce."

"Okay, I'll drink tea till the cows come home to avoid that."

The waitress brought them a fresh pot and some more cakes. Hayley was about to refuse them but caught the gleam of pleasure in her companion's eyes just in time. He had already consumed two eclairs, a cream slice and three pieces of Battenburg, but there was obviously room in the bottomless pit for more.

"I only hope she stays though," he said, almost out of nowhere.

"Stays? Who stays?"

Artie clammed up. "Er, oh, nothing."

"What do you mean? You hope she stays?"

"I was just thinking," he said at last. "I mean, it was a quick decision, wasn't it? You don't up sticks at a moment's notice, especially not when you're about to start your 'A' Levels."

"But it's the perfect time, don't you see?"

"Er, not exactly, no."

"It's just before she starts them. She can choose her subjects at her new school and go from there. It's not as if she's in the middle."

"No, that's true."

"It's just – " She paused.

"Just?"

"Well, there's something troubling her, I know, but she won't say what it is."

"Ah, I see."

"What do you see?" She glared at him now. "And for God's sake stop eating. You'll explode."

Artie looked contrite and returned a half-eaten Eccles cake to the stand.

"Oh, sorry, Artie, you carry on. I'm just a bit worried, that's all. I'm really glad she's home, but she's holding something back. It's like she doesn't know me well enough to confide in me."

"Well, you can hardly blame her, can you? You've not exactly been there for her for the past ten years. Sorry to say and all that."

Hayley sighed. "You're right, of course. But now she's here I'm going to make up for all the time I wasn't there for her."

"I know you are. Did – did you have any trouble getting her in the school, by the way?" Artie was wisely moving onto safer ground.

"Oh, none at all. Money speaks volumes. It helped, I think, that Natasha was brought up a Catholic, but I don't think it would really have been a barrier if she'd been a Muslim or a Seventh-Day Adventist."

Artie laughed. "No – money is all that matters these days. They have to keep up the standards."

Hayley poured out the tea and sipped it thoughtfully. Then she suddenly clattered her full cup into the saucer, spilling most of it in the process. "Of course!"

Artie was startled by her abruptness. "Careful," he grinned. "That waitress is giving you a dirty look."

"Oh, blow the waitress," said Hayley, mopping up the spillage with her napkin. "I've got more important matters on my mind."

"So it would appear," said Artie, helping her mop up with his own napkin now. The tea had gone everywhere. "Is it a Eureka moment?"

"You could say that. Grant Vaughan. The lying bastard."

"How so?"

"He's the man. He's the daddy!"

"What are you on about?"

"He's our man, all right."

"What makes you so sure – this time?"

"How, my darling little Artie, did he know there was *pesticide* in the chocolates?"

"How did he know? We must have mentioned it at some point. Or isn't it in the papers?"

"Oh, yes, it's in the papers, all right. But not about the *type* of poison. We never stipulated that. We never told the press – or anybody – that it was a pesticide."

"Oh, right," said Artie, seemingly not as enthused as Hayley. "But wouldn't it be a reasonable assumption?"

"No, it would be more likely that people would say 'arsenic' or 'cyanide'. Wouldn't they?"

"Yes, I suppose so. Especially those who read Agatha Christie a lot."

"Well, I think it's enough to ask him some more questions. Don't you?"

Artie smiled. "Yes, I believe I do."

36

Grant Vaughan could see from his study window a fresh fall of snow covering the too-early snowdrops in his front garden. He could also see those two police persons walking up the path again. What did they want this time? he wondered. Sighing, he clicked the mouse and powered down his laptop.

"Darling, the police are here asking for you," he heard his wife call from below.

"Be right down," he answered. Would the police never leave him alone? The last time had been a social call from the female one. Quite a looker, he had to admit, and she seemed genuine in her request for information about Amie's school. But he wasn't sure. Ever since her visit he had been wondering if she had been trying to catch him out about something, but he was pretty sure he hadn't fallen into any traps. Not that he had any worries, anyway. They had nothing on him. They were just fishing.

Of course, he wasn't sorry Zelda Caldicot was dead. At least not from the point of view of the reversion of the will. He was sorry for anyone who died prematurely but why pick on him? Just because of the will, he supposed.

When he entered the warm living room, Hayley and Artie greeted him with a smile and seemed relaxed. They hadn't come bearing warrants then, he reckoned.

"Hello, Detective Chief Inspector – Detective Sergeant," he said, addressing them as correctly as possible. He didn't want to antagonise them unnecessarily, he just wanted them to state their business, ask their questions, and go. All this police business was upsetting for Amie too, who was due back at school in a couple of days and was preparing for her 'A' Levels. Any suspicion her father was a murderer would be doing her no good at all.

"Hello, Mr Vaughan," said Hayley, still smiling. "Brass monkeys out there today. Even colder than last week."

"Yes, my snowdrops have had it, I'm sorry to say. Anyway, what can I do for you this time? Oh, do please sit down."

They sat. "Just one or two small points we'd like to clear up," said Hayley.

"Fire away."

"Tea, coffee, anyone?" Pilar had put her pretty head around the door.

"No, we're fine, thanks, Mrs Vaughan," said Hayley. She turned back to Grant. "Now, first of all, you told us you only met the victim once, didn't you? You had never heard of Zelda Caldicot before you were told about the will?"

"That's right. I went to see her about it – to see if she would – well, be reasonable, I suppose."

"Reasonable? In what way?"

"Just that, as I explained, I needed money for my daughter's school fees – and other things. I thought maybe we could come to a mutually beneficial arrangement. I didn't want to challenge the will in court if it could be avoided."

"I see. Didn't you think that Mrs Caldicot was entitled to your mother's bequest then?"

"No, not entirely. I'm glad that the bulk of the estate will come to my daughter when she's eighteen, but I need some of the money now. After all, it was for *Amie's* benefit, not mine. Amie had visited my mother regularly and they were fond of each other. I believe my mother would have relented if she'd known money was needed right now for my daughter. She wouldn't have made her wait three years."

"And what about *your* relationship with your mother?"

He shrugged. "Not so good. I might as well tell you we hardly had any contact."

"So, therefore, you could hardly expect Mrs Vaughan to leave all her worldly goods to you then?"

Grant was getting flustered now. Where was all this questioning leading to? They clearly thought he'd done away with Zelda Caldicot for the money. "Look, Detective Chief Inspector," he said, trying to control his rising temper, "I didn't expect a miracle, but I did expect something in the way of a hand out at least. My mother was a very wealthy woman. I didn't expect her to leave it to a complete stranger – "

"She wasn't a stranger to Mrs Vaughan," Artie piped up now.

"No, of course not to her. But it seems wrong to me that, just because this clairvoyant told my mother a pack of lies, she should cop the lot. It's unfair."

"Right. So we've established that you thought the will was unfair," said Hayley, looking pleased with herself. "Now we come to the actual murder."

"That, as I think I've already told you, had nothing to do with me."

"Well, I beg to differ. You see, the poison in the chocolates is an issue we need to address."

"The poison? What do you mean – address?"

"I'm afraid we have a little difficulty here. About the actual *type* of poison used."

"Well, I can't tell you what that was, can I? Surely your lab people can tell you that?"

"In the normal run of things, that's right. They can."

There was an ominous pause now. Pilar had slipped back into the room and was sitting on the arm of her husband's chair, gently rubbing his shoulder.

"So?" Grant patted Pilar's hand in gratitude for her unspoken support. Something was about to happen and he knew it wasn't going to be good.

"Of course *we* know what the poison was. The lab people, as you say, informed us. The only thing we don't quite understand is how *you* knew it too?"

"But I *didn't* know it. Don't know it. What are you getting at?"

"I distinctly recall you mentioning the *pesticide* in the chocolates – that you didn't put it there."

"I didn't! I don't understand this line of questioning." But he was beginning to.

"How did you know the poison was a type of pesticide, Mr Vaughan?"

"I – I read it in the papers. Or – didn't you tell me? Oh, I can't remember."

"No, you can't remember. You see, we withhold certain information from the media for just such a situation as this. To stop would-be confessors, and also to catch out the real culprit."

"So – that's it. Because I said it was a pesticide you believe it was me."

"Look at it from our point of view, Mr Vaughan. How else would you know that?"

"I think you're just clutching at straws because you can't find the real murderer. I said 'pesticide' because it was a natural assumption to make. Weed killer is a domestic poison readily available to anyone, I think you will find."

"Well, that told them," said Grant Vaughan after Hayley and Artie had left. "I thought they were about to get out the handcuffs."

"How can they think you would do such a thing?" said Pilar, tears standing in her eyes. "They are persecuting you."

"Yes, I believe they are."

He sat on with his wife by the fire, deep in thought, while she stroked his still healthy crop of hair, silver-white though it was. She rested her cheek on the top of his head, tears spilling unchecked.

"You – you didn't do it – did you?" she managed to say after a few minutes.

"You know me better than that," he said quietly. "Et tu Bruté?"

"Oh, darling, I'm sorry. I just needed to be sure. I want you to tell me everything. We have never had any secrets from each other – I will stand by you, whatever you have done."

"I swear to you on our daughter's life that I never poisoned Zelda Caldicot," he said grimly.

But, he thought, did he know someone who did?

37

Amie was probably the smartest girl in her class, both in terms of fashion and brains. Added to that, her Mediterranean good looks singled her out wherever she went, turning the heads of most of the red-blooded male population as she strode confidently on her elegantly long, slim legs. Although only just turned sixteen, she looked much older and she loved the admiration she engendered. All the girls in her class were envious of her, even though most of them still liked her as well. Even if she committed the unforgivable sin of being so beautiful.

Her best friend at school, Brooklyn, was almost her equal in looks and brains, so they stuck together, feeling superior in every way. Brooklyn was far less popular than Amie, however, due to her high-handed attitude and the way she tended to flaunt her good fortune in the other girls' faces. Amie was more modest in her behaviour, even if it was mostly of the false variety.

Today was the second to last before she had to return to school but she didn't want to return without seeing Luke again. She had only met him once but he had made a great impression on her. His childlike qualities appealed to her. She liked his simple outlook on life, his inability to see a middle ground. Everything was either black or white to him.

His mother had ordered the death of his pet. That was what he knew and understood. Whatever the reason for it, she had done it. It was the one incontrovertible fact. Amie had sympathised with him: most grown-ups could justify anything they did just by twisting words.

She was anxious to see how he was now, nearly two weeks after his mother's Christmas day death. She rang Luke's front door bell and waited impatiently. There was no movement. The house was still as if it had a secret and wasn't going to give it up. She rang again, much louder this time, keeping her finger on it much longer than necessary. It was clear there was no one at home.

Disappointed, she turned to retrace her steps down the icy, slippery path and as she did so a head popped up over the next door fence. It belonged to a rather attractive boy of about her own age.

"Hi," said the head. "You looking for Mr Caldicot?"

"Er, no. I was hoping to see Luke," she said, going over to Simon Rogers. "Do you know where he is?"

"Lucky old Luke," Simon whistled, almost under his breath. "Yeah, well, he doesn't live there at the moment. He's staying with a friend of his mother's."

"Oh, I see. Cool. Like, do you know where?"

"Not sure. Luke keeps texting me that he's coming home soon, but he hasn't so far. Are you Amie, by the way?"

"Yes. How do you know?"

"Luke has talked of nothing but you for days – on the phone and in his texts. At least, I think he must mean you. His grammar isn't much – as I expect you'd understand, but I get the gist all right. I think he's in love with you and I can't say I blame him."

She blushed at the compliment. She had to admit this boy was rather nice and – well, normal. Not as good looking as Luke but at least he had all his marbles. It was a wicked thought, but one had to be realistic she told herself. There really wasn't any future for her with someone with Luke's problems.

"Why don't you climb over and come in for a coffee?" Simon was saying, offering her his hand to help her. "I'm Simon, by the way."

She had her best jeans on, the ones with the most tears and patches, so she was reluctant to climb. If they got torn in the wrong place it would be a disaster. But she accepted his invitation by going back down the Caldicot path and through the Rogers gate and up the Rogers path. Like the young lady she obviously was.

"Are you on your own?" she asked, looking around the immaculate kitchen.

"Yep. Dad's at work and Mum's at one of her interminable coffee mornings," said Simon, pouring boiling water into the cafetiere.

"A bit like us then," she giggled.

He paused in the act of plunging. "Eh? Oh, yeah, see what you mean." He laughed.

"So, like, are you a good friend of Luke's?" she asked, enjoying the delicious coffee that only seemed to come from smart cafetieres like the one in the Rogers kitchen. It must have cost a fortune. The one they had at home was rubbish in comparison.

"I like to think so, poor chap. He's really quite intelligent, you know. Has his own logic, which works for him."

"He must have been, like, devastated by his mum's death."

"Well, it wasn't exactly a surprise to him, you know," he said enigmatically.

She looked at him knowingly. "It wasn't?"

Simon sat down opposite her and cradled his coffee mug. "No. I may as well tell you – he'd actually asked me to help him poison her."

Her eyes widened. She sipped her coffee more quickly than was good for her, starting a fit of coughing.

"Sorry – you all right? Didn't mean to shock you."

"No – no – you're all right. I – I actually, like, knew that."

"You did?" He went to the sink and poured her a glass of water.

She drank it gratefully, wiping her watering eyes. The coffee was good, but the side effect wasn't. More haste, less speed, she told herself.

"Yes. He mentioned to me that he was upset because his mum had had his dog killed and he wanted to do the same to her."

"That's his logic. An eye for an eye."

"He didn't really mean it, though. Did he?"

Simon shrugged, pouring out more coffee. "Drink it more slowly this time," he grinned.

"*Did he?*" she demanded, giving him one of her 'don't mess with me' looks.

"Yes, I think he did. Of course, when she did die, he was sad. But he seems to have taken it in his stride."

"That's good. I'm glad he's being looked after, anyway."

"You haven't asked me if I – we – actually *did* poison the chocolates, have you?"

"Haven't I?"

"No."

"Perhaps I don't want to know," she said, enjoying the wordplay between them. They were flirting, and she liked it. Simon Rogers was growing more and more attractive by the minute. She'd be able to tell Brooklyn she had a new boyfriend and make her jealous. She was always going on about Rupert and Freddie, and how they doted on her. Couldn't do enough for her. And both of them had their own cars: a Mercedes and Jaguar respectively. How the other half lived.

"Well, I didn't."

"Didn't what?" Her mind had wandered briefly.

"Didn't poison the chocolates, cloth ears!"

"Oh, that. No, I didn't think you had."

38

"Why is Dad looking so miserable, Mummy?"

Amie was on a high after her meeting with Simon. They had agreed to meet the next day, her last day before she had to return to school, and they were going to the pictures to see some new sci-fi epic and then going for a pizza afterwards. She was really looking forward to it, even though she didn't relish sitting through almost three hours of interminable special effects, and pizzas weren't her favourite food. But her father's distance and grim expression were putting a damper on everything.

Pilar put her arm around her daughter's shoulders and sighed. "It is the police again, my dear," she said as calmly as she could. "Your father believes they suspect him of murder. Murder, my darling. It is ridiculous!"

"Oh, mummy, they can't suspect him. They can't!"

"It is because of the will, my sweet. They have a strong case against him – they think so anyway. You see, your father said it was pesticide in the chocolates."

"Eh?" Amie looked at her mother in amazement. "Is that all?"

"It seemed little enough to me, but they said there had been no mention of the type of poison used. So your father saying it was a pesticide makes him a strong suspect. It is all very distressing."

"It's ridiculous. The police haven't got a leg to stand on. Pesticide! It would have been different if he had known exactly *which* pesticide. They can't arrest him for that."

"No, dear. They haven't. Obviously as he is still here."

"Where is he? In his study?"

"Yes, but I think he wants to be left alone."

"But I must talk to him," she protested. "Poor, poor Daddy."

"All right, dear. Whatever you say. See if you can cheer him up, you usually can."

Amie made for the stairs, but stopped abruptly on the second step. "*You* – you don't believe he did it, do you?"

Pilar seemed unable to look her daughter straight in the eye, apparently more interested in a speck of dust on the gleaming banister. She rubbed at it vigorously with her thumb.

"Mummy?"

"He swears he didn't, and of course I believe him. We have never lied to each other in all the years we have been together. And he knows he can tell me anything – anything. He would have told me if it had been true."

"But you suspected him, didn't you?"

"No – only – the will."

"How could you! I'll never speak to you again!" Amie disappeared up the stairs before Pilar could react to this.

"My darling – you don't understand."

Amie didn't hear these words as she pounded up the stairs to her father's study. She usually knocked when Grant was in his eyrie, but today she just burst in and rushed over to him, falling into his arms, sobbing.

"Daddy! Oh my Daddy!" she cried. She was Jenny Agutter at the end of *The Railway Children*, her favourite film when she was younger. The scenario was even similar – her father being wrongfully imprisoned! It just couldn't happen. And just when everything was going so well – almost everything, anyway.

"Amie, darling. What's wrong?"

"Nothing with me, Daddy. It's you! You couldn't poison anyone. Not even a fly!" She hugged him tightly.

He gently pushed her away and sat her down. The room Grant Vaughan called his study looked exactly like one, with its book-lined walls, mahogany desk and velvet-upholstered chairs. The only nod to the twenty-first century was Grant's laptop, open at a Wikipedia page on pesticides.

"You mustn't worry, my love," he said, smoothing her hair. "It's a mistake. That's all. They haven't enough evidence. I told them they were clutching at straws and they knew it."

"But Mummy said it was because you said the poison was a pesticide. Surely they can't suspect you just because you said that?"

"I think they do, darling." He returned behind his desk and stared absent-mindedly at his laptop.

"But why did you mention 'pesticide' anyway?"

249

"It – I thought – I'd heard it mentioned on the news. Or somewhere." He shrugged, looking small, smaller than she had ever seen her daddy.

"Somewhere?"

"Somewhere else."

He was looking at her now. She stared at him, then looked away.

The winter sun was streaming in through the windows of Grant's study, penetrating the dark corners of the room but, sadly, it couldn't penetrate the dark corners of their minds.

39

"Sit down, Mr Vaughan."

Hayley eyed her visitor with curiosity. She sat back in her chair and spread her arms on the desk. "To what do I owe this pleasure?"

He coughed nervously and crossed and uncrossed his legs several times. His chair creaked. She made a mental note to get it oiled when she next came across a maintenance man.

"I – I've come to ..." He trailed off.

"You came to?"

He leaned forward, his hands between his knees like a naughty schoolboy. She watched his face. It seemed to get more handsome every time she saw it.

"To – confess."

She sat bolt upright. She hadn't expected that. She had almost begun to believe he was innocent after all. Now, here he was, admitting he'd murdered a woman for her money. Money, she supposed, he thought was rightfully his.

"I see," she said, scanning her computer screen quickly for something she needed to have at her fingertips. She saw it eventually as she clicked the mouse urgently.

"So, let me get this straight. You have come to confess that you put poison in a box of chocolates and sent it to Mrs Caldicot anonymously, in the expectation she would eat those chocolates and die?"

He stared at the floor and crossed his legs again. "Yes," he said, almost inaudibly.

"Pardon?"

"Yes," he said, louder and more assertively this time.

"Right. I see. No need to shout." She knew she should caution him before they went any further, but something stopped her. "So, Mr Vaughan, now that you have so helpfully told me that you did the deed, perhaps you can also tell me exactly how you did it and by what means."

"What do you mean? You have all the facts. You don't need me to tell you anything. So, let's stop messing about and bring out the handcuffs."

She sighed and stared at her computer screen once more. "I need you to help me out here. I was told the name of the pesticide originally and a report was filed. Someone should have put it on the system, but I can't seem to find it. Technology, eh?"

"Well, I don't see how I can help ...." He looked almost disoriented now.

"But you must be able to. Come on, you've confessed now – no point in holding back information. What was the pesticide – the poison – called?"

"Why do you need to know? It's not that important, is it?"

"Of course it is. When you go for trial your defence barrister will need to know exactly what the pesticide was and how it worked, how it came to kill the victim – and whether you meant that to happen."

"I told you. I killed her. I wanted my mother's will to be under my control. I wanted my daughter to be able to continue her education at the school chosen for her by myself and my wife. We knew when we first sent her there it would be difficult to meet the fees every term, but we had saved up. Now the well's run dry and I need the money. I did it. Charge me. Please."

"Just as soon as you tell me the name of the pesticide you used." Hayley's features were hard, set into a mask of stone.

The door opened as she said this, and Artie strolled in, muffled up against the cold, carrying two cups of coffee. "Sorry to have been so long. There was an almighty queue at Starb-" He stopped as he saw Grant Vaughan swivel in his chair to look at him. "Oh, sorry, didn't realise you were here …"

"It's okay, Artie. Bring me that coffee. I need a caffeine fix right now." She gave him a meaningful look. "You'd better stay too."

Artie put the coffee down on the desk and turned to look at Grant Vaughan. "Good afternoon, sir," he said politely.

Grant managed a grunt in reply.

"I was just asking Mr Vaughan the name of the pesticide he used to murder Mrs Vaughan."

She smiled to see the look of surprise on her subordinate's face. He was well out of the loop, spending all his time in coffee houses.

"It's – isn't in the notes?" Artie's face was a picture of confusion.

"No. It isn't."

"Let me look." He made to come around her desk to look at the computer.

"No need. Not here." She gave him a warning glare. "So, please, Mr Vaughan, the name, please?"

"Oh, I can't remember. I just went into Robert Dyas and bought some strong weed killer."

Artie was staring at him. Hayley looked at Artie. They both smiled.

Grant looked hurt. "I can't see there's anything to laugh at. Just charge me. Get it over with."

"You think we're playing with you, don't you?" said Hayley.

"Well – aren't you?"

"You didn't kill Mrs Caldicot, did you?"

"I just told you. I did!"

"All we can do you for is wasting police time. Just get out."

Grant Vaughan groaned and leaned forward, his head in his hands. "This can't be happening," he muttered.

"Well, Mr Vaughan. I'm afraid it is. Show the gentleman out, please, Sergeant."

"I knew he wasn't our man," said Hayley, sipping her coffee gratefully.

"What? Just because he didn't remember the name of the pesticide? Don't think I'd remember it either. Great long mouthful."

"It's called chlorpyrifos."

"There you are, then."

"No, it's not just because of that. Although it was the clincher. He couldn't murder anyone, that one."

"But you've been saying it was him all along."

"I know. But he would never have confessed just like that, not if he'd really done it."

"Why not?"

"Think about it."

Artie seemed to 'think about it' and didn't seem any more enlightened.

The phone leapt into life. Hayley grabbed it. "Okay," she said after a moment. "Send her up."

"Shall I go?"

"Er – yes. I think you'd better. This will be better as a two-hander. I'll tell you all about it afterwards."

"Who is it? Do I know her?"

"You do." But she didn't elaborate.

Amanda-Thérèse Vaughan entered Hayley's office about a minute after Artie had left it. It was all go that afternoon.

"Hello," Hayley greeted the young girl. She had to hold her breath as she waited for Amie to sit down. It was astonishing how like her own daughter she was.

"Hello," replied Amie, obviously unaware of the mixed emotions she was stirring up. "I must speak to you." Her voice was flat, her face deadpan.

"Of course. I've just said goodbye to your father. You can only just have missed him."

"Oh, he's waiting for me in the car. I know he's been here."

"And does he know you're here now?"

"No. He thinks I've gone to Starbucks."

"I see. Well I understand there's quite a queue, so I don't suppose your father will expect you back too quickly."

"No."

There was a short silence.

"Well, Miss Vaughan. What can I do for you?"

"I just came to ask you to stop hounding my dad. He didn't kill that woman. He just couldn't have."

"And how can you be so sure?"

"I am, that's all. He's my dad."

"Do you know why he came to see me?"

"Er – the same thing. To ask you to stop harassing him."

"Then I expect it would surprise you to learn that he's confessed to the murder."

The look on the girl's face was a picture. Hayley watched her as she seemed to register shock, anger, sorrow and disbelief, all in the space of a few seconds. Finally she seemed to settle for sorrow.

"That's my daddy all over."

"All over? So you admit now that your father is an habitual murderer? Not what you just said." Hayley smiled, mostly to herself. This could be her own daughter sitting there. She felt a sudden surge of compassion for her.

"No, I mean – well, Daddy wouldn't let someone he loved take the blame."

Hayley stood up and walked up and down her small office. She had often requested a bigger one, in keeping with her high rank, but was always fobbed off with talk of 'cutbacks'. A word she had come to hate. If she had her way she'd expunge it from all English dictionaries.

Then she came and sat down behind her desk again. The silence was growing and the atmosphere was charged. She studied the girl out of the side of her eyes. Yes, it could be Natasha. They were alike as two peas.

"I think, Miss Vaughan, you have something to tell me?"

Amie sat on, not speaking. The clock on the wall made the only sound in the room. Hayley listened to its tick and found it strangely comforting. Then Amie cleared her throat.

"Chlorpyrifos acts on the nervous system," she began. She pronounced the pesticide's name perfectly without stumbling. She was obviously used to it. "It's considered to be only mildly toxic to human beings."

"Not so mild, I would have said," observed Hayley, more calmly than she felt.

"It's been banned for domestic use in America since 2001," continued Amie, as if she was reciting for some oral examination or presenting evidence in a court of law. "I chose it because I believed it would only cause mild discomfort."

"So, you had no idea how much of the stuff you were injecting into the chocolates? How *did* you do that, by the way?"

"I've a keen interest in chemistry – science in all its forms and I'm top of my class. My chemistry master thinks I'll do great things one day."

"What has that to do with the price of eggs?"

"I'm explaining how I came to put the poison in the chocolates." There was a note of impatience in her tone now. Amie's passivity seemed to be wearing thin. "Mr Kenwright says I'll find a cure for cancer some day. I've got the brains and the aptitude."

"Bully for you. Get to the point, Miss Vaughan."

"I'm getting to it. Mr Kenwright gave me the keys to his garden shed for the Christmas holiday. He went away with his family."

"Keys to his garden shed?" The conversation was verging on the surreal now. "And what, pray, would you want with his garden shed?"

"It's his private laboratory."

Hayley knew she should have guessed that. She nodded. "I see. Carry on."

"Well, that's it, really. Mr Kenwright's special interest is toxicology. He keeps all kinds of poisons in his shed – under lock and key. He trusted me to use the facilities. He encouraged me to experiment as much as I liked." She looked at Hayley slyly. "So I did."

It was all crystal clear to Hayley now. She had suspected Amie for a while, but had dismissed the idea as ridiculous. It would be almost like suspecting

Natasha of such a crime. It was unthinkable. But the idea kept recurring to her. And when Grant Vaughan confessed only a quarter of an hour ago, she knew for sure who the real culprit was. He would do anything to protect his daughter. Just like she would do anything to protect Natasha.

"Why did you do it?" Her voice was soft, coaxing.

"I didn't mean to *kill* her. You must believe me. I didn't know she had a heart condition. There wouldn't have been enough to kill her if she'd been well. She'd have just been sick for a few days. That's all."

"If I accept that, I still don't understand how you could wish another human being harm of any sort. You don't look cruel." She didn't. She looked like an angel. Just like Natasha.

"I'm not! No, I'm not. I care so much for people. That's why I want to save lives, not take them. I've been feeling terrible."

"Oh, poor you. But you still haven't answered my question."

"Why did I do it?"

"Yes."

"Because of poor Daddy. He so wanted me to continue at St Mary's. I did too. Of course I did. I was doing so well there. But he told me he couldn't afford to send me there anymore."

"But, if as you say you only intended to make Mrs Caldicot sick, that wouldn't have given you – or your father – access to your grandmother's legacy."

"No. I know. It was just to teach her a lesson." She paused. She had started to cry and Hayley fished out a tissue from her drawer. "There was another reason too," she said, blowing her nose.

"And what was that?"

"Luke."

"Luke?" Hayley called to mind the young, handsome boy with his child's mind. "What about Luke?"

"He was angry with his mother for killing his dog. That made me angry too. I can't stand cruelty to animals."

"You don't mind cruelty to humans, though?"

Amie didn't answer. Tears welled up in her eyes again. "He was so sad about his dog, I wanted to do something to make him feel better. I thought making his mum ill would, like, be about the right punishment for the poor dog's death."

"Did it occur to you that Mrs Caldicot had done the dog a kindness by having it put out of its misery?"

Amie looked at her stunned. "Wh-what do you mean?"

"The dog was ill, in pain. She took it to the vet for its own good."

"Luke never mentioned that."

If she half-closed her eyes, Hayley could see her own darling Natasha sitting there, confessing to murder. Murder she hadn't meant to commit. What would she do if it really *was* Natasha, not Amie, saying these things? If she charged this girl, her whole life would be blighted. A life that promised so much. Hayley realised she held the fate of Amie Vaughan in the palm of her hand.

She sighed as she thought of what the Chief Superintendent would say. A great wall of a man whose bite was far worse than his bark. Another unsolved case. She'd be in line for demotion if she wasn't careful.

40

Hayley's thoughts were in turmoil as she let herself into her flat, nearly tripping over a pile of bulging luggage by the hall door.

"Is that you, Maman?"

"Yes, love. You packed already? Good girl. All set for the off tomorrow?"

She found her daughter in front of the living room fire stuffing text books into her already over-filled rucksack.

"Here, let me do it," said Hayley, going over to her, glad of something to take her mind off what she had just done. Or, more accurately, not done.

"Don't fuss, ma chérie," laughed Natasha. Hayley realised that her daughter looked happier than she had seen her since her return. But somehow it didn't please her as much as it should have done. She already knew why, and waited for the words which she didn't need to hear, not now. Not ever.

"Can you give me a lift to the station? Now? I'm in a hurry."

Hayley tried to curb her rising concern. "But – but St Mary's isn't accepting pupils until tomorrow, darling."

"Oh, I'm not going *there!*" There was contempt in her tone. "I'm going home!"

"Home? But you *are* home, aren't you?" Hayley's stomach seemed to hit the floor.

"Paris! Patrice has texted me. He misses me. Says he was a fool – an idiot – to dump me. I could have told him that."

"So could I," said Hayley quietly. Today was turning out to be a very trying one indeed. There were days like that, she thought, days when it would have been better not to have got out of bed at all.

"Oh Maman, darling," cried Natasha, hugging her tightly. "Don't be sad. I'm happy! Be happy for me. I'll still come and see you – often. You know I will. It'll be just like I was away at school. You wouldn't be seeing that much of me even if I stayed in England anyway. Would you?"

The irony of this hadn't been lost on Hayley. Sending Natasha to the best school involved her being boarded out, only coming home some weekends. But it was a sacrifice she had been prepared, *wanted*, to make in order to give her daughter the very best education that England could offer. Much better than any French école, she'd hoped.

She had texted her ex-husband only that morning telling him all about the great school their daughter would be attending. He had been very angry about Natasha's defection, but he'd had to grudgingly admit that Hayley was doing right by her. She had been triumphant; it had been about time she'd got one over on Jean-Pierre. Now here was her daughter turning that triumph into a very hollow one indeed.

"Darling, are you sure? I mean, what if this Patrice gives you the elbow again?"

"Elbow? What is this elbow?" She sounded very French to Hayley at that moment.

"Oh, sorry," laughed Hayley. "Your grandfather was a cockney through and through. Some of his phrases have stuck with me."

"Oh, I know what you're saying, that Patrice will dump me again."

"Well – he's done it once …"

"I know it could happen again, I'm not stupid. But – well, I suppose I miss being in Paris after all. I – oh, you know. I love you but I also love mon père too. And he's done most of my bringing up."

That hurt. Hayley wanted to react but knew if she did she would lose her temper. Instead she took the rucksack from Natasha and pushed the books in with a strength that only comes with anger.

"Careful," admonished Natasha. "You'll bend or tear them."

"No doubt Daddy can buy you new ones," said Hayley, feeling like a sulky, defeated child.

Natasha tried hugging her again, but she shrugged her off. "Right. You've got everything? Good. I'll take some of the stuff down to the car. You bring the rest."

Artie rolled over and looked at her. He propped himself up on one elbow and traced her nose and mouth with a gentle finger, marvelling at her beauty. He could allow himself to appreciate it properly now that he had been invited into her bed and able to observe it at close quarters.

Bed hadn't been on the agenda to start with, he was sure of that. But after three bottles of wine and a box of tissues it became the next logical step. As logical a decision as any two drunk people could make, anyway. The wine had been consumed by both parties, while Hayley had got through the tissues on her own, her tears undiminished until practically the last one. Artie had been patience personified, tutting at the perfidy of daughters in between gulping down the rather indifferent plonk and passing the next tissue.

He had been surprised by her text. He had had to read it twice to make sure he'd got it right: *"Need to get drunk. Bring bottles. Now."* He hadn't expected anything, although he hadn't quite dismissed the possibility as completely out of the question. Part of him was ashamed of taking advantage of her misery, but he'd been wanting her from almost the first moment they had met. And it had been good. Very good. And not just for him, he hoped.

"How are you?" he asked her, as she opened her eyes. The dark grey orbs that looked at him were cloudy with puzzlement. "Remember me?" he smiled.

"Artie," she mumbled, slowly sitting up. She pushed her mussed hair back from her face. "I'm – I'm sorry – did – did I make a complete fool of myself?"

"No, of course not. You were lovely." He helped her straighten her hair. He was aware she was shielding her naked breasts from him, the same ones that had been on full display the night before. The snub hadn't been lost on him and his heart sank. Back to harsh reality, he supposed.

"Are – are you sorry it happened?" he asked now, turning away and preparing to get out of bed.

"Well, we work together. I'm your boss."

"So – that's it, then? Do you want me to ask for a transfer?"

"No. Don't be silly. It's just that – oh, no, I don't regret it. You were lovely." She reached out to touch his back, but he flinched.

She rested her head on it and sighed. Gradually he turned and took her in his arms. They lay like that for several minutes.

"Shouldn't we be getting to work?" he then asked, but making no attempt to move.

"What for? We've just got another unsolved case on our hands. Where do we go with it now?"

"Back to Charlie Caldicot, I suppose," he said, gently untangling himself from her arms. "If you're sure Vaughan isn't guilty."

"Oh, I *know* he isn't. Nor is Caldicot."

He looked at her questioningly. "Do you know something I don't?"

She seemed about to say something, but stopped. Flinging back the duvet, she stood on the uncarpeted wooden floor, her nakedness now on full display. She stretched and yawned while Artie watched her with delighted admiration, forgetting for the moment what he had just said. She may be getting on for the big four-o, he thought, but her body was in perfect shape.

"Do you?" he repeated when her nakedness had been hidden in a bra and knickers. She was definitely hiding something, and it wasn't just her body.

"Come on. We'd better get going. I'll shower first," was all she said.

41

Faith Desmond checked and rechecked the bookings list. Yes, she said to herself with satisfaction, she had contacted everyone on that list. They all knew that Zelda Caldicot would not be keeping their appointments now. She had expected someone to make a tasteless joke about 'due to unforeseen circumstances', but nobody had. Most of the clients had heard about her death anyway, being a reasonably high-profile murder case. Not nationwide, but it had caused quite a stir in the Cotswolds.

She stared out of the window at the woman now walking up to the front door of the consulting rooms. Rooms that had had hardly time to air before Zelda had been so cruelly forced to vacate them. Faith recognised the woman as she drew closer. She had met her with her sister at St John's church in Bibury towards the end of last year. She had recommended Zelda's psychic services to both her and her sister. They had been easy targets, both being widowed. The woman heading for Zelda's consultation room now had been the more recently widowed of the two, Faith remembered.

If there was one thing Faith prided herself on, it was her memory. The woman's name was Olive and she definitely didn't have an appointment.

As the bell rang for the second time, she made up her mind to answer it. Her first thought had been to let the woman go away. After all, Zelda wasn't here anymore, and if this Olive saw her she'd know that

Zelda had been a fraud all along. But then, she thought, what did it matter now? Zelda was dead. Nothing could hurt her now, least of all the loss of her reputation as a genuine psychic.

"Is that for me?" said a voice from behind her. It was a soft, deep male voice which Faith immediately recognised as belonging to Cornelius Gray. She turned to see him coming down the stairs.

"My secretary's gone to lunch," he continued. "I'm not expecting anyone though."

"Neither am I, but I know who she is. I saw her from the window. She's one of Zelda's clients."

"Oh, right. Didn't you inform all her clients about what happened?"

"Well, only the ones who had appointments," she said. "Anyway, most of them would know from the papers."

"Yes, you would have thought so, wouldn't you?"

Faith opened the door to Olive Dickinson. "Hello," she said. "What can I do for you? I'm afraid you don't have an appointment."

Now that Faith was inches from her, she could see how ill she looked. She'd remembered her as being quite a bonny woman in late middle age. Now her complexion had sallowed and it looked as if she'd lost a couple of stones in weight.

"No, I don't have time for appointments," said Olive. If she had remembered her, she didn't let on. Faith knew her face wasn't particularly memorable, which had been an asset in her line of work. "Can I see Zelda? It's important. Urgent."

"Please do come in," said Faith, a little flustered. It looked as if the woman was about collapse. "Come and take a seat in the waiting room and I'll be back in a moment. I'll get you some tea."

"Thank you," said Olive, following Faith into the waiting room. When the door was closed on her, Faith turned to Cornelius.

"She doesn't know," she whispered.

"She's dying," he said bluntly.

"Sssh! You think so?"

"I know so. The black aura is very prominent."

"What shall I say to her? It doesn't look like she can stand a shock."

"I'll go and talk to her while you make some tea," he said reassuringly.

"I supposed she was probably a fraud," said Olive, sipping her tea. She looked marginally better now, but Cornelius could see the aura getting darker all the time. "Even before I saw Faith just now. Madame Zelda didn't give me much confidence. Told me my Harry was waiting for me and was happy. Well, they all say that, don't they?"

"So you didn't believe her, then?" asked Cornelius. His voice was soothing.

"No, not really. But you buy into it all the same, don't you? Are you a psychic, then? I mean, I'm sorry if you are. I'm sure there are some genuine ones knocking about."

He laughed. "Yes, I'm a psychic medium, for my sins. But, tell me, why did you want to see Madame Zelda so urgently? Especially if you didn't think she was genuine?"

"I didn't know what else to do. You see, I've just been told by the hospital that my case is hopeless. They want me to go into a hospice as soon as possible. But I wanted to see if Harry would really be waiting for me. I'll go happily if he is."

Cornelius felt deeply sorry for her. He knew he wouldn't be able to categorically tell her that, although he was willing to try. He had been successful in contacting the recently passed over before they got to where they were going, so it would all depend how long her husband had been dead or just how quickly he'd got processed on his final journey.

"You came to see Madame Zelda to ask her to try and get in contact with your husband?"

"Yes. I knew it was unlikely, but I wanted to give it a try, I'm desperate. This death sentence has been such a shock to me. I need something – someone – to tell me it will all be all right."

That someone, he told her, wouldn't be Zelda Caldicot. She seemed to take the news in her stride, if a little tearfully.

"So, I've made a fruitless journey. I'm sorry, of course, for Zelda." She blew her nose.

"Look, why don't you come with me to my room upstairs? I've an hour before the next client. I'll do my best to get in contact with your husband, but I can't promise anything."

"Thank you. That would be very kind," said Olive, rising shakily to her feet. "How much do you charge?"

"This is on the house," he said, putting his arm around her frail shoulders and escorting her gently up the stairs.

"Were you able to help her?" asked Faith after Olive's departure some thirty minutes later.

"Yes, I think – hope so. I put her into a cab. She could hardly walk, poor thing."

Faith sighed. "Yes, she did look very ill."

"Anyway, I managed to make some sort of contact. It wasn't very clear but I managed to talk to a man called Harry Dickinson. I just hope it was the right one."

"Couldn't you be sure, then?"

"Well, I was, really. But the terrible thing was he didn't want to meet his wife again. I couldn't tell her that now, could I?"

"Oh, the poor woman," cried Faith. "Life can be so cruel sometimes."

"Death can be too," said Cornelius wisely.

Faith looked at him and nodded. He really was quite attractive in an understated sort of way, she thought. She would have been pleased to know that he was thinking just the same thing about her.

"How about a quick cuppa?" he suggested. "I've still got thirty minutes before my next client."

42

Charlie Caldicot was an unhappy man. All his life he'd relied on his rough-hewn good looks and charm. Women had always been drawn to him, especially the posh birds. They liked a bit of rough. But something had changed lately.

A single man once more, he thought he'd continue to have his pick. But it seemed he'd lost some vital ingredient all of a sudden. A cheerful, chirpy cockney 'sparrer' to his very kneecaps, he didn't feel quite so chipper these days. And those kneecaps had begun to creak. Surely he was too young to have arthritis? He was still only in his early forties, but he felt at least a decade older.

He used to enjoy his nights in the pub with his drinking pals, seeing who could chat up the most birds. He nearly always won. Life had been sweet. Then.

He stared at himself in the mirror and who he saw there seemed like a stranger. His once ruggedly handsome face was looking decidedly jowly now. The bags under his eyes looked like they were packed for a long trip abroad and, horror of horrors, his hair was starting to recede!

He felt his stomach. It was definitely on the increase. He breathed in and looked at himself sideways in the full-length mirror beside the front door. He'd just about pass with his clothes on, but he wouldn't stand a chance on a St. Tropez beach, that was for sure.

That was it then. Faith Desmond had deserted him. She didn't want him back. He'd kidded himself she'd murdered Zelda so she could get him back. It stood to reason she'd want him back now he had the money left to him by his dead wife. Like a shot. It seemed the most logical thing to him, but she'd been impervious to his cajoling, coaxing attempts at winning her back. So now he had to face it. She no longer fancied him, money or no money. He was fast coming to the conclusion that being rich wasn't all it was cracked up to be.

No, money wasn't everything. He never thought he'd say that, not even to himself. He was lonely. There. He'd said that too, now. Again, only to himself. But he was. Very lonely. Perhaps he should try once more with Faith? Smarten himself up a bit. Get a haircut – not too much off the top, of course. He could look dead sharp when he tried. But then, he thought, what was the point?

An aching void of loneliness had begun to engulf him, making him almost incapable of any kind of positive thought or movement. He hadn't had a decent meal for days, but now was past caring if he ate another meal ever again. Besides, the washing up was piling up in the sink and he'd broken the dishwasher on his first attempt at using it. Now there wasn't a clean piece of crockery in the place. Even if he'd wanted to eat there wasn't anything to eat it off.

Life for poor Charlie Caldicot had taken a definite turn for the worse. He picked up the Racing Gazette and tried to concentrate on the runners at Catterick. There was one called Blind Justice. It sort of leapt out of the page at him. Was that some sort of message, he wondered? Had he got his come-uppance at last?

He thought he was hearing things at first, but no, he was sure he'd heard the key turn in the lock. Faith! She'd come back after all. She must still have a key.

He got up and ran out into the hall. But it wasn't Faith Desmond. It was Luke.

"Hello, Dad," he said.

"I've told you before," grumbled Charlie. "Don't call me dad. Charlie's my name."

"Hello, Charlie," said Luke obediently.

"Well, what d'you want?"

"I've come back. I've got all my things here. Can I go up to my room?"

"S'pose so," shrugged Charlie. "'Ow long are you intending to stay then?"

"Forever and always," said Luke.

"Oh, you are, are yer? Well, we'll see about that. I 'aven't got much food in. And there ain't no clean plates, neither. Cor blimey, you got it made at Faith's. What'd you wanna come back 'ere for?"

What he'd give to swap places with Luke, he suddenly thought. All the time he'd regarded the boy as nothing but a simpleton and a bleeding nuisance, but now here he was, actually envying him. How the tables had turned.

"It's not home, Charlie. I want to be here, Charlie."

Charlie Caldicot wondered if Luke was about to launch into the Marlon Brando back-of-the-taxi speech in *On the Waterfront*. He knew he'd asked him to call him 'Charlie' but there was no need to overdo it. He hated Marlon Brando anyway. Some woman had once said he looked like him and not when he was in *The Godfather* either.

"All right. So you wanna stay 'ere? Okay then. Get stuck into the washing up. Make yourself useful."

Luke walked into the kitchen and stared at the piles of dirty plates, cups, saucepans and glasses in the sink. Not to mention the stacks of empty beer bottles under it.

"Why don't you put them in the dishwasher?" he asked.

"'Cos the bloody thing don't work. Duh."

Luke went over to it and stared at it for a moment. It was lit up like a Christmas tree.

"Well no wonder it doesn't work," he said. "You need to put rinse aid in and more salt."

He stared at the boy. What was the silly bleeder talking about? "Salt? You put salt in there?"

"Of course. Not ordinary salt, dishwasher salt," said the boy wisely. He rummaged in the cupboard under the sink next to the beer bottles. "Here," he said, fishing out a bag. "Here it is."

He opened a compartment in the dishwasher and proceeded to pour in the contents of the bag. When he had finished, he looked in the cupboard again and finally drew out a small bottle of liquid. He then proceeded to put that in a separate compartment.

All this time, Charlie watched in amazement. The boy seemed to know what he was doing. God knew how.

"Now let's put all this stuff in," directed Luke, now firmly in command.

"Don't see no point in doing that," muttered Charlie. "It don't work, I tell yer."

"Never mind. It will do."

They stacked the dishwasher between them, trying things in different places and getting into muddle after muddle. But eventually everything was in place.

"Now all we need is the washing powder."

"Ah, well, we ain't got none. After all that." Charlie laughed, realising for the first time that he didn't feel lonely anymore.

"Let's have a look," said Luke, still undeterred. He soon found what he was looking for. He held it out to Charlie. It was just a small tablet.

"That it?"

"Yes. *You* put it in, Charlie."

Charlie took it from Luke and examined it. "Funny thing, ain't it?" he said.

"You put it in there," instructed Luke.

Now the dishwasher was ready, Luke told him. He turned a dial and pressed a button. And, sure enough, it whirred into action.

Cor blimey, thought Charlie, perhaps Luke wasn't such a mental retard, after all.

"Can I have some beans on toast, Dad?"

Charlie Caldicot was about to remonstrate but then began to think. First of all, he'd heard his name mentioned enough times that afternoon as it was. Second, he rather liked being called dad, after all.

"Yes you can – son," he grinned.

"You won't burn them this time, though, will you?" Luke sat down at the kitchen table.

Charlie grinned. "I'll do my best, old son. I'll do my best."

43

Things happen for a reason. At least that's what DCI Hayley Pascal had always thought. But, for the life of her, she couldn't understand why her daughter had been given back to her only to be taken away a matter of days later. What had been the point of it all? Pulling out all the stops, not to mention all the money involved, to get her into that posh school only for her to bolt back home when some spotty-faced French youth clicked his fingers. Or, more accurately, clicked his mobile. What if she got back to Paris only to find him going with someone else? A day was a long time in the love lives of teenagers.

She'd said most of this to Artie two nights ago, between sobs and great quantities of cheap red wine. He had been sympathetic, but he couldn't really understand. Not being a parent himself.

She and Artie had deserted their posts yet again and were hiding in Starbucks while they knew the Super was on the warpath. Why hadn't they arrested Grant Vaughan? he'd wanted to know. He'd bloody-well confessed, hadn't he?

She watched her companion trifling with his Danish. Artie looked about to ask the self-same question. She could read him like a book.

"Before you ask, Artie. No I'm not going to charge Grant Vaughan."

"So you keep saying." He took a bite out of his Danish.

"You were going to ask me that, weren't you?"

"Well, it does seem a pertinent question."

They finished their coffees in silence, both deep in their own thoughts.

"I suppose we'd better go back. Show willing." Hayley looked out of the window at the driving rain. The snow had finally gone, only to be replaced by the monsoon season.

Artie sighed, agreeing.

They left Starbucks huddled under one umbrella. The station was only around the corner, but they were already wet through after only a few steps. "I think I'd prefer the snow back," said Hayley.

Artie suddenly stopped and pushed her into a doorway. "Before we go back, you must tell me the truth." He looked serious. She thought he'd planned to kiss her, but she could see his mind was definitely not veering in that direction.

She tried to look alluring, but it was difficult with a rain drop poised on the end of her nose. If she could get his attention on to her personally, he might stop asking awkward questions. But it was a vain hope.

"You didn't charge Vaughan because you know who did it, don't you?"

She shrugged, wiping the rain from her nose and lips. Still no response. "I – I….. Oh, Artie, don't ask."

"I've got to. Don't you see? I can't let you do this. It's Vaughan's daughter, isn't it?"

It all came tumbling out then. "She didn't mean to do it. She's got her whole life ahead of her…."

"Just listen to yourself! You and Grant Vaughan are both stupid! You'd both do anything for your daughters, wouldn't you? You sympathise with him, don't you? You'd do the same if it were Natasha, wouldn't you?"

She was crying now. "Leave me alone!" she screamed at him and, before he could stop her, she had rushed out into the rain, minus the umbrella.

She didn't know how long she'd been walking. It felt like hours, days. The rain had stopped and a weak sun was trying its best in the lowering sky. She walked through the empty park, hands in pockets, ignoring the appeal of a squirrel in her path. Then she turned and looked at it. It was probably a mother too, looking for nuts to take back to its young.

Life wasn't easy if you had children. You did your best for them all the time, but you weren't perfect yourself. What was right? What was wrong? Could she, in all conscience, let a crime go unpunished?

She thought of Natasha, now happy in Paris with Patrice. Amie was now safely back at school, or at least she supposed so. The only one who was miserable in the whole of this was herself. A demotion looming because she couldn't bring a criminal to book, and a daughter that didn't much care if she never saw her again. It wasn't a great prospect to look forward to.

Then there was Artie. What should she do about him? She was very fond of him, but she didn't love him. The sex was good and she had needed it that night.

But could they continue to work together now? Not only had they slept together, he now knew she was shielding a murderer. Not a great outlook for their continued working relationship.

As she came out of the park, she suddenly knew what she had to do. She had known all along, only she hadn't wanted to face it. But now she knew she had to. For her own self-respect, as well as for the respect of others. Artie, mainly.

Anyway, she'd had enough of ungrateful daughters, not to mention unsolved murders.

Printed in Great Britain
by Amazon

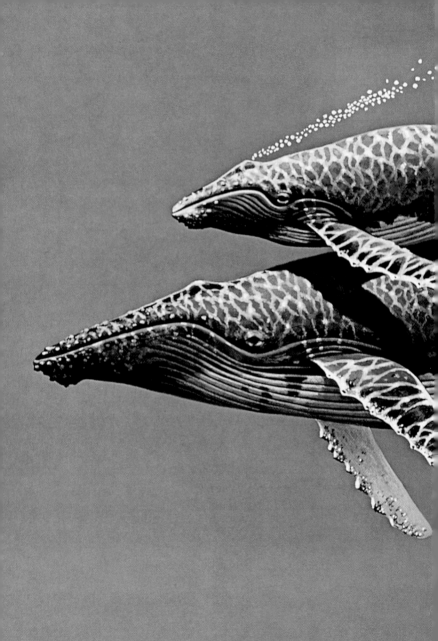

RICHARD ELLIS

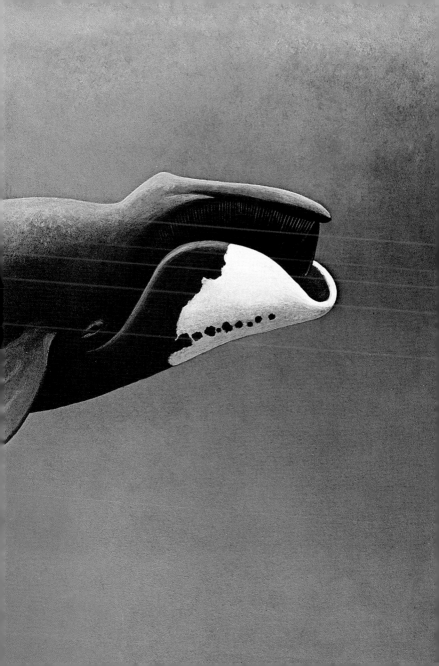

SOMMAIRE

VIE ET MORT
DES BALEINES

Yves Cohat et Anne Collet

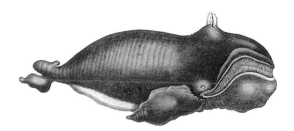

DÉCOUVERTES GALLIMARD
SCIENCES

La taille gigantesque des baleines a toujours fasciné les hommes; leur mode de vie a fait naître les mythes les plus fantastiques. Ce n'est qu'au XVIIIe siècle que les cétacés sont reconnus comme mammifères et non plus comme poissons. Les baleiniers des siècles suivants acquièrent des connaissances empiriques sur leurs comportements et leurs migrations. Mais la cétologie moderne ne débute que dans les années 1960-70 grâce aux nouvelles techniques et méthodologies scientifiques.

CHAPITRE 1

UN ANIMAL MARIN EXCEPTIONNEL

Que signifie ce saut majestueux d'une baleine à bosse (ou mégaptère) venue se reproduire dans les eaux abritées de la Nouvelle-Calédonie ? Certains comportements échappent encore aujourd'hui aux scientifiques, qui continuent à émettre des hypothèses.

La Bible et l'*Histoire naturelle*

Le premier récit mentionnant une baleine se trouve
dans la Bible. C'est la célèbre histoire de Jonas jeté
à la mer par les marins pour calmer la tempête qui
fait rage et menace de détruire le bateau. Jonas est
avalé par une baleine qui le régurgite trois jours plus
tard sur la terre ferme. Mais dans la Bible ne figure
pas le mot «baleine». On y lit seulement : «Dieu
avait créé un *grand poisson* pour avaler Jonas.»
Un autre animal biblique certainement identifiable
à une baleine est le Léviathan, qui «fait bouillonner
les abysses comme une chaudière.» Le psaume CIV,
25-26 le décrit ainsi : «Voici la mer grande et vaste
dans laquelle rampent des créatures innombrables,
tant grandes que petites. Là voguent les navires :
là se trouve le Léviathan, que Tu as fait pour jouer
au sein des eaux.»

   Pline l'Ancien, qui voyagea au Ier siècle en
Afrique du Nord, explique dans son *Histoire
naturelle* que la mer est si grande et si illimitée
que «ce n'est pas étonnant si on y trouve tant
de créatures étranges et monstrueuses».
Et Pline ajoute que dans l'«océan des Gaules»,
on a découvert «un énorme poisson appelé *physeter*
("souffleur" en grec, nom scientifique du cachalot),
émergeant de la mer à la façon d'une colonne
ou d'un pilier, plus haut même que les voiles
d'un bateau; et alors, il faisait jaillir,
et envoyait haut en l'air, une
quantité considérable d'eau,
comme si elle sortait d'un tuyau».

Le terme cétacé
provient du grec *ketos*
qui signifie «monstre
marin». À partir des
récits de chasseurs, les
artistes représentaient
souvent des animaux
fantastiques.

Le *Speculum Regale*

Presque tout ce qui a été écrit
sur les cétacés au Moyen Âge provient
de récits scandinaves et islandais. Le
principal de ces textes, le *Speculum Regale*
(milieu du XIIIe siècle), décrit diverses espèces
de cétacés vivant dans les mers autour de
l'Islande. D'après cette œuvre, les orques «ont
des dents comme celles des chiens» et ils sont
aussi agressifs envers les autres cétacés que le sont

«• Et Dieu parla du poisson. Et du fin fond du froid et des profondeurs noires, la baleine remonta vers les agréments du soleil et vers les délices de l'air et de la terre. Et elle vomit Jonas sur la terre sèche. •»

Herman Melville,
Moby Dick

Les légendes qui ont circulé autour des baleines ont inspiré d'innombrables représentations de très surprenantes créatures. À la vue de cette «baleine porcine» (gravure du XVIᵉ siècle), on peut penser que l'ancêtre des cétacés était sans doute un animal terrestre.

les chiens envers les autres animaux terrestres. Les orques s'assembleraient donc et attaqueraient les grosses baleines. Et, chaque fois qu'ils trouveraient une baleine isolée, ils l'épuiseraient en la mordant jusqu'à ce qu'elle en meure, «bien qu'avant de mourir elle puisse tuer un grand nombre d'attaquants de son souffle puissant».

Le *Speculum Regale* donne des descriptions de quelques monstres terribles parmi les cétacés, qui détruisent les navires et les hommes. Ils portent alors des noms bizarres : «cheval-baleine», «cochon-baleine» ou «baleine-rouge». Mais des espèces bien connues tels le cachalot ou le narval y figurent également. Ces monstres sont féroces et cruels.

Néanmoins, il cite aussi des exemples de «bons cétacés». Parmi ces derniers, le «conducteur de poissons» est particulièrement utile aux pêcheurs parce qu'il pousse les harengs et toutes sortes d'autres poissons depuis la pleine mer jusqu'au rivage. Ce qui est encore plus remarquable, c'est que, poussant vers eux tous ces poissons, il épargne navires et hommes, «comme si Dieu avait décidé qu'il en serait ainsi aussi longtemps que les pêcheurs se comporteraient de façon pacifique : mais qu'ils se querellent et se battent au point de verser le sang, le cétacé s'en aperçoit et bloque la voie vers le rivage, poussant tous les poissons vers le large».

Baleine diabolique et île-baleine

Au Moyen Âge, les marins islandais éprouvent une grande crainte pour ce qu'ils appellent les «baleines du diable». Il est même dangereux de prononcer leur nom en mer : si l'on en parle, elles s'approchent du bateau et essaient de le détruire... Le nom de «baleine» est donc tabou, et tout marin qui se rend coupable de le prononcer est privé de nourriture. Alors, lorsqu'ils veulent évoquer

Avant l'arrivée d'une foule nombreuse attirée par l'événement, deux hommes mesurent un globicéphale échoué sur une côte (gravure du XVIᵉ siècle).

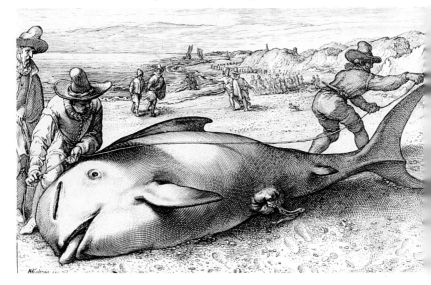

les cétacés en mer, les hommes les désignent sous le nom de «grands poissons». Ils pensent d'ailleurs que certains d'entre eux sont friands de chair humaine et qu'ils s'attardent une année entière à l'endroit où ils ont trouvé une telle nourriture. Ils évitent donc les hauts-fonds où des baleines ont déjà coulé des navires.

On trouve dans les folklores de nombreux pays des histoires de marins prenant par erreur une baleine endormie pour une île; la baleine se réveille et plonge, noyant les hommes. C'est en partie la légende de saint Brendan, l'abbé bénédictin irlandais qui, en 565, fait voile vers l'ouest sur l'océan Atlantique, à la recherche de la Terre sainte. Au cours de son voyage, il débarque avec ses hommes sur le dos d'une immense baleine. Le saint homme y installe tranquillement un autel et célèbre une messe. Mais il ne subit pas les conséquences tragiques de son erreur, et la baleine le laisse finir sa messe.

Mammifères ou poissons ?

Pendant longtemps, les hommes se sont contentés d'étudier les corps des baleines échouées sur les plages. Ces observations constituent la base de la

La légende de saint Brendan raconte la navigation du saint sur les océans. Dans cette histoire symbolique, Dieu est l'océan et l'Église, une nef sur les flots de l'éternité. Pour parvenir au paradis, il faut subir des épreuves. Saint Brendan et ses disciples doivent affronter trois mois de tempêtes puis un monstre marin «plus fort que quinze taureaux en furie». Ils rencontrent tantôt une île aussi blanche qu'un troupeau de brebis; tantôt une autre, noire et aride, qui s'engloutit devant le moine : c'est le dos du «plus gros des poissons vivants»! Ce moine voyageur a probablement atteint en réalité les îles Féroé (l'île aux brebis) et l'Islande (l'île noire).

«cétologie», la science des cétacés, dont on peut faire remonter l'origine à l'Antiquité.

Quatre cents ans avant Jésus-Christ, le philosophe grec Aristote range les baleines parmi les mammifères. Après lui, Pline l'Ancien affirme qu'elles sont des poissons. De nombreux naturalistes suivront Pline, mais Belon (1551) et Rondelet (1554), tout en persistant à classer les dauphins parmi les poissons, les décrivent avec des poumons et une «matrice» (utérus) comme les mammifères. Il faut attendre la dixième édition, en 1758, du *Systema naturæ*, écrit par le naturaliste suédois Charles de Linné, pour voir les cétacés définitivement classés parmi les mammifères. Quelques décennies plus tard, le zoologiste français

CONRADI GESNERI
MEDICI TIGVRINI
HISTORIÆ ANIMALIVM
LIBER IV.
Qui est de Piscium & Aquatilium animantium natura.

Cum Iconibus singulorum ad viuum expressis ferè omnibus DCCXII.

Editio secunda, nouis figuris, versus castigationibus non paucis auctior, atque etiam multo in locis emendatior.

Continentur in hoc Volumine,
GVLIELMI RONDELETII cognomẽ. Medicinæ Doctoris Regij in Schola Monspeliẽ. &
PETRI BELLONII Cenomani, Medici hæc omnium Latina nomina, de Aquatilium Quadrupedibus.

Emendatum quoad sic suam admissum.

Maioribus hactenus explicatum.

FRANCOFVRTI.
In Bibliopolio Andreæ Cambieri.
ANNO M. D. CX. CLII.

Le Suisse Conrad Gessner est l'un des premiers naturalistes à décrire les baleines dans le quatrième livre de son *Historia animalium* (1558). Deux siècles plus tard, grâce aux récits de quelques capitaines baleiniers comme William Soresby Jr. ou Charles Scammon, l'anatomie, la physiologie et la biologie des cétacés commencent à être mieux connues, et les zoologistes cherchent à reconstituer les animaux disparus. Des squelettes de baleines sont assemblés et exposés dans les muséums d'histoire naturelle des grandes villes européennes (gravure ci-dessous).

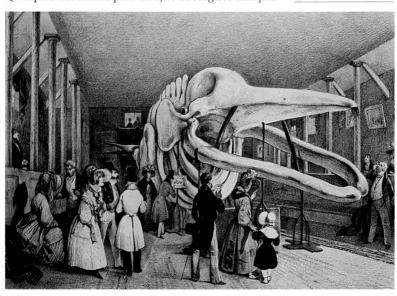

Cuvier écrit :
«La baleine est un
mammifère sans jambes
arrière.» Des squelettes
de baleines sont
reconstitués dans
les premiers musées
d'histoire naturelle.
Les zoologistes les
comparent à ceux des
mammifères terrestres
fossiles et déduisent que
les cétacés constituent
une très ancienne
famille de mammifères,
ayant probablement
des ancêtres communs
avec les mammifères
terrestres.

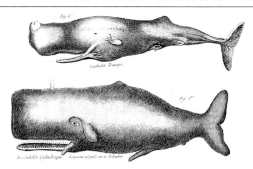

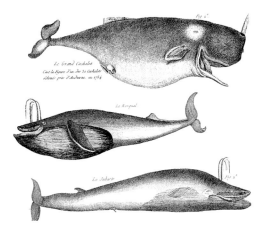

La longue évolution des cétacés

Il ne fait aucun doute
qu'à l'origine ces
mammifères se sont
développés sur terre.
Mais, compte tenu
du petit nombre de
fossiles découverts,
retracer le chemin qui a mené leurs ancêtres de
la vie terrestre à la vie aquatique serait hasardeux.

Les paléontologues reconnaissent le mésonix
comme étant l'ancêtre des cétacés primitifs. C'était
un carnivore terrestre, à l'allure de loup, au museau
allongé, qui possédait quatre pattes aux doigts
munis de sabots. Il vivait à l'éocène (il y a
cinquante-cinq millions d'années) dans les zones
marécageuses proches du littoral et pêchait
pour se nourrir. En quelques millions d'années,
les membres se raccourcissent, le museau s'allonge
et les narines migrent sur le sommet du crâne
pour faciliter la respiration lorsque la tête
de l'animal émerge à la surface.

Les naturalistes
représentaient les
animaux qu'ils n'avaient
jamais vus d'après des
descriptions de seconde
main. Ainsi, se fondant
sur des récits relatifs
à des échouages ou à
des observations en
mer, le zoologiste et
paléontologue Georges
Cuvier avait déterminé
trois espèces de grands
cachalots. En réalité
il n'y en a jamais eu
qu'une seule (ci-dessus,
une planche extraite
d'un de ses ouvrages).

L'adaptation morphologique la plus remarquable est la disparition du bassin et des membres postérieurs, qui procure au corps une forme parfaitement hydrodynamique. La locomotion est assurée par une nageoire horizontale, actionnée par les muscles puissants du pédoncule caudal. C'est le mouvement ascensionnel de la caudale qui propulse l'animal et lui facilite la montée vers la surface pour respirer.

Les organes généralement saillants chez les mammifères terrestres, comme les oreilles, l'appareil génital des mâles ou les mamelles, s'effacent. La peau devient lisse, elle se double d'une épaisse couche de graisse, à la fois protection contre le froid et réserve de graisse; l'œil s'adapte à la vision sous-marine, comme l'oreille interne qui se transforme pour mieux capter les ondes sonores dans le milieu aquatique; et les narines deviennent l'évent situé sur le sommet du crâne.

Si les cétacés ressemblent extérieurement aux poissons, ils n'en restent pas moins des mammifères, comme en témoignent leur sang chaud (les poissons sont à la même température que le milieu ambiant), leurs poumons qui filtrent

La gueule des mysticètes est dotée de longues rangées de lamelles appelées fanons dont la face externe est lisse. Lorsqu'ils sont écartés, on aperçoit les franges sur la face interne (ci-dessus).

Comme en témoigne le crâne fossile (ci-dessous) de cet archéocète, les ancêtres des baleines avaient des dents et des narines situées à l'extrémité du museau. Ce sont les plus anciens mammifères marins connus. Ils vivaient dans les mers peu profondes et les estuaires il y a 50 millions d'années.

l'oxygène dissous dans l'air (les poissons ont des branchies pour fixer l'oxygène dissous dans l'eau), leur reproduction vivipare (les poissons sont ovipares) et, bien sûr, les mamelles des femelles qui allaitent leurs petits pendant les premiers mois de leur vie.

Les mysticètes

La science de la classification, la taxonomie, distingue deux sous-ordres chez les cétacés : les mysticètes ou vraies baleines, qui possèdent des fanons, et les odontocètes, littéralement «cétacés à dents». Cette classification évolue encore de nos jours avec l'amélioration constante des connaissances, basées notamment sur les nouvelles techniques génétiques. On peut ainsi cartographier les gènes des êtres vivants et établir de nouvelles relations entre les espèces ou entre les familles. Chez les baleines, on distinguait récemment une seule espèce de petit rorqual, mais on admet dorénavant que la population de l'Antarctique forme une espèce à part entière.

Les mysticètes (baleines et rorquals) portent donc des fanons, lames cornées (faites de kératine

Chez tous les grands cétacés, les yeux sont situés sur les côtés de la tête, proches des commissures de la bouche. Pour observer le photographe, cette baleine grise doit pencher la tête et regarder d'un seul œil. Elle se nourrit de crustacés amphipodes, telles les puces de mer, qui vivent dans les sédiments des eaux peu profondes. Elle nage sur le côté (les baleines grises sont généralement droitières), pour remuer le sable avec ses lèvres très mobiles, puis aspire les petits organismes qu'elle a dérangés. Elle rejette enfin l'eau et les sédiments à travers le filtre de ses fanons.

comme les poils et les ongles) et souples qui sont
suspendues au bord du palais. Très nombreux
(jusqu'à 8 000 chez la baleine bleue), serrés les uns
aux autres, ils sont effilochés vers l'intérieur de la
bouche. Ils forment ainsi un piège parfait pour
retenir le krill et les petits poissons tandis que l'eau
de mer est rejetée au travers de ce filtre.

Actuellement, on distingue quatre familles de
baleines : celle des baleines franches ou Balénidés,
qui comporte quatre espèces (la baleine du
Groenland, la baleine franche de l'Atlantique nord
ou baleine des Basques, la baleine franche du Pacifique
nord et la baleine franche australe); celle des
rorquals ou Balénoptéridés, où l'on compte sept
espèces (le mégaptère ou baleine à bosse, le petit
rorqual, le petit rorqual antarctique, le rorqual
tropical, le rorqual boréal, le rorqual commun et
la baleine bleue ou grand rorqual). Enfin la baleine
grise, qui possède des caractères des deux groupes,
a été classée dans une famille dont elle est la seule
représentante. La baleine bleue détient le record
de gigantisme, avec une taille pouvant atteindre
35 mètres de long pour 150 tonnes.

La baleine grise porte
souvent des parasites
externes (ci-dessus).
La baleine des Basques
(ci-dessous) est
recouverte de callosités
encombrées
de crustacés, qui
prolifèrent sur sa peau.

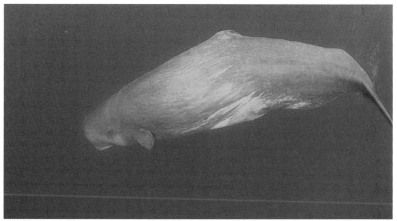

Les odontocètes

L'autre sous-ordre des cétacés, les odontocètes, comprend plus de soixante-dix espèces réparties en huit familles. Les plus connues sont les Delphinidés (dauphin, globicéphale, orque), les Phocoenidés (marsouin), les Monodontidés (narval et bélouga), les Physétéridés (grand cachalot, cachalot nain et cachalot pygmée). Il existe aussi plusieurs familles de dauphins d'eau douce : les Iniidés, les Pontoporiidés, les Platanistidés et les Ziphiidés qui regroupent une vingtaine d'espèces encore peu connues (mésoplodon, bérardie, ziphius, hypérodon, tasmacète…). Contrairement aux mysticètes, qui possèdent un évent double, les odontocètes n'ont qu'un seul évent.

Le cachalot (*Physeter macrocephalus*, «souffleur à grande tête») peut atteindre 18 mètres de long chez les mâles; à l'inverse des baleines les femelles sont beaucoup plus petites, ne dépassant pas 12 mètres. Le cachalot est immédiatement identifiable par son énorme tête qui représente le tiers de son corps. Sa mâchoire supérieure est dépourvue de dents et comporte des alvéoles correspondant aux dents de la longue et étroite mâchoire inférieure. Elle en possède une quarantaine, puissants cônes d'ivoire atteignant 18 centimètres.

Les cachalots (ci-dessus) détiennent des records de plongée exceptionnels. Ils peuvent rester plus d'une heure en apnée et, malgré les adaptations physiologiques que les biologistes ont découvertes, on ne comprend toujours pas comment ils réussissent à se passer si longtemps d'oxygène. Ils économisent certainement leurs ressources, notamment par une descente et une remontée à la verticale (le plus court chemin). Lorsqu'ils sont sur le fond, ils chassent le calmar géant à l'affût, attendant passivement que la proie s'approche, après l'avoir repérée grâce à leur sonar très perfectionné.

Le krill, l'aliment préféré des baleines

Le régime alimentaire des mysticètes est essentiellement composé de plancton, énorme magma d'éléments vivants charriés par la mer. Constitués de végétaux et d'animaux, ces organismes de petite taille dérivent au gré des courants dans les couches supérieures ou moyennes des océans.

C'est au sein de ce plancton que les baleines trouvent leur nourriture principale : le krill, crevettes pélagiques qui sont absorbées en énorme quantité après avoir été prises au piège du tamis que constituent les fanons.

Le krill se trouve en abondance dans les eaux froides des zones polaires. Vers la fin de l'hiver, les baleines entreprennent donc une migration de 3 000 à 8 000 kilomètres vers ces eaux froides. Les baleines franches, volumineuses, ne dépassent guère la vitesse maximale de 5 nœuds (9 km/h) lors de leurs déplacements, mais les rorquals, plus fins et plus puissants, peuvent atteindre 15 à 20 nœuds (28 à 37 km/h) en vitesse de pointe. Certaines baleines peuvent «marsouiner» (effectuer de petits sauts à la surface) sur de courtes distances, pour diminuer l'effort à

Le terme de krill regroupe des espèces différentes de petits crustacés, selon l'océan où ils se trouvent. En Antarctique, la plus abondante est l'*Euphausia superba* (ci-dessous) qui mesure entre 3 et 6 centimètres de long. Pendant la saison d'alimentation, une baleine en ingurgite plusieurs tonnes par jour, comme le montre (ci-dessus) cet estomac de rorqual dépecé.

La base de la chaîne alimentaire marine, constituée de phytoplancton ou plancton végétal, a besoin de lumière et d'éléments nutritifs pour se développer. Ceux-ci se trouvent dans les sédiments, sur le fond, là où l'eau est la plus froide. Il faut donc que ces eaux glacées, chargées de nitrates, puissent remonter vers la surface où la lumière pénètre pour permettre le développement du phytoplancton. C'est le cas dans les océans polaires et dans les zones d'*upwellings*, lorsque des phénomènes océanographiques créent des courants ascendants de masses d'eaux froides le long des plateaux continentaux (Pérou, Chili, côte ouest de l'Afrique…). La biomasse est donc plus abondante lorsque les eaux superficielles sont froides. Pour trouver les tonnes de krill dont elles ont besoin, les baleines passent l'été dans ces mers arctiques parsemées d'icebergs (à gauche, au Spitzberg). Le soleil ne se couchant pas, la lumière continue favorise la prolifération du plancton. Le repas des baleines à bosse (pages suivantes) est souvent accompagné d'oiseaux de mer qui grappillent le krill qu'elles font remonter vers la surface.

fournir (la résistance de l'air est nettement inférieure à celle de l'eau). Lors des longues migrations elles nagent beaucoup plus lentement (3 à 5 nœuds en moyenne). Pendant les quelques mois de l'été polaire, elles se livrent à une véritable «orgie» alimentaire : elles absorbent les tonnes de krill qui vont constituer l'essentiel de leur alimentation pour l'année entière.

Les seuls mammifères à se reproduire en pleine mer

Les baleines quittent les mers froides pour rejoindre les eaux tempérées ou chaudes (basses latitudes) lorsqu'elles veulent s'accoupler ou mettre bas. Elles sont sexuellement matures entre cinq et douze ans mais ne se reproduisent pas avant l'âge de huit à quinze ans.

Avec une gestation de dix à quatorze mois selon les espèces et un allaitement d'au moins six mois suivi d'une phase de repos, une baleine donne naissance tous les trois à quatre ans pendant la période la plus fertile de sa vie.

Les jumeaux sont très rares. En général,
ils n'arrivent pas à terme ou meurent rapidement
car la mère ne fournit pas suffisamment de lait
pour deux baleineaux. L'espérance de vie varie
d'une trentaine d'années pour les petites espèces à
près de cent ans pour les plus grandes. D'une façon
générale, la mortalité infantile est assez élevée
chez les cétacés, et l'on estime qu'une baleine
n'aura pas plus de quatre à huit petits qui
atteindront eux-mêmes l'âge de se reproduire.

Contrairement aux mammifères terrestres qui
naissent normalement la tête en premier, les cétacés
sortent par la caudale, de façon à monter respirer
en surface dès que la tête est dégagée. Lorsqu'il a
pris ses premiers souffles, le petit revient sous le
ventre de sa mère pour téter. Les cétacés n'ont pas
de lèvres normalement indispensables à la tétée
qui s'effectue par succion. Une particularité pallie
cette absence : les glandes mammaires sont
entourées d'un muscle circulaire de sorte que,
lorsque le baleineau se présente en face de la fente
mammaire qui cache le téton – hydrodynamisme
oblige –, la femelle érige d'abord son mamelon puis
presse sa glande mammaire pour que son petit
recueille directement le lait.

Le lait des mammifères marins est très riche en
graisse, car le jeune doit grossir – son lard est peu
épais à la naissance – et grandir rapidement.

Aucune naissance
de cétacé n'a été
observée dans la
nature, mais des mises
à bas de dauphins
ont été filmées en
captivité (à gauche).
La délivrance dure
environ une demi-
heure. Le cordon
ombilical est rompu
au moment où la tête
du petit sort du ventre
de sa mère. Il est
immédiatement poussé
vers la surface pour
prendre son premier
souffle. Lorsque
la mère va chasser,
une autre femelle
du groupe la relaie
auprès de son jeune.

Il contient jusqu'à 50 % de matières grasses et, chez le grand rorqual, on estime que la femelle peut produire quelque 500 kilos de lait quotidiennement, ce qui permet à son petit de grossir d'environ 100 kilos par jour pendant les premières semaines de sa vie.

La respiration, la plongée et le sommeil

«Elle souffle, elle souffle!» criait la vigie, du haut du mât; il savait repérer les baleines, à plusieurs kilomètres de distance par temps calme.
Son long cri a résonné pendant des siècles sur toutes les mers du monde.

Les baleines franches ont un souffle double, en forme de V, tandis que les rorquals émettent une seule colonne de vapeur, plus ou moins haute ou touffue selon les espèces. La forme et la taille relativement réduite des poumons, la position

Les baleineaux sont nettement plus clairs que les adultes à la naissance mais leur pigmentation fonce rapidement. Le jeune mégaptère, ci-dessus, n'a guère plus d'une semaine, à en juger par sa couleur. Pendant leurs premiers mois, les cétacés se laissent souvent «porter» sur le dos de leur mère, ou plus précisément, sur les filets d'eau créés par la vitesse de nage de l'adulte. Ils parviennent ainsi à maintenir le même rythme, malgré leur petite nageoire caudale.

particulièrement horizontale du diaphragme permettent aux cétacés d'expirer très rapidement.

Les records de plongée, et donc d'apnée, sont détenus par le cachalot, par quelques odontocètes de la famille des Ziphiidés et par plusieurs phoques. Des cachalots ont été retrouvés pris dans des câbles téléphoniques à plus de 1 000 mètres de profondeur, et récemment des sondeurs perfectionnés ont enregistré des groupes de cachalots par près de 3 000 mètres de fond. Les baleines ne plongent guère à plus de quelques centaines de mètres, pendant quarante à cinquante minutes au maximum. La plupart du temps, leurs apnées ne durent que dix à vingt minutes, entrecoupées de périodes de respiration lors desquelles l'animal reste en surface pour expirer et inspirer six à quinze fois en quelques minutes. Le rythme de la respiration varie bien sûr en fonction de l'espèce, de la taille de l'animal et de son activité.

Lorsqu'une baleine dort, elle reste quasi immobile sous la surface pour remonter respirer toutes les dix minutes en moyenne, en donnant un léger coup de

Les baleines grises du Pacifique est (ci-dessus) passent l'hiver en mer de Cortez, où elles se reproduisent, et entreprennent au printemps une longue migration en mer de Béring, au large de l'Alaska, pour se nourrir. Cette population, qui a failli disparaître sous la pression de la chasse industrielle, est très surveillée. Des survols aériens sont organisés tout au long de leur route pour dénombrer chaque année les effectifs. Malgré quelques captures autorisées pour les Inuits américains ou sibériens, leur nombre a nettement augmenté. On compte maintenant plus de 25 000 individus.

caudale. La respiration des mammifères terrestres est un acte réflexe; ils peuvent dormir profondément sans penser à respirer, pas plus qu'ils ne doivent penser à faire battre leur cœur ni à digérer leurs aliments. Chez les cétacés, la respiration resterait un acte volontaire. L'animal peut ainsi éviter le risque de respirer sous l'eau lorsque son taux de gaz carbonique augmente dans le sang lors d'une plongée prolongée. La baleine doit donc «penser» à respirer, même lorsqu'elle dort. On suppose alors qu'un seul hémisphère cérébral dort tandis que l'autre reste partiellement en éveil pour contrôler la respiration, et que le système de veille s'inverse pour que chaque partie du cerveau se repose alternativement.

Ainsi communiquent les baleines

Chez l'homme, la communication est essentiellement basée sur le langage, tandis que chez les animaux elle s'appuie sur bien d'autres critères, notamment sur les attitudes et les comportements. Le sens de leurs vocalisations

Tous les mysticètes ont un évent double : deux narines distinctes, tandis que les odontocètes n'ont qu'un seul orifice de la respiration sur le sommet du crâne. Mais seules les baleines franches (ci-dessus) émettent un double jet de vapeur. Les rorquals soufflent en une colonne unique, dont la forme et la hauteur varient en fonction de l'espèce et des conditions météorologiques. Hormis pour quelques espèces au souffle caractéristique (baleines franches et cachalots), seuls les spécialistes sont capables de les identifier sur ce critère.

nous échappe souvent, simplement parce qu'elles signifient moins que le contexte et les comportements qui les accompagnent.

Les baleines émettent des sons dont la fréquence varie de 20 hertz à 3 000 hertz en privilégiant les basses fréquences qui se propagent sur de longues distances sous l'eau. On a ainsi enregistré des rorquals qui se trouvaient à 30 kilomètres du microphone, et les analyses acoustiques montrent que leurs vocalisations sont audibles à plusieurs centaines de kilomètres, voire à plus de 1 000 kilomètres dans certaines conditions océanographiques. Chez les rorquals, qui vivent en solitaire ou en groupes restreints, des sons assez brefs et monotones sont répétés pour maintenir le contact entre les individus, notamment la nuit, ou lors des longues migrations.

Les mégaptères ou baleines à bosse sont les «chanteurs» les plus célèbres et les mieux étudiés. Chez cette espèce, seuls les mâles chantent, essentiellement en hiver lorsque les animaux se retrouvent dans les zones de reproduction. Ils répètent de courtes mélodies, parfois pendant plusieurs heures. Ces chants diffèrent d'une population à l'autre, ils évoluent en permanence

Pour comprendre ce qui se passe dans un groupe d'animaux, il faut pouvoir reconnaître chaque individu. L'étude du comportement des cétacés se base sur la photo-identification : chaque animal est identifié selon des signes morphologiques individuels. Chez les baleines franches, on utilise les amas de petits crustacés parasites qui forment des taches blanches, grises ou jaunes sur les sourcils et sur la tête (ci-dessus). Chez les baleines à bosse, le meilleur critère est la pigmentation de la caudale (ci-dessous) qui varie du tout noir au tout blanc, avec ou sans marques orangées.

au cours d'une saison, mais il faut plusieurs années pour que la phrase musicale soit entièrement changée. Chaque animal semble posséder sa propre signature sonore, ce qui permet de l'identifier à distance. On reconnaît aussi l'appartenance à un groupe selon certaines séquences employées, leur tonalité ou leur accent, qui sont communs à tous les membres.

Les mégaptères sont connus pour leurs sauts impressionnants. On les voit parfois jaillir à la surface avec une telle puissance que tout le corps apparaît quelques secondes avant de retomber en créant une immense gerbe d'eau.

Quant à la signification de ces chants, les observations montrent qu'ils auraient un rôle dans la manière de «marquer son territoire» en occupant un espace sonore, dans la façon de courtiser les femelles, dans l'expression d'agressivité à l'égard des autres mâles ou dans le but de communiquer un message (appel d'un autre partenaire, alerte pour le groupe, annonce de disponibilité sexuelle, etc.). La même mélodie aurait un effet ou un sens différent selon le contexte dans lequel le chanteur l'emploie. Les émissions sonores ont principalement une fonction d'identification, en indiquant à tous ceux qui les entendent le sexe du chanteur, son âge, son statut, ses activités et son état émotionnel.

Ces manifestations ont certainement un rôle dans la communication sociale. Le saut n'est peut-être pas porteur de message en lui-même, mais il agirait comme un point d'exclamation physique pour ponctuer un signal sonore précédent. Les jeunes sautent souvent, probablement pour s'entraîner à parfaire ce geste dont le sens semble important chez les adultes.

NAVTÆ IN DORSA CETORVM, QVAE INSVLAS PVTANT,
anchoras figentes fæpe periclitantur. Hos cetos Troluual sua lingua
appellant, Germani e Teuffeluual.

SIMILIS EST ET ILLORVM ICON APVD EVNDEM, CAPITE,
roftro, dentibus, fiftulis, quos mentium inftar grandes effe scribit, & naues euertere, nisi sono tubarum aut missis in
mare rotundis & vacuis vasis abfterreantur: quod & in Balthico mari circa
balænam Brunfvich dictam fieri diximus.

Au tout début du Moyen Âge, les Basques attaquent les baleines en pleine mer. Du IXᵉ au XVIᵉ siècle, ils détiennent le monopole de cette activité lucrative. Anglais et Hollandais vont suivre cette voie mais ce sont les colons de la Nouvelle-Angleterre qui deviennent les plus grands chasseurs. L'âge d'or des baleiniers américains, qui commence en 1835, va durer vingt-cinq ans.

CHAPITRE 2

LES CHASSES À LA BALEINE

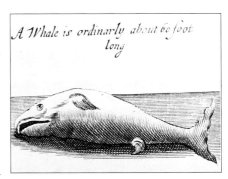

Les cétacés ont été abondamment représentés.
À gauche, une gravure du XVIᵉ siècle tirée des planches de l'*Histoire des animaux* de Conrad Gessner illustre un dépeçage et une attaque de «monstres».
À droite, une baleine tuée lors des chasses au Spitzberg (gravure du XVIIᵉ siècle).

Les Basques, précurseurs de la chasse

On ne peut dater précisément les premières chasses
à la baleine mais on peut estimer que la
récupération de cadavres échoués sur les rivages
remonte aux temps préhistoriques.

Au Japon, des fouilles archéologiques ont permis
de mettre au jour des harpons et des ossements
d'animaux qui laissent penser que la chasse aux
petits cétacés se pratiquait dès la période Jomon
(3000-300 av. J.-C.).

En Norvège, on pense que les baleines étaient
rabattues sur le rivage. Bloquées dans d'étroits
fjords, elles étaient ensuite achevées à la lance.
Cette technique – rabattage puis mise à mort –
se nomme le *grind*.

À partir du IXe siècle, la chasse prend une place
de première importance au Pays basque. Pendant
six mois de l'année, les baleines sont très nombreuses
dans la baie de Biscaye, car elles viennent mettre
bas dans les eaux chaudes de cette zone abritée de
l'Atlantique. Il s'agit de la baleine franche boréale
ou baleine de Biscaye *(Eubalaena glacialis)*,
que les Basques appellent dans leur langue *sarda*.

Fig. 2.

Chaque automne, les guetteurs basques se postent dans des tours au sommet des collines, ou à tout autre endroit surplombant la mer. Dès qu'ils aperçoivent un troupeau de *sardas*, ils donnent l'alarme en frappant sur des tambours, en sonnant les cloches ou en allumant de grands feux. Les barques sont alors mises à l'eau et guidées depuis la terre par ces guetteurs, tandis que les chasseurs rament vers leurs proies. À bord, il y a dix hommes : rameurs, harponneurs et barreurs. Les frêles canots s'approchent des baleines et les hommes les attaquent à coups de trident. Une fois tuée, la baleine est remorquée jusqu'au rivage, où elle est dépecée.

Très vite, la chasse à la baleine devient une activité primordiale dans la vie des Basques. Les premières entreprises commerciales voient le jour sur les côtes française et espagnole. On y fait le trafic de tous les produits baleiniers : viande, lard,

Les Japonais se sont lancés très tôt dans la chasse aux baleines qu'ils croisaient près de leurs côtes. Ci-dessus, une méthode de chasse particulière, l'*amitori*, pratiquée au Japon au XVI⁰ siècle. La baleine est prise au piège des filets lancés par les chasseurs qui l'ont coincée dans un endroit où la mer est de faible profondeur. À gauche, des harponneurs basques. Au XVII⁰ siècle, leur réputation de grands chasseurs de baleines franchit les frontières et ils initient d'autres marins à leur savoir-faire.

huile, mais aussi des fanons qui sont très recherchés.
La langue de *sarda*, considérée comme un met
délicat, est vendue sur les marchés de Biarritz,
de Bayonne et de Ciboure; le lard est salé et envoyé
dans toute la France.

Mais, vers le XVe siècle, les *sardas* cessent de
s'aventurer près des côtes basques. Les a-t-on
tellement chassées qu'il n'en reste plus? Ont-elles
compris ce qui les attendait dans la baie de Biscaye?
En tout cas, il n'y en a plus assez pour alimenter le
marché baleinier. Alors, les Basques abandonnent
leurs canots et s'embarquent sur des vaisseaux de
haute mer pour aller chasser les baleines plus au
nord. Ils arment des caraques, de puissants voiliers,
hauts sur l'eau, d'une vingtaine de mètres de long;
ils enrôlent des équipages originaires des ports

Lorsqu'une baleine
est tuée, elle est
amenée le long du
navire où le dépeçage
peut commencer.
Les trancheurs, retenus
par des «cordes
à singes», découpent
des bandes de lard
qu'un grand palan
permet de tirer à bord
(ci-dessus).

normands, pour les conduire sur les lieux de chasse. Eux-mêmes se réservent les activités «nobles» : le harponnage et le dépeçage. Quelque temps plus tard, les caraques sont remplacées par des caravelles, navires plus rapides et mieux adaptés à la mer, avec lesquels les Basques poursuivent les baleines jusqu'aux îles Féroé, au large de l'Islande. Face à ce nouveau type de chasse s'instaurent de nouvelles techniques de dépeçage et de conservation.
À présent, la baleine tuée est dépecée sur place. Cependant, la conservation pose de gros problèmes; dès que le bateau quitte le climat rigoureux des régions nordiques, le lard se détériore et dégage une odeur épouvantable. Les Basques imaginent alors de fondre le lard à bord et de le stocker sous forme d'huile dans des tonneaux rangés dans les cales.

Quand le lieu de capture est proche de la station côtière, les cadavres de baleines sont remorqués à terre par des canots et c'est sur le rivage que les dépeceurs découpent les lanières de lard. Débité en petits morceaux, il est mis à fondre dans des fondoirs circulaires en brique (en haut). L'huile obtenue est versée dans des bacs de décantation (des cuves à moitié remplies d'eau) puis transvasée dans les barriques (ci-dessus).

Les Hollandais, fondateurs
de la première industrie baleinière

Au XVIᵉ siècle, l'histoire de la
chasse à la baleine prend un
nouveau tournant : les
affrontements incessants entre
le royaume de France et la
couronne d'Espagne entraînent
le démantèlement des entreprises
florissantes des Basques.
Dans le même temps, deux pays,
la Hollande et l'Angleterre, se
battent pour la domination des
grandes voies maritimes.
Armant à leur tour des navires
baleiniers, Anglais et Hollandais
commencent par employer des
harponneurs et des écorcheurs
basques qui connaissent bien
le «métier».

   Mais bientôt, ayant parfaitement
assimilé la technique des Basques,
ils les renvoient chez eux sans autre forme
de procès, leur interdisant même de naviguer
dans les mers septentrionales! Désormais,
une concurrence acharnée va mener les Hollandais
et les Anglais à la poursuite des baleines
du Groenland.

   Dès le début du XVIIᵉ siècle, les Hollandais édifient
sur les côtes du Spitzberg de véritables stations
de chasse : de petites villes qui, en plus des fonderies
de lard, des magasins et des entrepôts, comptent
toutes sortes de commerces, des boulangeries,
des auberges et un temple. Grouillantes de monde
pendant la période de chasse, ces stations deviennent
des villes fantômes une fois les baleiniers partis.

   Nombreuses près des côtes, les baleines sont
prises en chasse par des canots légers avec six
hommes à bord. Quand les chasseurs sont
suffisamment proches de l'animal, ils lui plantent
un harpon relié par une longue corde à l'embarcation.
Sous l'effet de la douleur, la baleine entraîne

avec elle l'esquif. C'est la partie la plus dangereuse de la chasse : si la baleine plonge, il faut donner de la longueur; si elle nage en surface, il faut se laisser tirer. Quand elle montre des signes de fatigue, le canot s'approche et on achève l'animal à la lance. La baleine est ensuite remorquée sur le rivage.

Le cadavre est laissé là un ou deux jours avant que les dépeceurs commencent leur travail. Ils découpent le lard et le chauffe pour en extraire l'huile. Les tonneaux seront ensuite transportés par radeaux jusqu'au navire de haute mer qui les livrera dans les ports hollandais.

Mais, très vite, cette chasse si bien organisée épuise les populations de baleines franches qui venaient se refaire des forces en mangeant le krill, particulièrement dense dans les parages du Groenland. Elles émigrent vers l'ouest et on les retrouve beaucoup plus loin, vers le Labrador, au nord-est des côtes du Canada. Ce départ des baleines franches marque le déclin des grandes stations hollandaises.

Pendant plusieurs années, les côtes du Spitzberg sont confondues avec celles du Groenland, comme l'indique cette carte du début du XVIIᵉ siècle (à gauche). En 1623, la petite ville de Smeerenberg (ci-dessous) «jaillit» du sol stérile du Spitzberg, sous la seule impulsion de la chasse à la baleine. Véritable ville champignon, elle est une cité morte en dehors des saisons de chasse. À son apogée, dans les années 1630, Smeerenberg, que l'on appelle aussi la «cité du gras», compte jusqu'à 300 navires baleiniers et de 12 000 à 18 000 occupants saisonniers.

Les baleiniers de Nantucket chassent le cachalot

Dans la seconde moitié du XVIIᵉ siècle, dans les colonies anglaises d'Amérique du Nord, la Nouvelle-Angleterre, une industrie baleinière est en train de naître. Vers 1650, les colons mettent sur pied de petites entreprises de chasse. Comme autrefois au Pays basque, les baleines sont signalées par des guetteurs installés le long de la côte.

Après 1670, la chasse y est devenue une véritable industrie qui exporte ses produits, d'une part, vers l'Angleterre et ses autres colonies et, d'autre part, vers le reste de l'Europe. Sur toute la côte entre l'île de Long Island et le cap Cod, de nombreux ports se spécialisent dans la chasse à la baleine. Mais, à partir de 1690, l'un d'eux devient en peu de temps le premier port de chasse de la Nouvelle-Angleterre : Nantucket.

En 1712, Christopher Hussey, capitaine de navire à Nantucket, parti à la recherche de baleines franches, se retrouve au milieu d'un troupeau de cachalots. Or les chasseurs de baleines ont toujours fui les cachalots qui les effraient, parce qu'ils ont des dents (et non des fanons), parce qu'ils sont prédateurs

Les Indiens Kodiaks des îles Aléoutiennes à l'ouest de l'Alaska (ci-dessus) utilisaient des harpons empoisonnés à l'aconit qu'ils se contentaient de jeter sur la baleine, la blessant. Le poison, les vents et les courants faisaient le reste. La baleine morte venait s'échouer sur le rivage. En 1858, Von Kittlitz, un explorateur allemand, décrit cette technique : «La baleine meurt habituellement le troisième jour et le cadavre est alors rejeté sur une des îles; la tribu qui la récupère examine la blessure pour trouver la lance portant la marque de la tribu à laquelle appartient le chasseur. Ce village est alors prévenu et il partage le butin avec la tribu qui a chassé l'animal.»

(et non tranquillement brouteurs), parce qu'ils se déplacent en immenses troupeaux pouvant aller jusqu'à plusieurs centaines d'individus, et surtout parce que ces troupeaux leur ont toujours semblé avoir une organisation presque militaire.
Lorsqu'ils apercevaient de loin un troupeau, ils viraient de bord plutôt que de s'attaquer à lui.
En ce jour de 1712, Christopher Hussey ne fait pas demi-tour; il s'attaque à l'un d'entre eux et ramène le premier spécimen mort jusqu'à terre! Pour tout Nantucket, c'est un véritable exploit.

Cet événement marque le début de la chasse en haute mer. En 1715, Nantucket possède 6 sloops de chasse (navires à voile munis d'un seul mât). En 1775, au début de la guerre d'indépendance des colons contre l'Empire britannique, Nantucket est une station baleinière florissante qui fait d'énormes profits grâce à la chasse au cachalot. L'animal donne une huile meilleure que celle des baleines et il fournit du spermaceti, une substance extraite de sa tête, utilisée dans la fabrication de bougies, ainsi que des morceaux d'ambre gris que l'on trouve dans son estomac, très recherchés pour fixer les parfums.

À partir de 1715, les baleiniers d'Amérique portèrent leurs efforts sur la chasse au cachalot car sa valeur marchande est très grande : chaque individu fournit 10000 litres d'huile. En temps normal, ce cétacé à dents nage à une vitesse de 3 nœuds, mais ses poursuivants avaient la surprise de le voir accélérer sa course et tenir une vitesse de 10 à 12 nœuds pendant une heure. Le cachalot mâle, son harem et ses petits décrivaient un vaste circuit de migration que les chasseurs finirent par connaître. Entre 1842 et 1846, 20000 cachalots furent tués. Ci-dessus, une mère cachalot est en train d'attraper dans sa gueule son petit harponné par des chasseurs.

À cette époque, la production annuelle des colonies anglaises du Nouveau Monde est de 45 000 barils d'huile de cachalot, de 7 500 livres de fanons de baleine, de 8 500 barils d'huile de baleine.

La guerre de l'Indépendance américaine est une véritable tragédie pour l'industrie baleinière de la Nouvelle-Angleterre : la marine anglaise capture ou coule ses navires, attaque ses ports. Ses marins faits prisonniers ont le choix entre servir sur les baleiniers anglais ou aller croupir à fond de cale. Les flottes «américaine», hollandaise et française sont maintenant hors course : l'Empire britannique a le champ libre...

La suprématie de l'industrie baleinière anglaise et écossaise

En 1756, les flottes baleinières anglaise et écossaise réunies comptaient déjà 83 navires. Vingt ans plus tard, la guerre leur a permis d'étendre leur zone d'activité à tout l'Atlantique, des eaux polaires du Spitzberg en passant par les rivages canadiens jusqu'aux côtes orientales de l'Amérique du Sud.

À partir de 1790, l'activité connaît un nouvel essor : le navire baleinier *Emilia* franchit le cap Horn et fait une chasse providentielle dans le Pacifique! Ses cales reviennent littéralement pleines de spermaceti et d'huile de baleine... Les Anglais ne perdent pas de temps : en trois ans, ils envoient 23 bateaux dans l'océan Pacifique! Et ils en profitent pour implanter des ports baleiniers en Australie et en Nouvelle-Zélande.

Mais, au début du XIXe siècle, leur flotte baleinière commence à perdre du terrain : dans l'Atlantique, les animaux

Timothy Folger, commerçant aisé de Nantucket (ci-dessous), refuse de se rebeller contre l'Angleterre. En 1785, il conduit 300 loyalistes chasseurs de baleine en Nouvelle-Écosse (Canada) et y crée une pêcherie. En 1792-1793, la couronne britannique persuade les 300 loyalistes de s'établir dans le port de Milford Haven, au pays de Galles, pour renforcer sa flotte baleinière et tenter d'enrayer le succès grandissant du port de Nantucket.

se font de plus en plus rares, et la guerre contre la France fait des bâtiments anglais des cibles idéales pour les frégates de Napoléon : dans le Pacifique, le navire américain *Essex* en coule 12...
Les revers sont sérieux. L'Angleterre perd le monopole de la chasse. Dès 1815 et la paix signée entre Américains et Anglais, les ports américains se réorganisent. Leurs navires prennent à leur tour la route du Pacifique. Dans les années 1820, plus de 120 baleiniers sillonnent ses eaux.

Après le creux qui a suivi la guerre de l'Indépendance, la relance de l'industrie baleinière a été si vigoureuse que de nombreux marins américains, enrôlés de force sur les bateaux anglais, regagnent précipitamment la Nouvelle-Angleterre. En six ans, de 1835 à 1841, la flotte baleinière nord-américaine passe de 203 à 421 navires pour trente ports baleiniers. En 1846, la Nouvelle-Angleterre et l'État de New York comptent une cinquantaine de ports et 735 navires. Chaque port a sa «spécialité» : les marins de New London poursuivent les baleines franches; ceux de Stonington, les baleines franches et les baleines de l'Arctique, tandis que les petits navires de Provincetown traquent les baleines de l'Atlantique. Mais les deux très grands ports baleiniers, ceux qui resteront dans l'histoire, sont Nantucket et New Bedford.

Le *Charles W. Wanderer* (ci-dessus) était le joyau de la flotte de New Bedford. Dernier baleinier entièrement à voiles, il fit naufrage le 26 août 1924, à 13 milles du port. Un violent vent du nord le drossa vers les rochers et il fut entièrement brisé. Pendant quatre-vingts ans, le *Charles W. Wanderer* avait effectué 37 campagnes et rapporté près de 2 millions de dollars à ses armateurs.

L'âge d'or de Nantucket

Autour de 1820, Nantucket est le plus important des ports baleiniers américains. Ses quais croulent sous le poids des barils d'huile prudemment recouverts d'algues pour les empêcher de se dessécher au soleil. Le prix de l'huile ne cesse de monter et la demande en fanons de baleine est de plus en plus forte.

Dans toute la ville, des manufactures de préparation des huiles, du blanc et des fanons se sont implantées. Il y a aussi des voileries et toutes les entreprises qui fabriquent les harpons, les cordages métalliques et les rivets de cuivre. Vers 1830, 72 baleiniers quittent chaque année Nantucket. Les 30 000 barils qu'ils y rapportent fournissent au monde entier une huile précieuse, nécessaire à la lubrification des machines de la révolution industrielle naissante et à l'éclairage des grandes ville d'Europe et d'Amérique.

Mais peu à peu Nantucket perd de sa supériorité. Un banc de sable à l'entrée du port limite la taille des bateaux qui peuvent y pénétrer et les nouvelles zones de chasse découvertes dans le Pacifique nécessitent des baleiniers de plus en plus gros. Bientôt, le port de New Bedford supplante Nantucket.

❝Tout le monde n'était pas millionnaire, bien que l'industrie baleinière en ait fait quelques-uns, mais bon nombre de fortunes s'élevaient à plusieurs centaines de milliers de dollars, ce qui représentait une grande richesse pour l'époque. Il n'était pas rare de voir un capitaine prendre une retraite confortable à un âge encore jeune, après quelques campagnes réussies. Quant aux armateurs qui faisaient naviguer plusieurs bateaux en même temps, ils gagnaient souvent assez d'argent pour se retirer au bout d'un très petit nombre d'années, si les choses tournaient bien.❞

Cité par
A. B. C. Whipple,
in *Les Chasseurs
de baleine*

New Bedford, capitale de la chasse au cachalot

Dès 1842, l'industrie baleinière américaine affirme sa suprématie. Sur les 882 bâtiments engagés dans la chasse à la baleine sur les océans du monde, 652 sont américains. Pour la seule année 1851, New Bedford arme 249 navires. Sept années plus tard, les bateaux de New Bedford rapportent de l'huile et des os de baleine pour une valeur de 6 millions de dollars.

La chasse a apporté la richesse dans cette petite ville : le revenu par habitant y est l'un des plus élevés du monde. Tout est florissant, depuis les quais bourdonnant d'activité jusqu'aux maisons de maître sur les collines. Pratiquement toute la population vit de la chasse. Les rues sont peuplées d'une foule bigarrée d'Africains et d'insulaires des Açores ou des mers du sud. Dans les grandes corderies, des équipes d'ouvriers assemblent les filins destinés aux lignes des harpons.

Les tonneaux étaient embarqués vides et se remplissaient au fur et à mesure de la chasse. Une campagne réussie représentait environ 1 500 à 2 000 barils d'huile de baleine, un cachalot fournissant entre 20 et 40 barils.

" La voilerie de Front Street à New Bedford est fraîche et aérée, même par grosse chaleur. [...] Les artisans de la voile cousent paisiblement l'épais tissu, à l'aide de leur grosse aiguille triangulaire et de leur paume [morceau de cuir ajusté à la paume du couseur, équipé d'une pièce de métal pour mieux pousser l'aiguille à travers le tissu] [...]. Pour coudre la totalité des voiles du navire *Ulysse*, il faut des centaines de milliers d'aiguilles, onze cents mètres de toile et des kilomètres de fil recouvert de facilement vingt kilos de cire d'abeille. **"**
Cité par Jan Adkins, in *Wooden Ship*

En 1841, un artiste américain, Benjamin Russel, embarque à New Bedford sur le baleinier *Kutusoff*. Pendant trois années, il dessine toute l'histoire de la chasse, dans ses moindres détails. À son retour, il engage un peintre en bâtiment, Caleb Purrington, pour mettre l'épopée sur toile. *Le Panorama du tour du monde d'un baleinier* mesurait près de 500 m. Il était déroulé à la main sur l'estrade d'un théâtre pendant que le narrateur décrivait l'action. Cette scène (ci-contre) est l'une des plus célèbres de l'œuvre de Benjamin Russel. Elle relate les différentes étapes de la chasse. La flotte américaine est lancée en pleine action contre les baleines franches du Pacifique nord. À droite, un cachalot est harponné tandis qu'au centre un autre de ses congénères attaque une baleinière et la renverse. Les cales pleines d'huile et de fanons, les navires repartaient vers le port de New Bedford pour y vendre leur cargaison. (Pages suivantes, des chasseurs tuent une baleine tandis que d'autres capturent un ours.)

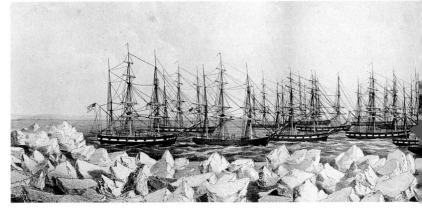

Un peu partout les fabriques de chandelles exhalent le lourd parfum du spermaceti. L'ambre gris dégage son odeur musquée, avant d'être expédié dans les parfumeries de Londres ou de Paris. À toute heure du jour ou de la nuit, les tavernes sont pleines de marins, les uns rentrant de la chasse, les autres sur le point d'y repartir.

Le déclin de la chasse traditionnelle

Dans la seconde moitié du XIXᵉ siècle, l'industrie baleinière américaine amorce sa régression. Les baleines se font de plus en plus rares, les bateaux doivent aller de plus en plus loin pour les trouver et ils reviennent souvent les cales vides.

La découverte d'or en Californie le 24 janvier 1848 déclenche une véritable ruée. Les désertions se multiplient à bord des navires. Les chasseurs de baleines se transforment en chercheurs d'or.

Dix ans plus tard, la situation s'aggrave encore : cette fois, on vient de trouver du pétrole en Amérique. Très vite, celui-ci remplace l'huile de baleine pour l'éclairage et, en quelques années, le prix de l'huile s'effondre.

Durant la guerre de Sécession (1861-1865), les baleiniers américains souffrent cruellement : marins engagés, équipages démantelés, bateaux coulés ou capturés par les corsaires des États du sud. Quand elle prend fin, les baleines ont déserté

Dès le mois de juin, les baleines grises de Californie viennent s'alimenter dans les eaux glacées du détroit de Béring. Les baleiniers américains les appellent des «brise-glace» car elles peuvent crever une épaisseur de glace de plus d'un mètre.

les côtes américaines. Les baleiniers restants sont obligés de s'aventurer loin dans les eaux du Nord, à la poursuite de la baleine franche. Mais, contrairement à leurs rivaux britanniques qui viennent d'adopter les bateaux à vapeur, ils se déplacent encore exclusivement à la voile. Ils se trouvent donc à la merci des éléments naturels, particulièrement rudes dans l'Arctique : ainsi, en 1871, la flottille américaine perd 34 navires, pris dans les glaces, près des côtes de l'Alaska, une véritable tragédie pour le port de New Bedford.

En 1871, 40 navires américains décident de rester dans le détroit de Béring pour continuer la chasse. À la mi-août, le temps se détériore rapidement et une partie de la flotte reste prisonnière des glaces. Le bilan est lourd. Cette catastrophe financière est estimée à 3 millions de dollars (à gauche et ci-dessous, deux peintures de Benjamin Russel illustrant le désastre).

Petit à petit, de nouvelles stations sont créées sous l'impulsion d'armateurs locaux sur la côte ouest des États-Unis (dans les lagunes de Californie et dans la baie de Monterey) et remplacent les ports moribonds de la Nouvelle-Angleterre.

Dans les dernières années du siècle, les financiers américains eux-mêmes se détournent de l'industrie baleinière; ils préfèrent investir leurs capitaux dans une nouvelle activité en pleine expansion : l'industrie du coton. La grande chasse traditionnelle disparaît lentement.

Au milieu du XIXe siècle, un chasseur de baleine passe en moyenne quarante-deux mois en mer. «L'océan est sa patrie», écrit Herman Melville. Le baleinier partage sa vie entre l'attente et la peur, la solitude et l'exaltation, les doux plaisirs des îles exotiques et la rencontre souvent violente avec des hommes d'autres cultures. Seuls des marins patients et courageux peuvent survivre à de tels voyages.

CHAPITRE 3

DES HOMMES ET DES BALEINES

Partis pour une longue aventure, les chasseurs connaissent des périodes d'ennui et de doutes. Les distractions sont rares à bord du baleinier. Un des passe-temps favoris des marins est de graver des dents (ci-contre) et des os de cachalot.

La route du Pacifique

De 1850 à 1860, la plus grande partie de la flotte baleinière américaine est mobilisée dans le Pacifique. Le cachalot, qui reste la prise la plus convoitée, y abonde : probablement plus de un million d'individus.

Le parcours du baleinier varie suivant l'époque de l'année, les migrations connues des cétacés ou la fantaisie du capitaine. Mais généralement les baleiniers passent le cap Horn pour atteindre le Pacifique en octobre ou en novembre et naviguer ensuite dans l'archipel des Galápagos. Puis ils se dirigent vers les îles Sandwich (Hawaï) avant de repartir vers le Japon.

Ils écument littéralement les eaux du Pacifique jusqu'à ce que leurs cales regorgent de barils d'huile. Ils font escale et provision de nourriture fraîche dans les îles, et peuvent rester ainsi plusieurs mois, voire une année entière, avant de reprendre la route qui les ramènera, via l'Australie, les côtes africaines et l'océan Atlantique, à leur port de départ, après avoir effectué un tour du monde.

Le «patron» et ses hommes

Le capitaine est seul maître à bord. Il n'a de comptes à rendre à personne, sauf au propriétaire du baleinier, au moment du retour. Il aime à se décrire ainsi : «De ce côté de la terre [à l'est du cap Horn], je dois le respect à mes propriétaires et à Dieu tout-puissant; de l'autre côté, je suis Dieu tout-puissant.» La discipline qu'il fait régner sur le navire est souvent rigoureuse et despotique.

Il doit être un excellent navigateur, connaître les mœurs des baleines et savoir les trouver. C'est un expert dans les différentes phases de la chasse : la recherche, l'approche, la poursuite, le harponnage, le combat et le dépeçage. Il peut prendre lui-même le commandement d'une des baleinières ou bien rester à bord pour diriger la stratégie générale de la chasse.

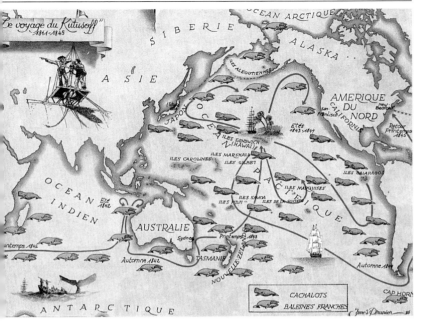

Comme il n'y a aucun médecin à bord, c'est lui qui panse les plaies et réduit les fractures.

Il est aidé dans son commandement par les seconds qui supervisent tous les travaux à bord et ont la responsabilité de la bonne marche du bateau. Ce sont eux qui achèvent à la lance la baleine harponnée et qui prennent en charge les opérations de dépeçage et de fonte de la graisse. Les harponneurs sont très importants; de leur adresse dépend le succès de la campagne. Le tonnelier fabrique les barils pour stocker l'huile. Il se charge aussi du rangement dans les cales. Il peut prendre le commandement provisoire du navire lorsque le capitaine et ses seconds sont tous embarqués sur les baleinières ou si une urgence le requiert. Le reste de l'équipage se compose du steward qui sert le capitaine et les officiers, du charpentier, du cuisinier et des marins qui fournissent, en plus de l'officier et du harponneur, les équipes de quatre hommes nécessaires pour la manœuvre des baleinières.

Ouverte dès 1789, la route du Pacifique est presque exclusivement utilisée par les Américains au XIXe siècle. La carte ci-dessus retrace le parcours du baleinier *Kutusoff* de New Bedford lors d'un tour du monde entre 1841 et 1845. On peut y voir des zones de baleines franches et de cachalots dans le Pacifique est.

À gauche, le capitaine Howland, qui entreprit plusieurs campagnes entre 1827 et 1844. En 1838, il ramena 3 000 barils d'huile à l'issue d'un périple de quatre ans à bord du *Magnolia*.

Pour les chasseurs américains, l'océan Pacifique, avec ses vents chauds et ses eaux limpides, ressemble à un paradis même si, aux mois d'août et septembre, il connaît de terribles cyclones où les vents peuvent atteindre 300 km/h. Les escales, très rares, sont fort appréciées par les équipages (ci-contre, une île du Pacifique). Ils en profitent pour cueillir des fruits frais car la nourriture à bord des baleiniers est très peu variée et mal équilibrée, à base de viande séchée, de riz, de biscuits, de haricots et parfois, de cervelle de baleine roulée dans la farine et frite à l'huile de baleine. Les tentations de déserter sont grandes et les capitaines sont obligés de prévenir leur équipage contre le danger de cannibalisme des indigènes. Malgré ce risque, les îles du Pacifique attirent bon nombre de marins qui fuient les conditions de vie à bord et les brutalités de leurs supérieurs, pour se réfugier sur les plages bordées de palmiers.

Un équipage venu de tous les horizons

Dans les premières années de la chasse, en dehors
des périodes où quelques Indiens ou quelques Noirs
remplaçaient parfois les effectifs manquants,
l'équipage du navire baleinier était composé de
Blancs originaires de la Nouvelle-Angleterre. Pour
ces hommes, la chasse était un simple gagne-pain
provisoire. Parfois, les plus habiles et les plus
expérimentés en faisaient une véritable profession,
qui leur permettait de subvenir aux besoins de la
famille restée à terre.

À partir de 1820, les besoins en hommes sont
tellement importants que l'on en recrute de toutes
origines et de toutes conditions : Basques et
Portugais, indigènes de Polynésie, de Mélanésie
ou des îles Sandwich, fort appréciés car beaucoup
d'entre eux se révèlent des harponneurs hors pair.

À ces vaillants gaillards se joignent des
aventuriers de tout poil : Espagnols, Suédois,
Français, Allemands, Irlandais ou Italiens. Cela
donne souvent des équipages instables et peu
homogènes, et surtout des hommes qui, peu
habitués à la dure vie des baleiniers, désertent à la
première escale. Malgré tout, de nombreux hommes
de valeur, excellents marins et chasseurs, s'illustrent
par leur courage et leur travail. En quittant la vie
à terre et leur famille pour de longues années,
ils partent assouvir une véritable passion.

Une si longue attente

Les premières semaines en mer sont monotones :
les zones de chasse sont encore loin, pas de
baleine... La seule distraction, ce sont les nouveaux :
ceux qui ignorent tout du maniement des harpons

Les *scrimshaws* sont
des os ou des dents
de cachalot gravés,
représentant souvent
des paysages de chasse.
Les marins fabriquent
aussi des objets comme
ce jeu de piquet.

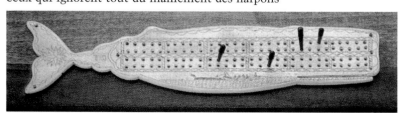

Au cours de ces interminables voyages, les chasseurs de baleines (ci-dessous, un harponneur de Nantucket, vers 1820) tiennent souvent un journal de bord en attendant la confrontation avec l'animal. À gauche, deux pages contenant le récit de neuf jours de campagne en novembre 1838 à bord du *William Baker*. Les dessins décrivent la chasse, et l'on peut y voir en haut à droite une baleinière brisée par un coup de queue.

et des embarcations. Ils s'entraînent sans relâche, car il est absolument vital que chacun à bord connaisse son rôle.

L'attente peut durer des semaines, des mois quelquefois. Le passe-temps favori des marins consiste à fabriquer des objets sculptés dans des os de baleine et des dents de cachalot. Un simple couteau de poche suffit à ce travail. Les dessins qui décorent ces pièces sont généralement gravés avec une aiguille à voiles, puis foncés en les frottant dans un mélange d'huile et de noir de fumée. Les créations peuvent aller de la simple épingle de vêtement à des objets de luxe, extraordinairement complexes et raffinés. Certains baleiniers se révèlent de véritables artistes.

Le navire baleinier (à gauche, le *Pequod* de *Moby Dick*, un trois-mâts carré.) est un bâtiment lourd, lent, résistant et spacieux. La vaste cale du navire est conçue pour abriter un grand nombre de barils d'huile. Il est lent mais d'une construction robuste, gréé en trois-mâts carré ou, plus souvent, trois-mâts barque (gréement léger, qui permet de manœuvrer avec six hommes pendant que le reste de l'équipage poursuit les baleines à bord des baleinières).

La baleinière (ci-contre) est une embarcation légère et rapide, très maniable. Sa forme est symétrique, allongée, pointue, permettant de naviguer aussi bien en avant qu'en arrière. Elle mesure environ 9 m de longueur sur 2 m de largeur et pèse 450 kg. Elle peut transporter six hommes dont un officier qui la dirige grâce à l'aviron de queue. Sur l'avant de la baleinière se trouvent les harpons (ci-dessous), reliés à la ligne dont plusieurs mètres sont lovés dans des baquets

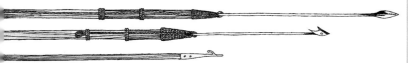

La fin tragique de la baleine

Une fois sur le lieu de la chasse, le rythme de vie change complètement. La nuit, les voiles sont carguées pour n'être déployées qu'au lever du jour. Pendant la journée, toutes les deux heures, un marin prend son quart de vigie sur une plate-forme située presque au sommet du mât. Soudain un cri : «Souffle, là... Elle souffle!» La vigie a repéré une baleine. Très vite, grâce à la forme de son souffle, on sait de quelle espèce il s'agit. Normalement, le jet de la baleine s'élève à 3 ou 4 mètres et dure trois secondes environ. On peut l'apercevoir à 6 milles à la ronde. À cette distance, il est facile de se tromper, et pour ne pas susciter, sur le pont, de branle-bas intempestif, certains veilleurs préfèrent attendre prudemment avant de crier le signal. Si elle projette la tête hors de l'eau, le guetteur crie : «Saute, là... Elle sau-au-aute!» et «Sonde là... Elle son-on-onde!» quand il la voit plonger.

On lance les baleinières à l'eau. Le capitaine ordonne de mettre en panne le bateau, en «brassant à contre» les voiles du grand mât. La poursuite s'engage, à la voile ou à la pagaie selon les

L'épisode de la chasse durant lequel la baleinière et ses occcupants sont traînés à toute vitesse (au moins pendant les premières heures) par l'animal harponné s'appelle le *Nantucket sleighride*, le«traîneau de Nantucket» (ci-dessus). Ainsi remorqués, les hommes doivent maintenir leur embarcation le plus près possible de leur proie et laisser filer la ligne si jamais l'animal sonde. Lovée dans de grands bacs au centre du bateau, la ligne va à l'étrave. Elle passe d'abord à l'arrière, autour d'un montant recourbé, le «tambour», pour revenir à l'avant sur un rouleau protégé par un taquet.

circonstances (force du vent, distance à parcourir, état de la mer). L'homme de poupe, l'officier responsable de la baleinière, ou «patron», la dirige grâce à un aviron de près de 7 mètres de long. À l'avant, jusqu'au moment opportun, le harponneur rame avec les autres. Les deux bras levés au-dessus de lui, il tient le harpon des deux mains et le projette avec force et précision sur le dos de la baleine. Une fois que le harpon est solidement fiché dans la chair du cétacé, l'officier crie : «Arrière toute!» À grands coups d'avirons, les marins s'éloignent de la baleine aussi vite que possible. Car les réactions de l'animal blessé peuvent être violentes, et il arrive souvent que les baleinières soient coulées à ce moment de la chasse, pour ne pas s'être écartées assez rapidement.

Puis la baleine harponnée nage en surface ou sonde dans les profondeurs. Dans le premier cas, les hommes de la baleinière se laissent traîner par leur proie tout en essayant de la freiner le plus possible. Dans le second cas, quand la baleine plonge, les hommes laissent filer la ligne. Si la longueur n'est pas suffisante, ils la doublent en ajoutant celle d'une autre baleinière.

La baleine a été harponnée. Un officier cherche son équilibre après avoir pris la place du harponneur, maintenant aux commandes de l'aviron de gouverne, pour achever l'animal. À l'arrière-plan, l'équipage du baleinier dépèce une baleine morte amarrée le long du bateau.

Parmi les grands dangers de la chasse figurent les coups de queue du cachalot blessé et le moment où, après avoir sondé, celui-ci refait surface. Personne ne peut lui échapper lorsqu'il surgit sous la baleinière, comme l'illustre l'aquarelle du Français Louis Garneray (1835) (pages suivantes).

Mais, si elle file complètement avant qu'ils aient pu agir, ils se contentent d'attacher des pièces de bois et de laisser le tout, avec l'espoir de les récupérer plus tard. Petit à petit, la baleine se fatigue et les hommes, halant la ligne, s'en rapprochent. L'officier échange alors sa place avec le harponneur. À lui la tâche noble : il saisit la lance et en frappe l'animal à grands coups, cherchant cette partie du corps que les marins appellent la «vie». Quand il est certain d'avoir porté le coup décisif, il fait éloigner l'embarcation de quelques mètres pour attendre la fin des soubresauts de l'animal. Et la baleine, enfin, au milieu d'une mer rougie par son sang, roule sur le côté... morte.

En général, il faut plusieurs dizaines de coups pour que la mort, provoquée par une hémorragie pulmonaire, arrive. Les hommes savent que la baleine va mourir lorsque son souffle se teinte de rouge. Ils appellent cela les «roses rouges», ou encore le *fleurry*. On plante alors sur le cadavre de la baleine un mât portant le pavillon de la baleinière... et la chasse continue. On repère les cadavres des baleines tuées grâce à ce pavillon.

Le dépeçage, une opération très complexe

Une fois la chasse terminée, le baleinier s'approche des prises. Le corps de chaque baleine est disposé le long de la coque, la tête vers la poupe, amarré avec

Amenée sur tribord, la baleine est littéralement «pelée», puis débitée en morceaux que l'on entasse sur le pont (à droite). Là, un mousse s'en empare et les découpe en minces lamelles semblables à des pages de livre, les «bibles»; cette façon de procéder permet une fonte rapide du lard. Les bibles sont ensuite plongées dans les marmites du fondoir. Après la fonte de la graisse, on verse l'huile ainsi obtenue dans un bac de refroidissement jusqu'à ce qu'elle soit tiède, avant de la transvaser dans les tonneaux qui sont entreposés dans les cales. A la fin de ces opérations, le navire empeste l'huile si fortement que certains marins rapportent que l'on peut sentir un navire baleinier à des milles de distance...

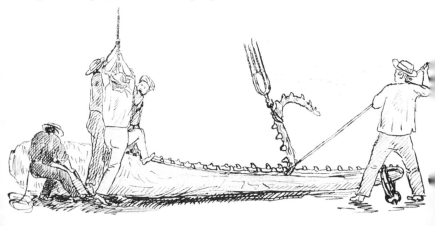

des cordes, une chaîne passée autour de la queue. On met alors en place, sur le flanc du navire, au-dessus de la baleine, le «chaffaud», plate-forme de découpage munie d'un garde-fou. C'est là que les écorcheurs travaillent. Ils utilisent des tranchoirs et des pelles coupantes à longs manches, avec lesquels ils dépècent la bête.

Au cours du dépeçage d'un cachalot, dès que cela a été possible, les matelots, après avoir enlevé la mâchoire inférieure, tranchent la colonne vertébrale, séparent l'énorme tête du reste du corps et l'apportent à l'arrière du bateau en attendant qu'on en ait complètement terminé avec le découpage et la fonte du lard. Alors, la tête est placée à hauteur du pont; on y fait un trou et, à l'aide d'un seau, un marin recueille avec précaution le spermaceti. On le porte immédiatement à ébullition pour qu'il ne se détériore pas avant la mise en tonneau. Durant les trois jours qui suivent, les tonneaux sont alignés le long du pavois tandis que l'huile refroidit. Quant à l'énorme carcasse du cachalot, cela fait longtemps qu'elle a été laissée à la dérive, pour la plus grande joie des requins.

Dans le cas d'un cachalot, la technique de débitage du lard reste la même que pour la baleine, à ceci près que quand le dernier morceau de lard a été détaché de la carcasse, les écorcheurs, à l'aide de leur long tranchoir, cherchent avidement dans les entrailles de l'animal le précieux ambre gris. A gauche, cette esquisse de 1855 montre des baleiniers en train d'extraire les dents d'un cachalot à l'aide d'un palan.

À la fin du XIXe siècle, l'invention du harpon explosif entraîne l'extermination de plusieurs populations de grands cétacés. Il faut attendre près d'un siècle pour que la Commission baleinière internationale intervienne efficacement. Aujourd'hui, malgré l'interdiction de toute chasse commerciale, plusieurs espèces sont encore menacées.

CHAPITRE 4

DE LA SUREXPLOITATION À LA PROTECTION

Tandis que le Japon continue à chasser des petits rorquals en Antarctique (à gauche), de nombreux pays protestent contre cette pratique, jugée cruelle. Les enfants, très sensibles à la protection des baleines, participent souvent aux manifestations, tels ces écoliers de Glasgow, en Écosse (ci-contre).

L'invention du harponnage au canon

En 1864, une innovation technique révolutionne la chasse à la baleine. Le capitaine norvégien Svend Foyn, maître chasseur de phoques, met au point un redoutable harpon explosif propulsé par un canon, d'une portée de 50 mètres. Une fois planté dans les chairs de l'animal, des barbillons s'ouvrent en étoile, brisant une fiole remplie d'acide sulfurique qui met le feu à une réserve de poudre. L'explosion provoque la mort de la baleine en quelques minutes, alors que l'agonie durait de longues heures avec un harpon classique.

Svend Foyn se fait construire un baleinier à vapeur, le *Spes et Fides*. Il y installe, à la proue, son canon lance-harpon. Au cours de la saison de chasse de 1868, il tue 30 rorquals. Jamais de mémoire de baleinier on n'avait vu cela : jusqu'alors on n'avait pas chassé les rorquals, trop rapides. Et surtout les rorquals ne flottent pas, une fois morts. Plus denses que l'eau de mer, ils coulent dès qu'ils cessent de respirer. Foyn a résolu ce problème de la flottaison

Svend Foyn (ci-dessus) est l'inventeur du harpon explosif– un harpon et une lance combinés en un seul engin – qui relègue au musée le vieux harpon à main et la lance des baleiniers traditionnels. Le harpon était à la fois un harpon et une lance combinés en un seul engin. Ce canon (ci-dessous) fabriqué en Norvège en 1925 est équipé d'un viseur. Il projette un grand harpon à tête pointue, aujourd'hui abandonné au profit d'un autre à l'extrémité en forme de cône.

en insufflant dans le ventre de l'animal tué de l'air comprimé, par un tuyau. Pour éviter que la ligne ne se rompe quand il se débat, Foyn conçoit des «amortisseurs» : une rangée de ressorts reliant le mât à une poulie dans laquelle coulisse le harpon.

Norvège, Russie et Japon : les nations baleinières

Les Norvégiens connaissent mieux que personne les concentrations des rorquals des mers arctiques.

Cinq compagnies norvégiennes s'établissent en Islande. Dès 1889, sur le site d'Onundardfjördur, s'élève la plus grande station baleinière jamais construite. En onze ans, on y dépèce 1296 baleines. En 1891, la Russie et le Japon se lancent à leur tour à la poursuite des baleines et mettent sur pied des industries florissantes. Au Japon, les stations ne possèdent pas de plan incliné contrairement aux stations norvégiennes; le cadavre de la baleine, amarré contre la coque d'un bateau, est découpé dans l'eau.

Mais, très vite, un nouveau problème se pose aux chasseurs norvégiens. Les «stocks» de baleines s'épuisent aux abords des côtes norvégiennes. Le gouvernement incite alors les compagnies baleinières à exercer leur activité en dehors des eaux territoriales. Dans un premier temps, les chasseurs se contentent d'aller installer de nouvelles stations un peu plus au nord : en Islande, dans les îles Féroé et l'archipel des Hébrides.

Jusque dans les années 1960, les Norvégiens et les Japonais chassaient les baleines à partir de Grytviken, port baleinier de Géorgie du Sud, une île britannique proche de l'Antarctique (ci-dessus, l'épave d'un navire-chasseur ou *catcher* à Grytviken). Les *catchers*, équipés d'un canon lance-harpon, rapportaient les baleines au port, où elles étaient dépecées. Plus de 800 personnes y travaillaient, pour fondre la graisse stockée dans d'immenses cuves, préparer les conserves ou sécher la viande, transformer les os en engrais ou réparer les bateaux. L'odeur âcre de l'huile de baleine est toujours perceptible derrière la rouille qui ronge aujourd'hui cette cité abandonnée.

Peu à peu, ils poussent de plus en plus loin de chez eux : sur les côtes du Labrador, puis à Terre-Neuve où l'on compte déjà dix-huit stations baleinières en 1905 et aussi vers l'Espagne, le Maroc, la côte pacifique de l'Amérique du Nord, l'Afrique et l'Amérique du Sud.

De 1914 à 1945 : la longue traque des baleines

Les Norvégiens mettent au point les premiers navires-usines, d'énormes bâtiments mouillant l'ancre dans une baie abritée; ils peuvent ainsi se déplacer d'un site à l'autre et travailler là où il est impossible d'établir une station baleinière à terre. Ils améliorent également le harpon de Foyn. En remplaçant la fiole d'acide par un mécanisme à retardement, on augmente la puissance de pénétration dans la chair et on facilite le chargement du canon.

L'approche de la Première Guerre mondiale ne ralentit pas l'essor de l'industrie baleinière norvégienne, bien au contraire : la demande en glycérine obtenue à partir de l'huile de baleine, avec laquelle on fabrique les explosifs, augmente. De nombreux instruments nouveaux sont

Une station côtière emploie de 200 à 300 hommes : directeur, contremaître, ingénieurs, forgerons, magasiniers, mécaniciens, équarisseurs, fondeurs, ouvriers, cuisiniers. Une équipe de dépeceurs découpe une baleine en une heure et demie; en moyenne douze baleines pouvaient être traitées par jour. Ci-dessus, des dépeceurs norvégiens tiennent les pelles coupantes avec lesquelles ils débitent les lanières de lard qui seront fondues en huile dans des chaudrons.

expérimentés pour la chasse : harpon électrique, harpon à tête plate, appareil lance-roquette. Mais ce sont les Japonais qui remportent la palme de la sophistication avec l'usage d'un sonar qui indique la direction dans laquelle nagent les baleines et la distance à laquelle elles se trouvent des bateaux.

De l'Arctique à l'Antarctique, on traque les baleines de toutes espèces, de toutes tailles, les jeunes comme les adultes, les mâles comme les femelles. Les prises annuelles sont considérables. En 1920, 12 000 grands cétacés sont massacrés; 15 000 en 1922; 17 000 en 1924; 27 000 en 1926; et 44 000 en 1931, dont plus de 30 000 baleines bleues harponnées dans l'Antarctique.

Les Japonais, qui s'intéressent à la pêche à la baleine en Antarctique, achètent en 1934 un navire-usine norvégien, l'*Antarctic*, et cinq chasseurs baleiniers. Rebaptisé *Tonan Maru*, ce navire-usine et sa flottille regagnent le Japon en chassant. Sur l'année 1937-1938, quatre stations baleinières dans l'Antarctique sont construites. Deux ans plus tard, la chasse japonaise en haute mer commence dans le Pacifique Nord.

Tristes vestiges de l'époque de la chasse, les squelettes de baleines ne sont pas rares sur les rivages des régions où on les pourchassait. Dans les zones froides et desséchées par les vents, la biodégradation est extrêmement lente. Les ossements de taille importante, comme ci-dessous la colonne vertébrale d'une grande baleine gisant sur une plage de Patagonie argentine, mettent plusieurs siècles à disparaître totalement.

La Seconde Guerre mondiale laisse un temps les baleines tranquilles. Mais, dès 1945, neuf navires-usines reprennent immédiatement les chasses en Antarctique : la Norvège en arme 6; la Grande-Bretagne, 2; l'Afrique du Sud, 1. L'année suivante, on en compte onze : 7 norvégiens, 3 anglais, 1 sud-africain. Le Japon obtient des puissances alliées l'autorisation de reconstituer sa flotte baleinière.

La Commission baleinière internationale

Le nombre des cétacés décroît de plus en plus. Le répit occasionné entre 1939 et 1945 n'a pas suffi à repeupler les eaux en baleines.

En 1946, une commission internationale siège à Washington pour envisager une solution. Dix-neuf pays, dont certains favorables à la chasse (le Japon, l'Afrique du Sud, la Russie), ratifient la Convention pour la réglementation de la chasse à la baleine et mettent en place la Commission baleinière internationale (CBI).

Trois ans plus tard, la première réunion de cette commission, qui se déroule à Londres, instaure, pour établir des quotas de capture, l'unité en baleine bleue : 1 baleine bleue équivaut à 2 rorquals communs, à 2,5 baleines à bosse ou à 6 rorquals boréals. La baleine franche et la baleine grise sont déclarées «espèces protégées».

La baleine bleue ou grand rorqual (à gauche) est le plus gros animal que notre planète ait jamais connu : les femelles peuvent atteindre 35 m de long, pour quelque 150 t (les mysticètes mâles sont plus petits que les femelles). En mer, quand sa longueur est difficile à évaluer ou s'il s'agit d'un jeune adulte, on reconnaît la baleine bleue à la forme arrondie de son museau.

La CBI interdit, en outre, la capture des baleineaux et des femelles pleines, pour toutes les autres espèces.

Mais ce système d'appréciation par quota est injuste et critiquable car il est basé sur des notions quantitatives et non qualitatives. Il ne tient pas compte de la rareté comparative de chacune des espèces. Ainsi, si un pays a un quota de 10 unités, il peut tuer indifféremment 10 baleines bleues, ou 8 baleines bleues et 4 rorquals communs, ou 60 rorquals boréals. En 1971, l'unité en baleine bleue est abandonnée. Une nouvelle procédure de gestion est adoptée. Cette fois, les quotas sont calculés par espèces mais dans la quasi-ignorance de l'état des populations.

Les baleines sont nombreuses en été au large de l'Islande et la chasse y est intense jusqu'au début des années 1980. Il est facile de les ramener vers les stations côtières pour les découper. Les cétacés ont trois estomacs successifs : un mécanique, un chimique et un pylorique. Ci-dessus, l'estomac mécanique d'un rorqual commun se répand sur l'aire de l'usine de Hvalfjördur.

L'URSS et le Japon poursuivent les chasses meurtrières

L'activité baleinière en haute mer se ralentit dans les années 1960 car les expéditions coûtent cher et la main-d'œuvre est rare. La Grande-Bretagne, les Pays-Bas et la Norvège cessent d'envoyer leurs navires dans l'Antarctique. Les deux premiers pays désarment complètement leur flotte; le troisième ne conserve que quelques bateaux opérant au large de ses côtes. En outre, dans les économies modernes, la chasse à la baleine n'a plus vraiment sa place : les produits baleiniers perdent leur intérêt, car certains peuvent être remplacés par de nouveaux produits. Par exemple, l'huile de jojoba, issue de la plante du même nom, se substitue à l'huile de spermaceti du cachalot et maintenant on utilise un fixateur chimique à la place de l'ambre gris.

Ce type de chasse ne reste rentable que pour l'URSS et le Japon, et pour des raisons bien précises : en URSS, l'industrie baleinière comble une déficience de l'industrie chimique; le pays est en effet incapable de produire en quantité suffisante des huiles de synthèse de grande qualité; au Japon, la viande de baleine fait partie de l'alimentation courante.

Lors de la saison de chasse soviétique de l'année 1961, 1 200 baleines franches du Sud, une espèce pourtant protégée, sont massacrées. Deux ans plus tard, les Soviétiques déclarent 75 baleines bleues tuées alors qu'en réalité ils en ont pris plus de 500.

Un moratoire sur la chasse commerciale

En 1972, un appel quasi unanime est lancé à la conférence des Nations unies pour l'adoption d'un moratoire de dix ans relatif à la chasse à la baleine. Les nations baleinières l'ignorent. Les mouvements d'opinion en faveur des baleines se développent

Formé de concrétion d'éléments indigestes dans l'estomac des cachalots, l'ambre gris se présente sous la forme d'une masse molle, sombre, à l'odeur nauséabonde. Exposé à l'air libre et au soleil, il durcit, s'éclaircit et perd son odeur. Il a la particularité étonnante d'être un excellent fixateur de parfum. Vendu au poids, son prix dépassait celui de l'or au XVIIIe siècle.

À gauche, un navire-chasseur japonais. La viande de baleine est très appréciée de la population nippone. Elle est à la carte dans les restaurants huppés – le steak de baleine peut être plus cher que le meilleur des caviars –, dans les commerces de détail ou sous forme de conserve (ci-contre).

et s'inscrivent dans les préoccupations de la CBI. Des organisations non gouvernementales comme Greenpeace mènent campagne pour stopper la chasse commerciale. Le 3 mars 1973, à Washington, vingt et un États signent le plus important accord mondial pour la protection des espèces vivantes, lors de la Convention sur le commerce international des espèces menacées d'extinction (CITES). Cette année-là, le Japon et l'URSS violent les quotas et tuent en toute illégalité plus de 6 000 baleines.

C'est en 1982, sur proposition de la France, que la CBI adopte enfin un moratoire sur la chasse commerciale. Il entre en vigueur en 1985-1986, interdisant toutes formes d'exploitation commerciale des baleines. Mais les pays membres peuvent faire objection à toute décision de la CBI, lorsqu'ils estiment qu'elle est contraire à leur intérêt national.

Le Japon fait objection à cette décision puis, par un accord bilatéral avec les États-Unis en 1984, retire son opposition en prévoyant de reconvertir sa flotte de chasse en flotte scientifique. Ce type de chasse est autorisée par la CBI et vise à obtenir

L'organisation Greenpeace, qui fut l'une des premières à revendiquer la protection totale des baleines, agit directement sur le terrain : en pleine mer, ses embarcations tentent de s'interposer entre le navire baleinier et l'animal. Sur cette photo, prise au large de l'Espagne au début des années 1970, le baleinier vient de tirer et le harpon a atteint sa cible. Le zodiac de Greenpeace a dû s'écarter. Devant l'étrave du navire, l'agonie d'une baleine commence.

des informations scientifiques sur des espèces. Elle n'est tolérée que pour le Japon, qui n'a le droit de capturer que 500 petits rorquals par an et seulement en Antarctique. Seuls quelques prélèvements biologiques sont nécessaires à la science. Selon le règlement de la CBI, rien ne peut interdire aux Japonais de vendre les morceaux de viande de baleine provenant des stocks congelés issus de ces chasses. Mais une étude récente menée par des scientifiques américains et néo-zélandais démontre que plus d'un tiers des rorquals sont capturés en mer du Japon, une zone où les petits rorquals sont peu nombreux.

De son côté, en 1993, le gouvernement norvégien déclare unilatéralement la réouverture de la chasse baleinière commerciale dans ses eaux territoriales de l'Atlantique Nord. Il maintient ainsi son objection au moratoire adopté par la communauté internationale sept ans plus tôt.

La baleine est touchée. Son souffle chargé de sang, le *fleurry*, indique que ses poumons sont atteints. L'agonie dure de longues minutes. Bientôt, la mer alentour ne sera plus qu'une vaste tache rouge : le sang des cétacés contient beaucoup plus d'hémoglobine que celui des mammifères terrestres.

Novembre 1998 : un navire-usine japonais quitte son port d'attache pour aller chasser les petits rorquals autour de l'Antarctique, devant des écoliers qui agitent leurs drapeaux, fiers de cette activité ancestrale. Dans ce pays, la chasse à la baleine reste valorisée en souvenir du temps où l'homme combattait ces géants avec de bien faibles moyens. Mais les navires-usines actuels ne laissent aucune chance à la baleine : ils sont équipés de sonars pour repérer les cétacés en plongée, de harpons explosifs, de treuils et d'une plage arrière pour hisser l'animal sur le pont, où il sera dépecé (pages suivantes).

Reconnaissant la nécessité de protéger totalement les cétacés, la CBI instaure en 1994 un sanctuaire dans le Pacifique Sud. Cette zone, située sous le 40e degré de latitude sud, est désormais plus étroitement protégée que lors du vote du moratoire en 1986.

Le 13 avril 2000, le Japon réaffirme son opposition aux mesures de protection d'espèces en voie de disparition lors de la 11e session de la CITES qui se tient à Nairobi. Il maintient une réserve concernant la commercialisation de sa baleine grise et de son petit rorqual, dont les ventes annuelles sont respectivement évaluées officiellement à 140 et à 500 unités.

La clause d'exemption aborigène

Le moratoire ne concerne que la chasse commerciale. Chaque année, la CBI alloue des quotas de captures aux populations dites aborigènes, tels les Inuits de l'Arctique canadien, américain et russe, ou certains Indiens des Caraïbes. On considère en effet que ces peuples ne sont pas responsables de l'extinction des populations de grands cétacés. Ils chassent les baleines depuis des millénaires et consomment toujours aujourd'hui la viande et la graisse de ces animaux. Cette activité leur permet de ne pas dépendre entièrement des subventions de leurs gouvernements respectifs.

Ainsi, 280 baleines du Groenland et 140 baleines grises pourront être capturées par les différents peuples de l'Arctique entre 1998 et 2002. Les Inuits de l'ouest du Groenland ont droit à 19 rorquals communs par an sur la même période, et au maximum à 175 petits rorquals sur cinq ans, tandis que ceux de l'est du Groenland ne peuvent chasser que 12 petits rorquals par an. Dans les Caraïbes, pour les habitants de Saint-Vincent et des Grenadines, le quota maximal est de 2 baleines à bosse par an entre 2000 et 2002. On remarque cependant que plusieurs associations de protection des baleines critiquent ces quotas de chasse aborigène en estimant qu'ils sont trop élevés ou injustifiés.

Les peuples de l'Arctique conservent les méthodes traditionnelles de chasse à la baleine. Le harpon à main est toujours en usage, tel celui employé par cet Inuit de l'Alaska qui poursuit une baleine du Groenland en mer de Béring (à gauche). Ils peuvent néanmoins utiliser des embarcations à moteur et non plus des kayaks pour poursuivre les baleines et les ramener vers la côte. Ci-contre, un groupe d'Inuits canadiens vient de dépecer un béluga (un odontocète). Toutes les parties comestibles sont réparties entre les membres du groupe, en respectant une hiérarchie ancestrale. Le lard de l'animal, ou *muktuk*, est un mets de choix, considéré comme la meilleure des friandises. Quelques morceaux, encore tièdes ou déjà gelés, seront consommés sur place.

En Indonésie, la chasse à la baleine traditionnelle est pratiquée encore de nos jours. Un jeune cachalot est mis à mort par les habitants de Lamalera puis il est remorqué vers la plage où tout le village va participer au dépeçage (pages suivantes).

Le *whale-watching* : une alternative économique?

Certains pays baleiniers ont cessé de pratiquer la chasse commerciale et se sont tournés vers le *whale-watching*, le tourisme lié à l'observation des cétacés.

Apparue en Californie en 1955, cette activité ne concernait alors que les baleines grises. Elle s'est étendue progressivement à d'autres régions des États-Unis, puis, dans les années 1970, au Canada et au Mexique. À partir des années 1980, ce tourisme écologique a connu une croissance considérable. En 1994, plus de 5 millions de personnes ont approché les baleines. En Islande, le *whale-watching* a triplé durant les trois dernières années avec plus de 27 000 touristes pour la seule saison 1998. En 1997, l'économie touristique de ce pays a généré dix fois plus de revenus annuels que celui apporté par la chasse dans le début des années 1980.

D'autres pays pratiquent cette activité lucrative : le Mexique, le Canada, l'Argentine, l'Australie méridionale, l'Afrique du Sud (région du Cap), le Portugal (les Açores), la Nouvelle-Zélande.

Plusieurs espèces de baleines viennent se reproduire près de la côte est des États-Unis. Si cette habitude a bien failli leur être fatale lors de la grande époque de la chasse en Nouvelle-Angleterre, elle est devenue un atout pour leur protection, puisque ces animaux représentent un enjeu économique important grâce au *whale-watching*. Cette activité a dû être réglementée, afin que les observateurs ne dérangent pas toujours le même animal et qu'ils ne restent pas trop longtemps à proximité. Les mégaptères (ci-dessus et à droite) sont très démonstratifs pendant la période de reproduction.

Depuis peu, la France et d'autres pays méditerranéens tentent de développer le *whale-watching*. Dans les Caraïbes, la Dominique et Sainte-Lucie commencent à profiter des bénéfices rapportés par cette activité. Ces îles développent des structures (hôtels, restaurants, magasins) favorisant ainsi la création d'emplois locaux.

Compte tenu de son extraordinaire développement, cette nouvelle forme de tourisme doit être rapidement contrôlée. En effet, de nombreuses règles élémentaires (techniques, vitesses et distances minimales d'approche, nombre de bateaux sur les zones) doivent impérativement être respectées pour ne pas perturber la vie sociale des cétacés.

Vers un monde sans baleines?

Selon la CBI, il ne resterait que 5 à 10 % des populations de certaines espèces.

Depuis 1967, date à laquelle les baleines bleues sont protégées, leurs effectifs ne se renforcent pas. Il y en avait 230 000 en 1930, il en reste peut-être 10 000 aujourd'hui. On estimait à 115 000 la population de baleines à bosse avant son exploitation, il en reste seulement 15 000, malgré sa protection totale depuis 1966.

La diminution dramatique de ces populations est due à différents facteurs : la pollution, le trafic maritime, la diminution des ressources alimentaires et un taux de reproduction très faible. En revanche, la population des baleines grises dans l'est du Pacifique, après avoir frôlé l'extinction, est estimée aujourd'hui entre 18 000 et 20 000 individus, soit 90 % de son stock initial sans qu'aucune explication scientifique, à ce jour, ne permette de comprendre ce phénomène.

Quant aux baleines franches de l'Arctique et de l'Antarctique, leur survie tient littéralement du prodige : elles ont été chassées sans discontinuer du VIIIe au XXe siècle, et on ne peut dire quel était leur nombre lorsque leur population était maximale. Il n'en reste actuellement que quelques milliers.

L'indispensable équilibre écologique des océans

Il est aujourd'hui impossible d'évaluer la population mondiale des grands cétacés, mais ils représentent indubitablement un pourcentage non négligeable de la biomasse des océans.

Comme tous les grands prédateurs, les cétacés jouent un rôle fondamental dans l'équilibre écologique marin. Cet équilibre est fragile, complexe et tous ses éléments sont interdépendants : ils sont liés les uns aux autres, comme les rouages d'une grande machine. Supprimer l'un d'entre eux, c'est prendre le risque d'enrayer définitivement le mécanisme.

À l'aube du IIIe millénaire, ce que nous savons des baleines, aussi populaires soient-elles, ressemble à la partie émergée d'un iceberg : les scientifiques restent incapables d'expliquer bien des éléments de leur biologie et la plupart de leurs comportements. Quant aux océans où elles vivent, ils appartiennent pour l'essentiel au domaine de l'inconnu total. Comment peut-on, dans une telle ignorance, protéger efficacement les cétacés et préserver l'équilibre écologique dont ils dépendent ?

De nombreuses nations reconnaissent la nécessité d'appliquer des mesures de protection dans le domaine de l'écologie, mais elles sont rarement

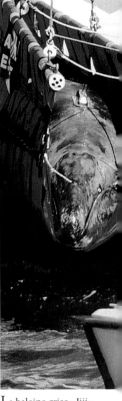

La baleine grise «Jiji» a été trouvée encore bébé, échouée le 11 janvier 1997 sur la plage de Marina del Rey, en Californie. Elle est restée un an en captivité au Sea Word de San Diego, avant d'être relâchée au printemps 1998 dans l'océan Pacifique (ci-dessus).

prêtes à investir suffisamment dans la recherche, pour saisir les relations fondamentales qui existent entre les êtres vivants et leurs milieux.

Pourtant, si l'homme a trouvé les «armes» pour détruire certains milieux, il doit connaître les «outils» pour les reconstruire. La première étape consiste à prendre conscience des dégâts, puis à envisager leurs conséquences sur notre environnement. Il semble évident que protéger la nature et tous ses habitants revient à prendre soin de nous-mêmes. Espérons que cet instinct de sauvegarde réapparaîtra rapidement, et que cette motivation sera assez forte pour que des actions nécessaires soient entreprises.

Pour l'alimenter, ses soigneurs ont dû inventer un lait spécial, puis lui donner jusqu'à 400 kilogrammes de poissons par jour. Grâce à ce régime, elle est passée de 4 mètres et 875 kilogrammes, à son arrivée, à près de 8 mètres et quelques tonnes lorqu'elle a été relâchée. Pendant sa période de croissance la plus forte, «Jiji» prenait un kilo et plus d'un centimètre par heure!

TÉMOIGNAGES
ET DOCUMENTS

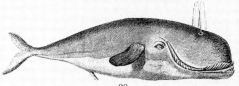

La baleine et la littérature

Tels des chasseurs du rêve, les plus grands auteurs du XIXᵉ et du XXᵉ siècle ont été captivés par le destin des hommes de la baleine et ont suivi les péripéties de ces marins hors du commun.

Le *Saint-Enoch*

Le lendemain 7 novembre 1863, le *Saint-Enoch* quittait Le Havre, remorqué par l'*Hercule* qui le sortit à l'heure de la pleine mer. Il faisait un assez mauvais temps. Des nuages bas et déchirés couraient à travers l'espace, poussés par une forte brise du sud-ouest.

Le bâtiment du capitaine Bourcart, jaugeant environ cinq cent cinquante tonneaux, était pourvu de tous les appareils communément employés pour cette difficile pêche à la baleine sur les lointains parages du Pacifique. Quoique sa construction datât d'une dizaine d'années déjà il tenait bien la mer sous les diverses allures. L'équipage s'était toujours appliqué à ce qu'il fût en parfait état, voilure et coque, et il venait de refaire son carénage à neuf.

Le *Saint-Enoch*, un trois-mâts carré, portait misaine, grande voile et brigantine, grand et petit hunier, grand et petit perroquet et perroquet de fougue, grand et petit cacatois, perruche, trinquette, grand foc, petit foc, clin foc, bonnettes et voiles d'étais. En attendant le départ, M. Bourcart avait fait mettre en place les appareils pour virer les baleines. Quatre pirogues étaient à leur poste : à bâbord celles du second, du premier et du deuxième lieutenant; à tribord celle du capitaine. Quatre autres de rechange étaient disposées sur les espars du pont. Entre le mât de misaine et le grand mât, en avant du grand panneau, on avait installé la cabousse qui sert à fondre le gras. Elle se composait de deux pots en fer maçonnés l'un contre l'autre, entourés d'une ceinture de briques. À l'arrière des pots, deux trous, pratiqués à cet effet, servaient à l'échappement de la fumée, et, sur l'avant, un peu plus bas que la gueule des pots, deux fourneaux permettaient d'entretenir le feu en dessous.

Voici l'état des officiers et des gens de l'équipage embarqués sur le *Saint-Enoch* :

le capitaine Bourcart (Évariste-Simon), cinquante ans;

le second Heurtaux (Jean-François), quarante ans;

le premier lieutenant Coquebert (Yves), trente-deux ans;

le deuxième lieutenant Allotte (Romain), vingt-sept ans;

le maître d'équipage Ollive (Mathurin), quarante-cinq ans;

le harponneur Thiébaut (Louis), trente-sept ans;

le harponneur Kardek (Pierre), trente-deux ans;

le harponneur Durut (Jean), trente-deux ans;

le harponneur Ducrest (Alain), trente et un ans;

le docteur Filhiol, vingt-sept ans;

le tonnelier Cabidoulin (Jean-Marie), cinquante-deux ans;

le forgeron Thomas (Gilles),
quarante-cinq ans;

le charpentier Ferut (Marcel),
trente-six ans;

huit matelots;

onze novices;

un maître d'hôtel;

un cuisinier.

Au total trente-quatre hommes,
personnel ordinaire d'un baleinier
du tonnage du *Saint-Enoch*.

L'équipage se composait par moitié
à peu près de matelots normands
et bretons. Seul, le charpentier Ferut
était originaire de Paris, faubourg

de Belleville, ayant fait le métier de
machiniste dans divers théâtres de
la capitale.

Les officiers avaient déjà été en cours
de navigation à bord du *Saint-Enoch* et
ne méritaient que des éloges. Ils
possédaient toutes les qualités qu'exige
le métier. Dans la campagne précédente
ils avaient parcouru les parages nord
et sud du Pacifique. Voyage heureux
s'il en fut puisque, pendant sa durée
de quarante-quatre mois, il ne s'était
produit aucun incident grave; voyage
fructueux aussi, puisque le navire avait
rapporté deux mille barils d'huile qui
furent vendus à un prix avantageux.

Jules Verne,
*Les Histoires
de Jean-Marie Cabidoulin,*
Hetzel, 1902

La mère et son petit

Nous faisions donc route vers le banc
d'huîtres dans une pirogue désarmée,
c'est-à-dire déchargée de ses harpons,
de ses lances et de sa ligne. Nous
étions sept : les cinq rameurs, le
capitaine et moi. À peine avions-nous
atteint le milieu du chenal par le
travers du cap Cachalot, qu'une
énorme baleine, accompagnée de son
nourrisson, de son cafre, vint sourdre
à l'avant du canot et nous asperger
d'eau salée.

Oh! Quelle figure fit le capitaine Jay,
en vue de cette baleine qui lui passait
devant le nez sans pouvoir l'amarrer!
Pas de harpons, pas de ligne, et pas
moyen de la signaler à nos canots,
partis depuis longtemps.

Et cependant, il ne pouvait
se résigner à laisser échapper une
si belle proie.

– Capitaine, voilà une lance, s'écria
le harponneur, une lance que j'ai prise
pour fusiller les cochons de la baie de
Togolabo.

D'un bond, le capitaine sauta à
l'avant du canot, et, brandissant sa lance,
s'écria :

– Attention, enfants! attention!

Le harponneur prit l'aviron de queue,
et, selon ses ordres, les matelots
nagèrent, scièrent, nagèrent et scièrent
encore.

Moi, content, heureux d'assister à
pareil tournoi, je me croisai les bras,
n'ayant pas d'aviron à manier; mais,
avant de les croiser, j'eus la précaution
d'attacher, avec un bout de bitord, mon
fusil au banc sur lequel j'étais assis.

Si l'embarcation chavirait, le fusil
ne serait pas perdu.

La mère baleine ne semblait pas
s'effaroucher de notre voisinage :
elle folâtrait, tournoyait sur elle-même,

soulevant de sa nageoire le petit cafre qui se fatiguait à la suivre.

M. Jay, sa lance en arrêt, attendait l'instant favorable pour frapper. Le moment vint, et la lance transperça, non pas la baleine, mais le cafre.

Je crus d'abord que mon capitaine n'avait pas visé juste... mais je compris bientôt sa prudence et son adresse. Il savait que, si le premier coup de lance ne tuait pas la mère, la mère s'enfuirait au loin et serait perdue pour nous; mais, en tuant le nourrisson, c'était arrêter, immobiliser en quelque sorte la mère : elle se laisserait massacrer sur place, plutôt que d'abandonner son cafre.

Et c'est ce qui arriva. – M. Jay put à loisir frapper un coup, deux coups, trois coups, dix coups... Le monstre se débattit, souffla le sang, fleurit et mourut... sans plus s'éloigner que s'il eût été amarré du harpon le plus solide. Admirable puissance de l'amour maternel qui domine l'instinct de conservation!

Je pouvais donc dire enfin que j'avais vu et touché une baleine vivante et même au plus fort du combat.

Je l'avais vue, et de si près, que j'étais couvert de son sang. Je l'avais touchée, et si bien, que mon bras faillit être broyé entre elle et le plat-bord du canot, alors que, faisant un élan à fleur d'eau pour se rapprocher du jeune blessé, elle longea la pirogue, jeta bas nos avirons posés en lève-rames, et, de même qu'un mouton abandonne un peu de sa toison au buisson qu'il côtoie, laissa, sur la peinture grise des bordages, les lamelles noires et pelliculeuses de son épiderme.

La manche de mon paletot était tapissée de ces pellicules. Je les secouai avec orgueil.

Nous abandonnâmes, bien entendu, la chasse aux ramiers et le banc d'huîtres. On planta un guidon de reconnaissance sur le dos de la baleine morte, et nous retournâmes à bord pour préparer les appareils du virage, tandis qu'un homme montant au sommet de la falaise d'Oli-Maroa, donnait, à l'aide d'un pavillon placé là tout exprès, un signal convenu pour ordonner à nos pirogues de rallier l'*Asia*.

On employa une partie de la journée à remorquer la baleine, et l'on se hâta de la virer.

Les Mahouris vinrent en foule donner un coup de main à nos hommes, et l'œuvre fut accomplie avant la tombée de la nuit.

À peine le dernier morceau de gras était-il monté sur le pont, que les canots des naturels se précipitèrent vers la carcasse flottante de la baleine, et la remorquèrent à sec sur la grève. Ce fut alors un spectacle burlesque et dégoûtant à la fois, que de voir cette tourbe d'hommes nus et armés de couteaux, les uns suspendus aux flancs de l'animal, les autres enfouis dans son flanc entrouvert, tailladant ses chaires en tous sens, et se choisissant d'énormes biftecks, que les femmes déposaient sur l'herbe, aux rayons du soleil.

Le soir, le feu du pauvre, comme celui du riche, s'allumait pour cuire ces friands morceaux.

Le festin commença d'abord par des cris de joie et des chansons improvisées en l'honneur des baleiniers, et, le lendemain, les prudentes ménagères suspendirent aux poteaux de leur *koamara* les pièces de viande réservées pour les temps de disette.

Alexandre Dumas,
Les Baleiniers,
Voyage aux terres antipodiques.
A. Le Vasseur et Compagnie Éditeurs,
Paris, 1858

La pêche à la baleine

À la pêche à la baleine, à la pêche
à la baleine,
Disait le père d'une voix courroucée
À son fils Prosper, sous l'armoire
allongé,
À la pêche à la baleine, à la pêche
à la baleine,
Tu ne veux pas aller,
Et pourquoi donc?
Et pourquoi donc que j'irais pêcher
une bête
Qui ne m'a rien fait, papa,
Va la pépé, va la pêcher toi-même,
Puisque ça te plait,
J'aime mieux rester à la maison avec
ma pauvre mère
Et le cousin Gaston.
Alors dans sa baleinière le père tout
seul s'en est allé
Sur la mer démontée...
Voilà le père sur la mer,
Voilà le fils à la maison,
Voilà la baleine en colère,
Et voilà le cousin Gaston qui renverse
la soupière,
La soupière au bouillon.
La mer était mauvaise,
La soupe était bonne.
Et voilà sur sa chaise Prosper qui se
désole;
À la pêche à la baleine, je ne suis pas
allé,
Et pourquoi donc que j'y ai pas été?
Peut-être qu'on l'aurait attrapée,
Alors j'aurais pu en manger.
Mais voilà la porte qui s'ouvre, et
ruisselant d'eau
Le père apparaît hors d'haleine,
Tenant la baleine sur son dos.
Il jette l'animal sur la table, une belle
baleine aux yeux bleus,
Une bête comme on en voit peu,
Et dit d'une voix lamentable :
Dépêchez-vous de la dépecer,

J'ai faim, j'ai soif, je veux manger.
Mais voilà Prosper qui se lève,
Regardant son père dans le blanc
des yeux,
Dans le blanc des yeux bleus de son
père,
Bleus comme ceux de la baleine
aux yeux bleus :
Et pourquoi donc je dépècerais une
pauvre bête qui m'a rien fait?
Tant pis, j'abandonne ma part.
Puis il jette le couteau par terre.
Mais la baleine s'en empare, et se
précipitant sur le père
Elle le transperce de père en part.
Ah, ah, dit le cousin Gaston,
On me rappelle la chasse, la chasse
aux papillons.
Et voilà
Voilà Prosper qui prépare les faire-part,
La mère qui prend le deuil de son
pauvre mari
Et la baleine, la larme à l'œil
contemplant le foyer détruit.
Soudain elle s'écrie :
Et pourquoi donc j'ai tué ce pauvre
imbécile,
Maintenant les autres vont me
pourchasser en motogodille
Et puis ils vont exterminer toute ma
petite famille.
Alors, éclatant d'un rire inquiétant,
Elle se dirige vers la porte et dit
À la veuve en passant :
Madame, si quelqu'un vient me
demander,
Soyez aimable et répondez :
La baleine est sortie,
Asseyez-vous,
Attendez là,
Dans une quinzaine d'années, sans
doute elle reviendra...

Jacques Prévert
Paroles,
Gallimard, 1941

Moby Dick

Rien n'a été écrit de plus beau, mais aussi de plus complet sur la baleine que le roman d'Herman Melville. Baleinier lui-même, l'auteur a rassemblé dans son chef-d'œuvre non seulement les qualités d'un fantastique écrivain, mais celles d'un observateur exceptionnel de ce qui fut la grande passion de sa vie : la chasse à la baleine.

Le capitaine Achab a juré la mort de Moby Dick *: la diabolique baleine blanche lui a enlevé une jambe voici quelques années. Depuis cette rencontre presque mortelle, il nourrit une haine furieuse contre l'animal et a juré sa mort. Depuis deux interminables journées, les hommes du* Pequod *se battent contre* Moby Dick, *retrouvée enfin après des années d'errance sur les océans. Achab est déchaîné, comme forcené. Les hommes, épuisés, voudraient renoncer. Personne ne peut encore savoir que ce troisième jour sera le dernier...*

Le matin du troisième jour se leva clair et frais, et une fois encore la vigie unique de la tête du grand mât fut relevée par les nombreuses vigies de jour qui mouchetaient chaque mât et presque chaque espar.

– La voyez-vous? cria Achab.
Mais la baleine n'était pas encore visible.

–Vous n'avez qu'à suivre son sillage. Il est infaillible. c'est tout. [...]
«Eh, là-haut! que voyez-vous?
– Rien, Sir!
– Rien! et c'est bientôt midi!
Personne ne veut donc du doublon? Voyez le soleil! Oui, oui, ça doit être ce que je pense. Je l'ai dépassée. Comment ai-je pu prendre l'avantage?

Oui, c'est elle qui me donne la chasse maintenant; ce n'est pas moi, c'est elle. Ça, c'est mauvais; aussi, j'aurais dû m'en douter. Fou! les lignes, les harpons qu'elle emporte la retiennent. C'est elle qui me donne la chasse maintenant. Oui, oui, je l'ai dépassée hier soir. Demi-tour... demi-tour. Descendez tout le monde, sauf la vigie régulière. Équipez les bras de vergue.

Dirigé comme il l'était, le *Pequod* prit le vent un peu de flanc et se mit à baratter la crème blanche de son propre sillage.

– Pour la gueule béante, il va maintenant contre vent, murmura Starbuck pour lui-même, tandis qu'il enroulait le grand bras nouvellement hissé sur la rampe.

– Que Dieu nous sauve! je sens déjà mes os mouillés dans moi, et, de dedans, ils mouillent ma chair. J'ai idée que je désobéis à Dieu en lui obéissant.

– Hissez-moi! cria Achab s'avançant vers le panier de chanvre. Nous la trouverons vite.

– Oui, oui, Sir.

Et immédiatement Starbuck obéit à l'ordre d'Achab qui, une fois encore, balança dans les airs.

Toute une heure passa. Élargi comme de l'or battu pendant des siècles et des siècles, le temps lui-même retenait sa respiration dans une attente vivante. Enfin, à trois quarts au vent, Achab découvrit de nouveau le jet, et, à l'instant, des trois têtes de mâts, trois cris s'élevèrent comme lancés par des vagues de feu. [...]

Il ordonna qu'on le descende et, regardant toujours autour de lui, il fut descendu doucement jusqu'au pont à travers l'air bleu.

En leur temps, les baleinières furent mises à la mer; mais lorsque debout, à l'arrière de son canot, Achab fut sur le point de descendre, il fit signe à son second (qui sur le pont tenait un des cordes de la poulie) et lui ordonna de s'arrêter :

– Starbuck!

– Sir?

– Pour la troisième fois, le vaisseau de mon âme reprend ce voyage, Starbuck.

– Oui, Sir, tu l'auras voulu.

– Certains vaisseaux quittent leur port et sont perdus à tout jamais, Starbuck.

– C'est la vérité, Sir, la triste vérité.

– Certains hommes meurent à la marée basse; certains en plein flux et je me sens maintenant comme une énorme lame avec une seule crête prête à retomber. Je suis vieux, Starbuck... une poignée de main, homme.

Leurs mains se touchèrent, leurs regards se pénétrèrent. Dans les yeux de Starbuck jaillirent des larmes.

– Oh, mon capitaine, mon capitaine!... noble cœur... n'y allez pas... voyez, c'est un homme courageux qui pleure, dans sa grande angoisse de vouloir vous persuader... alors?

– À la mer! cria Achab, repoussant le bras du second; équipage, soyez prêt! Tout de suite, le canot contourna de très près l'arrière.

– Les requins! les requins! cria une voix de la fenêtre basse de la cabine; oh, maître, mon maître, revenez!

Mais Achab n'entendit rien car, au même moment, il parlait lui-même très fort et sa barque filait.

La voix disait vrai. À peine s'était-il éloigné du navire que d'innombrables requins, montant sans doute du fond des eaux sombres, mordaient aux rames chaque fois qu'elles plongeaient dans l'eau, et ainsi accompagnaient le canot de leurs morsures. C'est une chose qui arrive souvent aux baleiniers dans ces eaux infestées de requins. Parfois les requins les poursuivent de la même façon presciente que les vautours planent dans l'Est, sur des régiments en marche. [...]

Les canots s'étaient à peine éloignés que, par un signal des vigies (un bras dirigé vers le bas), Achab sut que la baleine avait plongé. Mais, ayant décidé de rester près d'elle à sa prochaine remontée, il continua son chemin un peu par côté par rapport au navire. L'équipage, comme enchanté, gardait un silence profond tandis que les vagues droitement abordées martelaient et remartelaient le pont de la barque.

– Enfoncez... enfoncez vos clous, oh vagues! Enfoncez-les jusqu'à la tête! Vous ne faites que frapper sur une chose sans couvercle. Je ne peux avoir ni corbillard ni cercueil.. le chanvre seul peut me tuer! Ha!

Subitement, les eaux d'alentour se gonflèrent lentement en formant de larges cercles; puis elles se soulevèrent rapidement, comme si elles glissaient sur les flancs d'un banc de glace submergé en train de remonter rapidement à la surface. On entendit comme un grondement sous-marin et tous les hommes de l'équipage retenaient leur respiration quand couverte de lignes emmêlées, de harpons et de lances, une vaste forme s'élança d'un long saut oblique hors de la mer.

Enveloppée d'un mince voile flottant de brouillard elle plana une seconde dans l'air irisé, puis retomba lourdement dans l'océan. Projetées à trente pieds dans les airs, les eaux étincelèrent alors comme des gerbes de fontaines, puis retombèrent, brisées, en une pluie de flocons, laissant la surface tourbillonnante, comme crémeuse de lait nouveau autour du tronc marmoréen de la baleine.

– En avant! cria Achab aux rameurs; et les embarcations s'élancèrent à l'attaque; mais, enragée par les fers de la veille qui lui mordaient le dedans du corps, Moby Dick semblait possédée par tous les anges déchus tombés du ciel, jadis. Les longs rangs de tendons soudés qui s'étalaient sous la peau transparente de son large front blanc semblaient être noués ensemble quand, tête la première, elle arriva battant de la queue parmi les canots. Une fois encore elle les sépara brutalement, éparpillant les fers et les lances des embarcations des deux seconds, et défonçant un côté de la partie supérieure de leur proue. Mais elle laissa l'embarcation d'Achab presque intacte.

Tandis que Daggoo et Queequeg bouchaient les avaries et tandis que la baleine s'éloignait d'eux en se retournant, elle montra un de ses flancs tout entier et comme elle les dépassait de nouveau en coup de flèche, un cri s'éleva. Lié au dos du poisson, ligoté dans les emmêlements de lignes de la veille, on aperçut le corps à demi déchiqueté du Parsee : son vêtement noir était en loques et ses yeux exorbités étaient tournés en plein sur le vieil Achab. Le harpon lui tomba des mains. […]

Comme si elle avait décidé de s'enfuir avec le cadavre qu'elle portait, et que l'endroit de sa dernière remontée n'avait été qu'une étape de sa course sous le vent, Moby Dick maintenant nageait tranquillement en avant. Elle avait presque dépassé le navire qui jusqu'alors avait vogué dans la direction contraire et qui, pour l'instant, avait arrêté sa marche. Elle semblait donner sa plus grande vitesse et s'appliquer à suivre son propre chemin droit à travers la mer.

– Oh, Achab, cria Starbuck, il n'est pas trop tard, même maintenant, le troisième jour, pour renoncer. Vois Moby Dick ne te cherche pas. C'est toi, toi qui la cherches follement. […]

La Baleine Blanche était peut-être fatiguée par la chasse à toute vitesse de ces trois jours; ou peut-être la charge qu'elle portait ficelée sur elle l'empêchait-elle d'aller vite, ou bien le faisait-elle par ruse? Quoi qu'il en soit, elle allait moins vite, et en fait, le canot s'approcha d'elle une fois encore rapidement. À la vérité, elle n'avait pas une aussi bonne avance que la dernière fois. Les requins impitoyables accompagnaient toujours Achab à travers les vagues. Ils le suivaient sans répit et mordaient sans discontinuer les rames au point que, presque déchiquetées, elles laissaient dans la mer de menus éclats chaque fois qu'elles y plongeaient.

– N'y faites pas attention!… Ces dents ne font que donner plus de mordant à vos rames. Ramez toujours, la mâchoire du requin est un meilleur appui sur l'eau qui cède.

– Mais à chaque morsure, Sir, les rames diminuent.

– Elles dureront toujours assez! Tirez toujours… qui sait, murmura-t-il, si c'est pour se régaler de la Baleine Blanche ou d'Achab que ces requins suivent?… Mais ramez toujours!

Dans le film *Moby Dick* (1956) de John Huston, Gregory Peck joue le rôle du capitaine Achab qui affronte le redoutable cétacé.

– Oui, grouillez-vous, nous l'approchons! La barre, prends la barre, laissez-moi passer!

Et ce disant, deux rameurs l'aidèrent à passer à l'avant du canot volant toujours.

Quand le canot lancé de côté longea le flanc de la Baleine Blanche, elle sembla étrangement oublier d'avancer (comme la baleine le fait parfois) et Achab se trouva en plein dans la montagne de brouillard fumeux qui, rejeté par le jet, s'enroulait autour de sa grande bosse. Il était tout près d'elle quand, le corps bandé en arrière, les bras tendus, il lança son féroce harpon avec sa plus féroce malédiction.

L'acier et la malédiction s'enfoncèrent jusqu'à la garde dans la baleine détestée, comme dans un marais. Moby Dick se tordit de côté, roula spasmodiquement son flanc contre le flanc du canot et sans l'abîmer, le renversa si subitement que s'il n'avait alors été bien cramponné à la partie supérieure du plat-bord Achab aurait été une fois de plus jeté à la mer. Trois des rameurs qui ne pouvaient prévoir le moment précis du lancement du dard et n'étaient pas préparés à en subir les effets furent jetés à la mer, mais ils tombèrent de telle sorte qu'en un instant deux d'entre eux attrapèrent le plat-bord, et soulevés par une vague, purent se lancer encore dans le canot. Le troisième resta abandonné derrière, mais il flottait et il nageait toujours.

Presque aussitôt, avec une volte rapide, la Baleine Blanche se lança à travers la mer bouillonnante. Mais pendant qu'Achab criait au timonier de tirer la ligne et de tenir bon, et qu'il ordonnait à l'équipage de se retourner sur les sièges afin de pouvoir haler, la ligne, sous ce poids et ces efforts doubles, éclata dans l'air vide!

– Qu'est-ce qui éclate en moi? quel nerf a claqué?... toujours entier... les rames, les rames, sautez sur les rames.

En entendant le grand bruit du canot frappant la mer, la baleine se tourna pour présenter son œil vide à l'ennemi; mais dans ce mouvement, apercevant la masse noire du vaisseau qui approchait, et sans doute, voyant en lui la source de toutes ses persécutions, le prenant peut-être pour un ennemi plus grand et plus noble, elle chargea subitement sur sa proue approchante, claquant ses mâchoires parmi l'étincelante écume. Achab trébucha, sa main frappa son front.

– Je deviens aveugle; mais étendez-vous devant moi, que je puisse encore trouver mon chemin en tâtonnant. Est-ce la nuit?

– La baleine! Le vaisseau! crièrent les rameurs effrayés.

– Aux rames, aux rames! Apaise-toi jusque dans tes profondeurs, ô mer, pour qu'avant qu'il ne soit trop tard à jamais, Achab puisse une dernière fois, une toute dernière fois, faire son affaire! Je vois : le bateau, le bateau! Hâtez-vous mes hommes! Ne voulez-vous pas sauver mon bateau!

Mais tandis que les rameurs forçaient violemment leur canot à travers la mer battante, l'avant déjà frappé par la baleine céda et, presque en un instant, le canot provisoirement hors de combat s'enfonça au niveau des vagues. L'équipage pataugeait et éclaboussait, faisant de son mieux pour étancher et vider l'eau qui entrait à flots.

À ce même moment, au nid-de-pie, le marteau resta en l'air dans la main de Tashtego et le drapeau rouge l'enveloppa à demi, comme un plaid, puis flotta droit devant, comme si c'était son propre cœur qui flottait devant lui. Starbuck et Stubb, debout sur le beaupré, au-dessous, aperçurent en même temps que lui le monstre qui leur arrivait dessus.

– La baleine, la baleine!... Barre dessus; barre dessus! ô vous, toutes les bonnes puissances de l'air, soutenez-moi! Si Starbuck doit mourir, qu'il ne meure pas évanoui comme une femme. Barre au vent, je dis... fous! La mâchoire, la mâchoire! Est-là le paiement de toutes mes prières farouches? De toute la fidélité de ma vie? Oh, Achab! Achab! voilà ton travail. Doucement, timonier, doucement! Non, non! Barre dessus encore! Elle se tourne pour nous aborder. Ah! son front impitoyable se lance sur quelqu'un à qui le devoir commande de rester ferme. Mon Dieu, soyez maintenant à mes côtés! [...]

À l'avant du vaisseau, presque tous les marins restaient sans bouger; marteaux, morceaux de planches, lances et harpons machinalement tenus à la main, dans la position même où ils s'étaient élancés; médusés,

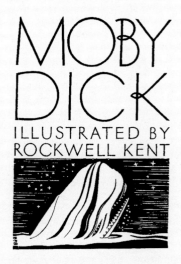

ils regardaient la baleine qui, de part et d'autre agitant sa tête prédestinée, jetait une large bande d'écume en demi-cercle devant elle.

Elle était le Jugement Dernier et la vengeance de la foudre et la malice éternelle, un homme mortel ne pouvait rien contre elle; le solide bélier blanc de son front frappa l'avant par tribord renversant hommes, planches et mâts. Quelques-uns tombèrent à plat sur leur visage.

Dans la mâture, les têtes des harponneurs furent secouées sur leurs cous de taureaux. Par la brèche, ils entendirent les eaux s'engouffrer comme des torrents de montagnes dans une crevasse. [...]

Plongeant sous le vaisseau qui s'enfonçait, la baleine fila en frémissant le long de la quille; puis se ravisant sous l'eau, elle s'élança de nouveau rapidement à la surface et très loin, de l'autre bord, mais à quelques mètres du canot d'Achab, elle s'immobilisa. [...]

Le harpon fut lancé. La baleine frappée s'élança. Avec une rapidité de flamme, la ligne coula dans la coulisse... se coinça. Achab se pencha pour la démêler, et il la démêla. Mais le rouleau volant l'attrapa par le cou, et, aussi silencieusement que par les Turcs qui étranglent leur victime, il fut emporté du canot avant même que l'équipage s'en aperçût. L'instant d'après le lourd épissoir en forme d'œil du bout de la ligne s'envola de la cuve vide, renversa un rameur et, frappant la mer, disparut dans ses profondeurs.

Un moment l'équipage, pétrifié, ne bougea pas; puis il se retourna.

– Le vaisseau? Le vaisseau, grand Dieu, où est le vaisseau?

Alors, à travers les vagues, ils virent son long fantôme s'évanouissant comme dans les brouillards de la fée Morgane!

Ses trois mâts seuls hors de l'eau, tandis que cloués par leur entêtement ou par une sorte de fidélité à leurs perchoirs hautains, les harponneurs païens gardaient leur vigie dans l'engloutissement même.

Des cercles concentriques saisirent le canot solitaire et tout son équipage; chaque rame qui flottait, chaque lance, animées et inanimées, se mirent à tourner en une ronde qui emporta hors de vue la plus petite épave du *Pequod*.

Une dernière vague recouvrit la tête de l'Indien du grand mât, ne laissant que quelques pieds de mât encore visibles avec toute la longueur du drapeau qui ondula paisiblement par une ironique coïncidence. Un bras rouge et un marteau sortirent de la mer et le bras clouait de plus en plus fermement le drapeau à l'espar qui s'enfonçait. Un de ces faucons de mer qui, de son gîte naturel, là-haut, dans les étoiles, avait suivi toute la chose, vint donner des coups de bec dans le drapeau que clouait toujours Tashtego. Et l'aile large et frémissante de l'oiseau se trouva un instant entre le marteau et le mât, et dans son dernier effort le sauvage englouti cloua l'oiseau du ciel au cri d'archange. Ainsi, son bec impérial appelant les dieux, le corps enveloppé dans le drapeau d'Achab, l'oiseau naufragea avec le vaisseau. Satan ne voulait pas s'engloutir dans les enfers sans arracher du ciel un morceau de vie.

Maintenant, les petits oiseaux voletaient en criant sur le gouffre encore ouvert. Une écume blanche et morne battit contre ses roides parois; puis tout s'égalisa; et le grand linceul de la mer se mit à rouler comme il roulait il y a cinq mille ans.

Herman Melville, *Moby Dick*,
Londres, New York 1851,
Gallimard, 1941

La Commission baleinière internationale

Au lendemain de la Seconde Guerre mondiale, la chasse commerciale baleinière décime des populations entières de cétacés. Une commission internationale se réunit à Washington pour envisager un remède à ces massacres. Elle adopte des mesures qui évoluent au cours des années mais qui s'avèrent être encore aujourd'hui assez ambiguës.

La création de la CBI

Le 2 décembre 1946, à Washington, les délégués de dix-neuf pays créent la Commission baleinière internationale (CBI) : l'Amérique du Sud, l'Argentine, l'Australie, le Brésil, le Canada, le Chili, le Danemark, la République d'Irlande, les États-Unis, la France, la Grande-Bretagne, l'Irlande, le Japon, le Mexique, la Norvège, les Pays-Bas, le Panama, le Pérou et l'Union soviétique.

Les dispositions qu'adopte la CBI visent quatre objectifs essentiels :
– protéger les immatures de toutes les espèces, afin de garantir l'existence des futurs reproducteurs;
– limiter «scientifiquement» le nombre d'animaux capturés;
– créer des réserves intégrales, notamment dans les zones de reproduction;
– prohiber toute prise d'animaux appartenant à une espèce en danger.

Au début de son existence, la priorité de la CBI n'est pas la protection des animaux mais de durs intérêts économiques. Elle forme, durant les quinze premières années d'existence, un cartel pour la stabilisation des prix de l'huile de baleine.

À partir des années 1970, lorsque les stocks très réduits ont commencé à menacer la rentabilité commerciale des baleines, la discussion sur la protection des mammifères marins a été sérieusement entamée. Il faudra attendre 1986 et la reconnaissance d'un moratoire de dix ans sur la chasse commerciale, pour que la CBI prennent des décisions plus protectrices.

Les limites de son fonctionnement

L'organigramme et le mode de fonctionnement de la Commission baleinière internationale ont été calqués sur ceux du Conseil de Sécurité de l'Organisation des Nations unies, et ces deux instances souffrent du même genre d'impuissance. La CBI. ne possède aucun moyen d'imposer ses décisions. Elle n'est habilitée à formuler que des «recommandations» ou des «suggestions». La souveraineté des gouvernements qui y sont représentés reste entière. L'Article 5 de la Charte stipule qu'une nation signataire peut toujours, si elle n'est pas d'accord avec une mesure de préservation ou avec un quota de captures, élever une «objection» dans les 90 jours : et la mesure ou le quota ne lui sont pas applicables! Si cela ne suffit pas, le pays mécontent conserve, bien entendu, la latitude de quitter purement et simplement la CBI.

Depuis 1946, les «objections» ont été nombreuses, et les défections également. Sans aller jusqu'à ces extrémités, les pays baleiniers ont eu la possibilité de constituer d'efficaces minorités de blocage : en effet, les décisions de la CBI ne doivent pas être prises à la majorité simple, mais aux trois quarts des voix.

Par ailleurs, les représentants des nations baleinières à la CBI sont le plus souvent les principaux actionnaires des sociétés de baleinage! Autant confier la garde d'un troupeau de moutons à des loups, ou celle d'un champ de laitues à des lapins. [...]

La CBI n'a fait que gérer la pénurie croissante de baleines. Les progrès qu'elle a accomplis lui ont surtout été imposés de l'extérieur, grâce aux pressions des «abolitionnistes». C'est un organisme qui a fait son temps. Greenpeace suggère qu'on le remplace par un comité scientifique responsable, dépendant uniquement du Plan des Nations unies pour l'Environnement.

La Fondation Cousteau préconise depuis des années la création d'une Haute Autorité de la Mer, internationalement reconnue, composée de «sages» indépendants de toute société privée ou étatique, et dont une des tâches les plus urgentes serait justement de veiller à la sauvegarde des baleines, au nom des droits des générations futures.

Les pays membres

Actuellement, la CBI compte 35 pays membres divisés en quatre tendances :

– les pays à tradition baleinière (Japon, Norvège, ex-URSS, Corée...) associés à des nations qui ont des intérêts économiques indirects dans la chasse baleinière (Antigua et Barbuda, Dominique, Grenade, Sainte-Lucie, Saint-Vincent et les Grenadines, Saint Kitts et Nevis, les îles Salomon);

– les pays disposant d'un quota de capture à titre de chasse baleinière de subsistance (Danemark pour le Groenland, les États-Unis pour l'Alaska, etc.);

– les pays protecteurs qui ne chassent pas ou plus et soutiennent des résolutions de conservation et de protection (Allemagne, Argentine, Australie, Autriche, Brésil, Chili, France, Inde, Italie, Monaco, Nouvelle-Zélande, Pays-Bas, Royaume-Uni, Suède);

– les pays mouvants qui surprennent par leurs votes sur certaines résolutions (Afrique du Sud, Chine, Espagne, Finlande, Irlande, Mexique, Oman, Suisse).

Il y a aussi des pays observateurs, non-membres qui n'ont pas de droit de vote (Canada, Iran, Islande, Maroc, Zimbabwe, Union Européenne), des organisations intergouvernementales et 70 organisations non gouvernementales, soit de protection de l'environnement comme Greenpeace, soit en faveur de la chasse comme les associations de promotion de la chasse baleinière japonaise.

Quelques dates marquantes

1982

Le grand tournant... Réunie à Brighton, en Angleterre, la CBI décide par 25 voix contre 7 et 7 abstentions, que toute pêche commerciale à la baleine devra avoir cessé en 1986. La CBI compte à présent 38 membres.

Aux 19 nations fondatrices sont venus s'ajouter de grands pays très peuplés, comme la Chine, l'Inde, l'Égypte, etc., mais aussi de petits États insulaires, très sensibles à la préservation des richesses marines : les Seychelles, Sainte-Lucie, Saint-Vincent, Antigua...

Le moratoire est voté en dépit des pressions et des intrigues des Soviétiques et des Japonais, bien qu'on assiste à des séries de marchandages surréalistes, où les affaires de baleines se trouvent mêlées aux chiffres de vente du café brésilien, aux aléas de la coopération économique seychello-nippone, aux retombées géopolitiques et idéologiques de la guerre des Malouines... Pour les amis des baleines, la meilleure surprise vient de l'Espagne, qui vote le moratoire alors qu'elle s'y était toujours opposée. Cependant, comme ils en ont la possibilité, le Japon et l'Union soviétique «objectent» dans les 90 jours, soutenus par la Norvège et le Pérou.

1983
Nouveaux progrès : le Pérou, le Brésil, la Corée du Sud et l'Islande acceptent le moratoire. À l'inverse, sous la pression du Japon, les Philippines, qui n'avaient jamais chassé la baleine, annoncent leur intention de capturer chaque année 200 rorquals tropicaux. Autre mauvaise nouvelle : on révise en hausse les quotas de captures de baleines franches du Groenland, dans le cadre de la «clause d'exemption aborigène».

1984
La conférence annuelle de la CBI se tient à Buenos Aires : à cette occasion, le gouvernement argentin décide d'élever un monument à la baleine franche, sur un îlot de la péninsule Valdes. Geste symbolique, qui accompagne une importante

réduction des quotas de capture autorisées (de 9 875 pour la campagne de 1983-1984, on passe à 6 837 pour la campagne de 1984-1985, la dernière avant le moratoire...). Le Brésil, le Japon, l'Union soviétique objectent, comme ils en ont le droit. La Norvège tente de trouver une astuce, en plaidant pour une chasse du «troisième type», ni commerciale, ni aborigène, et qui serait réservée aux «artisans», notamment dans l'Atlantique Nord.

1985
Les derniers pays chasseurs de baleines recourent aux ruses les plus élaborées pour poursuivre leurs activités de harponnage. Mais ils s'exposent à des sanctions de la part des États-Unis et des pays de la Communauté Européenne. Le hobby du baleinage perd des points. Le 5 avril 1985, le ministre nippon de l'Agriculture et des Pêches annonce que son pays mettra fin à ses activités baleinières en 1988. Promesse ferme, ou manière de tourner le moratoire?

1986
Le moratoire entre en vigueur. Le Japon, la Norvège et la Russie maintiennent leurs objections et continuent leurs chasses. L'Islande et la Corée du Sud prétendent effectuer une chasse scientifique. Des îles des Caraïbes, Sainte-Lucie et Saint-Vincent rejoignent les positions des pays baleiniers. Ce changement brutal dans leur politique de gestion des baleines coïncide avec de très gros investissements locaux dans des programmes d'aide aux développement des pêches... de la part du Japon.

1987
Depuis la proposition de moratoire sur la chasse commerciale, le Japon dit avoir

reconverti sa flotte commerciale en une flotte scientifique. Et, devant le vide juridique laissé par la résolution qui rend effectif le moratoire, le Japon, la Norvège et l'Islande programment une chasse scientifique.

1988
La Russie cesse son activité de chasse baleinière commerciale.

1989
La flotte de chasse scientifique japonaise traque le petit rorqual en Antarctique.

1990
Les pays baleiniers tentent d'élargir la gamme des espèces chassables au rorqual de Minke.

1991
La CBI adopte la RMP (Revided Management Procedure). L'Islande se retire de la CBI. Le moratoire sur la chasse commerciale est maintenu.

1992
La Dominique soutient les pays baleiniers en échange d'aides économiques. La Norvège lance la Commission de l'Atlantique Nord pour les mammifères marins avec comme ambition d'affaiblir l'autorité de la CBI dans la région.

1993
L'île de Grenade rejoint les États sous tutelle japonaise à la CBI, la Norvège reprend la chasse commerciale. Un trafic de viande de baleine, étiquetée comme étant des crevettes, destiné à la Corée du Sud et au Japon est révélé.

1994
La CBI reconnaît la nécessité d'un sanctuaire baleinier dans l'Antarctique.

Le Japon s'y oppose. Le ministère de la Pêche russe divulgue des documents secrets sur les falsifications effectuées durant les campagnes de chasse baleinière. Pour la première fois, le capitaine d'un baleinier norvégien est condamné pour dépassement de quotas. Le Japon commence un nouveau programme scientifique sur une population de petits rorquals dans le Pacifique Nord.

1995
Le comité scientifique de la CBI détecte une erreur dans le programme de l'ordinateur utilisé par les Norvégiens pour estimer la population de petits rorquals en Atlantique Nord.

1997
La flotte japonaise étend ses activités meurtrières à la zone VI de l'Antarctique. Des analyses d'ADN sur de la viande prélevée sur des marchés japonais et coréens prouvent la prise illégale d'espèces protégées. Le Japon propose une résolution visant à rendre secret les votes, ce qui lui permettrait de mieux dissimuler les accords qu'il passe avec des micro-nations.

1998
La Norvège s'auto-concède un quota de 670 petits rorquals, le double de celui qu'elle s'autorisait en 1993 lors de la reprise de la chasse norvégienne. Le Japon, aidé de la Corée du Sud, de la Chine et de la Russie, tente de créer une organisation de gestion de la chasse baleinière dans le Pacifique Nord. L'Islande annonce son éventuelle intention de reprendre ses activités. Le Japon tente d'appliquer sa chasse scientifique à une population de rorquals de Bryde.

Les produits de substitution

Au siècle dernier, des fortunes se sont édifiées sur le commerce des produits baleiniers. Mais rien aujourd'hui ne justifie plus que se poursuive une chasse meurtrière et de moins en moins rentable : tous les produits extraits de la baleine peuvent être remplacés par d'autres et bien souvent à un moindre coût.

Le collagène :
C'est une protéine extraite de la peau et des os. Une fois bouillie, elle donne de la gélatine qui est employée en cosmétique, en confiserie, en charcuterie et dans l'industrie photographique.
Substituts : matières d'origine végétale, algues.

Les dents du cachalot :
En ivoire, elles sont principalement utilisées pour les sculptures artisanales. Jadis, on en faisait des boutons ou des dés à jouer.
Substituts : matières synthétiques, plastiques.

Le foie et les glandes endocrines :
L'huile de foie de baleine est plus riche en vitamines A et D que celle de foie de morue. Elle est très employée dans l'industrie pharmaceutique. On extrait diverses hormones des glandes endocrines (pituite, hypophyse, pancréas, surrénales).
Substituts : carotène de carotte, huile de foie de morue, vitamine A de synthèse.

L'huile de baleine :
Jusqu'à la découverte du pétrole au XIXᵉ siècle et l'avènement de l'électricité, on l'utilisait pour l'éclairage, la fabrication des bougies et des savons. Aujourd'hui, elle a perdu de sa valeur et sert à la fabrication de produits explosifs, de fournitures pour l'industrie chimique et pharmaceutique et de substances de conservation.
Substituts : cires d'abeille, de paraffine, huile de colza, de jojoba, de lin.

L'huile de cachalot ou spermaceti (ou encore blanc de baleine) :
Une fois raffinée et filtrée, cette huile entre dans la confection de bougies de luxe, de cosmétiques : crèmes de beauté, rouges à lèvres, pommades et crèmes à raser. Elle peut servir également de lubrifiant pour moteurs, machines-outils et mécanismes de précision. Elle intervient enfin dans la préparation de solvants pour les peintures, d'encre d'imprimerie, de papier carbone, de plastiques et même de pâtes alimentaires.
Substituts : huile de lin, de ricin, de colza, huiles essentielles de citron et d'orange, crème d'avocat, lait de concombre, huile de jojoba.

Les os :
Les baleiniers les sculptaient pour en faire des ustensiles de cuisine, des aiguilles à tricoter, des pièces d'échecs, etc. Aujourd'hui, les os sont réduits en poudre et entrent dans la

composition des engrais et des aliments pour animaux.
Substituts : résidus de céréales, algues, restes d'abattoirs, etc.

La peau :
On en tirait une «eau de colle», matière gélatineuse qui permettait de confectionner des selles de bicyclettes, des sacs à main, des chaussures, ainsi que des lacets.
Substituts : matériaux d'origine végétale, animale (élevage) ou chimique.

Le sang :
Il est transformé en engrais.
Substitut : engrais d'origine végétale.

Les tendons :
Ils servent à faire des cordes de raquettes de tennis ou des fils de chirurgie.
Substitut : tendons d'animaux d'élevage.

Viande :
Elle est consommée au Japon, en Irlande, en Norvège, au Groenland et en Alaska ainsi qu'en Corée. Au Japon, elle ne représente que 1,70 % de l'alimentation carnée. Elle entre également dans la composition des aliments pour chiens et chats et dans l'alimentation des animaux d'élevage à fourrure.

Les viscères :
Ils sont cuits et séchés pour être transformés en engrais. Avec la bile, on fabrique des colorants et des vernis.

Substituts : engrais d'origine végétale; produits synthétiques, chimiques.

L'ambre gris :
Cette concrétion qui se forme dans l'estomac des cachalots est utilisée en parfumerie. Nauséabond quand il est frais, l'ambre finit par exhaler une agréable odeur de musc et se vend très cher. Cet ambre gris se compose surtout d'alcools non volatils comme l'ambréine, produit voisin du cholestérol. Substance très odorante, l'ambre gris fut un parfum recherché au Moyen Age. Il est encore employé de nos jours comme fixateur de parfums, ainsi que pour la confection de cosmétiques et de savons de luxe. D'autre part, il possède des propriétés antispasmodiques, utilisées en pharmacie. «Qui aurait imaginé qu'un parfum dont se délectent les belles dames et les beaux messieurs provient d'ignobles entrailles, bien plus, qu'il est la cause ou l'effet – on ne le sait au juste – d'une maladie de foie des cachalots?», écrit Herman Melville dans *Moby Dick*. Le plus gros bloc d'ambre gris fut trouvé au début du siècle dans le ventre d'un cachalot; il pesait plus de 450 kilos.
Substitut : fixateur 400.

TDC, Textes et Documents pour la Classe, octobre 1993, n° 661

Plante de jojoba.

Sauter comme une baleine

Des masses de plus de 30 tonnes, de plus de 15 mètres de haut, qui surgissent au-dessus de la surface des mers! Depuis toujours, les sauts des baleines ont impressionné les observateurs. Défi, code, jeu : ces sauts, dont certaines races sont coutumières, semblent avoir une signification sociale, et seraient des moyens de communication entre les baleines. Cet article de 1985 reste à ce jour le mieux documenté sur le sujet.

Le saut d'une baleine hors de l'eau est certainement l'action musculaire la plus puissante dans tout le règne animal. Lorsque l'on évalue l'énorme volume corporel et le poids qu'une baleine doit soulever pour sauter, on s'interroge naturellement sur la fonction de tels sauts. [..]

Au cours des siècles passés, les équipages des baleiniers ont observé à loisir les baleines qu'ils essayaient de capturer. Pendant des années les anecdotes rapportées par les pêcheurs constituèrent l'essentiel des connaissances sur le saut et autres comportements de la baleine. Les tentatives d'explication du saut étaient quelque peu anthropomorphiques : d'après les marins, les baleines sautaient soit pour se nourrir, soit pour s'étirer, soit pour s'amuser, soit pour fuir les espadons. Certains baleiniers interprétaient même ces bonds comme des «parades de défi».

Au cours de ces dernières années, des observations scientifiques en haute mer ont permis de rassembler des données quantitatives utiles sur le comportement des baleines et notamment sur leur saut.

Un travail herculéen

Lorsqu'un Mégaptère bondit, il soulève une biomasse équivalente à celle d'un ensemble de 485 personnes qui pèsent en moyenne 68 kilogrammes chacune. Les plus grands Mégaptères mesurent approximativement 15 mètres de long et pèsent quelque 30 tonnes.

Dans leurs sauts, les Mégaptères et autres baleines n'émergent souvent paresseusement qu'une moitié de leur corps, mais, parfois, ils bondissent complètement hors de l'eau. [...] Dans un autre type de saut, le marsouinage, des animaux marins sortent intentionnellement de l'eau au cours. d'une nage rapide entrecoupée de bonds horizontaux. Robert Blake, de l'Université de Colombie britannique, a calculé que, grâce au marsouinage, les petites baleines et les dauphins minimisent la force de traînée due au frottement de l'eau; les grosses baleines, au contraire, n'ont aucun intérêt à marsouiner et je n'ai jamais observé ce comportement chez les Mégaptères. [...]

Quelle quantité d'énergie la baleine dépense-t-elle au cours d'un saut? Quelle est la puissance qu'elle

développe lorsqu'elle sort de l'eau? J'ai simulé le saut de la baleine sur un petit ordinateur, d'après des mesures prises sur des photos de baleines en action. Au cours d'un saut complet, lorsque la plus grande partie du corps de l'animal s'élève au-dessus de l'eau à un angle d'environ 35 degrés, un Mégaptère adulte de 12 mètres franchit la surface à une vitesse de 15 nœuds (28 kilomètres à l'heure). Puisqu'il s'agit quasiment de la vitesse maximale qu'un Mégaptère peut atteindre, un saut complet correspond donc à la force de propulsion maximale de l'animal.

L'énergie nécessaire à un tel saut est d'environ 2 500 kilocalories, soit environ la ration alimentaire journalière d'un homme. Le métabolisme basal de la baleine – c'est-à-dire l'énergie qu'elle dépense au repos – est de quelque 300 000 kilocalories par jour. L'énergie consommée au cours d'un saut représente donc un peu moins du centième de son besoin calorique quotidien minimal. [...] Par conséquent, le saut n'est pas un effort particulièrement coûteux dans le budget énergétique journalier d'une baleine. Toutefois, une série de vingt sauts ou plus consomme beaucoup d'énergie, ce qui explique

pourquoi, au cours d'une série, les sauts sont de moins en moins vigoureux.

Les circonstances des sauts

Il est difficile d'expliquer pourquoi les baleine sautent. [...] J'ai passé plusieurs centaines d'heures, à bord de petits voiliers, à suivre les baleines dans leurs activités quotidiennes. Grâce à cette étude, à celles de R. Payne et d'autres chercheurs, nous savons définir dans quelles circonstances les baleines effectuent des sauts. [...] D'après les résultats de ces études, il semble que le saut soit principalement associé aux interactions sociales, notamment à des fins de communication chez les baleines adultes, et dans des buts ludiques chez les jeunes baleines.

Les baleines sautent quand un groupe de deux individus ou plus se scinde, ou quand deux groupes (parfois réduits à un seul individu) fusionnent. Souvent, les baleines sautent moins de 15 minutes après avoir, par exemple, battu la surface de l'eau avec leur queue ou leurs nageoires. [...]

Paradoxalement, il semble que les Mégaptères sautent moins en été, bien que les bandes se scindent et se regroupent plus souvent en été qu'en hiver; cependant, l'accouplement et la mise bas ont lieu en hiver et constituent des interactions sociales probablement plus importantes : ainsi les activités estivales. Ainsi, la fréquence des sauts n'est pas liée au nombre d'interactions sociales, mais plutôt à leur importance dans la vie des cétacés.

Un autre lien entre le saut et l'activité sociale apparaît lorsque l'on compare la fréquence des sauts dans les espèces de baleines. [...] Je pensais que les espèces où les individus sont les plus «dodus» devraient être les moins aptes à sauter, à cause de leur forme peu hydrodynamique; or, ce sont justement ces espèces qui sautent le plus souvent!

Au moment de la reproduction, les Baleines franches australes, les Baleines grises et les Mégaptères, les trois espèces les mieux étudiées, se rassemblent toujours aux mêmes endroits. Elles s'y alimentent rarement et survivent grâce à l'énergie stockée dans leurs épaisses couches de graisse. Les interactions sociales y sont fréquentes et quelquefois énergiques. C'est en ces lieux que les sauts sont les plus fréquents.

En revanche, le Rorqual bleu, le Rorqual commun et le Rorqual de Rudolphi, qui sont des baleines «minces», ne se rassemblent pas pour se reproduire, mais restent dispersées au cours de l'hiver. Ce comportement réduit probablement leur dépense d'énergie : elles ne s'encombrent donc pas de grosses couches de graisse. Pour trouver un partenaire, elles émettent probablement des sons puissants à basse fréquence (elles ont peut-être même un comportement monogame). Quoi qu'il en soit, il existe apparemment peu de contacts entre les individus.

On connaît très mal le système social de la Baleine du Groenland, du Rorqual de Bryde et du petit Rorqual. Il semble toutefois que les espèces les plus structurées socialement sautent plus souvent que les autres. Par exemple, le système social du cachalot – un cétacé pourvu de dents, qui bondit fréquemment – est particulièrement complexe.

Les significations possibles du saut

Quels autres indices ressortent de toutes ces observations? Plusieurs études indépendantes montrent, fait surprenant, que les baleines sautent davantage quand la vitesse du vent augmente. [...] R. Payne pense que les baleines utiliseraient le saut comme moyen de communication sonore – par le claquement émis lorsque la baleine retombe dans l'eau – quand le bruit du vent et des vagues couvre les vocalisations émises en temps normal.

R. Payne a également fait une autre découverte qui l'incite à penser que le saut tient lieu de signal : chez les Baleines franches australes, un saut en entraîne d'autres; autrement dit la probabilité qu'un individu saute augmente quand des baleines voisines sautent. [...] Dans de bonnes conditions, les baleines voisines doivent entendre le bruit produit par le saut de l'une d'entre elles sur une distance de quelques kilomètres. Ces observations corroborent l'hypothèse de R. Payne selon laquelle le saut a une fonction de signalisation. Lorsque d'autres baleines voient ou entendent le saut, un message leur est transmis : il «dit» au moins qu'une baleine a sauté.

Le saut est-il un moyen efficace de transmettre d'autres messages? [...] La question est de savoir si les sons produits par les sauts des baleines sont plus puissants, du moins pour certaines fréquences, que ceux produits par leurs vocalisations. On ne possède malheureusement que peu d'informations sur l'intensité sous-marine du bruit du saut. [...]

Le saut pourrait aussi signifier une agression, un défi, une démonstration de force ou une parade nuptiale. [...] Pendant les nombreux mois que j'ai passés en mer dans de petites embarcations, je n'ai jamais eu le sentiment que les sauts que nous observions étaient des agressions. De plus, un coup de queue de baleine est certainement plus dangereux.

Lorsqu'une baleine saute, elle montre sa force maximale à chacune des baleines qui la voient ou qui l'entendent. Par conséquent, le saut est peut-être utile dans la parade nuptiale, pour défier un adversaire ou pour exhiber sa force. Ainsi, les femelles choisiraient leur partenaire, du moins partiellement, en fonction de la force du saut des mâles, ou de leur capacité à soutenir un effort intense ou à faire beaucoup de bruit au cours d'une série de sauts. Une telle démonstration renseignerait les femelles sur la force et la résistance d'un mâle, et donc peut-être (indirectement) sur ses qualités génétiques. [...]

Le jeu des baleines

Le saut peut être aussi une forme de jeu, mais ce concept est assez flou, et on a souvent tendance à appeler jeu toute activité dont on ne comprend pas la fonction. Tout comportement inexplicable rentre alors dans cette catégorie, y compris le saut de la baleine. Les biologistes et les spécialistes du comportement considèrent actuellement que le comportement ludique existe chez les animaux, bien qu'il soit difficile à définir. [...]

Le saut a toutes les caractéristiques des activités que les spécialistes appellent des jeux : il apparaît dans un contexte social, il est souvent exécuté par de jeunes individus et, dans beaucoup de cas, il n'a aucune fonction évidente. Certains chercheurs ont spéculé qu'à travers le jeu les jeunes animaux développent leurs muscles; le saut remplit peut-être cette fonction chez les jeunes baleines.

Les sauts les plus spectaculaires sont ceux des plus jeunes baleines. Les petits des Baleines franches australes, des Baleines grises et des Mégaptères commencent à sauter à peine âgés de quelques semaines. Les sauts sont en général vigoureux et en longues séries. [...]

Ces résultats et hypothèses ne dégagent pas une fonction unique et évidente du saut, et les données incitent à penser qu'il en a plusieurs. Malgré les fortes corrélations entre les sauts et la vie sociale, et bien que les sauts aient toutes les caractéristiques d'une exhibition de force physique, rien ne permet de confirmer ces hypothèses avec certitude.

Personnellement, je pense que le saut sert souvent à mettre en valeur d'autres signaux visuels ou acoustiques émis par les baleines : c'est une sorte de point d'exclamation physique. Les baleines exécutent des sauts tout comme les gens élèvent la voix, gesticulent ou sautillent pour donner plus de poids à leurs messages. Les observateurs des baleines sont comme les curieux qui écoutent aux portes : ils ne retiennent que les traits frappants et ne comprennent pas le message.

Hal Whitehead,
Pour la science, mai 1985

Les baleines ne se suicident pas!

On découvre depuis très longtemps des cétacés échoués sur les plages. Les scientifiques s'interrogent sur ce phénomène : pollution, effet de groupe, maladies parasitaires? Des explications rationnelles mettent fin au mythe du désespoir des baleines.

Gravure du XIXᵉ siècle représentant un cachalot échoué.

En France, les échouages de cétacés sont recensés systématiquement depuis 1972. Jusqu'à la fin des années 1980 quelques petites centaines d'animaux étaient trouvés chaque année sur le littoral, puis brusquement les chiffres se sont emballés : 500 à 900 cétacés par an, dont une grande majorité de dauphins sur les côtes du golfe de Gascogne. Cette augmentation soudaine n'est malheureusement pas due à l'accroissement des populations, mais plutôt à celui de leur mortalité.

En examinant de près les différentes causes des échouages, on comprend que les nouvelles techniques de pêche, comme les chaluts pélagiques, sont à l'origine de ces échouages multiples. Les baleines représentent une très faible proportion (1 à 3%) des cétacés trouvés échoués, tant en Europe que dans le reste du monde. Chez nous elles vivent souvent plus au large de nos côtes,

et leurs populations sont bien plus réduites que celles des dauphins. La probabilité de trouver un dauphin mort sur une plage est beaucoup plus grande que pour une baleine.

Le suicide des baleines fait encore partie des mythes auxquels nous aimons croire, comme si la capacité de mettre volontairement fin à ses jours pouvait rapprocher la baleine de l'homme. Nous avons tant besoin de nous reconnaître chez les animaux que nous aimons. Pourtant il ne s'agit ni de baleines, ni de suicides.

Ces événements concernent en fait plusieurs espèces d'odontocètes (globicéphales, orques, cachalots…) que les Anglo-Saxons appellent *whales*, terme qu'ils emploient pour tous les cétacés de grande taille, y compris les baleines. Lorsqu'un troupeau de globicéphales (*pilot whales* en anglais) s'échoue sur une plage d'Australie ou d'Écosse, les médias francophones répercutent l'information en traduisant «baleine pilote». Mais, en français, le terme de baleine est réservé aux cétacés à fanons, les mysticètes (les globicéphales sont des gros dauphins, des odontocètes, ils ont des dents et non pas des fanons). Cette erreur linguistique est donc à l'origine de notre confusion. Aucune espèce de baleine n'a jamais été concernée par ces événements qui nous évoquent un suicide.

L'interprétation anthropomorphique du suicide provient du fait que, lorsque plusieurs dizaines, voire centaines, de globicéphales s'échouent vivants, il est difficile d'intervenir dans cette masse de gros dauphins (les adultes mesurent 4 à 6 m de long) qui s'agitent et crient sur la plage. Les sauveteurs ne peuvent manier qu'un animal à la fois pour tenter de le remettre au large, ils choisissent d'abord les jeunes, plus légers et faciles à manipuler. Mais les globicéphales sont probablement assez grégaires, de sorte que leur instinct de groupe prime souvent sur celui de l'individu. Le jeune dauphin, remis seul au large, n'aura de cesse que de rejoindre son groupe resté échoué au fond de la baie. Il revient donc vers sa famille, et nous interprétons ce geste comme un suicide volontaire.

Ayant compris leur erreur, les sauveteurs savent maintenant que pour réussir leur mission, ils doivent repousser vers le large plusieurs dauphins simultanément, en prenant soin qu'un animal dominant (parmi les plus gros) fasse partie du groupe.

Si ce n'est pour se suicider, pourquoi ces troupeaux de dauphins viennent-ils s'échouer alors qu'ils paraissent en bonne santé? Il s'agit probablement d'erreur de navigation, facilitées par la nature du terrain. On constate en effet que la majorité de ces échouages ont lieu au fond de baies sableuses, substrat qui renvoie mal l'écho du sonar que les dauphins utilisent pour se diriger. De plus, des anomalies du champ magnétique terrestre sont souvent repérées sur les lieux de ces types d'échouages, elles favoriseraient aussi la confusion des animaux. Enfin, un phénomène de «panique de foule» facilite probablement aussi ces tristes événements.

Anne Collet

Globicéphale échoué à Roscoff en Bretagne en décembre 1904.

LISTE DES CÉTACÉS*

CLASSE : MAMMIFÈRES
ORDRE : CÉTACÉS
SOUS-ORDRE : MYSTICÈTES

Mysticeti (Mysticètes, baleen whales)
13 espèces

Famille des *Eschrichtidae* (Eschrichtidés, eschrichtids), 1 espèce :
- *Eschrichtius robustus* (Baleine grise, gray whale).

Famille des *Balaenopteridae* (Baleinoptidés, balaenopterids), 7 espèces :
- *Balaenoptera acutorostrata* (Petit Rorqual ou Rorqual à museau pointu, minke whale).
- *Balaenoptera bonarensis* (Petit Rorqual Antarctique, Antarctic minke whale).
- *Balaenoptera edeni* (Rorqual tropical ou Rorqual de Bryde, Bryde's whale).
- *Balaenoptera borealis* (Rorqual boréal ou Rorqual de Rudolphi, sei whale).
- *Balaenoptera physalus* (Rorqual commun, fin whale).
- *Balaenoptera musculus* (Baleine bleue ou Grand Rorqual, blue whale).
- *Megaptera novaeangliae* (Mégaptère ou Baleine à bosse ou Jubarte, humpback whale).

Famille des *Balaenidae* (Baleinidés, right whales), 4 espèces :
- *Eubalaena glacialis* (Baleine franche de l'Atlantique Nord ou Baleine des Basques, North Atlantic right whale).
- *Eubalaena australis* (Baleine franche australe, Southern right whale).
- *Eubalaena japonica* (Baleine franche du Pacifique Nord, North Pacific right whale).
- *Balaena mysticetus* (Baleine du Groenland, bowhead whale).

Famille des *Neobalaenidae* (Néobaleinidés, neobalaenids), 1 espèce :
- *Caperea marginata* (Baleine franche naine, pygmy right whale).

CLASSE : MAMMIFÈRES
ORDRE : CÉTACÉS
SOUS-ORDRE : ODONTOCÈTES

Odontoceti (Odontocètes, tooth whales)
69 espèces

Famille des *Iniidae* (Iniidés, iniids), 1 espèce :
- *Inia geoffrensi* (Boutou, Amazon river dolphin).

Famille des *Lipotidae* (Lipotidés, lipotids), 1 espèce :
- *Lipotes vexillifer* (Baiji, Yangtse river dolphin).

Famille des *Pontoporiidae* (Pontoporiidés, pontoporids), 1 espèce :
- *Pontoporia blainvillei* (Franciscain, franciscana).

Famille des *Platanistidae* (Platanistidés, platanistids), 1 espèce :
- *Platanista gangetica* (Plataniste, India river dolphin).

Famille des *Delphinidae* (Delphinidés, delphinids), 34 espèces :
- *Steno bredanensis* (Sténo, rough-toothed dolphin).
- *Sousa chinensis* (Sousa du Pacifique, Indo-Pacific hump-backed dolphin).
- *Sousa teuszi* (Sousa de l'Atlantique, Atlantic hump-backed dolphin).
- *Sotalia fluviatilis* (Sotalie, Tucuxi).
- *Tursiops truncatus* (Grand Dauphin, bottlenose dolphin).
- *Tursiops aduncus* (Tursiops de l'océan Indien, Indo-Pacific bottlenose dolphin).
- *Stenella longirostris* (Dauphin à long bec, spinner dolphin).
- *Stenella attenuata (dubia)* (Dauphin tacheté du Pacific, pantropical spotted dolphin).
- *Stenella frontalis (plagiodon)* (Dauphin tacheté de l'Atlantique, Atlantic spotted dolphin).
- *Stenella clymene* (Dauphin clymène, clymene dolphin).
- *Stenella coeruleoalba* (Dauphin bleu et blanc, striped dolphin).
- *Delphinus delphis* (Dauphin commun, common dolphin).
- *Delphinus capensis* (Dauphin commun à long bec, long-beaked common dolphin).
- *Lagenodelphis hosei* (Dauphin de Fraser, Fraser's dolphin).
- *Lagenorhynchus albirostris* (Dauphin à bec blanc, white-beaked dolphin).
- *Lagenorhynchus acutus* (Dauphin à flancs blancs de l'Atlantique, Atlantic white-sided dolphin).
- *Lagenorhynchus obliquidens* (Dauphin à flancs blancs du Pacifique, Pacific white-sided dolphin).
- *Lagenorhynchus obscurus* (Dauphin obscur, dusky dolphin).

- *Lagenorhynchus australis* (Dauphin à menton noir, Peale's dolphin).
- *Lagenorhynchus cruciger* (Dauphin sablier, hourglass dolphin).
- *Cephalorhynchus commersonii* (Dauphin de Commerson, Commerson's dolphin).
- *Cephalorhynchus eutropia* (Dauphin noir, black dolphin).
- *Cephalorhynchus heavisidii* (Dauphin du Cap, Heaviside's dolphin).
- *Cephalorhynchus hectori* (Dauphin d'Hector, Hector's dolphin).
- *Lissodelphis borealis* (Lissodelphe boréal, northern right whale dolphin).
- *Lissodelphis peronii* (Lissodelphe austral, southern right whale dolphin).
- *Grampus griseus Grampus* (Dauphin de Risso, Risso's dolphin).
- *Peponocephala electra* (Dauphin d'Electre, melon-headed whale).
- *Feresa attenuata* (Orque nain, pygmy killer whale).
- *Pseudorca crassidens* (Pseudorque, false killer whale).
- *Globicephala melas* (Globicéphale noir, long-finned pilot whale).
- *Globicephala macrorhynchus* (Globicéphale tropical, short-finned pilot whale).
- *Orcinus orca* (Orque, killer whale).
- *Orcaella brevirostris* (Orcelle, Irrawaddy dolphin).

Famille des *Phocoenidae* (Phocoenidés, porpoises), 6 espèces :
- *Phocoena phocoena* (Marsouin commun, harbour porpoise).
- *Phocoena sinus* (Marsouin de Californie, vaquita).
- *Phocoena spinipinnis* (Marsouin de Burmeister, Burmeister's porpoise).
- *Phocaena dioptrica* (Marsouin à lunettes, spectacled porpoise).
- *Neophocaena phocaenoides* (Marsouin de Cuvier, finless porpoise).
- *Phocoenoides dalli* (Marsouin de Dall, Dall's porpoise).

Famille des *Monodontidae* (Monodontidés, monodontids), 2 espèces :
- *Delphinapterus leucas* (Bélouga, white whale).
- *Monodon monoceros* (Narval, narwhal).

Famille des *Physeteridae* (Physétéridés, physeterids), 1 espèce :
- *Physeter macrocephalus* (Grand Cachalot, sperm whale).

Famille des *Kogiidae* (Kogiidés, pygmy sperm whales), 2 espèces :
- *Kogia breviceps* (Cachalot pygmée, pygmy sperm whale).
- *Kogia sima* (Cachalot nain, dwarf sperm whale).

Famille des *Ziphiidae* (Ziphiidés, beaked whales), 20 espèces :
- *Berardius arnuxii* (Bérardie australe, Arnoux's beaked whale).
- *Berardius bairdii* (Bérardie boréale, Baird's beaked whale).
- *Ziphius cavirostris* (Ziphius, Cuvier's beaked whale).
- *Tasmacetus shepherdi* (Tasmacète de Shepherd, Shepherd's beaked whale).
- *Hyperoodon ampullatus* (Hypérodon boréal, northern bottlenose whale).
- *Hyperoodon planifrons* (Hypérodon austral, southern bottlenose whale).
- *Mesoplodon pacificus* (Mésoplodon de Longman, Longman's beaked whale).
- *Mesoplodon bahamondi* (Mésoplodon du Chili, Juan Fernandez beaked whale).
- *Mesoplodon peruvianus* (Mésoplodon du Pérou, pygmy beaked whale).
- *Mesoplodon hectori* (Mésoplodon d'Hector, Hector's beaked whale).
- *Mesoplodon mirus* (Mésoplodon de True, True's beaked whale).
- *Mesoplodon europaeus* (Mésoplodon de Gervais, Gervais' beaked whale).
- *Mesoplodon ginkgodens* (Mésoplodon ginkgo, ginkgo-toothed beaked whale).
- *Mesoplodon grayi* (Mésoplodon de Gray, Gray's beaked whale).
- *Mesoplodon carlhubbsi* (Mésoplodon de Hubbs, Hubbs' beaked whale).
- *Mesoplodon bowdoini* (Mésoplodon d'Andrew, Andrew's beaked whale).
- *Mesoplodon stejnegeri*, (Mésoplodon de Stejneger, Stejneger's beaked whale).
- *Mesoplodon bidens* (Mésoplodon de Sowerby, Sowerby's beaked whale).
- *Mesoplodon layardii* (Mésoplodon de Layard, strap-toothed whale).
- *Mesoplodon densirostris* (Mésoplodon de Blainville, Blainville's beaked whale).

* Liste des noms scientifiques (latins) et vernaculaires français et anglais.
Cette liste a été adoptée par la Commission baleinière internationale en juillet 2000.

LA PROTECTION DES DIFFÉRENTES ESPÈCES

La baleine franche de l'Atlantique nord, ou baleine des Basques :
- 12 à 15 mètres (maxi 17 mètres). 40 à 100 tonnes.
- Population mondiale : 800 à 1 000.
- Protection : totale depuis 1935.

La baleine franche du Pacifique Nord :
- 12 à 15 mètres (maxi 17 mètres). 40 à 100 tonnes.
- Population mondiale : 200 à 300.
- Protection : totale depuis 1935.

La baleine franche australe :
- 13 à 15 mètres (maxi 18 mètres). 50 à 100 tonnes.
- Population mondiale : environ 3 000.
- Protection : totale depuis 1935.

La baleine du Groenland :
- 13 à 15 mètres (maxi 19 mètres). 60 à 110 tonnes.
- Population mondiale : 6 000 à 8 000.
- Protection : interdiction de chasse commerciale depuis 1935; quelques captures aborigènes autorisées par la CBI pour les Inuits de l'Arctique.

La baleine franche naine :
- 5 à 6 mètres.
- Population mondiale : inconnue.
- Protection : n'a jamais été exploitée; protégée par le moratoire de 1986.

La baleine grise :
- 10 à 13 mètres de long. 20 à 35 tonnes.
- Population mondiale : 20 000 à 26 000.
- Protection : interdiction de chasse commerciale depuis 1935; quelques captures aborigènes autorisées par la CBI pour les Inuits de l'Arctique.

Le petit rorqual :
- 8 à 9 mètres. 6 à 8 tonnes.
- Population mondiale : environ 180 000.
- Protection : interdiction de chasse commerciale depuis 1986; quelques captures aborigènes autorisées par la CBI pour les Inuits du Groenland; captures scientifiques de 50 à 100 animaux par an pour le Japon dans le Pacifique nord-est et environ 300 captures annuelles par la Norvège en Atlantique Nord.

Le petit rorqual antarctique :
- 8 à 10 mètres. 6 à 10 tonnes.
- Population mondiale : 600 000 à 1 140 000.
- Protection : interdiction de chasse commerciale depuis 1986; environ 400 captures scientifiques annuelles autorisées par la CBI pour le Japon.

Le rorqual tropical, ou rorqual de Bryde :
- 11 à 13 mètres (maxi 14 mètres). 18 tonnes.
- Population mondiale : environ 90 000.
- Protection : interdiction de chasse commerciale depuis 1986; quelques captures probables non autorisées en Indonésie.

Le rorqual boréal, ou rorqual de Rudolphi :
- 13 à 15 mètres (maxi 21 mètres). 20 tonnes.
- Population mondiale : 55 000 à 100 000.
- Protection : interdiction de chasse commerciale depuis 1986.

Le rorqual commun :
- 18 à 22 mètres (maxi 26 mètres). 40 à 100 tonnes.
- Population mondiale : environ 120 000.
- Protection : interdiction de chasse commerciale depuis 1986; quelques captures aborigènes autorisées par la CBI pour les Inuits du Groenland et quelques captures probables non autorisées en Indonésie.

Le grand rorqual, ou baleine bleue :
- 24 à 27 mètres (maxi 33 mètres). 80 à 160 tonnes.
- Population mondiale : 1 500 à 5 000.
- Protection : interdiction de chasse commerciale depuis 1967; quelques captures probables non autorisées en Indonésie.

Le mégaptère, ou baleine à bosse :
- 13 à 15 mètres (maxi 17 mètres). 20 à 50 tonnes.
- Population mondiale : environ 15 000.
- Protection : interdiction de chasse commerciale depuis 1966; quelques captures aborigènes autorisées par la CBI pour Saint-Vincent et les Grenadines.

Le grand cachalot :
- 10 à 15 mètres (maxi 18 mètres). 15 à 45 tonnes.
- Population mondiale : environ 2 000 000
- Protection : interdiction de chasse commerciale depuis 1985.

BIBLIOGRAPHIE

Guides

- Cawardine M., *Baleines, dauphins et marsouins*, Bordas, 1996.
- Dumont J.-M. et Marion R., *Cap sur les baleines*, Nathan, 1997.
- Moreau A., Levet V., *Mammifères marins du Monde*, Arthaud, 1991.
- Sifaoui B., *Le Livre des dauphins et des baleines*, Albin Michel, 1998.
- Sylvestre J.-P., *Baleines et cachalots*, Delachaux et Niestlé, 1989.

Ouvrages de vulgarisation scientifique illustrés

- Cousteau J.-Y. et Paccalet Y., *La Planète des baleines*, Robert Laffont, 1986.
- de Beaulieu F., Hussenot E. et Ridoux V., *Mammifères marins de nos côtes*, Chasse Marée, 1994.
- Cox V., *Baleines et dauphins*, Soline, 1989.
- Diolé P. et Cousteau J.-Y., *Nos amies les baleines*, Flammarion, 1972.
- Duguy R. et Robineau D., *Guide des mammifères marins d'Europe*, Delachaux et Niestlé, 1982.
- Du Pasquier Th., *Les Baleiniers français de Louis XVI à Napoléon*, Veyrier et Kronos, 1990.
- Geistdoerfer P., *Grands Animaux sous la mer*, Gallimard Jeunesse, 1985.
- Harrison R. & Bryden M., *Baleines, dauphins et marsouins*, Bordas, 1989.
- Martin A., *Baleines et dauphins*, France Loisirs, 1992.
- Williams H., *Des baleines*, Aubier, 1988.

Récits et essais

- Benedeit, *Le Voyage de saint Brendan*, 10/18, 1984.
- Bullen Fr., *La Croisière du cachalot. A bord d'un baleinier 1875-1878*, Phébus 1989.
- Collet A. et Sich M., *Danse avec les baleines*, Plon, 1998.
- Collet A., Ross G. et Saladin d'Anglure B., *Baleines, un enjeu écologique*, Autrement, 1999.
- Collodi C., *Pinocchio*, Le Livre de poche, 1983.
- Coloane, Francisco, *Le Sillage de la baleine*, Phébus, 1998.
- Hervé-Gruyer, Ch., *Les Enfants Dauphins à l'école du vent, de la mer et de l'aventure*, Gallimard, 1990.
- Melville, H., *Moby Dick*, Londres, New York 1851, traduit par L. Jacques, J. Smith et J. Giono, Gallimard, 1941.
- Kipling, R., *Histoires comme* ça, Gallimard, 1984.
- Philbrick, N., *La Véritable Histoire de Moby Dick*, Jean-Claude Lattès, 2000.

Sites Internet

- Centre de recherche sur les mammifères marins de La Rochelle :
http://www.crmm.univ-lr.fr

- Commission baleinière internationale :
http://www.ourworld.compuserve.com/homepages/iwcoffice

- Greenpeace :
http://www.greenpeace.org

INDEX

CRÉDITS PHOTOGRAPHIQUES

ÉDITION ET FABRICATION

DÉCOUVERTES GALLIMARD
COLLECTION CONÇUE PAR Pierre Marchand
DIRECTION Élisabeth de Farcy
COORDINATION ÉDITORIALE Anne Lemaire
GRAPHISME Alain Gouessant
FABRICATION Corinne Chopplet
PROMOTION & PRESSE Valérie Tolstoï assistée de Doris Audoux
SUIVI DE PRODUCTION Madeleine Gonçalves

VIE ET MORT DES BALEINES
ÉDITION Paule du Bouchet et Élisabeth Le Meur
ICONOGRAPHIE Anne Lemaire et Élisabeth Le Meur
MAQUETTE ET MONTAGE PAO Valentina Leporé
LECTURE-CORRECTION Marianne Ganeau
PHOTOGRAVURE Arc-en-Ciel

Yves Cohat, docteur ès lettres, est anthropologue. Il est spécialisé
dans l'étude des techniques pratiques et des stratégies des communautés
de pêcheurs de l'Europe du Nord; il observe la façon dont celles-ci peuvent
influencer l'organisation sociale et économique de leur production.
Il est l'auteur de nombreux articles et ouvrages de vulgarisation scientifique.

Anne Collet, docteur en sciences, dirige depuis 1995 le Centre de recherche
sur les mammifères marins de La Rochelle. Membre expert de plusieurs
instances scientifiques nationales et internationales, elle a participé
à de nombreuses missions de recherche et d'observation
et a publié en 1998 *Danse avec les baleines* (Plon).

*Dépôt légal : septembre 2000
Numéro d'édition : 95538
ISBN : 2-07-053513-4
Imprimerie Editoriale-Lloyd, Italie*